Never After

Dan Elconin

SIMON PULSE
New York   London   Toronto   Sydney

This book is a work of fiction. Any references to historical events, real people, or real locales are used fictitiously. Other names, characters, places, and incidents are the product of the author's imagination, and any resemblance to actual events or locales or persons, living or dead, is entirely coincidental.

W

SIMON PULSE
An imprint of Simon & Schuster Children's Publishing Division
1230 Avenue of the Americas, New York, NY 10020
First Simon Pulse paperback edition October 2009
Copyright © 2009 by Dan Elconin
All rights reserved, including the right of reproduction in whole or in part in any form.
SIMON PULSE and colophon are registered trademarks of Simon & Schuster, Inc.
For information about special discounts for bulk purchases, please contact
Simon & Schuster Special Sales at 1-866-506-1949
or business@simonandschuster.com.
The Simon & Schuster Speakers Bureau can bring authors to your
live event. For more information or to book an event contact the
Simon & Schuster Speakers Bureau at 1-866-248-3049 or visit
our website at www.simonspeakers.com.
Designed by Sammy Yuen Jr.
The text of this book was set in Caslon.
Manufactured in the United States of America
10 9 8 7 6 5 4 3 2 1
Library of Congress Cataloging-in-Publication Data
Elconin, Dan.
Never after / by Dan Elconin. — 1st Simon Pulse paperback ed.
p. cm.
Summary: When sixteen-year-old Ricky Darlin is lured away from problems at
home by Peter, who later abandons him on the Island, Captain Hooke and his
crew rescue him and enlist his help in capturing Peter so they all can return home.
ISBN 978-1-4169-7967-8 (pbk)
[1. Fantasy. 2. Adventure and adventurers—Fiction. 3. Characters
in literature—Fiction. 4. Pirates—Fiction. 5. Islands—Fiction.]
I. Barrie, J. M. (James Matthew), 1860–1937. Peter Pan. II. Title.
PZ7.E358Nev 2009
[Fic]—dc22
2008055002
ISBN 978-1-4169-9697-2 (eBook)

Acknowledgments

First and foremost I'd like to thank my editors, Michael del Rosario and Emilia Rhodes, for not killing me.

Many thanks to my acquiring editor, Anica Rissi, for somehow seeing potential in the catastrophe that was my rough draft.

A big thanks to my cover art designer, Sammy Yuen. I'm actually hoping people judge my book by its cover.

Thank you to Bernadette Baker-Baughman and Gretchen Stelter, my agents, my friends, and freakin' badasses.

Thank you to Britney Wade, who helped me with just about everything (even with writing her own acknowledgment).

Thank you to all my teachers, who never stopped telling me my writing was phenomenal, and to my parents and Hank Benjamin, who never stopped telling me it sucked.

Thank you to Steve Cornell and Bill Madigan, two of the world's best stand-up comedians/motivational speakers/teachers.

And last but far from least, I'd like to thank my best friends Nick Vogel and Tom Megolmedomb, who each paid me ten bucks to mention them.

Chapter 1

"Now wake up, mate. I'm comin'."

I awoke slowly, the dream lingering like an afterimage. I clung to it, trying to pull myself back in, but it slipped away into the darkness of reality. . . .

Another few seconds and I was wide awake. The dream already seemed like a distant memory. It had been a good dream, I remembered that much. Something about the Island . . .

The clock on my nightstand read 11:38 p.m. I stared at the ceiling for a few minutes, trying to remember more of the dream, but as always, the details drifted tantalizingly just beyond my conscious reach. Finally I gave up and, yawning, rolled onto my side and closed my eyes.

It came from outside, behind me—a faint crunch of dry leaves.

My eyes snapped open. Automatically I drew my covers tighter around my shoulders, hairs prickling all over my body. I listened intently but didn't dare roll over to look out the window behind me.

It was your imagination, I told myself. *You were practically asleep, so—*

Another crunch.

And another.

It wasn't my imagination.

Panic and adrenaline shot through me like electricity, and I frantically scrambled out of bed and lunged for the stairs—then saw the closed door. The memory of slamming it flashed behind my eyes, and I froze while reaching for the doorknob. What the hell was I going to do, run scared to my mommy? I couldn't do that, especially not now.

Another crunch—leaves being stepped on, I was almost certain.

Suddenly feeling courageous—or perhaps just reckless—I spun around and peered out the window.

Nothing.

From across the room, in the darkness, I couldn't see much of anything. Still, I let out a breath of relief. I listened another five or ten seconds, but heard nothing more.

It was probably just an animal. A raccoon, maybe a squirrel.

But what if it wasn't? What if it was a robber? Or worse . . . ?

Hell, maybe it's Santa Claus getting a head start.

I snorted, smiling, and my anxiety abated a bit. I decided I was being ridiculous. Scaring myself. Totally overreacting.

Nevertheless, I knew I probably wouldn't sleep again tonight unless I investigated a bit.

I slowly tiptoed up to the window and scanned the roof of the garage, which my room sat on top of. Nothing. From inside the window, though, I could see little to either side. Trying to pretend to myself that I wasn't afraid in the slightest, I unlocked the window, slid it open, and—

The cheerful voice of a boy, seemingly right in my ear: "Boo."

2

I yelped, leapt back, and tumbled backward over my bed, crashing to the carpet behind it. I quickly peeked over the mattress, my heart going crazy, just as a dark, humanlike figure swung down from the roof of my room and perched on the windowsill.

After some careful consideration, I decided I'd seen enough. I scrambled to my feet and lunged for the door—but never reached it. Something grabbed my collar *(How the fuck did it move so fast?!)* and yanked me backward. I landed on the bed on my back, and before I could move, the figure was standing astride my waist. A boy's shadowy face loomed over me, eerily backlit by the moonlight, and for one heart-stopping moment, I was certain I was about to die.

Then the boy grinned broadly and said in a cheerful, Australian accent, "G'day, Ricky."

Hearing my name in his voice, I realized instantly:

This boy seemed somehow . . . *familiar* . . .

The boy backflipped off the bed—yeah, *backflipped*—and landed lightly on the floor in front of me. "No worries, mate," he said. "I'm na here to hurt ya."

I sat up slowly, my heart still freaking out, and glanced at the door. Common sense was advising me, *DON'T JUST SIT THERE, YOU DUMBASS*, RUUUUNNNN!!! But the boy's casual friendliness and distinct familiarity won me over.

I eyed him up and down. Seeing my inspection, the boy did a dainty pirouette, like a girl showing off a dress. He looked about my age, sixteen. He was lean and deeply tanned, and had a friendly face, twinkling blue eyes, and scruffy blond hair. He wore only a pair of dirty, tan shorts that looked like something an American Indian might have worn.

And for just an instant, I thought it looked like his right hand and wrist were glowing very faintly—as if his skin had absorbed a mist of pale light. It was just barely perceptible, though, and the next instant my mind had dismissed it as a trick of the moonlight.

"Who are you?" I asked, my voice slightly shaky.

"My name is Peter," the boy said, and he bowed theatrically, "...and I'm from the Island."

My breath caught.

After a moment, I said, "Which island?"

Peter grinned. "*The* Island."

"There's a lot of islands in the world."

His grin widened. "In *this* world, yeah."

That sentence seemed to whirl around the inside of my skull for a good five seconds, gathering momentum, before it slammed into my brain.

Then I said, "Holy shit."

I dashed into my bathroom and locked the door. I filled a cup to the brim with cold water from the sink and dumped it over my head. In movies, getting doused with cold water makes you more lucid and alert; in reality, I now discovered, it makes you more wet and cold. In the mirror, my eyes were puffy and bloodshot with dark circles underneath, my hair was sticking up in all directions, and my face was dripping wet.

So at least I *looked* perfectly sane.

I ripped the door open.

Peter was gone.

I carefully scanned the room three times, leaned out the doorway and looked to either side, and peered under my bed.

Nothing.

I let out a long, shaky sigh of relief and slumped against the door frame. "Jesus Christ," I whispered.

I must have been hallucinating. That was the only even remotely reasonable explanation I could think of—reasonable, perhaps, but hardly comforting. In fact, the notion that I was hallucinating was almost as disturbing as the notion that that kid was real and from the Island.

Can stress cause hallucinations? Probably not, or I'd be in a mental institution by now. Not counting high school, that is. Though even by the standards of the last few months, today *had* been extremely stressful.

I stayed slumped against the door frame for three or four minutes before I started trudging back to bed, still wondering what—

"Boo."

"JESUS *FUCK*!"

Peter was standing *right behind me*. Cackling.

"Where the fuck did you come from?!" I cried, looking around wildly. It was impossible. I'd looked around the entire room and he hadn't been there. There was nowhere to hide, no way in hell he could have popped up right behind me like that.

"Sorry 'bout that, mate," he laughed, "didn't mean to scare ya. Well, alrigh', I s'pose I did. But look, why don't we start over, ay? I just wanna talk."

"No." I stepped back, shaking my head. "You're not real. I'm not talking to you."

He frowned, looking politely puzzled. "Oh really?" He made a show of looking around. "Then may I ask *who* you're talking to?"

"I'm not talking to anybody, I'm hallucinating."

He grinned. "Oh, well, that must be a relief, ay? I'm not real, you're just batshit mental."

"I'm not '*mental*,'" I said, somewhat uncertainly. "It's just stress."

His grin widened. "Stress, ay? That a new name for LSD?"

"I'm not on drugs, either, all right?" I snapped.

"Well lemme just ask ya somethin', mate—when ya first saw me and ya started runnin' for the door, somethin' pulled ya back onto the bed, remema that? If I'm na real, how d'ya explain that?"

Oh shit. I'd forgotten about that. I stared at Peter, trying to act unfazed—more for my own sake than his—while groping frantically for an explanation. Finally, I said, "I tripped."

"Ah," he grinned and pointed at me, "so you admit it."

"Admit what?"

"You're on LSD." He threw his head back and cackled.

I covered my face with my hands. "I need to see a psychologist."

"Change a' heart, ay?"

I dropped my hands and looked at him sharply. "What'd you say?"

"Neva mind. Listen, mate . . . ya say ya stressed out, righ'? Well, I just happen to know the perfect way to relieve stress. So why don't ya just have a seat and let me explain, ay?"

My eyes gravitated toward the door—but again Peter's mirthful friendliness and my overwhelming wonder got the better of me.

I studied Peter again and frowned a bit in frustration. I still could not connect him with any specific memory—I felt almost certain I'd never seen him before—and yet somehow he seemed unmistakably familiar. . . . "Do I know you?" I asked.

"'Course ya do, mate. Ya know me from ya dreams—ya just havin' a bit a' trou—"

"Whoa, wait a sec," I said, staring at him quizzically, "did you say . . . from my *dreams*?"

"Uh-huh. Like that dream ya just had. The one about the Island."

My eyes widened. "How the . . . you . . . ?"

He grinned. "How'd I know 'bout that dream? I was *in* the dream, mate. Don't ya rememba? I told ya to wake up 'cause I was comin' to see ya."

I felt like an explosion had gone off inside my head—suddenly I *did* remember that. "But—but that's impossible, how'd you—"

"To make it simple, mate—very simple—I can communicate with ya through dreams. Which is how I told ya 'bout the Island. Oh, did I mention I live there?"

My mind was starting to spin crazily. "The Island's not real."

"And neither am I, righ'?" He laughed. "The Island *is* real, mate. But I couldn't just walk up to ya on the street one day and start *talkin'* 'bout it—ya woulda thought I was bloody mental. But people are much more open-minded in their dreams. So that's where I went first. I showed ya the Island through ya dreams. So that when I came tonight, I'd already have my foot in the door, ya see?"

My mind was now spinning so fast that the room itself seemed to be rotating. I knew what he was saying was impossible . . . and yet I could think of no explanation that *was* possible. Why else would Peter be so familiar when I was so certain I'd never seen him before? How else could he know about the Island? About my *dreams*?

"I can prove it, if ya want," Peter said, somewhat quietly. "I can show ya the Island. I can *take* you there." He was grinning at me eagerly, almost hungrily, his eyes sparkling. "Come with me," he said, nodding toward the open window.

That took me a beat to process. "What, like right now?"

Peter nodded. "Right now, mate."

I opened my mouth, but found I was too surprised to even think, much less speak.

Peter said, "Just think of it as, like . . . runnin' away from home for a bit."

That gave me a little jolt. I remembered, just hours ago, eyeing the door to the garage and—

"Ya were just thinkin' 'bout runnin' away, weren't ya?"

I looked at him sharply. "How the hell'd you know that?!"

7

"Ya told me yaself. In that dream ya just had. I know 'bout every-thin', mate—that's why I'm here. I know 'bout the last few months. I know 'bout today. And I know how much ya been wishin' ya could go to the Island. Well, now ya can stop wishin'. And hell, mate, why *not* get away? What's keepin' ya here?"

Nothing, I thought. And my throat tightened.

"I can come back whenever I want, right?" I asked.

"Yeah, a' course." Peter grinned. "I can't guarantee you'll want to, though."

"Where exactly is the Island?"

His grin widened. "It ain't on any maps."

"Then how do you get there?"

"You'll see. You'll like it there, I promise ya that. It's the most *wonderful* place. " He paused a moment, beaming at me excitedly. "So how 'bout it, mate?"

An actual escape to the Island, I thought wonderingly. An oppor-tunity to experience what before I could only imagine.

Quite literally, a dream come true.

I smiled slowly. "Yeah. I'm coming."

Chapter 2

"Then let's go already!" Peter said, and vaulted lightly through the window.

"Ya know we could just use the back door," I said, cocking a thumb over my shoulder.

"No need," Peter said.

That didn't seem like a very good argument, but I shrugged and started clambering out the window anyway. I stopped halfway, though, perched on the sill. The garage roof was fairly steep, there were virtually no handholds, and the edge of the roof was almost fifteen feet above the concrete driveway.

"Whoa," I said. "Uh, Peter? I'm not sure I can get down there—not without breaking my legs. I don't know how the hell you got up here."

"I flew."

"I'm serious, man, I don't think I can get down there."

"I'm serious too. And we're na goin' down."

I gawked at him. "Huh?"

He grinned. "We're na goin' down, mate. We're goin' *up*." He pointed skyward.

I looked up stupidly, as if expecting to see a ladder conveniently descending from the heavens, then cocked an eyebrow at Peter. "I suppose you own a helicopter or something? Island Airlines?"

"No, I can fly."

I snorted, smiling.

Peter just stared at me.

"You—you're kidding, right?" I said, my smile faltering.

He spread his hands innocently. "Would I kid ya, mate?"

I studied his face. "Are you serious?"

"I'm serious."

"Seriously?"

"I'm seriously serious. Seriously."

I eyed him incredulously another moment. Then a grin tugged at my lips. "All right, Superboy: Prove it."

Peter smiled—and my smile vanished. My heart seemed to stall as I watched his feet lift slowly off the roof. I leaned down and peered under his feet, then looked above his head for wires or something—but as far as I could tell, he really was levitating a foot in the air.

"Holy shit," I said.

Peter nodded. "Seriously."

"You can fucking fly."

"I commend your observational acuity." He dropped lightly back onto the roof. "And so can you."

I looked at him like he was batshit mental. *What?*

"You can fly too, mate."

I gave a burst of laughter. "Yeah—until I hit the ground."

"No, I'm serious, mate—seriously serious. It's quite simple, actually. Close ya eyes."

I narrowed my eyes suspiciously. "Why?"

"I'm gonna teach ya how to fly."

"I can't learn how to fly with my eyes open?"

"Just trust me, mate, it's important. Close ya eyes and keep 'em closed."

Though somewhat reluctantly, I went ahead and closed my eyes.

Peter's voice dropped a little. "Now all ya need to do is believe, Ricky," he said earnestly. "*Believe* ya can fly. Ya know 'The Little Engine That Could'? Fuck him. Don't *think* ya can, *believe* ya can. I know it sounds stupid, but ya can't fly if ya don't believe."

"All right, I believe."

There was a short pause.

"Really?" Peter said in surprise. "Well, that was easy."

"Hell, at this point, I'd believe just about anything."

"Alrigh' then—grab on."

I felt his forearm touch my hand, and without opening my eyes, I gripped it.

I noticed immediately that something didn't feel quite right, but it was so subtle that it took me a moment to pin it down: His arm felt cooler toward his hand than toward his elbow. And as I concentrated on this sensation, I noticed that the skin toward his hand also seemed to have a strange texture—somehow it felt coarse and slippery at the same time.

"Ya prepared for takeoff?" Peter said.

Immediately forgetting about what Peter's arm felt like, I shrugged and said, "What the hell."

"Just rememba, mate: Don't stop believin'."

"Just call me Journey, baby."

"Who?"

"Never mind. Let's go, I'm ready."

"Alrigh' then," Peter said, and he sounded like he was almost giggling with excitement. "Hang on."

I concentrated on believing. Though I probably didn't have to concentrate. Believing is easy when you don't think—and thinking is difficult when Journey is stuck in your head.

For a long moment, nothing happened.

Then I thought I heard a very faint ringing or clinking—it sounded as if the driver of a Hot Wheels toy car were jangling his keys in my ear. For some reason the sound made the hairs stand up on the back of my neck. I couldn't tell whether it was a distant loud sound or a nearby soft one—or was it just my ears playing tricks on me?

I was just about to ask Peter if he heard it too, when he called out, "Goiiinnnggg *UP!*"

I was yanked up and forward so fast that it felt like my arm almost popped out of its socket. Suddenly I was rocketing skyward at unbelievable speed, g-forces wrenching down on me, cold air blasting my face and roaring in my ears. Gripping Peter's wrist as tight as I could, I pried my eyes open and looked down. We'd only been flying for a couple seconds, yet we were already thousands of feet high—the ground resembled a starry sky, a black expanse strewn with countless pinpoints of light. I looked up. A blanket of low clouds loomed up ahead, faintly luminescent in the moonlight, approaching impossibly fast. I shut my eyes again just as we plunged into them; icy vapor prickled my skin and filled my lungs.

Then suddenly Peter jerked his forearm out of my grasp. I felt a heart-stopping jolt of terror. I didn't fall or even decelerate, as far as I could tell, just kept rocketing skyward. I opened my eyes and peered around frantically through the thick, rushing clouds, but Peter had vanished.

"PEEETTTEERRR!" I screamed as loudly as I could, but could barely hear myself over the roaring wind.

What happened next turned my whole world upside down—literally. I felt no change in speed or direction, and yet somehow, when I burst out of the clouds, I was no longer rocketing upward but plummeting straight down, headfirst. The darkness of night was suddenly gone, replaced by clear, blinding sunlight. Thousands of feet below, a misty, green, mountainous land lay bordering a vast ocean.

I squeezed my eyes shut and tried for a few seconds to concentrate on believing I could fly, but there was no effect. I started frantically flapping my arms and legs like wings, but this just set me to tumbling uncontrollably.

Apparently, without Peter, I couldn't fly at all.

I was going to fall all the way to my splattery death.

Panic flooded my mind. I flapped my limbs faster, furiously, even knowing it was useless, and screamed, "HEEEELLLLLPP—!"

A *whoosh* overhead, something grabbed my collar and yanked me sideways, and suddenly I seemed to be sliding along the air like a puck gliding on ice, feeling nearly weightless. It was Peter—and he was laughing hysterically.

"YOU *ASSHOLE*!" I screamed, which made him laugh even harder. "IF YOU *EVER* DROP ME AGAIN—"

He dropped me again. Instantly, gravity wrenched back down on me and I plummeted, tumbling, the world whirling and flipping sickeningly.

"PEETTTTERRRR!"

He nose-dived and easily grabbed my collar again, still cackling. I quickly grasped his wrist, and this time decided to shut the hell up.

"Sorry 'bout that, mate," Peter said through his laughter. "Couldn't help myself."

I scowled, but kept silent. We started gliding in wide circles, spiraling slowly downward. My body was a melee of jarring sensations—

heart hammering, head swimming, stomach churning. Nevertheless, I couldn't help looking down. We were still dizzyingly high.

And then, quite suddenly, wonder overcame my anxiety. "I'm flying," I said blankly, as if only now realizing it. I moved my arms and legs like I was swimming—the air felt substantially thicker than normal, as if partly liquid, while my body felt as if it were filled with feathers. The sensation was very unsettling—but even more thrilling. I felt a smile blooming on my face, then laughter bubbled up out of me, and then I howled with exhilaration, "I'm *FLYYYYING!*"

Peter chuckled. "Seriously."

"Is that it?" I asked excitedly, pointing down. "Is that the Island?"

"No," Peter said drily, "it's Iraq."

I slowly ran a hand through my hair. "Holy shit," I said softly. The Island was much bigger than I'd imagined, spreading for miles before fading into the distant haze; I could only wonder how far it stretched beyond that. Other than the size, though, the Island looked exactly as I'd imagined. The land was carpeted in lush, tropical greenery. Rolling hills and jagged mountains rose through the tattered mist. The pristine white beach seemed to shine in the sunlight. And the turquoise water was so clear that even from this height I could see an extensive coral reef just offshore.

We headed for a relatively small mountain abutting the shoreline. Covered in lush greenery dappled with gray rock, the mountain was shaped like a lopsided hump, with the seaward side slightly steeper than the landward side. About halfway up the sea side was a jagged, gaping orifice, the entrance to some sort of cave. Sticking out from the bottom lip of the opening was a stone ledge shaped roughly like a tongue.

Peter lowered me onto the ledge. The instant I let go of his wrist, gravity came crashing back down on me. My knees buckled and I stumbled slightly, but it only took me a couple seconds to get used to my normal weight again. Peter landed beside me.

I peered down the arched, tunnel-like cave, extending horizontally about thirty feet into the mountainside. A row of torches on either side of the tunnel provided a dim, flickering glow. At the end of the tunnel was a small, arched opening in the stone, like an undersized doorway.

"What is this?" I asked.

Peter nodded toward the opening. "That openin' down there leads to a tunnel that goes inside the mountain. My home."

"You live here?"

He nodded. "Inside the mountain, yeah."

I walked up to the tip of the ledge. I soaked in the view. Listened to the gentle rumble of the surf. Breathed in the fresh, salty scent of the ocean. The tropical air was intoxicating, the humidity perfectly offset by a cool breeze.

The Island was real.

It was hard to believe, but pretty impossible to deny. My many questions for Peter—*How can you fly? Are we still on Earth? Why'd you bring me here? Can we order a pizza?*—were temporarily forgotten. I couldn't move. I couldn't speak. I couldn't even think. I could only stand there gaping, letting my senses feast.

A splitting pain exploded at the base of my skull and—

Chapter 3

Lying on my side. Staring blankly forward. The darkness felt good on my half-lidded eyes, cushioning them like a plush pillow. Thinking faintly that it seemed darker than usual . . .

Suddenly I remembered. My eyes snapped wide.

No! I thought desperately. It couldn't have been a dream, it was so real! It felt *so real*!

I rolled onto my back—and realized I was tied up: thin ropes bound my wrists and ankles, and another circled my neck. And I wasn't in my bed, but on a cold, stone floor. I sat up, and a bolt of angry pain shot through my skull. I froze until the pain subsided to a dull throb.

Finally, I remembered blacking out.

Somebody must have knocked me unconscious.

Peter. Who else could it have been? But no, I couldn't believe that. Peter was so friendly—why the hell would he knock me out?

And why am I tied up? Where am I? What the hell is going on?!

I looked around, fighting panic. I was at the end of a roughly round, stone tunnel, about eight feet in diameter, with craggy walls and a relatively smooth floor. About forty feet ahead, the tunnel curved sharply to the left; from beyond the curve came a faint wash of firelight.

I guessed this was Peter's cave, but couldn't be sure. That would probably mean it really *was* Peter who had knocked me out and tied me up. But *why*? It made no sense.

I tried to think calmly but fear clouded my mind. Besides my rapid breathing, the only sound was the distant, echoing drip of water every couple seconds, as if from a leaky faucet. The air was clammy.

And there were smells—almost imperceptibly faint, yet somehow overpowering: urine. Feces. Vomit. And something even fainter, yet infinitely worse: rot.

My pulse quickened and my throat tightened, making my breath wheeze. The silence and darkness seemed to close in around me. . . .

I shut my eyes and forced myself to listen to my breathing and heartbeat, willing them to slow. After several seconds, I moved to lean my back against the wall—and as I did, my foot hit something.

And it moved.

I jerked my leg back with a gasp, and stared at the spot where my foot had been. For a moment I saw only solid blackness—then my eyes adjusted somewhat, and I made out a large mass sprawled on the ground. The tunnel was so dark I would never have seen it if I hadn't been looking for it. I leaned forward, and as my eyes adjusted a bit more—

A body.

A strangled gasp escaped me, and I scrambled backward until the rope caught and jerked me to a stop—the collar cut into my neck but I barely noticed. I pressed my back against the wall as if trying to pass through it, panic filling my mind like a deafening shriek. In my mind's eye the body sat up, its head a black hole, its rotting hands reaching for my face, and I try to back away but I can't go any farther, I can only scream—

But the body didn't move, and after about five seconds, the surge of shock and panic in my mind receded a bit, allowing rational thought to squeeze back in. I'd immediately assumed the body was dead, perhaps because of that rotten smell—but the smell was extremely faint, and the body was right next to me. It was possible the person had died very recently, but it seemed just as likely that he was simply unconscious—after all, *I* had been unconscious. It was probably another captive. In fact—

"Peter?" I croaked eagerly.

No response. My heart sank just as quickly as it had leapt. It could still be Peter, of course—he could just be unconscious—yet I suddenly felt irrationally certain that it wasn't him. As my mind continued to settle, the idea that Peter had done this to me was seeming more and more reasonable. The thought gave me a nauseating chill.

"Hello?" I said.

Still no response. This time I think I was relieved.

As much as I wanted to stay as far away from the body as possible, I had to at least know whether it was alive or dead. So, very slowly, I started crawling toward it. My heart thudded like a suspenseful drumbeat. The stillness suddenly seemed magnified. I was constantly expecting the body to bolt upright, but it didn't move. I stopped a couple feet away from the body, reached a hand out very, very slowly—and slapped the foot.

I immediately jerked my hand back and gasped a bit out of reflex—but the body didn't move.

I waited several seconds, then slapped the foot again.

No reaction.

18

I waited another few seconds. Then I slowly reached out and lightly gripped the leg right above the ankle. The skin was cool, but I could feel warmth underneath. Holding my breath in cautious excitement, I quickly slid my hand up the body until I found the neck and pressed two fingers against the carotid artery.

There was a pulse.

My breath escaped in a burst and my heart gave a tentative hop. I started running my hands lightly over the body. I guessed it was a girl because she had long hair, smooth, soft skin, and gentle facial features. Oh, and breasts. Which my hands happened to graze. Her body was slender and firm. Judging by her size—and her breasts—I guessed she was in her teens. (I realized this might be the only situation I'd ever encounter in my life in which I'd probably feel better feeling up a male.) Her clothes were frayed, dusty, and coarse like animal hide, and she was tied up like me. I felt nothing else unusual.

I debated for a moment trying to wake her up. I knew so little about what was going on that I was paranoid, so although she seemed to be just a normal human girl in the same situation as me, I figured she could be dangerous. On the other hand, she might be able to answer some of my questions and maybe even help me escape.

I decided to risk it.

Cue the dramatic music.

I shook her shoulder and said quietly, "Hey. Hey, wake up." No response. I shook her a bit harder and spoke louder: "Wake up. C'mon, wake up." I started lightly slapping her cheek. "Wake *up.*" I tried for about ten more seconds, but she didn't respond.

I blew out a breath and sat back on my haunches, wondering what to do. For the moment, I decided, there was nothing I could do about the girl. So, with an effort, I shut her out of my mind. She was hardly the only issue at hand anyway.

I fingered the rope around my neck. It wasn't chokingly tight, but tight enough that I couldn't possibly free my head. The other end of the rope was tied around a small metal ring embedded in the floor. For several minutes, I tried every way I could think of to get free—tried to squeeze my head through the loop, untie the knots, uproot the metal ring, chew through the rope, snap it with brute force.

But nothing worked.

So I went to Plan B.

"HEEELLLLPPPP!" I screamed as loud as I could. Loud, eerie echoes filled the tunnel, seemingly mocking me. "SOMEBODY HEELLLPPP!"

A distant voice: "Where are you?"

My heart leapt. Was that Peter? It was definitely a boy's voice, but so distant and distorted that otherwise I couldn't tell. What if it *was* Peter? What would that mean?

I decided I didn't care who it was. I was in no position to be choosy.

The voice repeated, louder, "Where are you?!"

"I don't know," I called, "but I need help, I'm tied up. Is that you, Peter?"

A slight pause. "Just hold on. I'll come find you."

Not Peter, apparently. Who, then?

I waited tensely, blood pounding in my temples, trying to ignore those sickening smells and that eerie, maddening *drip . . . drip . . .* A couple minutes passed, and I was just about to call out again when a shadow crossed the firelight up the tunnel; I shrunk against the wall, holding my breath. A moment later, a boy rounded the bend and stopped, silhouetted by the firelight. His knees were bent and his shoulders hunched, like he was sneaking around, and held out in front of him with both hands was a—

A sword.

"You down there?" he called softly.

Well, I thought with an inward shrug of desperation, *swords can cut ropes.*

"Yeah," I called back.

"Sick." He reached out a hand like a blind man and started walking slowly toward me. "I can barely see, so sorry if I run into you."

"As long as that sword doesn't run into me," I said, only half joking. The boy laughed shortly, but said nothing. "Uh . . . just outta curiosity . . . you're not gonna kill me, are you?"

"Depends. Are you a Yankees fan?"

I frowned quizzically. "Uh . . . no . . . ?"

"Then no, I'm not gonna kill you."

Straining my eyes, I could just see the boy as he came up to me. "I'm right here," I said, and reached out and touched his bare shoulder. I instinctively tensed for a blow—but none came. "Could you help me, I'm tied u—"

"Yeah, I know," he said. "Just gimme a second for my eyes to adjust and then I'll cut you loose."

"Who are you?"

"Your savior."

"Wow. Not much of a Second Coming."

"Huh?"

"Never mind," I said. "Where's Peter? Do you know Peter?"

"Peter's a dick—that's why his name's Peter. Just be glad he isn't here."

"And why the hell am I tied up?"

He smiled thinly. "Like I said, Peter's a dick. Listen, I'll—what the *fuck*?!" The boy jumped back, sweeping me against the wall with one arm and pointing his sword at the girl, who I'd completely forgotten about. "Who the hell is that?!"

"I don't know," I said. "It's a girl. She was here when I woke up."

He looked at me sideways. "Is she alive?"

21

"Yeah, just unconscious. I already tried to wake her up but I couldn't."

The boy leaned forward and put his face out toward the girl—it looked like he was smelling her. After a couple seconds, he felt her neck for a pulse. Then he started trying to wake her, speaking in her ear and shaking her. As she continued to not respond, his efforts became more and more vehement. Finally, after almost a full minute, he sat back on his haunches and muttered, *"Shit."*

"Excuse me," I said as politely as I could, "would you mind telling me what the fuck is going on?"

"Later," the boy said distractedly. "Right now we gotta hurry." He drew a knife from his rope belt and sawed through the collar around the girl's neck. He started sawing through the rope around her wrists too, but after just a few strokes he stopped, hesitated a moment, then withdrew the knife, leaving the rope intact. Then he sawed through all my binds. "Now c'mon," he said, "we gotta get outta here." He slung the girl over one shoulder with surprising ease and started striding swiftly down the tunnel. I followed close behind.

As we rounded the bend, we passed a dim, wall-mounted torch. I couldn't see the girl's face, but I saw that she had black hair and brown skin—I guessed she was Hispanic. I also noticed that the boy was dripping wet. I almost asked why, but then decided I should probably wait.

The unbroken tunnel twisted and zigzagged incessantly. On and on we strode, slowing cautiously at corners and bends, accelerating past torches. The faint, widely spaced torches provided the only light.

About a minute after we'd started walking, the boy was rounding a corner when he suddenly jumped back, bumping into me. He looked around quickly, then pressed his back against the wall, grabbed my sleeve, and pulled me alongside. "Don't move," he breathed.

I froze, my heart thumping so hard it made me slightly nauseous. I fought to rein in my bucking anxiety as I wondered why we were hiding. The nearest torch was around a bend behind us; our immediate surroundings were almost completely black. I listened intently but heard nothing except that ubiquitous *drip . . . drip . . . drip . . .*

Then suddenly I smelled it—the same rotten smell I'd noticed earlier, but now suffocatingly strong, filling the tunnel like a thick cloud. A second later I felt, more than saw, something moving just a couple feet in front of me. For one heart-stopping moment I thought it was coming for us, and I recoiled against the wall, my mind screaming with panic—

And then it was past us, continuing down the tunnel, the smell rapidly fading. Slowly, half reluctantly, I started turning my head to look. . . .

The boy grabbed my arm and yanked me around the corner.

After we'd rounded another bend, I whispered, "What the hell *was* that?!"

"I'll explain later," the boy said distractedly. "We're almost there."

A minute later, the tunnel branched into two; we took the right branch. After several more twists and turns, the boy stopped beside a torch and started running his hands over the floor, sliding his fingers along the countless cracks in the stone.

After almost a minute, I whispered, "What are you looking for?"

"This," the boy said, and he stuck his fingers deep into a crack and, with a grunt, pulled upward. A jagged square of rock popped loose, revealing an opening about the size of a manhole cover. The boy slid the stone aside, picked up the girl again, and hopped through the opening. I lowered myself carefully after him into a cramped space enclosed by rock. The boy dragged the stone back into place, shutting us in near blackness.

After about thirty seconds to let our eyes readjust, the boy said, "All right, let's go," and started moving.

I took one step and banged my head against a rock jutting down from the ceiling.

"And watch your head," the boy added.

"Thanks," I said acidly, grimacing and rubbing my head.

The boy squeezed through a narrow gap in the rocks, inched forward another few feet, then stopped and turned around. Just beyond him, the floor abruptly fell away. "All right," he said, "there's a drop right here, so you're gonna have to climb down, all right? It really isn't that hard—but if you *do* fall, you'll probably kill yourself. Or you'll land on me and I'll die, which is worse. So just take your time, all right?"

I nodded. "Yeah, all right."

The boy had left the girl's wrists bound, and now he slipped one of his arms through her arms so that she'd hang from his shoulder.

"Hey, uh," I said uneasily, "don't you think she's too heavy for that?"

He laughed. "You're lucky she's unconscious."

"Seriously, are you sure you can get down there?"

"Nope," he said lightly. "But I'll find out."

Then, grunting with exertion, he lowered himself over the edge and started climbing down as if on a ladder. I leaned forward and peered over the edge. The roughly tubular cave dropped straight down. In the darkness, I could only see about ten feet down; I couldn't see the bottom. I swallowed with difficulty, my mouth suddenly dry. But then I thought, *He's doing it with another person on his back. Stop being a bitch.* And I started climbing down.

It was surprisingly easy—the coarse, notched rock offered plenty of handholds, and the drop was only about twenty feet. (There was no way in hell I could have done it with another person on my back, though—the boy must have been incredibly strong.) My limbs and chest got scraped up, but I didn't die, so I can't complain.

When we reached the bottom, we started crawling through a series of downward-sloping tunnels, the boy carrying the girl on his back. The rock was moist, and there were small puddles in some places. I was kind of grateful for the near-blackness, because I think if I could see just how tight these spaces were I would have gotten claustrophobic.

We'd been crawling along for about five minutes when I thought I heard something. I stopped.

The boy looked back. "What's the matter?"

"Listen," I whispered. It was a very faint, distant, continuous rumble. "You hear that?"

"That rumbling sound?"

"Yeah."

"That's just the river, don't worry about it. C'mon."

The rumble got gradually louder as we progressed. Five minutes later, we stopped at a gaping crevice in the floor. I peered through it into a tunnel-like cavern. Ten feet down was a rushing, roaring river, which flowed out of the cavern through a broad, underwater opening. Daylight streamed in through the opening, making the river glimmer and buoying my heart—I'd thought I might never see daylight again.

"All right, listen up," the boy said loudly over the roaring water. "We're gonna drop down into the river. The current'll take you through that opening and outside. I'm gonna go first. Wait about five seconds, then go in after me. Stay close to this side of the river, and once you're outside, try to climb onto the bank. Got it?"

I nodded. "Yeah, I got it."

The boy covered the girl's mouth and pinched her nose shut with one hand, then casually stepped through the crevice. They slid into the water feetfirst and instantly disappeared. I counted five seconds, gazing nervously along the careening, foaming river, then held my breath and jumped in. The water was freezing, but I barely had time to notice. The powerful current sucked me underwater, flung me through the opening like a rag doll, and launched me outside like a cannon, all in barely two seconds. The moment I surfaced, the boy grabbed my collar and dragged me onto a muddy bank.

He helped me to my feet. "You all right?"

"Yeah."

"Then c'mon, let's go."

Before I could respond, he raced off into the jungle along the river, the girl once again slung over his shoulder. I stumbled after him, nearly blinded by the sunlight. Even carrying the girl, the boy weaved effortlessly through the foliage, obviously familiar with the terrain, and I struggled to keep up. The muggy air seemed to weigh me down.

After a couple minutes, he mercifully slowed to a jog, still following the river. Without stopping, he took what looked like an undersized coconut out of his pocket, kissed it quickly, then put it back.

After maybe fifteen long minutes, we stopped. The boy laid the girl down by the edge of the river, sawed through her binds with his knife, and threw them into the river. He cupped some water in his hand and trickled it into her mouth; she coughed a little, but I saw her throat work as she swallowed.

Even with her face sickly, her shoulder-length hair disheveled, and her skin smeared with dirt, she was very pretty. She was lean, and her naturally dark skin, her black hair, and something about her face or eyes, I think, gave her an alluringly exotic aura. Her blouse and capris appeared to be made of the same material as the shorts Peter had worn. Neither the blouse nor the capris accentuated her curves at all, but the rips in the clothes provided tantalizing glimpses of skin.

I noticed all this inadvertently in one look; I really wasn't checking her out. Nevertheless, I gave myself a little mental slap. *Can't you at least wait till she's conscious before you start being a pig?* I said to myself.

To which myself replied: *You say pig, I say teenage guy.*

I also got my first good look at the boy. He was about my age, maybe slightly older, and fairly tall. He looked like a stereotypical surfer—bronze skin, longish, disheveled blond hair, and a cheery face. And he was impressively ripped, particularly his upper body.

Despite carrying the girl, he didn't seem winded at all; I, however, was doubled over and heaving for breath, feeling like I was dying. And death didn't sound all that bad—my lungs probably wouldn't hurt so much if I was dead.

"You shouldn't bend over like that," the boy said. "Stand up straight and put your hands on the back of your head. Opens up the lungs so you get more air."

I eyed him quizzically. "What're you, a PE teacher?"

He grinned. "Nah. I'm a PE teacher's dream come true, though."

"You're a good retirement plan?"

"What?"

I shook my head. "Never mind."

"Name's Alex Starkey, by the way." He extended his hand. I hesitated automatically, glancing at his hand, then back at his face. He grinned. "Don't they still shake hands in reality, or have I been gone that long?"

I hesitated another beat, wondering what the hell that meant, then slowly reached out and shook his hand. "Ricky Darlin."

He nodded approvingly. Then he picked up the girl again and started striding briskly along the river. Groaning inwardly, I followed alongside. After a couple minutes, when I was breathing easier and reasonably confident I wasn't going to die, I asked, "What did you mean, 'in reality'?"

"What?"

"You said, 'Don't they still shake hands in reality.' What do you mean by 'in reality'?"

For just an instant the boy hesitated, looking uncomfortable—but the instant passed so quickly I didn't take much notice. "Back home," he said, "where you and I both came from. That's reality."

I cocked an eyebrow. "And . . . all this . . ." I waved around. ". . . *Isn't* reality?"

"Not exactly."

I waited a couple seconds, but he didn't elaborate.

"What the hell does that mean?" I asked.

"Well . . . a lotta things—*most* things, actually—are just like they are in reality: you, me, the trees, the water, the birds—well, most of the birds. But then some things . . . well . . . uh . . . ya know what, there's really someone else who should explain all this. I'd probably just confuse you even more."

I had so many other questions I didn't bother pressing him. I ran my hands through my hair, trying to decide where to start. "All right—you said you know Peter, right?"

"Unfortunately."

"And he's the one that tied me up?"

"Yeah. Probably knocked you out, too, huh?"

I nodded faintly and touched the base of my skull. A dull ache remained, though I'd forgotten about it until now. "How the hell could he do that?"

"Probably just with a rock or something."

"No, I mean . . . he seemed so . . ."

"Cool? Friendly?" Alex looked at me sideways, smiling thinly. "Yeah. He's a hell of an actor, I'll give him that much. It's that Australian accent that got me. If he'd had a New York accent I woulda kicked his ass in a heartbeat."

"So why'd he do it?" I asked, frowning.

"I wish I knew."

I raised an eyebrow. "You have no idea?"

He pursed his lips and shook his head. "Your guess is as good as mine."

I nodded toward the girl. "Who's she, then?"

He looked at her face thoughtfully. "I'm not sure."

"But you have an idea?"

"Yeah," he said slowly, "but . . . well, it's complicated. And you probably wouldn't believe it anyway."

"Well, no offense, but I'm not sure I believe anything you're saying."

He laughed darkly. "Trust me . . . you'll start believing soon enough."

"All right, fine, then who are *you*? I mean, why'd you rescue me? How'd you get here?"

"Well, basically, the same thing happened to me that happened to you. Peter convinced me to come to the Island, flew me over here, then knocked me out, tied me up, and threw me in his caves. I'm not really sure how long I was in there—longer than you, though, I can tell ya that much. You got the express service. But anyway . . . I just sat there until I got rescued."

"Who rescued you?"

"The Captain—same guy who came up with the plan to rescue you. And the others, for that matter. He's our leader, basically. That's why we call him Captain." I opened my mouth, but Alex raised a hand to stop me, looking vaguely uncomfortable again. "*He* should be telling you all this, not me. He can explain a lot better than I can. We'll be there in just a bit."

I didn't bother asking where "there" was.

After another couple minutes, Alex said, "Here it is." He walked up to a thick, towering tree and swept an arm out to push aside the dense ferns around the trunk, revealing a sort of chasm in the ground between two gnarled buttress roots.

I eyed the opening warily; it looked big enough for a person to duck into. "That some kinda giant gopher hole?"

Alex smiled thinly. "It wasn't a gopher."

I cocked an eyebrow at him.

He shook his head. "You don't wanna know."

I figured he was probably right. "So where's it go?" I asked, nodding toward the opening.

"We call it the burrow. Our home away from home." Alex stepped forward and ducked into the opening—but then paused and looked back at me. "Oh, and, uh . . . watch your head." He grinned.

Before I could respond, he turned back and continued into the opening. I followed cautiously. The opening led to an earthen, downward-sloping tunnel, about as wide as a car but so low we had to almost crawl.

We'd gone about ten feet when a faint, gruff male voice up ahead said, "Alex?"

"No, it's Peter," Alex said.

"Did ya get him?"

"*Them*, actually."

At the end of the tunnel was a large opening in the ground. Alex hopped through the opening, dropping about five feet. I followed and emerged into a roughly rectangular earthen chamber, about thirty feet long and twenty feet wide, lit only by the daylight spilling down the tunnel. Gnarled tree roots bulged from the walls and ceiling. Several brightly colored quilts lay scattered about the floor, and another hung on the far wall like a painting. In the center of the room was a small fire-pit ringed with stones.

A man and a boy stood before us, waiting to meet us. The man, who I presumed was the Captain, was tall and wiry, with shoulder-length, curly black hair, a scraggly beard, and a very crooked nose. His body and face were so weather-beaten that it was hard to tell how old he was; at first glance he looked middle-aged, but looking closer, there was something about him—I really don't know what—that made me decide he was much younger, probably only early twenties. The boy was about my age, black, average height and build, and had tousled, shoulder-length dreadlocks. They both wore trousers of the same material as Peter's and the girl's clothes; the boy also wore a baggy Packers Brett Favre jersey.

"Don't get comfy, lad," the Captain said in a grave, English-accented drawl. "We're settin' sail."

"What?" Alex said in surprise and confusion. "Where we going?"

"Anywhere but here."

"*What?* What the hell are you—" Alex broke off, seeming to suddenly realize something.

"Oscar's gone," the Captain said.

Chapter 4

Alex's mouth fell open. He looked like he'd been socked in the stomach. "She—she's dead?"

"No, unfortunately," the Captain said grimly. "Not yet, anyways. Which is why we gotta get outta here."

"We're gonna rescue her?" Alex said with a mix of hope and skepticism.

"Lad, ye know as well as I do that that'd be bloody suicide. If not worse. We're leavin' 'cause ye can bet your arse Peter's gonna try and get Oscar to lead him to the burrow. Now, we all know Oscar's tougher 'n hardtack, but . . . the devil only knows what he'll do to her."

"Jesus Christ," Alex said weakly, slumping against the wall. He stared blankly ahead for a few seconds, his mouth still hanging open, looking almost hypnotized. Then suddenly he wheeled toward the Captain, his demeanor fiercely gung ho. "We gotta do *something*, Cap. We can't just—*abandon* her—"

"If ye can think of a decent plan, lad, I'd love to hear it."

"We are still trying to think of one," the boy said with strained hopefulness.

"But I ain't losin' anyone else," the Captain said. "We don't wanna waste her sacrifice. We still won today, mind ye—we lost one but we gained two."

"Actually I think we only gained one," Alex said.

"Why? Is she dead?" the Captain asked, nodding at the girl in Alex's arms.

"No, just unconscious. But take a closer look."

Alex laid the girl down on a quilt. The Captain and the boy stepped up to her and bent over, hands on knees, studying her.

After a moment, the boy said, "She looks like . . ."

"Bloody hell," the Captain murmured in awe. He studied the girl up and down for another few seconds, his mouth ajar. Then he blew out an angry breath, wheeled around, and started pacing. "Well that's just bloody *marvelous*," he ranted to himself, gesticulating frenetically. "What the hell are we s'posed to do with her?"

Suddenly he stopped pacing and looked straight at me. Our eyes locked for what felt like an unnaturally long moment. His gaze was so piercing that a few hairs stood up on the back of my neck.

Then he glanced at Alex. "Does he know yet?"

Alex shook his head.

The Captain turned back to me and forced a small smile. "Me apologies for this welcoming—or lack thereof, I should say." He walked up to me and extended his hand. "James Hooke."

I shook it. "Ricky Darlin."

"Welcome aboard, lad."

The boy walked up to me too. His eyes seemed doleful and weary, but his smile, though not much bigger than Hooke's, was warm and genuine. "Nigel Mason," he said, extending his hand. I shook it. "Nice to meet you, man," he said.

"Yeah, you too."

"I imagine ye got a few questions," Hooke said to me, "and I'll answer e'erythin' I can in just a bit. But righ' now we gotta pack up and go. I reckon it'll take two trips."

"Where exactly are we gonna go?" Alex asked.

"I got a spot in mind," Hooke said. "Now c'mon, let's get movin'."

Crammed into one corner of the room were some folded quilts, wicker baskets, coils of rope, reddish clay pots of various shapes and sizes, and an array of knives, swords, spears, axes, and round wooden shields. We divvied everything up among ourselves, and just managed to get everything at once, though not without a little creativity (Alex wore one of the pots like a hat).

After hauling our loads up the tunnel, we set off into the jungle in single file. I noticed almost immediately that Hooke was extremely edgy; his head jerked and his eyes darted about constantly.

Just as I was about to start asking questions, Hooke spoke, in a near whisper: "Alrigh', lad. Now, I'm sure you're wonderin' why you're here—why'd Peter bring ye here, why'd he knock ye out and tie ye up and all that, righ'? Unfortunately, we don't know. All we know is that 'bout once or twice a year, as bes' we can reckon, Peter flies to reality, brings back some lad, usually a teenager, then knocks him out, ties him up, and throws him in his cave. After that, we don't know what he does."

"What do you think he does?" I asked.

"Honestly, lad, your guess is as good as ours."

"Whatever it is, though," Alex said, "we doubt it's very pleasant— at least, not for the kid."

"So why me?" I asked. "I mean, of all the people in the world, why'd Peter choose me?"

"Well, we don't know the main reason," Hooke said. "We don't even know why Peter brings lads here at all, so it's kinda hard to say how he picks 'em. But—well, lemme ask ye somethin', lad: What was goin' on at your home afore ye came to the Island?"

"What do you mean?"

"Well . . . was there anythin' *unusual* goin' on? Any kinda, like . . . problems?"

I drew my head back, shocked. How could he possibly know anything about that?

After a beat—just long enough to see my reaction—Hooke said, "Ye don't have to answer that, lad. Ya see, all the lads Peter brings out here to the Island—all the ones I know of, anyway—they all had some kinda problem back home. Some reason they wanted to get away. Somethin' that made 'em more willin' to say 'aye' when Peter asked 'em to fly away with him."

"But obviously," Nigel said, "there's millions of troubled teenagers—hell, that's practically redundant—so that can't be the main reason."

"Well, why didn't he just kidnap me?" I asked. "I mean, just grab me outta bed and fly away?"

"Well, again," Hooke said, "we don't really know. But me guess is it's something like this: Ye gotta *believe* in the Island to get here. Ye gotta *believe* ye can fly, and ye gotta be *willin'* to fly. So for a long time, Peter works on convincin' ya that the Island really is real—and he does that with dreams. I got no idear how it works, but somehow, he got *into* your dreams, and introduced himself. Told ye 'bout the Island. Advertised it, basically."

"Otherwise," Alex said, "when he showed up at your house and offered to take you here, you woulda beaten him over the head with a baseball bat."

"Or declined in some other fashion," Hooke said. "Ye understand, lad?"

"Yeah, I think so." Suddenly I remembered something. "Oh

35

yeah—back in the burrow you asked Alex if I knew something yet, and he said no. What was that about?"

For a moment Hooke didn't respond in any way, and I thought he hadn't heard me. Then he slowed to a stop. I noticed he took a deep breath before turning around. His face was grim.

A worm of dread wriggled into my stomach.

"Let's take a break, lads," Hooke said.

I glanced back. Alex and Nigel were setting their loads down in silence—and not looking at me. Suddenly my mouth and throat felt dry. I set my stuff down too.

Hooke took another breath and cleared his throat. His eyes were on mine, but somehow he didn't seem to be really looking at me. "Alrigh', lad—there ain't any easy way to say this, so I'll just get it o'er with." He took one more breath, then spoke slowly: "As far as we know, only Peter has the power to fly—the power to move between here and reality. So, to get back to reality, we have to capture Peter—and at the moment, we don't know how to do that. So, what that means is . . . ye can't go home. Yet. You're stuck here with us, for a while."

I felt like an explosion had gone off right next to my head. My ears were ringing and my brain seemed to be working slow and laboriously.

Jesus fucking Christ, why hadn't this occurred to me before? Why would these people be living here unless—

I fought to stay calm and think clearly. *It's probably not as bad as you think,* I told myself. *You're just assuming the worst.*

"How long is a while?" I asked. My voice was surprisingly, deceptively calm.

"Howe'er long it takes to capture Peter," Hooke said.

"How long is that?"

"We don't know, lad."

"Well how long do you think it'll be?"

"Honestly, lad, it'd be pointless to guess."

"All right, fine," I snapped, my anxiety facilitating irritation, "then how long have you guys been here?"

Hooke hesitated.

"A few weeks?" I prompted.

Hooke looked away uncomfortably.

"Months?" I pressed, a note of panic seeping into my voice.

Still Hooke said nothing. I looked at Alex and Nigel; they, too, were tight-lipped and avoiding my eyes.

"*Years?!*" I cried.

"Alex and I have been here for about a year," Nigel said. "Cap's been—"

The dam shattered; panic flooded through me with gut-wrenching force. "I thought all we had to do was capture Peter?!"

"Well, aye," Hooke said uncomfortably, ". . . but . . . that's a lot easier said than done."

"Why?!" I demanded. "Why can't you just . . . *catch* the little fucker?!" I grasped at the air as if I were grabbing the back of Peter's collar.

"'Cause he can fly," Alex said. "And 'cause he's . . . protected."

"Have you ever *tried* to catch him?"

"Aye, we've tried," Hooke said.

"We're always trying, really," Nigel said.

"So when are we gonna try again?"

"I'm sorry, lad," Hooke said. "I just can't say."

"So what if we never catch him?"

They all answered at once: "We will."

"But what if we don't? What if we *can't*?"

No answer.

"Holy fuck," I breathed, and turned away, covering my face with my hands. The unspeakable answer to my last question filled my

mind: *You'll never go home. You'll be stuck here for the rest of your life.*
Just the possibility seemed too staggering and horrible to be real.
Suddenly my head swam and my throat seemed to close up—I felt
like I was drowning.

But they said we'll get him, I told myself desperately, *they said we
will, they said—*

But they couldn't say when, and they'd already been here a year.
How much longer would it take? Another year? Two? Twenty?

But my life, was all I could think in response, and the inconceiv-
able enormity of that simple fragment swallowed my mind like a
black hole. I slumped against a tree, feeling a sort of crushing small-
ness that I'd never felt before.

My life.

Someone put a hand on my shoulder.

I looked over. It was Nigel. He opened his mouth but hesitated
a moment, then closed it, and instead gave my shoulder a gruff
squeeze. He didn't have to speak. His dark eyes mirrored my anxiety, and for some reason, that was comforting—suddenly I didn't
feel quite so lost.

"We are gonna get Peter someday," Hooke said softly. He was
gazing skyward, his eyes murky—he seemed to be speaking as much
to himself as me. "Someday soon."

"It really isn't so bad here, though," Alex said, smiling at me
feebly. "I mean . . . things could be a lot worse."

"Yeah," Nigel said drily. "At least the weather's nice."

"And," Alex said soberly, placing a hand on his chest, "you could
not have asked for better company."

I smiled—genuinely—but only for a moment. I breathed a
shaky sigh and sat down with my back against the tree. The others
politely pretended to ignore me.

My life.

Even as I consciously clung to the hope that I'd get home within a few months, the possibility that I'd be stuck here for a significant portion—if not the rest—of my life, dominated my mind as if it were a probability or even a certainty.

My whole fucking life. Everything. Gone.

Yeah, my life had been fucked up in many ways—yeah, I'd been angry, depressed, whatever—but that didn't mean I'd wanted to throw my life away completely and permanently. I'd just wanted a vacation. And if I knew I was only going to be here for a few days, a couple weeks, maybe even a month or two, I wouldn't have been homesick at all. But knowing I might never go home, or not for a long, long time—that changed everything.

Suddenly I missed my life.

My parents, my relatives, girls, foods, drinks, books, magazines, TV, movies, sports, music, video games, the Internet, girls, driving, hot showers, my bed, sleeping in on weekends, sleeping in class, getting good grades on tests I hadn't studied for, even the bittersweet things like talking to my old friends and antagonizing my teachers and making my classmates laugh and talking openly with Dr. Komori, plus my future, which was its own boundless category. Oh, and girls.

There was just so much. Too much. I felt like a fat chunk of my heart and lungs had been ripped out, leaving a wheezy, aching emptiness in my chest. And I knew the pain would only get worse with time.

And that was only the pain of loss. A new pain had bored into me and now seemed to be clawing and biting at my very soul.

Guilt.

My parents would be miserable. Worried sick. Wondering what happened to me, whether I was okay. They'd probably feel guilty themselves. And every day their fears would grow and their hopes would wane. Eventually they'd have to assume the worst.

If I never got home, I might as well have murdered them. Actually, that might have been more merciful. And even to me, even at the moment, that seemed melodramatic—I *wished* it was melodramatic—but I knew it was true. I was their only child. I was their life. And now I was gone.

And what made that so much worse was that part of me had wanted it. Part of me had wanted to hurt them.

Why? For Christ's sake why in the *fuck* would I want that?

"Hindsight," I said, "is a bitch."

Alex nodded solemnly. "Word."

Nigel stared at him.

This wasn't final. I could still make this right. I *had* to make this right.

So stop feeling sorry for your pansy-ass self and fucking do it.

"All right," I said, and the strength of my voice surprised even me, "so lemme get this straight—to get home, we have to capture Peter, right?"

"Aye, lad," Hooke said.

"And that's the *only* way to get back?"

Hooke nodded. "Far as I know."

"There aren't even any ways that you think *might* work?"

"I already tried e'erythin' I thought migh' work. Nothin' did."

"So if we *do* get Peter, you're sure we can get back, right?"

Hooke opened his mouth but hesitated uncomfortably. My heart plummeted like a brick.

"Not exactly," Hooke said carefully.

"What do you mean, not exactly?" I demanded, panic rising in me again. "Why? If he could fly us here, why couldn't he fly us back?"

"Oh, I got no doubt he's *capable* a' flyin' us back—I just seriously doubt he would."

"Why?"

"'Cause if he did," Nigel said, "we'd kill him. And he knows it."

"You mean we'd kill him once we got back?"

"Yeah," Nigel said.

"Why?"

"Two reasons," Hooke said. "One, if we let him go, he'd go righ' back to kidnappin' innocent lads; and two, he migh' be afeared we'd find a way to *stop* him from kidnappin' lads, so he migh' try and kill us just to be safe. And keep in mind, it don't even matter whether or not we'd *actually* kill him—it only matters whether or not he *thinks* we would. And ye can bet your arse he's thought it through. The last thing he'll wanna do is take us back."

"But it doesn't matter what he wants," I said. "If we capture him, we can make him do whatever the hell we want."

"That's true," Alex said. "When we're on the ground."

"What do you mean?"

"Just think about it," Alex said. "When we're on the ground, if we want him to go somewhere, we can just drag him if we have to, and there's nothing he can do about it, right? But as soon as we're in the air, he's got more control than us—he's flying us, we're not flying him."

"And that's just too damn dangerous," Hooke said. "We can't just hold on to him, like hold his hand or somethin', 'cause he could pro'ly just shake us off and drop us. So we'd have to tie him to us with ropes. But there's still all sorts a' things he could do—he could dive down and bash us against some rocks, he could scrape us against a cliff, he could fly us back to his mountain, he could—well, ye get the idear."

"So if we're not gonna let Peter fly us back, how *are* we gonna get back?"

"Well, we don't know yet," Hooke said. "But if there is another way, we figure Peter'd be the one to know it."

"*If* there's another way?!" I cried in horrified disbelief. "You're not even sure there *is* one?!"

"Well—no," Hooke said uncomfortably, "but—"

"Do you even have any reason to *think* there is?!"

"We don't got any reason to think there ain't."

"And I don't have any reason to think punching myself in the face won't get me home, that doesn't mean it *will*!"

"It won't," Hooke said soberly. "I've tried."

I rubbed my face hard with both hands, fighting to stay calm. "Even if there is a way, why would Peter tell us? You just said, he doesn't want us back in reality."

Hooke smiled darkly. "I'm pretty confident we can . . . uh . . . *persuade* him to tell us."

"But what if we can't? Or what if there really is no way? What do we do then?"

"Well," Hooke said, "then I s'pose we'll have to decide whether we wanna take the risk and let him fly us. There are things we could do to minimize the risk, like tyin' him to us, maybe starvin' him for a few days to make him weak—but that should still only be a very last resort, if anythin'."

I shut my eyes and pinched the bridge of my nose. The notion that getting home was very difficult was bad enough; the notion that it might be impossible was significantly worse.

But "might be impossible" still meant "possible," didn't it? There was still hope. Not much, but enough. Enough to subsist on.

"All right," I said, "so I don't get it—what's so hard about catching Peter?"

"Well, there's a few things," Alex said. "For one, he can fly. If he sees us coming for him, all he needs is a second," Alex said, snapping his fingers, "and he'll be up and outta our reach. Think about trying to catch a bird."

"So what if he doesn't see us coming?" I said with a shrug. "We just grab him before he can fly away?"

"It's not that easy," Alex said.

"Why not?"

"'Cause he's protected."

"By who?"

"By *what*, more like," Hooke said grimly. "His Boys."

"His *Boys*?"

"The Lost Boys, is what we call 'em. There be Lost Girls, too, but there really ain't no difference far as I'm concerned."

"So who—er, what are they?"

"Well, it's kinda hard to explain," Hooke said. "They're like people—kids, mostly—at least they look like kids—who ain't completely alive but ain't completely dead. They're like . . . well, they're like corpses, only they can still move around."

"Zombies," Nigel said.

"*Zombies*?" I said, looking at Nigel skeptically. "You gotta be kidding me."

He shook his head. "I wish I was."

"Hell," Alex said, smiling, "you practically met one already."

"I did?" I said.

"Remember back in the cave, that thing that walked past us?"

"That was a *zombie*?"

Alex nodded. "That was a Lost Boy, yeah."

"Why do you call 'em Lost Boys?"

"'Cause when you look at their faces, in their eyes, it's like there's no one in there," Nigel said. "It's like they're gone. Lost. It's kinda hard to explain, but when you see one up close, you'll understand."

"So what do they do, exactly?" I asked.

"Whate'er Peter tells 'em to," Hooke said. "They live—er, exist,

I s'pose—to serve him. He uses 'em as servants, hunters, fishers, all sorts a' things—but mostly he uses 'em as guards. And he's got a small army of 'em."

"So can you, like . . . *kill* them?"

"Oh, aye. Just gotta cut off the head or destroy the brain. They're actually pretty easy to kill—they ain't great fighters. See, I said they're partially dead, righ'? Well, methinks they're partially *decayed*, too. Physically and mentally. They seem to be a little weaker and slower 'n' a normal human, and methinks their bones're easier to cut through. And they're a *lot* stupider. They basically can't do nothin' unless Peter tells 'em to. The problem, ya see, is Peter's got a lot of 'em—scores and scores of 'em. And we only got—what?— four, now. Not a fair fight, ya see."

"When I snuck into the caves to get you," Alex said, "Cap, Dread, and Oscar were attacking on the other side of the mountain, trying to raid the main entrance. But it was a trick—a diversion. And it worked: Peter sent most of his Boys out to fight them, so there were none—well, almost none—in the caves. Otherwise we never woulda gotten outta there alive."

I'd barely heard his last couple sentences; a realization had just struck me like a kick in the chest. Horror sprouted in the pit of my stomach.

Don't jump to conclusions, I told myself, knowing it wasn't much of a jump. *You don't know enough, you could easily be misunderstanding something.*

"You were talking about Oscar before, right?" I asked.

"Aye," Hooke said.

"And—Oscar's a girl?"

"Yeah," Alex said. "Her real name's Mariah. We nicknamed her Oscar 'cause she—well, she . . ."

I wasn't interested in her nickname. My throat was starting to tighten, making it hard to breathe and talk. "And she got captured by Peter?"

"Aye," Hooke said. "She got surrounded by Boys and then Peter came and managed to disarm her."

"And this—this was while she was helping to rescue me?"

"She was helpin' with the diversion, aye."

Hooke's tone was nonchalant—I knew he knew what I was thinking, and he was trying not to make me feel guilty. But it didn't help. For the second time today my throat seemed to close completely and I felt like I was drowning. I clenched my teeth, swallowed with difficulty, and forced myself to breathe.

"So what's gonna happen to her?" I asked.

"Well," Hooke said, "me guess is Peter's gonna try and get her to lead him to the burrow."

"So he's gonna, like . . . torture her?" Just saying the word "torture" seemed to grind me inside.

Hooke shrugged, still feigning nonchalance. "Possibly, I s'pose."

"And then what'll happen to her?"

"Well, I'm guessin' Peter'll do the same thing to her that he does to all the other lads he brings to the Island. But again, what that is, I got no idear."

"So basically," I said—and suddenly I wanted, almost needed, to cry, or scream, or something—"she's dead."

"Not necessarily," Hooke said. "Like I said, we got no idear what—"

"But you're assuming she's never coming back."

Hooke didn't respond.

I closed my eyes and covered my face with my hands.

I'd been able to stomach the guilt over my parents largely because the damage I'd inflicted on them was reversible. But this girl was, for all intents and purposes, *dead*. Because of me.

45

I couldn't stomach that, not on top of everything else. I felt like I'd ingested an acid that was slowly but steadily eating away at me from the inside out, and I desperately wanted to vomit it up but I just couldn't, and I wondered with sick horror when it would stop, whether it ever would, and the pain was so deep and raw that I felt I'd do almost anything to make it stop.

And maybe there was something I could do.

She wasn't dead yet, was she?

"And you said we're not gonna do anything to save her, didn't you?" I said.

"There's nothin' we *can* do, lad," Hooke said.

"She risked her life to save mine and now we're just gonna let her die."

"We *all* risked our lives to save yours," Hooke said. "And we're not *'letting'* her die. If there was anythin' we could do, we'd do it, but—"

"Try!" I burst out. "That's what we can do, we can at least *try!"*

"We *are* tryin'. We're tryin' to think of a way to rescue her that might actually work."

"You guys just rescued me, didn't you?"

"Exactly. So Peter'll be more paranoid than ever. I reckon he'll have at least twenty Boys surroundin' her at all times and he won't let her leave his own sight. And plus, when we rescued you we had four well-trained fighters. Now we only got three."

"I'll fight," I said with all the indignation and courage I could muster.

"Aye, but ye've ne'er handled a sword afore in your life."

"Well we should at least, like . . . I dunno, go scout out his mountain or something. See if there's any holes in his defenses."

"Peter'll be expectin' that, and he's already got lookouts hidden all 'round the base of the mountain. Goin' anywhere near there would be a major risk."

"She was willing to risk *her* life, shouldn't we return the favor?"

"Ye seem to keep forgettin', lad," Hooke said, an edge in his voice and expression for the first time, "that we just *did* risk our lives, righ' alongside her. We ain't cowards, but we ain't idiots, either. We *are* willin' to risk our lives, but we ain't willin' to commit suicide."

"I don't understand how you can do this," I said exasperatedly. "How you can just sit here doing nothing when you know—"

"Don't be givin' me no holier 'n' thou bilge," Hooke growled. "Ye only wanna rescue her so bad 'cause ye feel guilty. If she got captured in some way that had nothin' to do with ye—"

"But she didn't, it has *everything* to do with me! She saved my fucking *life!*"

"Aye," Hooke said, his tone softening somewhat, "and ye should be grateful. But not guilty. Ye got absolutely nothin' to feel guilty about."

"She's dead because of me," I said, my voice suddenly quavering. I fought back tears.

"No, lad. She's dead because a' Peter."

"Still—she sacrificed her life to save mine. I owe her."

"Aye, ye owe her respect. Respect for her sacrifice. If we go do somethin' stupid and ye get killed—if *any* of us get killed, really— we waste that sacrifice. And 'member, we *all* rescued ye, not just her. Ye owe us, too. And we need ye, lad. We need e'ery man we can get."

"Which is another reason to save her! She's—"

"WE *CAN'T* SAVE HER!" Hooke bellowed furiously. I was shocked into silence. Hooke looked around nervously, then spoke to me with quiet intensity. "This argument is pointless, not to mention loud and therefore dangerous. If ye really wanna help Oscar, do what the rest of us are doin'—try and think of a plan. Otherwise, do us all a favor and keep your mouth shut."

Hooke glared at me for another moment. I glared right back. That all-too-familiar thrill was blazing inside me.

It all started with the note from my mom: "Please excuse Ricky Darlin from class at 10:45 for a doctor's appointment." Later I'd wonder whether the attendance lady would have been at all more accommodating—which probably would have averted this whole incident—if my mom had replaced "doctor" with "psychotherapist."

When I went to the attendance office before school to get the official pass out of class, there was a line. Naturally, just as I got to the front of the line, the first bell rang.

The attendance nazi—er, lady—was known among students as Armstrong. She looked to be in her late thousands and was the human equivalent of the DMV.

When I slid my note across the counter, Armstrong said in her deep, gravelly voice: "The bell just rang. Class is starting in five minutes." She really *did* sound like Louis Armstrong.

"So *that's* what that bell means," I said. "And here I thought it was God's cell phone. Can I have a pass, please?"

"You have to get to class."

I must have argued with her for over four minutes before she grudgingly spent the eight seconds it took to fill out the official pass. I snatched it and immediately started sprinting up the deserted hallway.

"You forgot to say thank you!" she called irritably.

I called back over my shoulder, "I didn't forget!"

The second bell was going to ring any second, and my quarterly allowance of lates for Ms. Fulsom's class was already exhausted—if I was late one more time, I'd have to go to Saturday school. I blew past a campus supervisor who shouted at me to slow down, skidded around a corner, lunged for the door—

48

And the bell rang.

I cracked the door open and peeked in. The room was fairly noisy, and Ms. Fulsom was at the whiteboard with her back to me, meticulously writing the definition of "alliteration" for today's lesson on literary devices—and yet somehow, the instant I took one ginger step into the room, her head whipped toward me.

"Dammit," I muttered through gritted teeth.

Ms. Fulsom raised her eyebrows. "Excuse me?"

DAMMIT! I thought.

"Mr. Darlin, did you just say the D-word?"

Instantly the entire class stopped whatever they were doing and turned toward me, hungry for some entertainment—and I wasn't going to disappoint them. I never did. I loved antagonizing my teachers, especially Ms. Fulsom. Twentyish, blond, and busty, Ms. Fulsom could easily pass for a Playboy Playmate if not for her invariably boring attire. A first-year teacher, she was almost incapable of being stern, and she looked even cuter when she tried. But the main reason I liked antagonizing her, and all my teachers, was the thrill it gave me. Such reckless defiance is exhilarating. Liberating.

I frowned in mock puzzlement. "Which D-word? Dumb?" I shook my head gravely. "I didn't say dumb. I would never say dumb."

Several audience members snickered. "Dumb" was one of Ms. Fulsom's countless forbidden "D-words." The first week of school, she'd told our class she had at least one taboo word for every letter of the alphabet—and I'd promptly exclaimed, "Holy *crap*! You must know even more bad words than *I* do!" The class had laughed, and she'd been so embarrassed she overlooked the C-word.

"No, Mr. Darlin, I thought you said the *other* D-word. The bad one."

My frowned deepened with concern. "Which one? Dick? Dyke? Dildo? Dipsh—"

"Okay, Mr. Darlin," Ms. Fulsom interrupted loudly as the audience laughed. "I suppose I might have misheard you."

I started toward my seat, suppressing a triumphant grin.

"But," she snapped.

I froze, wincing a bit, and thought: *Dammit.*

"You *were* late."

I held up my pass. "I have a pass."

Her eyes narrowed suspiciously. "You have a pass that explains why you were late to class?"

"Well—no—but the reason I was late is 'cause I was at the attendance office getting *this* pass."

"I'm sorry, Mr. Darlin, but that doesn't excuse you. Managing your time is your responsibility."

"Well I would have gotten here with time to spare if the attendance lady wasn't such a B-word."

The audience guffawed.

But apparently I'd gone too far for Ms. Fulsom. Her eyes narrowed in what seemed to be serious anger. "I do not like your attitude today, Mr. Darlin," she said, her voice like thin ice.

The threat in her demeanor made defiant anger spark and sizzle behind my eyes. "I don't give a damn if you like it or not."

A girl in the audience gasped.

Ms. Fulsom's nostrils flared and her voice rose to a near-yell: "And I certainly don't like the way you're speaking to me, either."

"Well I don't like your dumb '*D-word*' rule, and I *DON'T* GIVE A *DAMN* THAT *DUMB* AND *DAMN* ARE *D-WORDS!*" I turned to the audience, smiled, and said, in my best teacher's voice, "And that, class, is what you call *alliteration.*"

A beat passed in shocked silence.

Then the audience howled with laughter. One guy fell out of his chair.

Ms. Fulsom no longer looked much like a Playmate. She looked more like Satan. "GET OUT OF MY CLASSROOM!" she screamed, stabbing a finger toward the door. "STRAIGHT TO DETENTION! *NOW!*"

Smiling smugly, I twirled on my heel and walked to the door—but there I paused a beat, twirled back around, and bowed theatrically. Then before Ms. Fulsom could respond, I kicked the door open and strutted out.

A moment later, sauntering down the hall, I faintly heard applause.

I spent the rest of that period in the detention center. Detention wasn't really punishment, just a quick fallback for desperate teachers.

The real punishment came later.

Chapter 5

As we started walking through the jungle again, I realized the sun was almost touching the horizon. I'd been so absorbed in our dialogue, I hadn't noticed the changing light.

We walked in silence. I was glad we were in single file so that we didn't have to look at one another. The languid transition from soft, pink-orange sunlight to deep blue darkness clashed with the clusterfuck that was my emotions.

After what felt like almost an hour, we stopped in an area of particularly dense vegetation and hid the stuff from the burrow amid the underbrush.

As we were doing this, Nigel said, "Hey Cap—what do you think about hiding out by the burrow tonight, just to see if anything happens?"

"Too risky," Hooke said. "Peter'll be expectin' it. So he won't go straight for the burrow, he'll have his Boys search around the burrow first, and pro'ly even hide out and wait for a while."

"But don't you think we should try and see whether or not he comes at all?" Alex said. "'Cause, I mean, there's definitely a chance Mariah won't tell him. So if he doesn't show up in the next few days—"

"We could move back in," Hooke finished. "Problem is, Peter's gonna assume we already packed up and left. So what he'll do is stay away from the burrow for a while—weeks, maybe even years—to make us think he doesn't know. Then we move back in, and we're screwed."

"So you're thinking we'll never go back to the burrow, no matter what happens with Peter?" Nigel asked.

"Well, I don't know 'bout ne'er, but certainly not for a while. So we migh' as well make ourselves at home. And I think we should start by tryin' to get some sleep."

We fashioned five beds from quilts (one for the girl, who was still apparently as unconscious as ever).

"Since we're out in the open," Hooke said, "we're gonna need a lookout."

"Every night?" Nigel asked, clearly not looking forward to the idea.

"Pro'ly, aye."

"I'll take first shift tonight," Alex said. "I'm not sleepy at all."

Alex sat down with his back against a tree. He took from his pocket the small coconut I'd seen him kiss earlier, right after rescuing me, and starting rolling it around in his hands. The rest of us got into our quilts and exchanged good nights.

Then silence.

I was both physically and mentally exhausted—yet I didn't even think about trying to sleep. Gradually, the shock continued to wear off, the recognition that this was all really happening continued to sink in, and the fear and pain continued to grow.

I thought about my life—though in some ways it seemed like someone else's life. I couldn't seem to remember how I'd felt before coming to the Island. I remembered the *fact* that I'd been angry and depressed and *why* I'd been angry and depressed—and I still thought I'd had the right to feel that way—yet I couldn't seem to remember what those feelings had felt like. Which was bizarre, because I *did* remember how all-consuming those feelings had seemed at the time.

I thought about my parents. I'd left reality around midnight, and I couldn't have been here more than five or six hours, so my mom was probably still sleeping. They had only a few more hours of ignorance, of peace of mind—relative peace of mind, at least.

When they realized I was gone, they'd be worried sick right from the start. But at first they'd cling to simple reasonableness. Surely he just ran away, they'd tell themselves, trying hard to believe it. Surely he'll come skulking back in just a few hours. I wondered how long they'd wait before calling the police. How long it would be before their seemingly overblown parental anxieties became full-blown, unequivocal fear and anguish.

Even though the notion of never seeing my parents again was unthinkable, I wouldn't say I "missed" them—I had no immediate desire to see them. Not yet, anyway. And I think this was because I loved them but didn't especially like them. Liking is based mostly on interaction; love is based partly on interaction but mostly on something else. Something deeper. What that something is, I don't know—I don't know if anyone knows—but I did know that even if I went a very long time without interacting with my parents at all, the essence of our relationship wouldn't change. Our love wouldn't change.

But do you really love them?

The fact that that question would even occur to me made me feel sick. Of course I loved them.

But to some degree, I hated them too. I hated them for what they'd done.

Of course, love and hate are not mutually exclusive. And some-times hate can seem much more powerful than love—it certainly had in my case. But now I could see that hate isn't necessarily more powerful, it's a different kind of power. Hate is a sprinter; love is a marathoner.

More than my life or my parents, though—somewhat to my surprise—I thought about Oscar. I kept imagining what she looked like. My image of her changed constantly, except that her face was always bright, smiling, innocent. I wondered what was happening to her right now. Was Peter torturing her? How? Beating her? Cut-ting her? Burning her? Holding her head underwater? Raping her? There were so many sickeningly horrible possibilities—many, I fig-ured, that were too horrible to even occur to me.

And what was her ultimate fate? The fate that should have been mine? The fate that she had saved me from?

And how many people would miss her? How many would be devastated by her loss? Parents, siblings, friends—when all was said and done, how many lives had I fucked up in all?

I tried to counter these torturous thoughts with much the same arguments Hooke had used.

This really wasn't my fault at all. I hadn't intended for any of this to happen. And if Peter hadn't gotten me, he would have gotten someone else.

My mind accepted all that; my heart didn't. Besides, I wanted to rescue Oscar not so much to atone for my sins (real or not) as to repay her. I could atone for my sins in countless ways, but there was really only one way I could repay her. And there was no question I owed her. I owed her my life.

I owed the others too. And they needed me.

She needed me more. Their lives were not at stake.

I couldn't forget about my parents.

55

What about *her* parents?

But none of that even mattered. I *couldn't* rescue her. It was suicide.

So Hooke had said. But I didn't trust Hooke. I didn't *dis*trust him, necessarily—I just didn't know him. He'd helped save my life, but that was at least partly because he wanted more fighters. And he had seemed callously quick to dismiss Oscar as lost. When Alex had heard about her capture, by contrast, he'd pushed to do something about it.

But I didn't have to take Hooke's word for it—all I had to do was use common sense. Oscar was valuable to Peter, and Peter had just had a captive snatched right out from under his nose—of *course* the security was going be tight.

But we didn't know the specifics. There might be a flaw. A hole. We should at least scout out Peter's mountain to thoroughly assess the situation.

There was no way I could get the others to go along with that. Hooke wouldn't even consider it, and Alex and Nigel deferred to him.

Peter would be expecting a group action—going solo might have advantages.

And only then did I realize I was actually, seriously considering doing something. And as soon as I realized this, I knew I *had* to do something. I had to try. Because now that I was at least somewhat willing to take action—now that I was looking at it as a real possibility and not just a comforting fantasy—I'd never be able to forgive myself if I didn't. I had to at least go to Peter's mountain and see for myself.

You're doing this purely for your own benefit, hissed a voice in the back of my mind. *You know you're not actually gonna rescue her, you just wanna make some token effort to appease your guilty conscience.*

No, I resolved. If I saw a decent opportunity to save her, I would take it.

You're gonna die, the voice taunted.

Maybe. Or probably? But if I didn't go, I'd die inside. Yes, that was disgustingly melodramatic, but I believed it. I had to do this. I *wanted* to do this.

You want a sword shoved inside you?

Your mom wants a sword shoved inside her.

I smiled a tiny bit. And that decided it. If I was seriously leaning toward risking my life like this and was still chipper enough to make a "your mom" joke, I knew I could do it.

As soon as the decision crystallized in my mind, cords of fear lashed around my body and squeezed with suffocating force. But it wasn't enough to hold me down. A sort of energy was pulsing through my veins like high-voltage electricity. The thrill of righteousness, I thought. And perhaps even the thrill of adventure.

First things first.

I was pretty sure it had been well over an hour since we'd all said good night. Judging by the sounds of their breathing, Hooke, Nigel, and the girl were all unconscious. Alex had started yawning about five minutes after saying he wasn't tired at all, and was now doing a set of push-ups, sit-ups, or similar exercises every few minutes to (I surmised) stay awake.

Perfect.

I sat up in my quilts. At the sound, Alex's head whipped around and his hand shot toward the hilt of his sword, but when he saw me he immediately relaxed, dropping his hand.

"Hey," I whispered, getting up.

"Hey man. You all right?"

"Yeah, I'm fine. But there's no way in hell I'm getting to sleep anytime soon. You want me to take over for you?"

"Uhh . . ." Alex hesitated, considering. I suddenly wondered if he suspected my intentions. But after a couple seconds he said, "Yeah, that should be all right. All you really gotta do is stay awake.

Just if you hear or see anything at all—even if you think it's just an animal, even if you think you just imagined it—wake one of us up right away. And if you start getting sleepy at all, just wake someone up and switch with 'em. All right?"

"Yeah, all right."

"Thanks man." Alex clapped me on the shoulder and, yawning, stepped over the sleeping bodies and got into his quilts.

After ten or fifteen minutes, I was confident he was asleep. I whispered, "Hey guys," a few times, just loud enough so that if someone was awake they'd definitely hear it. There was no response.

Cue the music.

The *Mission Impossible* theme, perhaps, I thought wryly.

I crept around until I found the hidden array of weapons. I slung a sword over my back and stuck a knife in my pocket. I whispered, "Hey guys," a few more times to make sure everyone was still asleep. Then—part of me hoping I was remembering my directions incorrectly—I set off at a brisk walk. I planned to find the river and follow it to Peter's mountain.

And then?

Rescue Oscar.

Good plan.

Fear weighed on me like heavy chains, trying to drag me down. But that energy, that tingling thrill, drove me on. It was almost like an out-of-body experience—I knew the fear was there, yet I couldn't really feel it.

I moved as stealthily as I could, which felt about as stealthy as a stampede of elephants. As the minutes slid by, the dark jungle seemed so unvarying and unending that I started to feel as if I were swimming in the middle of the ocean.

As the minutes neared an hour, I started to think I might be going the wrong way.

On the one hand, that thought was enormously appealing—I wouldn't have to risk my life but would still know I'd tried my best to help Oscar. On the other hand, I truly wanted to save her and felt disgusted at my other, selfish motives.

And on a third hand, I could hardly stand the thought of having to face Hooke after failing to even find the river. I wanted so badly, almost *needed*, to show him up. To prove myself. His last words to me—"Keep your mouth shut"—still reverberated in the back of my mind, and deep inside me, almost buried amid all my other emotions, defiant anger growled, like a small but powerful engine.

I heard the river, like a rumbling whisper, about thirty seconds before I stepped onto the bank.

Relief and fear surged inside me simultaneously and crashed into each other. The fear prevailed. The fear was growing. But it still wasn't enough.

I turned right and continued walking, much slower now, placing my feet very carefully with every step. Whenever I made a not-particularly-quiet sound, I'd freeze and hold my breath for a few seconds—but every time the jungle remained eerily still.

I wondered if I should check the burrow first. Hooke had said Peter would be expecting that and might have a trap set up—but he'd said basically the same about Peter's mountain. Not to mention he'd said this whole thing was bloody suicide. But I had to be careful not to let—

I froze.

I thought I'd heard something.

It had been just barely audible over the sounds of my movement and the river, so faint that it took me a moment to process it.

It sounded like a distant cry from somewhere up ahead.

And it sounded like a girl.

It was also so faint that I immediately wondered if I'd imagined it—a product of hope and/or dread, perhaps? My breathing and heartbeat both seemed to stop of their own accord to better my hearing. For a few seconds I heard nothing but the river. Then I realized that blended in with the soft roar was another sound.

Vegetation rustling.

Movement.

Lots of movement.

And I was pretty sure it was headed toward me.

Chapter 6

Whatever was left of that uplifting energy withered away in seconds, giving way to another kind of energy that exploded through me like a dam burst: panic. Before, I think, I'd subconsciously felt divinely protected, felt that because I was doing good, nothing bad would happen to me. That delusional bubble had now popped. Suddenly it seemed impossible to me that I'd been stupid enough to come all the way out here, to think I could rescue Oscar from Peter and a goddamn army of zombies all by myself.

Panic tried to seize control of my body, tried to make me sprint away, but with enormous effort I fought it off. I had come this far, I was at least going to assess the situation. Confirm that it was impossible, if nothing else. I had to. Otherwise I'd always wonder.

The movement seemed to be hugging the river, so I crept about fifteen yards away from the water and lay down on my stomach behind a bush. I had to struggle to keep my breathing under control. My heart battered my rib cage. My whole body felt like gelatin.

Just seconds later I saw the movement, about fifteen or twenty yards up the riverbank. At first it just looked like a dark blob sliding and melting through the vegetation, but as it got closer I saw that it was a clump of people, between twenty and thirty I estimated, striding briskly along the bank. It was too dark and I was too far away to discern anything else.

Lost Boys, I assumed. Was Oscar and/or Peter among them?

It doesn't matter, said a voice in my head—the voice of fear hiding behind reason. *There's at least twenty of them. There's nothing you can do.*

Probably not. But I'd expected a lot of Boys. There still might be a way. I had to know the specifics.

The conflicting arguments canceled each other out in my mind, and in the resulting vacuum of decision and command, my body seemed to act of its own accord. As the group passed me, I slipped into their wake, staying about ten or fifteen yards behind them.

I had no plan—other than to try to think up a plan. And, in the meantime, tail the group without being detected. Which wasn't easy for a stampede of elephants such as myself. Fortunately, both the group and the river were also noisy.

I'd been following the group for about a minute when I heard, from within the group, a girl cry out in pain—then, in chilling contrast, Peter's casual voice: "Bloody hell, lass, I've seen coral move fasta 'n' you."

Then I heard what I assumed was Oscar's voice, which shocked me. I would have expected her voice to be terrified, pleading, perhaps broken by sobs; in fact it sounded not only completely unafraid, but irritated and almost belligerent: "Maybe you shouldn't have clubbed my leg, you dumb fuck."

"Maybe ya shouldn't be such a bitch, you noisy cunt," Peter said lightly.

"All things considered, I think I have a right to be a bitch to you."

"You can have all the rights ya want. I have weapons. Now please—I'd hate to wreck that fine body. So kindly shut up."

"Why? C'mon, Petey, let's chat. It'll make the time pass faster."

"Keep in mind ya time alive might be quite limited."

"I know. Really says something about your company, doesn't it? And honestly, how can you stand the stench of these fuckers?"

I heard an astonishingly loud slap. I heard nothing from Oscar, but probably only because she was so shocked. Judging by the sound, Peter must have slapped her across the face about as hard as he could.

"You've got quite a mouth, lass," Peter said conversationally. Then, with sinister amusement: "Perhaps I can make better use of it, ay?"

"But you don't need a *big* mouth for that."

Peter laughed, seemingly good-naturedly. "You like insultin' me, don't ya? Does it make ya feel more powerful? That's ya big fear, isn't it? Not bein' in control?"

"That must be it, Sigmund. And hey, maybe I hate you so much 'cause your name's Peter!"

Peter laughed heartily. "Ya know, lass, I might just keep you around."

"I'm honored."

"You can entertain me. In more than one way. But for the moment, please, shut up."

Oscar didn't shut up, but we were now passing a stretch of the river that was narrow, rocky, and fast, and the roar drowned out her words.

My only chance, I'd decided, given the numbers, was to take Peter hostage. But that wasn't much more of a plan than "Rescue Oscar." *How* was I going to take Peter hostage? I had only one idea: Get ahead of the group, climb a tree, and then jump down on him. But there were two main problems with that. One, there was a good chance it was too dark to pick Peter out from the group from above. And two, Peter was expecting a rescue attempt, and since he was well protected on all sides, I was sure he was ready for an attack from above—it was too obvious.

I needed something that would get me close enough to pick Peter and Oscar out. And something unexpected. Creative.

And then, suddenly, I had it.

The river was loud and fast. The darkness was thick. The Boys were numerous and crowded close together, almost swarm-like, and they looked about my size. Plus, Hooke had said they were stupid.

There was a good chance this would work.

There was a very good chance it wouldn't.

But if they noticed me, there would probably be at least a couple seconds of confusion, so I could probably just bolt.

And—more important than anything else—I might capture Peter.

If I was going to do this, I had to do it very soon—I needed the river to be loud and fast.

I hesitated for about three more seconds—three seconds that contained an eternity's worth of mental war, three seconds in which the entire universe seemed to hold its breath, three seconds that centered around a decision that would drastically affect and might even end my life.

Actually, it might have been four seconds.

Then I faintly heard Peter laugh over the roar of the river—a playful, almost childlike, yet horrible laugh—and the decision was made.

After scanning the ground for a moment, I picked up a rock about the size of my fist, then sped up a little, closing on the group. I kept an eye on the rearmost members of the group for any indication that I'd been detected, but the river muffled the noise of my movement even better than I'd expected—I could barely hear it myself. Though my heart was in overdrive, fear seemed to be bouncing off me.

When I was about ten feet away, that horribly familiar stench of rot snaked into my nostrils. Then I was five feet away. Still the group seemed oblivious of me.

This was it. The moment of truth.

The first one, anyway.

Before fear and doubt could take root and make me waver, I pitched the rock almost as hard as I could to the left of the group. Its rustling flight through the underbrush was just audible over the river and sounded much like a small animal.

Perfect.

The head of every Boy I could see snapped toward the sound, and in the same moment I stepped quickly forward and melted into the outer layer of the group. For a few seconds my whole being felt tense enough to snap as I waited for a Boy's head to whip toward me. But even when they turned forward again, apparently dismissing the sound of the rock, none of them seemed to notice that their group had gained a member.

I was just inches away from multiple Boys. The stench was so thick I could taste it; I think I would have gagged if I hadn't been so focused elsewhere. I had a morbid urge to try to see a Boy's face—but the urge to not die was stronger.

Facing straight forward, heart hammering, I slowly slid between two Boys. It was so dark and the Boys were so bunched up that I was hoping my movement through the group would go unnoticed. I was edging toward the middle of the group, where I assumed Peter and Oscar were. They had stopped talking, which was unfortunate—their voices would have helped me pick them out. My eyes darted about constantly, looking for Peter or Oscar or any indication that I'd been detected.

I slid past another Boy—and his head turned toward me.

It felt like my lungs spasmed violently as panic seized me. Automatically I sped up slightly to get away from the Boy. Even as I did this, I knew it was a bad move; I shouldn't have reacted at all. At my abrupt acceleration, another head turned toward me—then two more—

I was just about to try to ram my way out of the group and run for it when I glimpsed, through a fleeting gap between several Boys, Peter and Oscar. I could only tell it was them because Peter's right hand was gripping Oscar's hair. In his left hand, at his side, I was pretty sure I saw a knife.

There was no time to think; I just acted. I quickly shouldered past one Boy, squeezed between two more, and just as I saw a flurry of rapid movement out of the corner of my eye, I shoved one last Boy aside and threw myself at Peter.

As my chest slammed into his upper back, I grabbed his left forearm with my left hand and whipped my right arm around his neck in a headlock. His grip on Oscar's hair broke as I continued barreling forward with him, crashing into as many Boys and creating as much chaos as I could.

"RUN, OSCAR, RUN!" I screamed.

I had no idea what happened to her. Peter started struggling wildly and trying to fly away—his body suddenly felt as light as a balloon—but I maintained the headlock, so his legs and torso swung outward as if something was pulling at his feet. I spun around as fast as I could, swinging his body, smashing him into one Boy, then another, then two more.

Then suddenly Peter stopped trying to fly—his weight returned and he dropped like a bag of bricks, wrenching out of my grasp. Before I could even react, he shot off into the air.

I immediately exploded into a desperate dash, crashing through the group.

"STOP HIM!" Peter screamed.

But it was so dark and chaotic that none of the Boys caught on to me in time. When I burst free of the group, I heard some of them rushing after me, but I was already far enough ahead. I covered the remaining ground in three bounding strides, made one last, flying leap, and plunged into the river.

The water was freezing, but I barely noticed. The current seized me like innumerable strong hands and sent me flying downstream. For just a moment, it seemed to be working exactly as I'd hoped— then a large, jagged rock slammed into my stomach, snagging me to a halt.

Still completely underwater, I was about to maneuver myself around the rock, but then I got an idea. I hesitated for an instant, debating it. Then I saw and felt two bodies go whooshing through the water right past me—the Boys were jumping into the river.

I decided. I wrapped myself around the rock and waited.

I sensed a few more Boys whoosh past—one would have hit my legs if I hadn't pulled them out of the way. Then there was nothing but the rumbling, tumbling waters. I stayed under for close to a minute, until it felt like my lungs were screaming and trying to burst out of my chest; then, holding onto the rock, I poked my head above water, sucked in a blissful breath, and scanned the bank.

It was clear.

Chapter 7

The instant I awoke, I nearly had a heart attack—but quickly looking around, I saw that I was still in the same place and was still, apparently, alone. I didn't remember falling asleep. Judging by the sun, it was midmorning.

Last night I'd spent hours searching for the hideout. Eventually I'd grown too worried about running into Peter or a Boy—no doubt they were out searching for me and Oscar. So I'd sat down in a densely vegetated spot, intending to keep watch all night.

I'd decided that in the morning I'd check the burrow. Even though the group last night had been following the river, I couldn't believe that Oscar had been leading them to the burrow—the way she'd spoken to Peter, there was no way in hell he'd broken her, and surely she'd realized that as long as she withheld the location of the burrow, Peter wouldn't kill her. If I was wrong, and Oscar *had* told Peter where the burrow was, he'd likely have a trap set up. But I'd decided that risk was less than the risk of being alone and out in the open for God knew how long while Peter and his Boys were scouring the area.

And besides all that, I was agonizingly anxious to know if Oscar had escaped.

During the rescue, I hadn't perceived any sign of a struggle apart from mine and Peter's, so I was pretty sure she'd made a clean getaway.

Or a Boy had killed her instantly.

Which would have been completely out of my control. I'd done everything I could for her. I'd done a hell of a lot. I'd very seriously risked my life for her.

But that didn't make me feel the slightest bit better. My conscience was a joke compared to her life.

Gripping my sword tightly at my side, I tiptoed slowly to the river, then proceeded even more slowly along the bank, checking the base of every tree for the tunnel. I felt almost like I was tweaking—my eyes and ears seemed extra sensitive, and my muscles seemed to be quivering to launch into action.

After at least two hours, I spotted the tunnel. I immediately snapped my sword up and frenetically scanned the surrounding jungle, my heart suddenly redlining—but nothing happened, and I detected nothing suspicious. Peter and his Boys might be *in* the burrow, though. I ducked into the tunnel and listened, not breathing.

After a few seconds, I faintly heard Alex's voice, then Nigel's.

Still not breathing, I scrambled down into the burrow.

Hooke, Alex, and Nigel were sitting around a big bunch of bananas to one side of the room. I felt a waterfall of relief as I saw Oscar, sitting with her back against the wall across from the others.

They all looked up at me—and awkward silence ensued. No one seemed to know what to say; I certainly didn't. When I tried to make eye contact with Oscar, she immediately looked down. Her face, neck, and arms were covered in bruises, but otherwise she looked fine. I also realized the unconscious girl wasn't there. I was about to ask what had happened to her, just to say something—

Alex pointed at me, as if pointing me out to myself. "You," he said, "are one crazy-ass motherfucker."

Nigel grinned. "Hey Ricky, where's your shining armor?"

"Oh," I said, cocking a thumb over my shoulder, "I left it up top with my white horse."

Nigel laughed.

Alex hopped to his feet and hurried over to me. "You, my heroic homie, never received a proper welcome, did you?" he said, slinging his arm over my shoulders and leading me forward. "So as long as we already got one new introduction to make, I think we should redo the others."

"Alex," Nigel said, sounding nettled, "he does not need to know your—"

Ignoring him, Alex clapped Hooke on the shoulder and said, "This here's the Captain. We call him Cap."

Hooke was staring at me rather coldly, his eyes narrowed slightly. A tiny chill tickled the back of my neck, but I held his gaze.

"Ye got guts, lad," Hooke growled. "I ain't sure 'bout brains, but ye sure as bloody hell got guts." Then his face broke into a wide, jolly smile. "You're a foine addition to this crew."

He stuck out his hand; I couldn't help smiling back as I shook it.

"When we started calling him Captain, it kinda got to his head," Alex said to me, a bit quietly, as if then Hooke wouldn't hear. "Now he thinks he's the captain of an old sailing ship or something."

"Aye," Hooke said loftily, "and a damn foine cap'n I am, ay lads?"

Alex said to me matter-of-factly, "Cap's a few fries short of a Happy Meal."

"And some nuggets, too, if ya ask me," Nigel said.

Hooke's eyes narrowed. "Ye best mind what ye be sayin', lads, or I'll throw both your arses overboard."

Alex smiled at me. "See what I mean?" Before Hooke could retort, Alex pointed to Nigel and said, "And that's Dread."

Nigel rolled his eyes.

"'Cause of his dreadlocks?" I said.

"No," Alex said, "'cause he eats like a pregnant American whale. He's the dread of buffet owners worldwide." Alex grinned, clearly proud of himself. "I think it's an awesome nickname."

"I think it's a juvenile and offensive nickname," Nigel said.

"*I* think it's an awesome nickname," Alex repeated importantly.

"I rest my case," Nigel said.

"Ahh," Alex waved him off, "Dread just likes to argue with me about everything."

"I don't argue with you about anything, *you* argue with *me*."

Alex smiled at me. "See what I mean?"

"I don't *argue* with you, Alex," Nigel said patiently. "I just occasionally express my disbelief at your never-ending displays of dumbassity."

"What does 'dumbassity' mean?" Alex said.

Nigel rolled his eyes and looked at me. "See what I mean?"

Alex leaned toward me, feigning confidentiality. "Dread likes to show off the size of his vocabulary. I think he's compensating for something."

"Alex likes to show off the size of his brain," Nigel said. "It makes his balls look bigger by comparison."

Alex opened his mouth to retort, but Oscar interrupted: "I can't tell whether you two are comparing how big your packages are or how big your mouths are. But I can think of a way for you to measure both at the same time."

"*That*," Alex said to me, rolling his eyes, "is Mariah Bell. I call her Oscar, 'cause she is a royal grouch."

"And look," Mariah said, spreading her hands and looking around, "I even live in a trash can."

Alex smiled at me. "See what I mean?"

"Go to hell, Alex," Mariah said carelessly.

Alex winked at her. "I'll save you a seat."

"She's probably already got reservations," Nigel muttered.

Despite her bitchy expression, Mariah was hot. She was markedly dirtier than the others, yet her face was curiously dignified, and her dirty skin made her green eyes seem all the more sparkling and intense. She was lean and athletic-looking, but her T-shirt and denim capris were baggy and hid her curves. Her skin was a perfect bronze, and her brown, disheveled hair was cut short, not even halfway down her neck. I thought she'd look much better with longer hair—and better still with a smile—but otherwise I had no complaints.

I looked away before she could catch me staring. I had a feeling she wouldn't appreciate my attention.

"So what's your nickname, Alex?" I asked.

Hooke, Nigel, and Mariah all answered at once: "Asshole."

Alex shrugged. "Most good athletes are assholes, especially the handsome ones."

"So what's *your* excuse?" Nigel said.

"Hey, where's the other girl?" I asked. "The unconscious one?"

"She snuck off last nigh' while we was out lookin' for ye," Hooke said.

Before I could ask who she was, Alex abruptly said, "So Oscar—are you gonna say thanks to Ricky or what?"

Mariah glanced at Alex like he was a particularly annoying fly that she would very much like to crush, then looked away again.

"Thanks, Ricky," she deadpanned, not even glancing at me.

Alex's eyes narrowed. "Well shit, Oscar, don't outdo yourself."

"Alex," I smiled breezily, "it's all right—"

But it was too late.

Mariah half sneered, half scowled at Alex. "What the fuck do you want me to do, give him a thank-you kiss? Or maybe a thank-you blow job, so then you can at least watch?"

"Well at least then you wouldn't be able to talk for a while," Alex said icily.

Mariah glared at him for a long moment, her expression oozing with loathing. Then she started striding toward the tunnel. "Go fuck yourself, Alex."

"I could use some assistance," Alex said.

Climbing up into the tunnel, Mariah said over her shoulder, "Use Nigel."

Nigel had just been about to bite down on a banana; hearing his name, he paused and looked up—with the banana still shoved in his mouth. It seemed to take him a moment to process what she'd said. Then he yanked the banana out of his mouth.

After a beat, he said blankly, "Whoa. I think I just lost my appetite."

Alex slammed his fist against the wall. "*God*, she pisses me off," he muttered. "And dammit, now my *fucking* hand hurts!" he yelled.

"What's her deal?" I asked. "She just really homesick or something?"

Alex sighed and shook his head, massaging his hand. "We don't know. That might be part of it, but . . . there's gotta be something else, too."

"Like what?"

"Well, remember, all the kids who come here, they all had some kinda issue back in reality, right? Some reason they wanted to get away."

"Yeah," I said, "so what was Mariah's issue?"

"That's the thing," Nigel said, "we don't know. She never talks about it—*refuses* to talk about it. So we figure, whatever her issue was, she just never got over it, and that's why she's such a grouch. That's the best theory we can come up with anyway. Either that, or she's an agent of Satan dispatched from the fiery depths of hell for the express purpose of bugging the shit out of us."

"Or," Hooke said, raising a finger, "she's a feminist."

"We've tried to be friendly and all," Nigel said, "but she just blows us off. She keeps to herself a lot, doesn't talk much—hell, this is the most I've heard her say in a long time. And it probably doesn't help that she's the only girl, either."

Alex finally handed me the banana I deserved, and I downed it so fast I could have been in a porno. I hadn't eaten in a long time—not since—

Not since dinner with my mom.

The banana in my stomach seemed to turn to stone. I grabbed another banana anyway and tried not to think of home.

As I ate, I recounted the rescue to the others, as Mariah hadn't known the whole story. Then Hooke said we should all "take a bath" in the river. We stripped to our underwear and waded into the river. The water was invigoratingly chilly.

I didn't realize quite how dirty the others had been until they started washing off—and as they became clean, I was unnerved to notice that they all had a variety of scars, some of which looked pretty ugly. The ugliest of them all—and the most bizarre—was across the front of Hooke's thigh. It was two horizontal rows of penny-sized, reddish-purple spots. The rows were about six inches apart; the spots were about a half inch apart. I debated for a moment asking him how he'd gotten the scar, but decided that might be rude.

When we were back inside, Hooke told Alex and Nigel to go fishing while he went and chopped wood.

"Lad, why don't ye stay here and rest up," Hooke said to me. "Ye got your first lesson this evenin'."

I opened my mouth to ask *My first lesson on what?* but Alex gave a snort of laughter and said, "So what was last night, a pretest?"

"Are ye all right bein' here by yourself?" Hooke asked me.

I opened my mouth to ask about the lesson again, but then Nigel said, with a smile, "Cap, he just took on Peter and like thirty Lost Boys all by himself. I think he can handle an empty room all by himself."

"Aye, alrigh'. But mind ye, lad"—Hooke pointed at me sternly—"don't go wanderin' off. Ye can go outside, but be real bloody careful—stay alert, and stay close enough to the tunnel that ye can dive in real quick if ye see or hear anythin'. I reckon there's gonna be a lot more Boys round here real soon."

Suddenly, with a twinge of anxiety, I thought of something. Surely they'd checked with Mariah—but just in case . . . "Do you know what Mariah told Peter? 'Cause last night they were walking along the river—"

"She wasn't leadin' 'em to the burrow," Hooke said. "She told him we live in a cave in the cliffs on the shore—it was part of her escape plan. Unfortunately, the easiest way to get to the shore is to follow the river. So now, even if Peter don't really believe her, he's gonna be sendin' out a lot a' Boys to search the cliffs just in case, and they'll all follow the river—right past the burrow. Now, the burrow's pretty bloody hard to find—"

"Hell," Nigel said wryly, "sometimes *we* have trouble finding it, and we know where it is."

"But me point is this," Hooke said. "The tunnel entrance may be really hard to spot, but a person ain't."

As soon as the others had left, I realized they still hadn't told me who the unconscious girl was. But I didn't think about it much.

Only one thing in the universe seemed to matter right now: Mariah was okay.

The comfort and security of the burrow—at least relative to the jungle—suddenly made me feel pleasantly drowsy. I flopped face-first onto a quilt and closed my eyes.

Chapter 8

I jerked awake, knowing even before my eyes were open that someone was standing over me. For an instant panic gripped me and I almost bolted to my feet—

Then I saw that it was Hooke. He was standing just a couple feet away, ramrod straight, his feet wide and arms folded. I got the impression he was trying to tower over me—which wasn't particularly difficult, since I was lying down. He was staring down his crooked nose at me with a stony expression. My panic faded, but I remained on edge.

"Ye 'wake now, lad?" Hooke said.

"Yeah."

He nodded toward the wall behind me. "Go 'head and sit up."

I slowly sat up and leaned my back against the wall, never taking my eyes off him. "What's going on?"

"Nothin'. Just listen." He cleared his throat—for dramatic effect, I think. "Now, I ain't sure if you're brave or mental, but either way, ye obviously ain't too shy 'bout puttin' your arse on the line—and this crew needs lads like that. But ye gotta get your priorities in order. If you're gonna be part of this crew, ye gotta do what's best for the crew."

That thrill of defiance started sizzling through my veins. "Mariah's part of the crew, isn't she?"

"She's one person. Ye gotta do what's best for the majority."

"Oh," I said with acid sarcasm. "So in other words, I have to do what you say. That's what this is about, isn't it?"

"Not at all. We do what the majority wants."

"Alex wanted to rescue her, I know that, and I bet Nigel did too."

"Well of course we all *wanted* to rescue her. But we also realized it'd be suicide."

"No," I said fiercely, stabbing a finger at him, "you *told* them it'd be suicide."

"They was free to challenge me."

"But you knew they wouldn't. They defer to you."

"They *choose* to defer to me. I didn't name meself Cap'n, lad, *they* did. They know I know more 'bout the Island than anyone else and they know I'm usually right."

"But not always," I said, letting a note of triumph seep into my voice. "You were wrong this time."

"No, I wasn't," Hooke growled dangerously. "What ye did was bloody stupid. Ye just got bloody lucky."

"I didn't get lucky!" I exclaimed indignantly. "I went looking for an opportunity and I found one!"

"It wasn't worth the risk."

"Mariah's life wasn't worth the risk?"

Suddenly Hooke's voice rose sharply, striking a booming, powerful tone of finality: "The very small chance a' savin' her was not worth the very large chance a' ye dyin'. If ye'd died, any other rescue attempts we made would be significantly harder and we'd be even farther from

78

capturin' Peter and stoppin' him from kidnappin' innocent lads."

Hooke paused—and the silence that followed was just as loud and powerful as his voice. I had no response, due only partly to surprise. I'd never thought about it quite like that . . .

"Start seein' the big picture, lad," Hooke said, less loudly. "And get your priorities in order."

Then he turned on his heel, strode across the burrow, and disappeared up the tunnel.

Leaving me to grapple with the monster of a question he'd just awakened:

What if I'd failed and died?

I'd been fully aware how bad this would have been for Hooke, Alex, and Nigel—but I'd never thought about how bad it would have been for their family and friends, everyone who grieved for them as much as my parents grieved for me, and an untold number of innocent kids, and all *their* family and friends.

Thus that monster of a question awakened an even bigger one:

In risking my life to rescue Mariah, had I done the right thing?

I'd thought I was doing the right thing at the time—but why had I thought so? To answer that, I had to look at my deeper motives. And the deepest I could go was: I'd rescued her because I'd wanted to, because I'd thought it would make me feel better.

Which didn't inherently mean I was being selfish. Everyone always does what they want to do most, what they think will make them feel best. Even someone who, for example, gives all their money to charity, does so because they think it will make them feel better than using the money any other way.

But had my core selfish drive gone too far? Had my desire to make myself feel better tricked me into thinking I was doing the right thing when really I wasn't?

Rescuing Mariah had increased our chances of capturing Peter.

But had I failed and died, I would have decreased them. Thus, the potential gain and the potential loss had been equal.

So it all came down to one question: Which had been greater, the chance of succeeding or the chance of failing and dying?

Even in retrospect, I couldn't answer that. My plan had been good, but I could think of many ways it could easily have gone bad.

But really, retrospect was irrelevant. Hooke had told me that the risk was too great before I'd rescued her. And I'd had no good reason not to listen to him—he'd proven he was willing to risk his life by saving me, and Mariah was more valuable than me.

So the real question was: Why hadn't I listened to Hooke?

And the answer was: I hadn't wanted to.

About ten minutes after Hooke had left, Mariah dropped in. When she saw me, she stopped, glanced around to see if anyone else was in the burrow, then just stared at me. I was debating whether to smile and wave or to run and scream when she finally spoke: "What you did last night—I mean . . . ya know . . . rescuing me and shit—that was really fucking stupid. You know that, right?"

I let my head fall back and bump against the wall. "I've heard."

"Well maybe you should hear it again. You're not a hero, you're an extremely lucky dumbass. And you're not gonna get lucky twice. You keep thinking you're a hero and you'll be dead before you know it. And what the fuck are you smiling at?"

My smile widened; I couldn't help it. "I thought I'd rescued a damsel in distress, but I'm starting to think I got the dragon."

"Oh, is that why you were so eager to rescue me?" she said, sneering with disgust. "Some macho fantasy about saving the poor helpless female and winning her heart?"

Indignation flared in me. "I rescued you 'cause I—" I was going to say something like *'Cause I think it's wrong to let someone die when*

80

you might be able to do something about it. But then my voice and indignation faltered, and I heard myself say, "—'cause I felt guilty."

"But you would have liked it, wouldn't you?" she challenged. "If I was a classic damsel in distress? Fawning all over my hero?"

My smile returned. "Well, I'll admit, I'd rather have a damsel fawning over me than a dragon spitting fire in my face."

"Well I'm terribly sorry to disappoint you," she said, sounding somewhat pleased that she'd disappointed me. "But I didn't ask you to save me."

"And I'm not asking for anything in return," I said, trying to sound conciliatory. "Look, the dragon thing, that was just a joke, okay? I'm not . . . judging you or anything. I mean, hell, you were willing to sacrifice your life to save mine—that makes you a good person in my book."

"Bad people can do good things."

I raised an eyebrow. "Are you saying you're a bad person?"

She smiled thinly. "I'm like Mother fucking Teresa. I'm just saying your take on good and bad is stupid."

"Yeah, you're probably right. I should judge people by something other than their actions. Appearance is pretty reliable . . ."

"Judging people at all is stupid. 'Cause you can never know a person completely, and everyone's capable of bad."

I smiled. "So you're paranoid."

She shrugged. "Better safe than sorry."

"Just 'cause you're safe doesn't mean you're not sorry."

Mariah didn't respond in any way, even when I stayed silent for several seconds. My curiosity tingled. Her lack of response seemed out of character; I wondered if it meant anything.

"Paranoia and society generally don't mix well," I said.

"Maybe you haven't noticed, but this isn't society."

"A group of people living together, that's *a* society."

She smiled darkly. "There's a few pretty big differences between the 'society' here and society in reality."

"You're still interacting with other people. It's the same basic concept."

"No. It's different. Very different."

"How?"

She stared at me for a moment, and I got the impression she was sizing me up in some way. "Think about it," she said. Then she turned around and started toward the tunnel.

"Hey wait," I said.

She stopped, but didn't turn back, and said impatiently, "What?"

"Are you . . . uh . . . okay and everything?"

Now she did turn back, looking annoyed at my ambiguity. *"What?"*

"I mean, like . . . Peter didn't hurt you too bad or anything?"

"Oh." She shook her head with an expression of careless dismissal. "Nah. He just smacked me around a bit. Fortunately he doesn't actually like hurting people, I don't think—he just doesn't mind it. He's not sadistic, he's just extremely, completely selfish. Which really isn't a whole lot better. But anyway—he prefers the psychological approach over the physical."

"What do you mean, the psychological approach?"

"Well, like mind games and shit. He tries to get into your head. And ya know, I think he likes it. I think maybe, because he interacts with people so rarely, he's fascinated by them, by how they think and feel and shit. So he likes fucking around with them to see how they'll react."

"Did you learn anything else? About Peter or anything?"

"Nothing we couldn't have guessed."

"Like what?"

"Like he's getting really pissed at us. And paranoid. And desperate. I'd bet he's gonna start trying a lot harder to hunt us down."

"So you didn't learn anything that might help us capture him?"

"No."

Her answer was immediate and certain—surely she'd already thought of that and considered it extensively. I'd expected this answer, but I still felt a pang, a reminder of the deeper anguish. My eyes dropped, and I didn't know what to say.

"I'm sorry," Mariah said, and her voice was almost completely flat—but I thought I detected the slightest hint of sincerity.

Then she turned around and started for the tunnel again.

"One more thing," I said, and again Mariah stopped but didn't turn back. "Cap said you had an escape plan last night?"

"Yeah?"

"What was it?"

"I was gonna try to lose 'em in the—" She broke off, then turned to face me, a wry smile teasing her lips. "You don't know about the cove yet, do you?"

"The cove?"

Her smile widened—and darkened. "You'll find out soon."

Then before I could respond, she turned around and jumped into the tunnel.

I was wondering about the cove a minute later when I heard someone coming down the tunnel again. I looked up, and a moment later Mariah dropped back in—and, to my surprise, she just stood there and stared at me, expressionless. Our eyes locked, and there was a moment of silence that I can only describe as weird.

"Thank you," she said, a little quietly.

I blinked, taken aback. "For what?"

"For saving my life, dipshit."

Then she turned around and was gone again.

Chapter 9

When Alex and Nigel walked in about an hour later, they were deep in a loud, heated argument over who would win in a fight, Maggie Simpson or Stewie Griffin. Even though I barely knew Alex and Nigel, I was glad to see them. The moment I greeted them, they both seemed to completely forget the argument.

"Cap's not back yet?" Alex asked me, frowning curiously.

"No, he came back a while ago with the wood," I said, "but then he left again right away."

"Did he say where he was going?" Alex asked.

"No."

"Did he take a spear with him?" Nigel asked.

"I don't think so, no."

"That's odd," Nigel said.

"That's Cap," Alex said, and this seemed to settle the matter.

Alex and Nigel sat down, and we started talking. I was eager to learn more about the Island, but they seemed even more eager for a "reality check." So I recounted everything significant I could remember that had happened in reality in the past year. (Alex cussed nonstop for almost three minutes upon hearing the Yankees had won the World Series.)

I also told them today's date, which they used to calculate how long they had been on the Island and their ages. Alex had been here thirteen months, Nigel eleven. They were both seventeen, Nigel a few months older. Mariah had been here two months and was sixteen.

"And Cap?" I said.

"Well," Nigel said, "Cap insists he's been on the Island for, uh . . . 'untold centuries.' But we suspect his math is a bit off. We figure he's been here for something like three to five years and he's in his early twenties."

During the reality check, Mariah walked in, looking surly. Alex enthusiastically hummed "The Imperial March" from *Star Wars*. Mariah didn't respond.

As I started running low on news I could remember from the past year, the reality check started turning into one of those chill conversations that meander from one inconsequential topic to another. And although I can scarcely remember a single thing we talked about, the conversation made me completely forget about all my questions about the Island.

There's nothing quite like just hanging out and talking with your friends. It is its own category of joy—simple and subtle, yet incomparable.

And like so many other things in life, it's hard to fully appreciate until you don't have it.

"Ricky, you seem a bit . . . *tentative*—which is completely understandable. It's hard to talk about such an emotional subject, especially with someone you just met. But again, I'm here to listen to anything you have to say. Anything. So please, feel free to be completely open with me. Okay?"

"Completely open, huh?"

"Yes." She smiled sweetly. "So let me ask that last question again, and just try to be as open as possible with your answer: How do you feel now?"

I held her gaze for another moment, then looked down. After several seconds, I took a breath and let it out in a little sigh. "Well," I said—but then broke off.

"Go ahead, Ricky," she said gently. "Just say whatever comes to mind."

I glanced up at her, then back down. I hesitated another few seconds. Then I leaned forward, putting my elbows on my knees, still looking down. "All right—if you really wanna know the truth . . ."

"Yes?"

I took a deep breath. "Right now I feel very uncomfortable."

"You're uncomfortable with the situation at home?" she said with tender understanding.

"No, I'm uncomfortable sitting in this chair. It's too high, the arms are too far apart, and the cushions are too hard. And as long as I'm being open, I gotta tell ya, it's also the ugliest chair I've ever seen. I mean, it's so ugly it's *scary*. I'm afraid it's gonna eat me. Aren't you supposed to have a couch? You should get a couch. There's nothing better than a couch at making people spill their innermost thoughts and emotions. Except alcohol. I'd go with the couch, though, 'cause not even alcohol could make this chair seem attractive."

Dr. Komori leaned back in her office chair, crossed her slender legs, and studied me for a moment with the faintest hint of a smile. She was Asian, thirtyish, and bookishly hot, with shoulder-length black hair and sleek, wire-rimmed glasses. My parents had made me see a psychologist over my vehement objections; so of course, now that I was here, I was determined to act like a total jackass.

Not that that was difficult.

"As far as I'm aware," Dr. Komori said, "that particular chair hasn't eaten anyone before—but just to be safe, would you like to sit in my chair instead?"

I grinned. "Sure. Do I get your notepad too?"

"If you'd like. I'm afraid I don't have any crayons, though."

My grin widened wolfishly. This might be some fun after all.

I let her keep her notepad, but we did switch places. I sat backward in her office chair; she climbed—literally *climbed*—into the enormous, gray, leather armchair, which vaguely resembled an angry hippopotamus. Though I imagine an angry hippo might be slightly more comfortable to sit on.

Besides the hippo-chair, her office was tastefully conservative. It was spacious, white, and well lit by a large window with a sprawling view of a freeway. Framed diplomas covered the wall above her glass-topped desk. Two mini palm trees flanked the hippo-chair—perhaps to simulate its native habitat.

For Dr. Komori's sake, I hoped this particular hippo was not hungry hungry.

Dr. Komori looked down at the notepad in her lap, tucking a stray lock of hair behind her ear. "Okay. So . . . your parents have gathered that you're feeling somewhat . . . *angry.*"

"Wow," I said. "And they're not even psychologists."

She looked at me for a moment, then cleared her throat. "Why don't we take a step back. Do you know why we're here, Ricky?"

"No, but if I see God, I'll ask Him."

Again a smile teased her lips. "Listen, Ricky . . . I think I understand how you're feeling. You feel like you shouldn't have to be here, you think this session is going to be useless, and you don't want to cooperate with me."

"I see why they gave you a Ph.D."

"And I think you should know that many of my patients feel the same way—at first. But once they *do* start cooperating—once they start opening up and talking—they realize it feels good. And if you give me the chance—if you cooperate with me—I think, in the end, you'll be happy you did. Besides, it couldn't hurt, right? So isn't it worth a shot?" She waited a couple seconds; I didn't respond. "Whaddaya say?"

"I've already said what I say. Nice speech, though. Well-rehearsed."

She just stared at me for a long moment. Then she said, "Let's talk about school." She looked down at her notepad again. "So . . . you're a junior in high school . . . and it's been—what, five weeks since school started?"

"Five weeks, five geological eras, something like that."

She raised an eyebrow. "What do you mean by that?"

"My school sucks like a broke, crack-addicted vacuum cleaner, that's what I mean."

"Ah. I see. So, uh . . . is there a particular reason you don't like school?"

"You mean besides the fact that it's school?"

She paused a moment. "What about friends, Ricky?"

"I prefer *Seinfeld*, actually. Despite Jennifer Aniston."

"And what about *your* friends?"

I smiled wryly—I knew my parents had talked to her about this. "Please, Dr. Komori, feel free to be completely *open* with me."

She frowned quizzically. "Excuse me?"

"What you really meant to ask is, do I *have* any friends. Right?"

She hesitated uncomfortably. "Well . . . your parents seem to think you—"

"I know what my parents think," I said, waving her off irritably. "So . . . you wanna know if I have any friends?" I shrugged. "Depends on your definition of 'friend.' I'm actually probably considered 'popular' by most people, but . . . that doesn't mean much to me. I'd much rather have one good friend, one *real* friend, than have the whole school just know my name."

"Have you actually *tried* making friends with anyone?"

I snorted. "You can't *'make'* friends. It just happens. And with these kids at school . . . it just ain't happening. They don't really like *me*, they just like being *around* me, ya know? Funny guys are always 'popular' like that. Same with guys who break the rules."

"Do you break the rules, Ricky?"

I smiled to myself. "Only the dumb ones."

Chapter 10

"Where were you?" Alex asked when Hooke strode in.

"In your mother," Hooke said briskly, then looked at me and nodded toward the tunnel. "C'mon, lad, let's get started."

"Started on what?" I asked.

"Your combat trainin'."

"Or as I liked to call it," Alex said, "Ass-Kicking 101."

Alex grabbed two long, smooth wooden shafts shaped roughly like swords, and he, Hooke, and I climbed up the tunnel and set off into the jungle, heading away from the river.

As we walked, Hooke cleared his throat in that wannabe-dramatic way, looking intense. "Alrigh', lad," he said to me. "Now, there be four basic reasons you'll wanna know how to fight. The first, obviously, is to pick up chicks. Girls love a guy who knows how to use his sword." He grinned and winked at me.

"Now, the second reason: good ol' self-defense. This island's dangerous, alrigh'? At any moment—*any moment*—ye could be viciously attacked by a soulless, bloodthirsty, sword-wieldin' fiend. And don't think I'm exaggeratin'—ye don't know Mariah like we do."

I laughed.

"And the fourth reason: Like I told ya, if ye wanna get home, first we gotta get Peter. And to do that, we're pro'ly gonna have to fight through a small army a' Lost Boys. So, if gettin' back home's important to ye, then it's important ye learn how to fight."

Judging by his behavior toward me, Hooke might as well have forgotten our quarrel. Hell, given his mental condition, maybe he had. He had, after all, apparently forgotten the number three.

Soon we came to an area of relatively sparse vegetation. Over the next couple hours, through demonstration and hands-on exercises, Hooke and Alex taught me basic sword-fighting technique, the importance of agility, balance, and timing over power, how to move fluidly yet unpredictably (like a "drunk sailor on a rollin' deck"), and various other lessons.

Hooke concluded, "But sword-fightin's jus' like sex. I can tell ye 'bout it all the livelong day, but ye can only truly master your sword through hard, sweaty, hands-on practice."

So I fought Alex with the wooden swords. With so much more experience, Alex could kill me almost effortlessly, so he let me attack without striking back. Still, even applying all the lessons I'd just learned, I couldn't even touch him. He was like a machine. His reflexes were startling, his parries seemingly instantaneous. He wielded the sword as smoothly as if it were an extension of his own arm—whereas I was so clumsy I was probably more dangerous to myself than to him.

Hooke coached me for about fifteen more minutes, then strode off into the jungle—but not toward the burrow, I noticed.

Alex and I continued practicing. Even fighting a halfhearted opponent and resting every couple minutes, I was exhausted after only about a half hour.

I dropped my sword and slumped against a tree. "This is kinda tiring," I gasped.

"Yeah," said Alex, who wasn't even sweating, "conditioning's just as important as anything else Cap just taught you. But you'll get used to it real quick. You're off to a really good start, by the way."

I snorted. "Are you kidding? I didn't even hit you *once*."

"I didn't expect you to—hell, your first day, that woulda been incredible. I can just tell, though. You got ... *drive*. See, skills and conditioning are really important, obviously—but the difference between a good fighter and a great fighter is how much you wanna win, and how fierce and crazy you can get. It's like that one quote: 'It's not the size of the dog in the fight, it's the size of the dog's balls.'"

Alex walked over to a nearby tree and stood under a low, horizontal bough. He shook his arms to loosen them up, then jumped, grasped the bough with both hands, palms facing his body, and did thirty-six chin-ups (I counted). Then he dropped back to the ground and started stretching his arms.

"Do you guys have to use your sword a lot?" I asked.

"We don't *have* to a lot, no. But we practice a lot."

"How much?"

"At least a couple hours every day."

I raised my eyebrows, a bit surprised. "Every single day?"

"Yep."

"There's not even one rest day?"

"Not anymore."

"What do you mean, not anymore?"

"Well, before Oscar got here, we basically just practiced whenever we felt like it, which was usually just a few times a week. But right after we rescued Oscar, Cap told us to start practicing every day."

Alex jumped up and grasped the bough again, palms facing outward this time, and did twenty-nine pull-ups. Then he dropped back down and started stretching his arms again.

"Why did Cap tell you to start practicing every day?" I asked.

Alex smiled slightly. "That's a good question. I've been trying to figure it out myself."

I eyed him quizzically. "Why don't you just ask him?"

"I have, and he just says he thinks it's a good idea in general. But I don't buy that. I think he might be working on a plan."

"A plan for what?"

"For capturing Peter."

My heart leapt so high that it seemed to get stuck in my throat, because for a few seconds I couldn't breathe.

"Cap's crazy, but he doesn't do anything without a reason," Alex said. "Now, whether it's a *good* reason, that's a whole different question. But anyway—when he told us to start practicing every day, I figured he might be working on a plan that involved a lot of fighting—either a plan to capture Peter or one to rescue another kid. But there really wasn't much fighting when we rescued you. I could understand if he'd just told *Oscar* to practice every day, but not all of us. He must have a better reason."

"Have you asked him about it?"

"Yeah, and he just said the same thing he always says—that he has an idea but he's still working out the details."

My heart plummeted just as fast as it had leapt. "Then it's bull-shit. If he really had a plan, he'd tell us."

"Actually, no. Cap never tells us his plans until they're totally ready, like all the exact details and everything."

"Why?"

"I'm not sure, actually. Maybe he doesn't wanna get our hopes up too much in case the plan doesn't work out, but he doesn't wanna say there's no plan at all 'cause that would discourage us. And also, I think he's a little too wrapped up in the idea of being the leader."

"But that's stupid," I said. "If he told us what his idea was, the rest of us could all think about it and work on it too—ya know, brainstorm."

"Cap knows way more about the Island and Peter and all that than the rest of us put together, and in my experience, he thinks of everything—he doesn't need our help."

It was certainly possible, maybe even probable, that Hooke's revealing his plan wouldn't help—but that wasn't an adequate reason not to reveal it, because it still *might* help, and it certainly couldn't hurt. Hooke probably did know more about the Island than the rest of us combined, but in devising a plan, creativity was at least as important as knowledge. And no matter how creative and meticulous Hooke was, it was always possible he could miss something—something that someone else might catch.

But I could tell that Alex wasn't the right audience for this argument.

"But ya know, keep in mind," Alex was saying, "there's a pretty good chance I'm completely wrong about all this. It can be pretty hard to follow Cap's thinking. Hell, I don't even think *Cap* follows Cap's thinking half the time."

Alex did another set of chin-ups, but this time I didn't count. I was thinking.

When Alex was done, I said, "You've tried catching Peter before, right?"

"Yeah. Twice."

"How?"

"Well, the first time—well, first of all, you should know that one of the big problems with catching Peter is that he almost never comes out of his cave. His Boys get his food and water and firewood and stuff like that, so the only time he comes out regularly is either to hunt for birds or to take a bath. Now, he hunts a lot—like almost every day—but he stays in the air most of the time, and it's basically impossible to track him from the ground.

"But then about once a week he comes out and washes off in this little lake really close to his mountain. That's how we tried to get him the first time—tried to sneak up on him while he was taking his bath. But he had Boys standing guard all around him, and one of 'em saw us, and Peter took off."

"And the second time?"

"Second time we tried to trick him. Cap hid in the jungle at the bottom of the mountain and waited till Peter came out of his cave, and then started yelling up to him, saying he wanted to talk to him, right? He was gonna offer to tell Peter how to find me and Dread in exchange for taking him home. But me and Dread were actually hiding way up in the trees on either side of Cap. We figured Peter would drop down a little to listen to Cap, and then me and Dread could jump him from above. But he never came low enough—he just hovered right above the treetops the whole time. Cap talked to him for a while, tried to trick him into coming lower—but it turned out Peter was just stalling while his Boys moved in."

Alex did yet another set of pull-ups, but again I didn't count.

I had to talk to Hooke. If Hooke really did all the planning all by himself, that had to change. I wasn't at all sure I could help, but if there was any chance at all—and there was—I wanted to try. I wanted to do whatever I could. I had to. And I was going to.

I took a breath, suddenly feeling energized, and picked up my sword.

"All right, Alex, I'm ready."

Alex cocked an eyebrow at me, looking half skeptical, half impressed. "You wanna keep going?"

"Yeah. I'm not gonna be able to walk in the morning, but let's do it."

He grinned. "That's what she said."

• • •

I couldn't sleep.

I tried for what felt like hours, tossing and turning, keeping my eyes stubbornly shut. I even tried counting sheep jumping over a fence, but at two hundred seventy-eight I lost my patience and started blasting the sheep with a shotgun. This was enormously entertaining, but not particularly conducive to sleep. Finally I gave up trying and lay on my back, staring at the black ceiling, thinking of home.

As the minutes dragged by like mortally wounded sheep, I began to feel claustrophobic; the burrow, which usually felt fairly homey, now felt too much like a coffin. So I slipped outside. The cool, open air was refreshing. I sat with my back against the tree, gazing skyward through a gap in the canopy. Stars almost completely filled the cloudless sky, like a coat of brilliant white spray paint on black canvas.

After maybe fifteen minutes, Mariah came up and stood outside the tunnel without noticing me. She hugged herself like she was cold and gazed skyward. She looked pensive, and somehow almost . . . *vulnerable.*

"Hey," I said softly.

She jerked around, startled. When she saw me, her expression hardened.

"Can't sleep?" I asked.

She looked away. "I never sleep very well."

"Why not?"

She glanced at me sideways, sneering slightly. "You got your own problems to worry about." Then she turned around and ducked back into the tunnel.

I looked skyward again. After a few seconds, I said quietly, "I think she likes me."

If only the sky could laugh.

Chapter 11

"BLOODY *FUCK*!"

"What the—"

"Holy *sh*—"

"GET UP, LADS, GET UP!"

Frantic movement and shouting. Darkness. Someone dragged me to my feet and pushed me against a wall.

"SWORDS OUT!" Hooke screamed. "BACKS AGAINST THE WALL!"

Swords hissed out of scabbards. Hooke and the others quickly fanned out with their backs to the wall, knees bent, swords raised.

Across the burrow, eerily silhouetted by the pale moonlight leaking down the tunnel, stood a line of about a dozen humanlike figures.

"HOLD, LADS!" Hooke shouted. "HOLD!"

We all froze—and, abruptly, time itself seemed to freeze. The figures remained inhumanly still. I could only make out their outlines. At least some of them appeared to be holding swords or spears at their sides. One figure stood a couple steps in front of the others, as if the leader. There was no movement in the burrow, no sound except for my frantic heartbeat. The chaos of the last few moments magnified the sudden stillness.

Then, after maybe five seconds, a drawling man's voice came from the apparent leader: "Nice swords."

I sensed Hooke, who was next to me, flinch slightly, as if in surprise. A beat passed in silence.

Then, all at once, the figures burst out laughing. It sounded like they were all men.

"That's what she said," Alex murmured, as if from a daze.

The leader instantly stopped laughing and his head snapped toward Alex. "That's what who said?"

I could almost feel Alex tense spasmodically. "Never mind," he said quickly.

"Ye speak English?" Hooke said weakly, incredulously.

The leader's head turned slowly toward Hooke. After a moment, he drawled, "No, I don't."

The men laughed again. My eyes had now adjusted enough that I could see what they looked like. Or at least, I thought I could. I was having some trouble believing what I thought I was seeing.

Because what I thought I was seeing was North American Indian braves.

The figures were indeed all men, in their early twenties to early thirties. Each held a sword, spear, or hatchet or two at his side and stood as straight, stiff, and still as a flagpole. Their bodies were sinewy, their expressions stony and faintly proud, their skin so bronze it was almost red. Most had shoulder-length ponytails; a few had completely shaved heads; one had braided pigtails. They all wore animal-skin trousers, and some wore feathers in their hair and bracelets and necklaces made of yarn, beads, and shells.

And I couldn't put my finger on it, but there was something

about them, beyond their weapons, that made them seem distinctly, eerily lethal.

And the leader seemed the most lethal of them all. He looked to be in his late twenties. His height and build were average for the group. His face was lean, almost gaunt, but not unhealthily so. He had a short Mohawk, which gave his head and face a sleek, fierce look, as if the Mohawk were a racing stripe. A large shark or crocodile tooth dangled from each ear, and there was a metal ring in his nose septum, like a bull. At a glance, he didn't look significantly different from any of the other men. But his body language, his voice, and especially his dark, somewhat sunken eyes set him apart, exuding the cold, assured intensity of a loaded gun.

"How'd ye find us here?" Hooke asked—and something about his tone made me think he dreaded the answer.

"Lily was partly conscious at times," the leader said. "Just enough to remember."

Suddenly Hooke spoke very rapidly. "We rescued her from Peter, we was gonna bring her back, I swear, it's just—"

The leader laughed scornfully—he was laughing at Hooke's anxiety. "Don't worry. If we wanted you dead, you wouldn't have woken up."

Hooke hesitated a beat, probably not sure how to take that. "Right," he said uncertainly. "So, uh—now that ye've put our minds at ease—why are ye here?"

"We came to thank you. For rescuing Lily. I am Prince Panther, chief of my people. Lily is my sister. And to repay you, I have decided not to kill you for stealing from us."

I sensed Alex, Nigel, and Mariah relax somewhat. One of them let out a quiet breath of relief.

Hooke, however, did not relax. When he didn't respond immediately, I looked over at him, and got the impression he was thinking fast. After a long moment, he said, "That's it?"

Panther's eyes narrowed. "What's it?"

"That's the only way you're gonna repay us. By not killin' us."

All of our heads whipped toward Hooke and we gaped at him in horrified disbelief, telepathically screaming, *WHAT?!*

"Sounds fine to me," Nigel hissed at Hooke out of the side of his mouth.

Panther's eyes narrowed further, half curiously, half threateningly. "Do you not value your lives?"

"Yes," Alex said quickly.

Panther raised his eyebrows at Alex in surprise. "You do not?"

Alex's eyes widened as he realized his mistake. "No! I mean—no, we do not . . . *not*—not we—do not—"

As Alex continued stammering, Panther looked back at Hooke and said quizzically, "Does *he* speak English?"

"Barely," Nigel said.

"*We* value our lives, aye," Hooke said, shooting Alex a murderous glance. "'T's just wonderin' how much ye value your sister's life. She's worth more'n a few swords and knives . . . and quilts and pots . . . and other stuff—ain't she?"

Panther's whole body seemed to swell, as if it were physically filling with indignation. His voice became menacing—no, more than menacing. Bloodthirsty. "Do you dare to dishonor me by implying that I am a poor brother?"

Hooke didn't miss a beat. He straightened up to his full height, puffed out his chest with equal if not greater indignation, and said, "Do *you* dare to dishonor *me* by implying that *I* would dare to dishonor *you*?"

Despite the extreme tension, I choked back laughter, and Alex pretended to cough violently to disguise a guffaw. Panther just kept glaring for a few seconds, probably not sure if Hooke was serious.

Finally he asked, "What are you trying to say, then?"

"Here," Hooke said, "lemme put it a different way. You're sayin' ye won't kill us 'cause we rescued Lily, righ'? But if we *hadn't* rescued her, ye wouldn'ta known where the burrow's at, so ye wouldn'ta been able to kill us anyways. So, in effect, we rescued her for nothin'."

Again Panther glared silently; Hooke stared back unflinchingly. No one moved nor made a sound.

Finally Panther said, "How about I give you five of our finest swords? And I will trade five more for your pretty squaw."

It took us all a moment to realize what—or rather, who—he was talking about. Alex had another, even more violent coughing fit. Hooke, Nigel, and I all struggled to bite back smiles, and none of us fully succeeded.

Mariah, however, neither laughed nor smiled. Instead, she held up both her fists and extended her middle fingers.

Alex choked and started coughing for real; Hooke, Nigel, and I suddenly succeeded in not smiling; we all gaped at Mariah in incredulous horror. I waited for the Indians to howl savagely and charge forward to avenge such a naked insult—

But Panther frowned curiously and raised his own middle fingers. "What does this mean?"

Hooke was caught off balance—he opened his mouth but I could tell he drew a blank—he looked like a deer in headlights—

"Thank you," I said—and even I was surprised by how casual I sounded. "It means thank you. For calling her pretty."

"Ah." Panther inclined his head toward Mariah. "You're most welcome."

Hooke, Alex, and Nigel visibly relaxed. I glanced at Mariah. She gave me a false, sneering smile and did a fierce "up yours" gesture.

I smiled warmly. "I love you too, Oscar."

Alex and Nigel smiled at me appreciatively. I looked away from Mariah before my face melted.

Hooke cleared his throat, looking uncomfortable. "Your offer's quite generous, but, uh ... as ye can see, we already got swords. Very fine swords, I might add. And as for the squaw ..." He hesitated a moment and glanced at Mariah, who looked distinctly homicidal. "Well, we can talk 'bout that later."

"What do you want, then?" Panther said.

"Well, first of all, I's hopin' ye could just answer a few questions. That be alrigh'?"

Panther grunted noncommittally.

"Fantastic," Hooke said. "First of all, d'ye know any way to get off this island?"

"Yes," Panther said, and my heart just had time to leap into my throat before he said: "Swim."

The men laughed.

"Is there any other way?" Hooke asked.

"Ask Peter," Panther said.

They laughed again.

"Speakin' a' Peter," Hooke said slowly, ". . . what ye gonna do 'bout him?"

"What do you mean?"

"Well, I mean, he was gonna kill your sister. Surely ye want revenge."

"No. He had the right."

Hooke eyed him curiously. "What d'ye mean?"

"Peter had the right to kill Lily."

"He had the *right* to kill your *sister*?" Hooke said incredulously.

"Yes. My people have an agreement with Peter—we have our territory, he has his. Lily trespassed on Peter's territory. If one of Peter's braves trespasses on our territory, we have the right to kill him also."

"But we ain't talkin' 'bout a bloody *zombie*, we're talkin' 'bout a

102

young, fully alive girl! Ye think she deserves to *die* for, what, pickin' flowers in the wrong field?"

"She was not 'picking flowers,'" Panther said contemptuously. "She was looking for a Rare Singer."

"A Rare Singer?" Hooke said. "What's that?"

"A bird. An extremely elusive and sacred bird. Several days ago we heard a Rare Singer singing. Rare Singers almost never sing, because Peter loves to hunt them, and if he hears them—"

"Ne'er-birds!" Hooke said abruptly.

"What?"

"Sorry," Hooke said. "I know the birds you're talkin' 'bout. Go on."

"So Rare Singers only sing when they're in great trouble. We went out to find the Rare Singer, to help it. Lily went too. She got lost and accidentally crossed into Peter's territory. Peter came flying in to find the Rare Singer and found Lily instead."

"And that's alrigh' with ye?"

"The agreement is the only thing that keeps the peace between my people and Peter. We must honor it."

"But she's just a kid!"

"She is a princess and a warrior. And she knows the agreement."

Hooke opened his mouth to continue arguing but hesitated a moment, then closed it. He paused another moment, and I could almost see his mind working, switching gears. He cleared his throat. "So ye'd say Peter's your enemy, righ'?"

"What do you mean?"

"Well, ye got this truce with him, aye . . . but wouldn't ye kill him if ye got the chance?"

Panther's eyes narrowed. "What are you trying to say?"

Hooke licked his lips. "Listen . . . we wanna get off this island, and the only way to do that is through Peter, righ'? So we'd both like to get our hands on him, wouldn't we?"

"What are you trying to say?" Panther repeated, his voice becoming dangerously impatient.

"I'm sayin' we join forces and get Peter. I'm not sure exactly—"

"No. Absolutely not."

"How many men ye got?"

"That doesn't matter. We have no idea how many braves Peter has."

"Then what if ye just attacked as a diversion, and me and me lads handled the rest? Ye wouldn't even have to fight, really, just get their attention and—"

"But no matter what we do, if we fail to capture or kill him, there will be war. There is peace now, and has been for a long time. Why risk it?" Hooke opened his mouth to continue arguing, but Panther cut him off: "What else do you want?"

Hooke faltered for a moment, thrown off. "I—well—nothin', I s'pose. For now. But—if e'er we do need somethin'..."

"Perhaps we'll be able to help," Panther said, a tad grudgingly. "You're welcome to visit our village. Do you know the way?"

Hooke opened his mouth to answer, but then the men laughed.

Hooke smiled uneasily, understanding. "Aye. Methinks I 'member."

"Farewell then," Panther said, inclining his head toward us, just slightly. "And thank you again."

And he flipped us off with both hands.

Then he turned on his heel, strode regally to the tunnel, and jumped up into it. The others swiftly filed in after him.

After the last one had gone, silence remained. I looked around at the others; they were all staring toward the tunnel, looking somewhat dazed.

After about five seconds, Nigel drily voiced what seemed to be the prevailing sentiment: "Whoa."

Alex took that small coconut out of his pocket, pressed it to his lips for a couple seconds, then put it back. "Why the hell didn't you accept the swords, Cap?" he asked.

Hooke eyed him quizzically. "What the hell are we gonna do with a bunch a' extra swords?"

"Who cares?" Alex said. "We woulda gotten rid of *her*." He jerked his head toward Mariah. Mariah carelessly flipped him off. "You're welcome," Alex said.

"Were those . . . uh . . . Native Americans?" I asked.

"Native Islanders," Hooke said. "They live in a village several miles from here." He shook his head wonderingly and said, mostly to himself, "I had no bloody idear they speak English."

"You've never, like, interacted with 'em at all before?" I asked.

"Well, I stole a bunch a' stuff from their village o'er the years—weapons, quilts, pots, clothes—basically e'erythin' we have, actually. But I ne'er really needed to *talk* to 'em, and I had no idear if they'd be friendly—and mind ye, a lot a' things on this island ain't. So I just figured, why risk it?"

"And so that girl you were talking about—Lily—she was the one in the cave with me, right?" I asked.

"Aye. I had no idear she was conscious at all afore she snuck off. Had no idear she was a bloody princess, either."

"And what's the deal with the Rare Singers?"

Hooke smiled darkly. "They're one a' the big reasons you're here and not rottin' away in Peter's cave."

I eyed him curiously. "What do you mean?"

"Ne'er-birds—we call 'em Ne'er-birds—are extremely rare birds. In all me years on the Island I ne'er seen one—which is why we call 'em Ne'er-birds. I only heard 'em a few times."

"So what do they have to do with me and Peter?" I asked.

"Well, 'bout a month after I 'scaped from Peter, I just happened to be snoopin' round his mountain when I saw him come outta his cave and fly off to reality—and just a couple minutes later, the Ne'er-birds started singin'. That was the first time I heard 'em, and I've ne'er heard anythin' like it. It was like the whole island got turned into a giant aviary. There was pro'ly only twenty or thirty birds singin' total, but their songs was so loud and carried so far, I could hear 'em from all the way 'cross the island. They sang for 'bout two or three hours, I'd reckon—then I saw Peter come flyin' back with a lad, and righ' away, e'ery one of 'em stopped. After that, I didn't hear a single Ne'er-bird sing for almos' a year—not till Peter left for reality again.

"Ya see, lad, Peter goes out and hunts birds just 'bout e'ery day—for fun, I assume. And the Ne'er-bird must be his favorite target—pro'ly 'cause they're so rare—or maybe they're rare *because* he hunts 'em so much. At any rate, he's hunted 'em enough that they've *learned*. They've learned to shut up whene'er he's on the island. 'Cause if they make noise like I heard 'em do while Peter's here, chances be he'll come track 'em down.

"But soon as one Ne'er-bird sees Peter leave for reality, he takes the opportunity and starts singin' his arse off. Ya know, to try and get a mate, or a record deal, or why ever the hell birds sing. And then the other Ne'er-birds hear the first one singin', an' pretty soon they're all singin'. And that's how we know when Peter picks up another lad. If it weren't for Ne'er-birds, I wouldn'ta known when to come rescue any a' ye lads, an' ye'd pro'ly all be dead. Or worse."

Chapter 12

We cooked breakfast, as Hooke had somehow determined that dawn was near. (When I asked him how he knew this, he said he could tell time using the position of the stars. I decided not to point out that he hadn't gone outside.)

As I was cooking a skewer of seafood, Hooke pointed to it and said, "Ye best savor that, lad. 'Cause that'll be your last free meal."

"What do you mean?"

"From now on you're gonna help put bread on the table."

"We don't have bread," Nigel grumbled.

"Or a table," Alex said lightly.

"Shut up, lads," Hooke said, then to me: "Today you're gonna learn how to fish." He nodded at Alex and Nigel. "Ye two can take him to the tide pools."

Alex smiled crookedly at Nigel. "Let's take him to the cove first."

"The cove?" I said, and glanced at Mariah, who continued to ignore everything but her breakfast. "That was part of Mariah's escape plan, wasn't it?"

"Yeah," Nigel said. "It'll just be a quick detour."

"Well actually," Alex said, "with Dread, it probably won't exactly be *quick*. Dread walks about as fast as a quadriplegic turtle."

I looked at Nigel, expecting a comeback, but he was staring at Alex, looking almost unnerved. "You know what quadriplegic means?"

"Yeah," Alex said breezily. "It means your legs got amputated."

Nigel nodded to himself, looking relieved.

"So what's at the cove?" I asked.

Alex grinned. "You'll see."

When the sun was up, Alex grabbed a basket, and he, Nigel, and I headed out. We followed the river for about a half mile until it spilled into the ocean; then we turned left and proceeded parallel to the beach, keeping just inside the tree line. I gazed seaward, through the vegetation. The seascape was almost surreally perfect, like a postcard: deserted, pristine beach; clear, turquoise sea glistening in the sunshine; deep blue sky scattered with fluffy white clouds; all framed by palm trees and tropical ferns.

"Remind you of home?" Alex asked.

I looked over at him. "Huh?"

He nodded toward the beach. "The beach. It remind you of San Diego?"

I shrugged. "Yeah, a little, I guess." I'd actually just been thinking how much better this beach looked than any I'd been to in southern California. "So where you guys from?"

Nigel smiled proudly. "Green Bay, Wisconsin, baby. Land of the cheese, home of the Packers."

"Cambridge, Massachusetts," Alex said. "But right before Peter came to me I moved to New York. Which is *why* Peter came to me, actually."

That made my ears perk up. "Rough move?" I asked.

Alex smiled thinly. "Yeah, I'd say it was pretty, uh . . . *brutal.*" He said "brutal" with a curious, wry emphasis.

"What do you mean?" I asked.

"Well, the move sucked in a lot of ways, ya know. I had lived in Cambridge my whole life. Same house and everything. Then one day my dad got a job transfer, and just like that," he snapped his fingers, "we lived in New York." He shook his head in (I assumed) bittersweet reminiscence. "I had so many friends in Cambridge. And good ones, too, ya know? Some of 'em I'd known my entire life. And then suddenly they were all gone. And I kept telling myself I'd make new friends real fast, but . . . that just didn't happen. And ya know, without friends, school is like . . . it's just . . . well . . ."

"School," I said.

"Yeah," Alex said, nodding. "It's like prison, basically, just more boring. And less civilized. I mean, hell, friends are the only reason I *go* to school."

"Needless to say," Nigel deadpanned.

"Well, friends and baseball," Alex said. "And that was really the only thing I was even kinda looking forward to about the move: My school had a really good baseball team. Unfortunately, they also had a really good pitcher. He had started on varsity since he was a freshman, and he was a senior now, and he was the star of the team. Problem was . . . I was better than him. And I was a sophomore.

"It was pretty clear that I was better just in the first day of try-outs. After the second day, he came up to me while I was alone and threatened me. Said this was his year, and I could have the next two. Said I better start fucking up my pitches or he'd fuck 'em up for me. I said we'll just let the coaches decide. I mean, I felt bad for him—well, I *had* felt bad for him before he threatened me—but I take baseball really seriously, and I'd worked really hard for a really long time to be as good as I was. There was no way in hell I was gonna fuck up on purpose.

"So I kept playing as good as I could—and still better than him. Then after the fourth day of tryouts, I was walking to work when that fucking fucker and three of his friends came outta nowhere and surrounded me. I tried to run but they pushed me back. I started trying to talk to 'em, but none of 'em said a thing. The fucker just walked right up to me and took a swing at my face. I'm pretty used to hard things coming at my face—"

"I bet you are," Nigel said.

Alex gave him an evil look. "I'm used to *baseballs* coming towards me really fast," he clarified to me, "so my reflexes are pretty good—so I managed to dodge that first punch. Then I swung back as hard as I fuckin' could and nailed that fucker dead in the face. I'm sure I at least broke his nose. Hopefully a hell of a lot more. But after that I didn't get another punch in. They overpowered me. Threw me to the ground and just beat the shit outta me for a good few minutes. And then left."

"Jesus," I said.

Alex laughed a little. "Yeah. So, eventually I got to the hospital. It was nothing too serious—I had a concussion, some bruised ribs, needed stitches in a couple places—mostly it was just a shitload of bruises. And honestly, sometimes I think all that mighta been worth it just for the opportunity to sock that fucker in the face. But the real damage was mental, ya know? I was . . . traumatized. So when Peter came that night—and I had already been having dreams about the Island ever since the move—so . . ." Alex shrugged.

Nigel grinned at me. "And ya wanna hear something funny about all that? When Cap rescued him, Alex was wearing one of those 'I Heart New York' T-shirts."

I laughed.

Alex smiled and shrugged. "My parents bought it for me for my birthday. I felt like I had to wear it sometimes." He looked down, and his eyes seemed to lose focus; his smile faded, became sad, bitter, then disappeared. "Ya know, Ricky . . . if there's one thing you're gonna learn on the Island, it's to appreciate your life back home."

Nigel smiled a bit. "Alex the sentimentalist."

Alex eyed him quizzically. "*What?* I'm not a sentimentalist. And what the hell's religion have to do with this anyway?"

Nigel looked like he hadn't the slightest clue how to respond.

As soon as I was confident I could open my mouth without laughing, I asked, "So what about you, Nigel? Why'd you come here?"

"My, uh . . . my dad died."

I flinched as if I'd been slapped in the face; I hadn't expected anything so serious. "Jeez, I . . . I'm sorry. I didn't mean to—"

Nigel shook his head and waved me off. "Nah, it's all right. He, uh . . . he was a cop. He pulled over some guy on the freeway one day, told him to get outta the car, and, uh . . . the guy pulled a gun and shot him. Turned out the car was stolen. They never caught the guy."

"Jesus," I said softly. "I'm sorry."

Nigel nodded in thanks. "I started getting dreams about the Island just a couple nights after it happened. And the dreams were always really fuzzy to me when I woke up—but I always remembered very clearly that while I was in the dream—while I was on the Island, ya know—I had this amazing feeling of . . . kind of . . ."

"Peace," I said. "Bliss."

"Yeah," Nigel said, nodding. "And so then Peter came a couple weeks later and offered to take me to the Island for real. And I think I knew I only got that feeling 'cause it *wasn't* real, 'cause it was just a dream—but I guess I just wanted the feeling so bad, I just said yes."

Nigel smiled thinly. "And actually, ya know, coming to the Island did kinda help. Took my mind off it, at least. I mean, hell, living with Alex is horrible enough to overshadow almost anything."

Alex clapped him on the shoulder. "Don't mention it."

"Seriously, though," Nigel said thoughtfully, "the Island's kinda like the ultimate, universal therapy. At least, it was for me. It helped me through all sorts of problems."

"Yeah, by replacing them with bigger ones," Alex said, eyeing him skeptically. "You don't think the Island's made your life better, do you?"

"No," Nigel said slowly, "but I think it's made *me* better. As a person."

"Well that's true," Alex admitted. "You're not chunky anymore."

"Chunky?" I said in amused surprise—Nigel looked almost as fit as Alex. "Nigel used to be chunky, huh?"

"I was not *chunky*," Nigel said testily. "I was just . . . *hefty.*"

"Right," Alex said drily. "And the Michelin Man is just big-boned."

As Alex said this, he absently took the coconut out of his pocket and started tossing it up and down. Before Nigel could retort, I said to Alex, "Hey, what's the deal with that coconut? I've been meaning to ask you abou—"

"'*That*' coconut, as you so casually refer to it," Alex said, "is not just any coconut." He held the coconut up like a diamond. "This coconut . . ."

". . . is *magical*," Nigel whispered in mock wonder.

Alex stabbed a finger at him. "*Never* mock my nuts. Coco- or otherwise." He cleared his throat. "As I was saying—*this* coconut," he held it up again, "is a *lucky* coconut."

Nigel just smiled cynically.

"Lucky, huh?" I said, trying not to smile myself. "Why's that?"

"Well ya see, I wanna keep my arm in shape for when I get back to reality and start pitching again, right? Have you noticed that quilt that's hanging up on the wall in the burrow?"

"Yeah," I said.

"Well that's my target. I folded it up so it was about the size of a strike zone and then nailed it into the wall with a spearhead. Pretty clever, huh?"

"Ingenious," Nigel said drily.

Alex ignored him. "My only problem was, I didn't have a baseball. I thought about using a rock, but I couldn't find one that was round. So I started using coconuts—I'd pick 'em before they were done growing, when they were still about the size of a baseball. And they worked great—there was just one problem. Once in a while I'd miss the strike zone—the coconuts would hit the hard wall instead of the soft quilt, ya see—and after a few days they'd split open. So every week I'd have to go through a whole pile of coconuts. But then a few months ago"—he smiled fondly and started tossing his coconut up and down—"I came across this baby. Just about the perfect size and weight for a baseball, and guess what? After all this time, it still hasn't broken open. And it never will, 'cause it's lucky." He gave the coconut a loud, wet kiss.

Nigel rolled his eyes and muttered, "Christ."

"I carry it in my pocket wherever I go," Alex said. "You need a lucky charm on this damn island. So anyway . . . there ya have it. The story of my lucky coconut."

"So you were really like a great pitcher, huh?" I said.

Alex nodded, smiling proudly. "Hell yeah I was. I was the best damn pitcher on the East Coast."

Nigel snorted. "Probably 'cause batters got distracted by your massive head."

"You know, Dread," Alex said, "there's a difference between being arrogant and knowing you're actually good."

"Yeah," Nigel said. "It's called being *really* arrogant."

Alex shoved Nigel. Nigel shoved him back, and Alex tripped and fell into a bush. Nigel looked back at him, laughing tauntingly, and walked straight into a tree.

I laughed so hard I almost died. Literally. I couldn't breathe for like three minutes.

When I finally recovered, I asked, "So why'd Cap come to the Island? What's his story?"

Alex and Nigel exchanged a look.

"We don't know, actually," Alex said. "The only time we ever asked him about it, he said the crew of his frigate mutinied and deserted him here."

Nigel smiled. "Hell, I doubt he even remembers the real story."

"So what about you, Ricky?" Alex asked. "What's your story?"

I gave a slight, wry laugh and looked down at my feet, somewhat embarrassed. "It's lame, that's what it is."

"What do you mean?" Alex said.

"I dunno, I mean . . . I just thought my life was so shitty, ya know, and . . . now suddenly it's like . . ."

"You realize you were being a little emo bitch?" Alex suggested.

I laughed. "Basically. And especially after hearing your story, Nigel . . . I just had no right to be bitter or whatever."

"Rights are bullshit," Nigel said. "Ya know, after my dad died, people would tell me I had the right to be like pissed off at the world. But, first of all, I still had a hell of a lot to be thankful for. Ya know, there's always plenty of people in the world a lot worse off than you. But more importantly, what's the fucking point? Being pissed off at the world is just stupid. It's stupid, self-indulgent, counterproductive bullshit." Nigel fell silent for a long moment, and his expression darkened. "Just wish I'd realized that earlier."

"It's fucking amazing how fast everything can change," I said, half to myself.

"Your life, you mean?" Alex said.

"Well," I said, "more like . . . your perspective on life."

"Your perspective on life *is* life," Nigel said. "Life's what you make it."

A few seconds passed in silence as the simple yet profound power of that notion sunk in.

Then Alex said, "In other words: Life's a bitch. Make it *your* bitch."

Nigel looked at him in irritation. "Thanks, Alex. I say something eloquently profound and you make it chauvinistically crass."

"No," Alex said, "you said something painfully sappy and I made it fuckin' funny."

Nigel rolled his eyes.

"So c'mon, Ricky," Alex said. "Conclude the emo trilogy."

"Let's talk about grades," Dr. Komori said.

"Okay. Well, first of all, are you familiar with the alphabet?"

"You got nothing but As from kindergarten all the way up through tenth grade, is that right?"

"No. I got a B on a quiz once."

"And now suddenly your grades have dropped to Bs and Cs. Why is that?"

"I am protesting the widespread disproportionate emphasis on grades as a measure of academic merit."

She raised her eyebrows, looking surprised and slightly impressed. "Is that true?"

"Hell no, but it got two of my teachers to stop bugging me."

Her eyebrows settled. "Are you *trying* to get bad grades, Ricky?"

I laughed. "If I was actually *trying* to get bad grades, don't you think I could do better than Bs and Cs?"

"So you just don't care as much anymore, is that it?"

"A sixteen-year-old not caring about school? I dunno. I guess anything's possible."

"But this isn't about you being sixteen, is it? It's about you being angry."

She paused for several seconds, inviting me to respond. I just stared at her.

"Would you like to explain to me now *why* you're angry?" she said.

I opened my mouth to politely decline but hesitated a couple seconds. Then I blew out a "fuck it" sigh and looked away. "The move. All right? I'm angry 'cause we moved. I didn't wanna move, and I told my parents that more times than I can remember, but . . . we moved anyway."

"Well, the *reason* you moved is pretty important, isn't it?"

I didn't respond.

"As I understand it, your parents couldn't afford two houses in Santa Barbara. They moved to Alpine so their houses could be fairly close to each other—that way you could regularly see them both. So really, they moved because they *had* to, isn't that right?"

My whole body seemed to clench like a fist. "My mom didn't *have* to have an affair," I spat fiercely. "My dad didn't *have* to refuse to go to marriage counseling. They didn't *have* to get a *divorce!*"

Several seconds passed in loud silence. Dr. Komori stared at me expressionlessly; I glared back, a faint pounding in my head.

Dr. Komori cleared her throat. "Why don't we talk about the divorce and the move some more."

"I'll tell you why we don't," I said acidly. "'Cause it's pointless. We can talk about the divorce and the move all you want, it can't

116

change the fact that my family's split in half and all my friends live two hundred miles away."

"It can't change those things per se, no—but it might change how you feel about them."

"No it won't."

"How do you know? Have you ever even tried talking about this before?"

"I don't need to try, I just know."

"Well why not try anyway? What could it hurt?"

I glared at the wall and didn't respond. After about five seconds, she said, somewhat challengingly, "Do you *like* being angry, Ricky?"

"Look, I can't *help* the way I *feel*," I said exasperatedly.

"Actually, Ricky, you can," she said with sudden, shocking severity. "It's easy to think that how you feel is determined solely by external factors, things like the divorce and the move. Then you can just stop trying—you can just lie back and feel sorry for yourself. But really, *you* determine how you react to these external factors; in large part, you *can* control the way you feel. That's what I'm trying to help you with. That's what being a therapist is all about."

"Another moving speech," I muttered.

"Now, I'm not saying you can just switch off your anger. But you can't stay angry forever, right? And until you *do* resolve your anger, you'll continue to be unhappy."

"I'm not unhappy *because* I'm angry!" I cried. "I'm angry because I'm unhappy, 'cause I'm fucking *miserable*, and it's THEIR FUCK-ING FAULT!"

Chapter 13

"There it is," Nigel said quietly, pointing. Through the vegetation, about thirty yards ahead, I could see a break in the shoreline—the mouth of some sort of inlet.

"All right, slow down," Alex whispered, extending an arm across my chest. "And stay quiet."

"Why?" I whispered, frowning with uneasy curiosity.

"So they don't hear us," Alex whispered.

"*They?*"

Nigel held a finger to his lips. "Shhh."

We stopped and crouched at the edge of a roughly circular cove, about forty yards across, enclosed by craggy, ten-foot cliffs. In the center of the cove, rising from the greenish water, was a massive rock formation that looked a little like a castle.

And scattered on this castle were—

"What the fuck . . . ?" I breathed.

They looked like a cross between a man and a dolphin. Roughly human-sized, they were completely hairless, their skin sleek and dark blue, almost black. They had big, round, shiny eyes, squashed, upturned noses with slitted nostrils, and no discernible ears. A curved fin protruded from the top of their heads. Their arms and legs were humanlike, but their hands and feet were webbed, like duck feet, with inch-long talons. About a dozen of them lay sprawled on the castle, mostly motionless. Then a fin surfaced near one edge of the cove, racing across the water, and for a fleeting moment the creature leapt clear into the air, its gleaming body horizontal, skimming the water like a dolphin, before slipping back under and disappearing.

"What are they?" I whispered wonderingly.

"Mermaids," Alex said.

"Mermaids?" I said, looking over at him incredulously, then back into the cove. *"Those* are *mermaids?"*

"Well, that's just what we call them," Nigel said. "We have no idea what they really are. But they do look half human, half fish, don't they?"

"This cove is like their home," Alex said. "Once in a while you'll see one of 'em in the ocean or in a river or lake, but there's always some here."

Two more fins surfaced, one chasing the other. A mermaid clambered out of the water onto a rock and shook itself like a dog, spraying water. Another jumped off the top of the castle, did a lazily graceful flip, and slid into the water with barely a splash. Several others stood on the castle, ramrod straight, facing us.

I frowned. I was pretty sure none had been standing before.

"Hey you guys," I whispered. "I think they—"

A mermaid exploded out of the water directly below us, leaping halfway up the cliff, hissing loudly. We scrambled back frantically; Alex and Nigel whipped out their swords; I half turned, ready to run . . . then heard a splash—the mermaid falling back into the water. Presumably.

"Jesus *Christ*," I gasped, heart jackhammering.

Alex and Nigel glanced at each other, laughed slightly, and lowered their swords.

"Should we get outta here?" I asked anxiously.

"Nah, it's all right," Alex said, smiling at me reassuringly. "He was just trying to scare us."

"Well, I'd say he succeeded," I said. I pressed a hand to my chest, as if to keep my heart from bursting through. "Are mermaids dangerous?"

"Very," Nigel said. "They're territorial. They can't do much on land, so we're safe up here—but if we went in the water, they'd try to rip us apart. Cap says a long time ago he was trying to fish not far from here and a bunch of 'em attacked him, and he had to fight 'em off with his sword. He says they can get pretty fuckin' scary when they're mad."

"Oscar's escape plan was to lead Peter and that group of Boys here," Alex said. "She was hoping it was dark enough that they wouldn't see the drop-off until they were right in front of it and then she could push a bunch of 'em in and jump in herself. Then she figured the mermaids would go crazy, and maybe in all the confusion she could slip away."

"There's a hell of a lot of things that could have and probably would have gone wrong," Nigel said, "but it was still pretty damn clever, especially considering the circumstances she was in when she thought it up."

"You really don't have to worry about mermaids, though," Alex said. "As long as you leave them alone, they'll return the favor."

"Yeah, well, uh . . ." I stepped back and cocked a thumb over my shoulder, "I think I'll stay back here just in case."

Alex grinned at me and clapped me on the shoulder. "C'mon. Let's go fishin'."

"These fish don't have limbs by any chance, do they?" I said drily.

On our way back, we stopped at a network of tide pools and quickly collected every shellfish in sight. Nigel told me the tide brought in more every night. We picked up Hooke and some barbed fishing spears at the burrow, then set off again. Hooke told me the shellfish weren't enough to feed everyone, so every day they also went to the swamp and spearfished.

The swamp was about a half mile away. Low, gnarled trees and tall reeds rose from the still, knee-deep water, casting mottled shade. The air was muggy and smelled faintly of rotten fish. Frogs croaked, birds called, insects buzzed.

Hooke briefly taught me the basics of spearfishing, like how to throw the spear and how to aim slightly past the fish to offset the light refraction. "But spearfishin's just like sex," he said. "To truly master your spear, ye gotta get your hands wet. And your feet."

So with that puzzling and mildly disturbing notion in mind, we started wading slowly through the swamp, hugging the shore, Hooke towing the basket through the water. We positioned ourselves side by side, about five feet apart, to cover the most area possible.

Whenever Hooke, Alex, or Nigel spotted a fish within several feet, they launched their spears with deadly power and mechanical precision (Alex and Nigel competed to outfish each other). I tried—and tried and tried—but it was much harder than they made it look. The fish were small, fast targets, the light refraction confused me despite Hooke's pointers, and my throws were clumsy and inaccurate. I didn't hit a single fish.

Retrieving my spear after my eight hundred fifty-seventh miss (just estimating), I blew out a frustrated breath and said, "I don't know how the hell you survived out here on your own, Cap. I woulda starved to death the first week."

Alex snorted. "Dread woulda starved to death the first *hour*."

Nigel ignored him.

"Don't worry, lad," Hooke said to me. "Took me weeks to hit me first fish." He smiled. "And I had a bloody lot a' time to practice too."

"What *did* you do out here with all that time, all by yourself?" I asked.

Hooke shrugged. "Slept. Fished. Hunted. Chopped wood. Walked round the Island. Went swimmin'. Practiced fightin'. Named all me fingers and toes. Discussed and debated philosophy with 'em. By the way—turns out me left pinky toe is a bloody genius." Hooke lifted his left foot out of the water and said toward it, "Ain't that right, Mr. Mullins?" Mr. Mullins didn't respond. Hooke put his foot back down. "But anyways—anythin' to pass the time, really."

"Sounds kinda boring," I said, smiling.

"Aye, lad, that it was. And lonely, too. Hell, I's alone for so long, even *Alex* made good company."

Nigel laughed.

"I love you too, Cap," Alex said.

"How'd you rescue Alex?" I asked Hooke.

"Ah," Hooke said with a grin of triumphant reminiscence. "A bloody brilliant strategy, that's how."

"Brilliant strategy my firm, sexy *ass*," Alex said.

Nigel winced.

"So what was it?" I asked.

Hooke shrugged breezily. "I climbed up Peter's mountain, took out the guards at the main entrance, and then I found Alex and we escaped. Simple and brilliant."

"Simple and sui-fucking-cidal," Alex said. "When Cap found me he was already being chased by about fifteen Lost Boys. By the time we got outta the cave, Peter's whole damn army was after us."

Hooke shrugged again. "It worked, didn't it?"

"Barely," Alex said.

"Well, I admit," Hooke said, "if I could do it o'er again, I would *not* have done the same thing . . . I woulda just left Alex with Peter." He and Nigel laughed.

"I love you too, Cap," Alex said.

"So what about Nigel?" I asked. "How'd you rescue him?"

"Well," Hooke said, "after I rescued Alex, Peter got Dread pretty quick, just 'bout a month later. See, whate'er it is Peter gets from them lads, he must *need* it—'cause whene'er I rescue one, he always gets another real quick. Anyways, I knew this time Peter'd be ready for another straight-on raid. So here's what we did instead: The night Peter went back to reality, me and Alex climbed up the mountain and hid righ' outside the main entrance. Peter came back with Dread the next mornin', and soon as they landed on that ledge, we jumped 'em. We almost got Peter, too, but he managed to fly away in the knick a' time. But anyways . . . we got Dread and then we got the hell outta there."

"So what about Mariah?" I asked.

"Well, Mariah didn't come for a long time. See, after we rescued Dread, Peter got another lad in just like a week. I wanted to rescue that one too, but I couldn't see any way to do it. There was a good fifteen Lost Boys at the main entrance, who knows how many more inside the caves. I s'pose we coulda tried to fight our way through, but at that point, I's the only one who really knew how to fight. So we had to let that one go."

"Peter didn't go back to get Mariah until about two months ago," Alex said. "When he left, before he got back, the three of us went to scout out his mountain. Now, his Boys patrol the base of the mountain twenty-four seven, ya see, and while we were there, I heard one of 'em coming straight at me. I didn't have any time to hide, so without even thinking, I dove into the river. The current sucked me under the mountain, and when I came up for air I was in that cavern inside the mountain—you know the place I'm talking about. Anyways, I stayed there for a while, 'cause I wasn't sure if that Lost Boy had seen me or not . . . and while I was in there, I just happened to see this hole in the ceiling. I climbed up into it, and then I just kept on climbing and climbing till I saw some light shining through a crack in the rock. I pushed on the rock and felt it give a little. So I kept pushing, and after a while, the whole rock just popped loose. And there I was, in Peter's cave."

"So anyways," Hooke said, "we waited till Peter came back and tied up Mariah. Then we went into the river, climbed up through the openin', and snuck round the caves till we found her. See, I'm pretty sure Peter don't know 'bout that openin'—otherwise he'd have it guarded. And he definitely don't know that *we* know 'bout it. He put a bunch of his Boys at the front entrance, thinkin' that would stop us, so there weren't many Boys *in* the caves. And plus, it's pitch-black in there. We snuck in, cut Mariah loose, and snuck out without anyone seein' us."

"So how long do you think it'll be before Peter gets another kid?" I asked.

Hooke shrugged. "I dunno. But soon, I'm sure. He's hungry now."

"And so am I," Nigel said, "so let's shut up and get some fish."

Chapter 14

After almost an hour, I still hadn't speared a fish, and had used every cussword I know at least once (I couldn't even imagine what Ms. Fulsom would have done if she'd been here. Probably shot me. And/or herself).

"Don't worry 'bout it, lad," Hooke said to me. "If ye want, ye can head on back to the burrow now. I reckon we can handle the fishin' for today."

I gladly accepted the offer. Nigel escorted me until we could see the tree outside the tunnel, then he headed back to the swamp. I shuffled down the tunnel, lowered myself into the burrow—

And froze.

Mariah was sitting against the wall to my right, hugging her knees, her forehead resting on one knee. She hadn't noticed me. She was crying silently, her eyes closed but tears leaking out.

A panic of indecision seized me. My first instinct was to fly back up the tunnel and pray she didn't notice me. Girls in general are tricky terrain; crying girls are far trickier. And crying Oscar was a fucking minefield.

But then I realized this was a perfect opportunity to show Mariah how sweet I could be. I could sit down beside her, ask her very tenderly what's wrong, maybe even put my arm around her, and then maybe she'd—

I mentally shook myself. I was being a delusional asshole.

"Hey," I said softly, trying not to startle her.

And I hit a mine.

She started violently, eyes snapping open. I instinctively started walking toward her—but she reacted like I was charging to attack. Looking panicked, she scrambled to her feet, pressed her back against the far wall, and reached for the knife at her waist—at which point I decided I was never talking to a crying girl again. But then she abruptly froze, as if finally recognizing me. Her panic-stricken expression turned into a scowl.

"I'm sorry," I said quickly, stepping back, "I didn't mean to—"

"What the fuck are you doing here?" she snapped fiercely. "I thought you guys were fishing."

"I came back early, I . . . I'm sorry. Are you okay?"

"I'm fine," she said stiffly. "You just . . . startled me."

"I'm sorry."

"Yeah, you've said that three times."

"I'm sorry." She looked at me sharply. "I mean I'm sorry for saying I'm sorry. And I suppose I'm also sorry for saying I'm sorry for saying I'm so—"

"Ricky, just shut up, all right? You're not funny."

"Ouch. I think I would have preferred the knife."

Mariah turned away, cleared her throat, and briskly wiped her cheeks.

"You sure you're okay?" I asked.

"Yes, I'm *fine*," she said exasperatedly.

I couldn't help smiling a bit. "So were those tears of joy?"

126

"What?" she snapped, feigning scorn at my obvious crazy talk. "I wasn't crying."

"Fair warning—if you say you had something in your eye, I'm gonna make a dirty joke."

Mariah glared at me silently for about five seconds, eyes smoldering. I stopped smiling but refused to look away. Her eyes were absolutely beautiful—and they scared the shit out of me. I half expected them to start shooting out laser beams or lightning bolts. Possibly even both.

Finally she said, "So I was crying, so what?"

I shrugged. "Nothing, I just . . . wanted to know if there's anything I could do."

She sneered slightly. "I don't need your help. I'm sure me crying fits nicely into your little 'damsel in distress' fantasy, but—"

"Whoa!" I said, holding up my hands in a "slow down" gesture. "What the hell are you talking about? What is it with you and this whole 'damsel in distress' thing?"

"Ya know there's a reason the 'damsel in distress' thing is so popular in books and movies and stuff. It's 'cause guys get off on it. They get off on feeling like girls are weak and helpless and dependent on them. But I'm not that kind of girl."

"And I'm not that kind of guy," I said with seriousness bordering on indignation. "Look—I don't think you're a damsel in distress, all right? And I don't think I'm Prince Charming. I am charming as fuck, but technically I'm not a prince. All I did was ask if there's anything I can do. That's what you're supposed to do when you see someone crying. Why can't it be that simple?"

"'Cause human nature isn't that simple."

I eyed her curiously. "What do you mean by that?"

She sighed, kind of sadly, and looked away, and for just an instant I thought she was going to start crying again. But then she said with careless curtness, "Ricky, just leave me alone, all right?"

I hesitated for a long moment, considering continuing the conversation, but my survival instinct won out. She clearly didn't feel like chatting, and I didn't feel like being incinerated by a combined laser/lightning attack. So, sighing inwardly, I crawled back up the tunnel.

Walking on autopilot, I returned to the swamp and found the others. I told them I'd gotten bored and wanted to try spearfishing again. Hooke reproved me for walking here alone, but I barely heard him. My mind was still stuck back in the burrow with Mariah.

There were a few main reasons I couldn't (and didn't particularly want to) stop thinking about her.

She was hot. And she was the only girl here. So no matter how appalling her personality was, I was biologically required to have at least a little bit of a crush on her.

I was also curious about her. *Why* did she have such an appalling personality? Because there was no way in hell it was natural. I figured homesickness and her past were probably part of it—but I found it hard to believe that those two things could fully account for such over-the-top hostility. I had a feeling there was something else. A missing piece to the puzzle.

And I felt bad for her. There was obviously some kind of pain, serious pain, underlying (and perhaps intentionally buried beneath) her hostility. And I wanted to know what it was. I wanted to help her.

Which raised an interesting question: *Why* did I want to help her?

Part of it was straight-up compassion. Like most people, I think (I hope), I just like helping people.

But another big part of it was that she was pretty. Which doesn't really make much sense.

Mariah was partly right: Guys do have a thing for damsels in distress. But only if they're pretty. Generally—as shitty as it may be—the prettier the damsel, whatever her distress, the quicker most guys will be to come to her aid.

Mariah had said guys get off on feeling like girls are dependent on them. But I knew that wasn't true for me—although you can never fully know your unconscious—and though surely some guys did get off on that, it didn't seem to explain why guys like helping girls more the prettier they are.

One might think it's because guys hope their help will eventually be rewarded sexually—and I'm sure sometimes that's true. But not always, not even usually. I remember one time Ms. Fulsom dropped a stack of papers during class—quite possibly because of something I'd said, though that I couldn't remember—and half the guys in the room practically fought each other in their race to help her pick them up. I'd bet my ass a male or less attractive female teacher would not have gotten nearly such eager assistance. But only in their wildest dreams would my classmates expect Ms. Fulsom to sexually reward them for helping her pick up some papers. It was the same with me and Mariah. I wanted to help her partly because she was pretty, but I didn't expect—I fantasized, maybe, but certainly didn't expect—that she would reward me in any way, other than perhaps not to kill me.

So what is it, then? Perhaps guys just like having an excuse to be physically close to pretty girls. Perhaps they just want pretty girls to like them for vanity's sake. I honestly don't know.

But I did know that, whatever the reasons, I wanted to help Mariah.

We returned to the burrow a little after noon. Lunch was water, bananas, and what the others called "Oscarberries"—berries that looked like cranberries and were shockingly sour. Oscar herself was wearing a stony expression and avoiding my eyes. When our eyes finally did happen to meet for a moment, hers narrowed slightly and seemed to say, *If you tell anyone, I'll fucking kill you. And if you don't, I might just kill you anyway.*

After lunch, Alex practiced pitching with his coconut and the quilt on the wall. I don't know much about baseball, but it looked to me like Alex was every bit as good as he'd claimed. Though this didn't stop Nigel from taunting him incessantly.

"Ya know what, Dread," Alex snapped at one point, "maybe I should use your *head* as my target."

"Maybe you should use your own head," Nigel said. "It's so big even *you* could hit it."

Alex practiced for about a half hour. Then he, Nigel, Mariah, and I went and practiced sword-fighting in the same clearing where I'd had my training yesterday (no one seemed to know where Hooke had gone). While Nigel stretched, I watched Alex and Mariah duel.

I only had to watch for about a minute to be astonished at how good Mariah was. Even though she'd only been on the Island for a couple months, she and Alex appeared to be almost evenly matched.

Even more astonishing was how fiercely they fought—it looked like they were honestly trying to kill each other. Hell, maybe they were. They'd lunge at each other and exchange a furious flurry of swings, then back off and slowly circle each other, then clash again. In just a few minutes they were both panting, dripping sweat, and scowling murderously.

I asked Nigel, "Is Mariah really good, or is Alex just going easy on her?"

Nigel smiled wryly. "Well, if you asked Alex, he'd say he's going easy on her. But as you can probably tell, he's actually working his ass off."

"So how the hell'd Mariah get so good?"

Nigel shrugged. "She worked at it. Practiced a lot, took it real seriously. She was a soccer player back in reality, so she's athletic. And she's Oscar, so she's ferocious."

"So who's better, Alex or Mariah?"

"Well, Mariah's a little faster, I think, but Alex is stronger, and he's got a lot more experience. He usually wins. But Mariah makes him work for it every time. She always fights like this—like she's got something to prove, almost, ya know?"

Chapter 15

My quilts were perfectly comfortable, but I wanted my bed. Or even one of my desks at school.

I went outside and sat with my back against the tree again. The tropical air was intoxicating—and toxic to negative thoughts. I found myself hoping that Mariah would come up again. But after something like a half hour she hadn't, and I was finally starting to get sleepy, so—

"Hello?"

For an instant the only thing I registered about the voice was that it was female, and I started to get excited, thinking it was Mariah. But the next moment I realized the voice wasn't Mariah's and hadn't come from the direction of the tunnel.

Panic yanked my body into action. I leapt to my feet and scrambled several steps away from the voice, then spun toward it, wishing I had a weapon—

"No wait, please," the voice said anxiously.

It was coming from just a few yards away. I frantically scanned the area where it seemed the voice's owner should be, but saw nothing but dark jungle.

"I mean no harm," the voice said. "I'm Lily. You rescued me from Peter."

I blinked in surprise; my panic stalled. After a moment, I said stupidly, "Lily?"

"Yes." The darkness shifted a few yards away, and Lily stepped timidly into a patch of moonlight.

I'd thought she was very pretty when I'd first gotten a good look at her after we'd escaped from Peter's mountain; she looked even prettier now. She looked healthy, her skin was clean, even a little radiant, her eyes were bright (not to mention conscious), and her hair was in a neat ponytail. She also had a sword slung across her back. Lily, warrior princess.

"And you're . . . Ricky, aren't you?" she said.

I blinked again and eyed her curiously. "How'd you know that?"

"I was partly conscious at times after you rescued me. And I remember you in particular."

"I'm flattered."

She smiled. "You should be."

That caused a bump in my train of thoughts. It hadn't seemed sarcastic at all. In fact, it had kind of seemed flirtatious. But that was probably just wishful thinking. I know better than to think I know a girl's intentions. If there's one thing I do know about girls, it's that I don't know shit about girls.

"So you just came back to see me again or what?" I said.

She smiled again. "Sorry, but no." Then she quickly grew serious. "And I'm sorry for coming so late at night, but this was the only time I could sneak away. Panther refused to let me come here—he's absurdly and infuriatingly overprotective."

That caused another mental bump. I remembered the way

Panther had talked about Lily—for instance, how careless he'd seemed when saying Peter had had the right to kill Lily. He certainly hadn't struck me as the protective type—but of course, I barely knew him.

"Anyway," Lily said, "I wanted to thank you myself for rescuing me. I imagine Panther's thank-you was somewhat . . . less than generous?"

I shrugged. "It had the essentials. Like not killing us."

I thought I saw a flash of something like resentment in her expression. "Well, I want to do something more for you than not kill you." She paused a beat. "You want to capture Peter, right?"

My ears perked up, along with every other bit of my being. "Yeah."

"I want to help with that. However I can."

My heart sank a little—I'd thought she might know a way. "Well, thank you—really—but I think all we really need is more people, more fighters. And Panther seemed pretty opposed to helping us with that. So unless you can change his mind . . . ?"

"Unfortunately, no, I can't," she said, her voice and expression tinged with that resentment again. But then the resentment was replaced by determination. "But I can fight myself. I know it's not much, but I am quite well trained."

I narrowed my eyes curiously and somewhat skeptically. "You'd risk your life like that for us?"

"Of course. I owe you nothing less."

I was sorely tempted to just accept her offer—given how few people we had, one more fighter, especially a trained one, could make a huge difference. But I had to say it: "Lily, you don't owe us a thing."

Now Lily's eyes narrowed. "Do you not want my help?"

"No, it's not that at all, believe me. But we have no right asking you to risk your life for us."

"You're not asking, I'm volunteering. You all voluntarily risked your lives for me, didn't you?"

"Actually *I* didn't, no—"

"But you would have."

That threw me off for a moment. It seemed a tad odd for a near-stranger to compliment my theoretical gallantry. "That's not the point. The others didn't rescue you just to rescue you. They needed fighters."

"Then they should get a fighter, no?"

"They did: me. Which is who they intended to rescue anyway. They never intended to rescue you."

Lily smiled at me appreciatively. "That's very good of you, Ricky. Very selfless." Then her smile vanished. "But I don't want to help you just to repay you." Her voice was suddenly filled with a quietly profound resolve, which seemed to stem from some buried but sizable anger. "I want to stop Peter."

I raised my eyebrows slightly, questioningly. "Panther said you guys had this agreement with—"

"Panther is a coward," she snapped with such sudden ferocity that I promptly scribbled a mental note: *Do NOT fuck with Lily.* But the next moment she blinked, as if coming out of a trance, and the ferocity was gone. She looked away and down in embarrassment. "I'm—sorry, I . . . I wasn't planning on getting into . . . any of that." She smiled at me a little. "I never thought you'd resist my offer. But . . . perhaps it would be good to tell you. Do you want to hear it?"

Having no idea what she was talking about, I shrugged. "Sure. I mean, if you wanna tell it."

She hesitated a moment. "I do . . . but . . . only to you, I think."

I eyed her curiously. "Why only me?"

Another, longer hesitation. "That would be easier to explain afterward, if you don't mind."

"Okay," I said, frowning a little in confusion. "Uhh . . . you wanna sit down? There's no chairs, but . . . there's a tree." I gestured to the tree over the burrow.

Lily laughed. "There's several, in fact. But this one looks fine. So, how much did Panther tell you about the agreement?"

"Only that there is one, really."

"Okay. Well, before the agreement—and I can't tell you how unreal this still seems to me—but before the agreement, Peter and my people had always been very friendly with each other. Just about everyone in my village knew him personally, and as far as I know, everyone quite liked him. He'd come to our village all the time, at least a few times a week, and just chat and banter with whoever he saw. Sometimes he'd even have a meal with us. He was good company. He was, indeed, our friend.

"But we were never his friends. That's quite clear now. We were just a source of entertainment to him. Playthings. Peter, I think, is like a child in some ways: He has a constant need to be entertained, and he has such an ego, he sees the world as his playground—even the people in it. And so he had no qualms about—well, I'm getting ahead of myself.

"About a year ago, a boy about my age went hunting and never came back. No one had any idea what happened to him. We searched for him for about three days—then Peter kidnapped one of the searchers, a girl about the same age. This time one of the other searchers saw it happen."

"Do you know why he kidnaps people?"

"I wish I did. When he kidnapped me, I was kept tied up in his cave, in the dark, with just enough water to keep me alive—and that was it. Nothing else happened to me. I never even saw Peter. One of his braves would bring me the water, and other than that, I was alone the entire time. It seems like he was trying to weaken and demoralize me for some reason—but as for the reason, your guess is as good as mine."

"And Peter had never kidnapped any of your people before?" I said, frowning a little.

"No."

"Why'd he suddenly start, then?"

"Again, I wish I knew. But I doubt we could answer that without knowing why he kidnaps people in the first place."

I nodded in agreement. I remained curious, though.

"So anyway," Lily said, "our leader at the time, Prince Red, went to Peter and demanded he free the captives and explain himself. Peter claimed he had no idea what Red was talking about—but he refused to let us search his caves. So that night, Red led a small group of our best warriors in a rescue attempt. But Peter was ready, and the attempt failed. Badly. Red was killed, which left Panther in command.

"Later that same night, Peter and an army of his braves attacked my village, tried to wipe my whole people out. But we were ready too, and we fought them off—but not before we lost many. A great many.

"The next morning, Panther went to Peter and they made the agreement—they split up the island between themselves. Panther gave up far too much, in my opinion. We lost much of our best fishing, hunting, and gathering lands. Sometimes we've gone hungry. But we can all live with that if it means no more lives are lost."

"Of course, that's no small 'if.'"

"Peter never respected the agreement completely. Several times we spotted his braves going through our territory. But they were nowhere near our village, so we—"

"They were probably searching for us," I said.

"Yes, that's what we figured. And so Panther decided it wasn't worth risking war. He decided to do nothing about it. The braves didn't spot us when we spotted them, so Peter would never know. I'm still not sure this was the best thing to do—but as long as my people were safe, I was content.

"Then Peter captured me. I assume Panther told you I accidentally trespassed on Peter's territory?"

"Yeah."

"That's a lie. I'm completely certain I was well within our boundaries—and I'm almost completely certain Peter knew it too. And of course I told Panther all this—but he continues to tell my people I trespassed. I've argued with him that he has to confront Peter, warn him that if he breaches the agreement again, we'll retaliate. But Panther says—to me, in private—that such a confrontation could end up leading to war, and one breach of the agreement isn't enough to risk that. But it won't be just one. Now Peter knows he can kidnap my people without any retaliation—I have little doubt he'll continue to do it. And Panther says we'll continue to do nothing. He says it's better to accept a few losses than risk devastation. But that risk is all but negligible. Peter entered the agreement because the war was just as devastating for him—he's not going to start another one unless he absolutely has to.

"The reality is, Panther has only his own interests at heart. He knows that if there's any combat—be it a war or a reprisal—he'll have to be right in the middle of it—or else give up his title. And even though he knows the risk of combat is small, it's even less risky—for him—to just keep Peter happy."

"Why don't you just tell your people the truth yourself?"

"Because Panther told me that if I did that, he'd just tell everyone I was lying. He'd say something like, Peter did horrible things to me while I was in his cave, and now I'm trying to start a war with him because I want revenge. Some people would believe me, but most—and especially the men—would listen to Panther."

"And there's nothing else you can do?"

"I could think of only one other thing. And that's what I'm doing now."

"And you're sure you can't change Panther's mind?"

She sneered slightly. "I'd have to change his character first."

After a moment, I said, "I'm guessing Panther didn't really refuse to let you come here because he's overprotective."

Lily laughed coldly. "Well, he did refuse to let me come here, but not at all because he's overprotective."

"So why, then?"

"Well, partly it's that, if he let me help you, people might see it as an acknowledgment that Peter had done something wrong. But mainly, again, it's the risk. Even though, again, it's negligible. Even if Peter found out I was helping you, Panther could just say I'd been doing so without his knowledge or permission—which would be perfectly plausible, because Peter would figure that I in particular would like to get my hands on him. There's no way he'd start a war over that."

We were silent for several seconds as I tried to digest everything she'd told me.

"All right," I said, "so why don't you wanna tell all this to the others?"

Lily hesitated uncomfortably for a beat. "I'm just a little worried that if they knew everything I told you, they'd refuse my help for fear of angering Panther. Especially since he knows where your home underground is."

I felt a stab of anxiety in my chest. "Is there any chance he'd tell Peter where the burrow is?"

"None at all," Lily said with complete certainty. "Peter is still Panther's biggest threat, and Panther very much wants that threat removed—he just doesn't want to take any personal risk in the process. You and your friends are the answer to his prayers. So, again, you have absolutely nothing to worry about—but as long as the others don't need to know, and as long as you don't mind, I'd rather they not."

"That's fine," I said. After a moment, I frowned and asked, "Why'd you tell me, then?"

"Because I know you're not scared to take a risk. And I know you're not scared to stand up to your leader."

I eyed her quizzically. "How would you—" Then it hit me. "Oh. You remember that."

She smiled at me. "Quite well."

I didn't know what to say. Lily just kept smiling at me. I looked away and down, uncomfortable—and not just because her implied admiration embarrassed me. I also wasn't sure I deserved it.

I was about to explain this to Lily when she said, "Someday you'll have to tell me how you managed to rescue her all by yourself. But right now I really have to get back. If someone notices I'm gone, there will be trouble." She smiled at me and offered her hand. "It was a pleasure to meet you, Ricky."

I smiled back and shook her hand. "Yeah, you too." Brilliant repartee, Ricky.

Lily seemed to hold my hand and my gaze for just the slightest moment too long. But again, that was probably just wishful thinking.

Then she said, "I should be back soon," and she got up and flitted off into the darkness.

Chapter 16

I was lying in my quilts, my thoughts and emotions pinballing between home, Peter, and Lily, when the connection suddenly crystallized in my head.

Peter, who'd previously always been friends with the natives (at least ostensibly), had suddenly kidnapped two teenage natives about a year ago.

Hooke had rescued Alex and Nigel about a year ago.

That didn't seem like a coincidence.

I'd just started thinking about this when I heard a rustle of fabric a few yards away. I looked over and recognized Hooke's wiry figure as he slid out of his quilts and started tiptoeing toward the tunnel. I immediately dismissed him, figuring he was probably just going out to "use the head," as he would say. But then someone stirred in their quilts—and Hooke froze.

My eyes snapped back to him; I was careful not to move my head. Hooke remained still for several seconds, his head turned toward whoever had stirred, seemingly making sure the person was asleep. Then, apparently satisfied, he fluttered to the tunnel and disappeared.

My mind raced. Hooke had gone away for hours several times over the past two days without any of the others seeming to know where he went. The others didn't seem to find this suspicious at all—but they hadn't just seen Hooke sneak out of the burrow in the middle of the night.

If I confronted Hooke about this, whether now or later, he'd probably just make up a story. The only way I could think of to find out what he was really doing was to follow him. Without being detected. Which would be very difficult, what with me being a stampede of elephants and all. And Hooke was probably more like a mouse. But if he caught me, he'd just be catching me catching him. So I figured it was worth a try.

I got out of my quilts and hurried to the tunnel—but then I hurried back and slung on my sword. I felt kind of stupid carrying it—if I actually had to use it, there was a decent chance I'd decapitate myself just trying to unsheathe it. But I was thinking about being caught weaponless by Lily. It had turned out I hadn't needed a weapon then, but next time . . .

I rushed up the tunnel and poked my head outside. No Hooke. I stepped out of the tunnel and turned in a circle. After a few seconds, I heard a tiny rustle of vegetation about twenty yards away, just barely audible over the murmur of the river. I looked in that direction but saw nothing but still, dark jungle. After a moment, I heard another rustle—slightly farther away.

I started sneaking in that direction, moving as stealthily as I could while maintaining at least a slow walking pace. Every ten or fifteen steps I'd pause for a moment, watching and listening. On my fifth pause I heard another rustle, off to my left. I turned accordingly and kept moving.

After about ten more pauses, though, I hadn't heard anything else. I stopped for about a minute, listening. Nothing. I continued walking in the same direction for a few minutes on the off chance I'd hear him again. Still nothing.

I gave up. I walked to the river and started following it back to the burrow.

I wasn't particularly disappointed. I'd known it was very unlikely I'd be able to tail Hooke all the way to wherever he was going. And it was probably better we hadn't had a confrontation now—now I had more time to think.

Should I tell the others about Hooke sneaking out and try to get them to confront him with me? If we all confronted him, I thought it was more likely we'd get the truth out of him. But since the others seemed to trust him so much, I wasn't at all sure I could get them to back me—I might even antagonize them. I didn't want to risk that. Plus, if I didn't go to the others first, when I confronted Hooke myself I could threaten to go to the others if he wasn't open with me. Whether I'd carry out that threat—

I froze, suddenly realizing I hadn't been keeping track of how long I'd been walking. Five minutes? Ten? How long had I pursued Hooke? It couldn't have been much more than five minutes—and I'd probably been going a little faster on the way back. I'd been checking trees for the tunnel entrance since a minute or two after I'd started back, but I hadn't been paying much attention—could I have passed it?

Shit.

I walked for a few more minutes in the same direction I had been, meticulously checking every tree within ten yards of the river. Nothing. Now I was almost certain I'd gone too far. I turned back and walked for what I thought was about ten minutes (I was starting to seriously doubt my sense of time). Still nothing.

143

I stopped and turned in a slow circle, a panicky feeling of helplessness starting to gnaw at my chest, making me feel a little short of breath. The jungle, especially in the dark, looked completely uniform to me—there was absolutely nothing to indicate how far I'd gone. I kind of felt like I was on an inescapable treadmill—like no matter where I tried to go, I wouldn't get anywhere, my surroundings wouldn't change. It felt kind of nightmarish.

In more than one way, in fact. It was probably just because I was getting anxious, but the jungle seemed different than it usually did. A thin fog hung in the air, and this plus the pale moonlight produced an eerie atmosphere—one in which certain shadowy shapes seemed grotesquely lifelike. Hanging vines became tentacles; bushes became hunched predators; logs became giant snakes; branches became withered, grasping hands. The silence was total except for the low whispering of the river. And it was colder than usual—that I know wasn't my imagination. My breath formed little clouds, which disappeared almost instantly.

A chill skittered down my spine. And not because of the cold.

I turned around again and continued walking, checking trees I knew I'd already checked. I was trying to walk as quietly as possible, but suddenly the crunch of leaves underfoot seemed unnaturally loud. After another few unsuccessful minutes, I stopped again—

—and thought I heard a fleeting rustle of movement behind me.

My chest tightened almost painfully as I spun around and gazed intently into the darkness . . . but the jungle was as still as ever. I stood there watching and listening for a full minute, not moving, breathing, or blinking, my heartbeat sounding like a drum in my head: *Dum. Dum. Dum.*

But nothing happened.

I swallowed hard and licked my dry lips. Probably just my imagination . . . or maybe a rabbit . . .

I turned back and continued walking, trying to pretend to myself that that little interlude hadn't happened—but nonetheless listening intently.

And I'd only been walking for a few seconds when I heard, maybe twenty yards behind me, very faint rustling.

Something was following me.

And I had a feeling it wasn't a bunny.

Panic exploded in my head, totally blinding rational thought, and my body threw itself into an all-out sprint, heading at an angle from the river. My pursuer didn't let me go as I'd desperately hoped—I heard it speeding after me.

I ran as fast as I could, feeling like I should be able to go so much faster, wanting, *needing* to go faster. Within twenty seconds my legs and lungs were screaming with pain, but my mind was so high on adrenaline that I barely felt it. I could no longer hear my pursuer over the noise of running and didn't dare look back, but I felt horribly certain it was right behind me, that any moment now it was going to rip me to the ground.

After maybe a minute—it felt like a nightmarish eternity—I burst from the jungle onto the beach, and heard my pursuer about a hundred yards back. With a splash of relief but a wave of fresh panic, I raced off into the jungle again, parallel to the beach.

But suddenly I seemed to have lost my momentum. Exhaustion overtook me—my side cramped and I could barely breathe—I knew I couldn't run much—

I didn't see the drop until one foot was already over the edge. I cried out and desperately tried to reverse my momentum, but it was too late. For one heart-stopping moment I plummeted, panicking wildly, certain I was going to fall to my death—then plunged into deep, lukewarm salt water.

I scrambled to the surface, coughing, looking around. Craggy, ten-foot cliffs loomed around me, enclosing a circular inlet. I heard a small splash somewhere behind me but barely noticed. I quickly grabbed onto the cliff to climb back up, but then stopped. By the time I reached the top, my pursuer might have caught up, and besides, I was too exhausted to run much farther.

I looked back into the inlet. About twenty yards away, a mass of boulders loomed in the mist like a mini mountain. Less than ten yards away, a flat, circular rock, about four feet across, bulged from the water like a giant stepping-stone.

An agony of indecision seized me for one long moment. Then I heard my pursuer, far away but approaching, and promptly decided. I pushed off the cliff, swam to the stepping-stone, and ducked behind it, clinging to it—it protruded just high enough to hide my entire head.

After ten or fifteen seconds, I heard my pursuer stop at the edge of the cove. I huddled closer to the rock and listened intently, not breathing. There was silence for about ten more seconds . . . then slow footsteps. To track its movement, I peeked around the edge of the rock.

It was a Lost Girl—I knew the instant I saw her. In the sickly moonlight, she looked like a withered, walking corpse—gaunt, almost skeletal, with ghostly white skin, long, dark, disheveled hair, and tattered, grimy clothing. She was walking slowly along the edge of the cove, a spear at her side, her head turned toward the water— looking for me.

I was suddenly regretting my decision to hide. I'd hoped the Girl would run right past the inlet, but somehow she seemed to know I was here. Now I was trapped. If she saw me . . .

There was a small splash somewhere behind me.

The Girl's head snapped toward the sound. I jerked back behind the rock, my heart nearly jumping out of my chest, praying she hadn't seen me.

I didn't even think about the splash until a bizarre sound arose from the same direction—a long, high-pitched, warbling whistle superimposed with rapid clicks, like a cross between a dolphin and some exotic bird. I looked back, saw a flash of shadowy movement at the bottom of the rock formation—and suddenly I understood.

Mermaids.

This was the mermaid's cove.

Another whistle joined the first. Then two more.

They're territorial, Nigel had said. *If we went in the water, they'd rip us apart.*

Oh shit.

The whistling stopped abruptly. Several shadowy shapes melted out of the rocks and slipped into the black water.

Panic flooded my mind, and I scrambled frantically onto the rock, out of the water, and stood facing the mermaids—I couldn't see them underwater but knew they were headed for me.

The Girl, you dumbass!

Just as I spun around, she threw her spear. I ducked desperately and both heard and felt the spear pass just inches overhead. Looking up, I saw her dive into the water.

Suddenly I remembered my sword. I unsheathed it—without decapitating myself, fortunately—and spun around just as a mermaid burst out of the water, launching halfway onto the rock. It hissed so loudly it hurt my ears, its mouth opening impossibly wide, revealing multiple rows of small, jagged teeth, and grasped at my leg. I swung my sword wildly and slashed her upper arm, feeling the blade tear through the flesh and grate against the bone, feeling blood spray my forearms. The mermaid screeched horribly and darted back underwater.

I raised my sword again and quickly looked around—then saw a wake leading toward the rock formation. They were retreating. Temporarily, at least.

The Girl.

I spun around, scanned the water, but saw nothing. She wouldn't be visible until she surfaced—which might be too late.

But then I realized this was a perfect opportunity: I could simply swim to the cliff, climb up, and escape. Nothing was stopping me.

I sheathed my sword, and was just about to dive in when something burst out of the water right behind me and tackled me. A clammy, bony arm clamped around my neck in a headlock, and as I fell forward, a familiar, rotten stench filled my mouth and nose like a mist.

Then I plunged into the water.

Without having taken a breath, I immediately felt like I was suffocating. My whole body screamed for air. I tried to claw up to the surface, but the Girl dragged me down. I tried to pry her arm off my neck, but she was too strong. I reached back and tried to push her away—

My elbow touched something hard.

The hilt of my sword.

Knowing this was my last chance, I unsheathed the sword, gripped it with both hands, and drove the blade back into the Girl's face as hard as I could. I felt the blade bore into her skull, grinding against bone. She immediately released me, and I pushed off her, leaving my sword, tearing for the surface.

I exploded out of the water and sucked in a long breath, opening my mouth as wide as I could and closing my eyes in blissful relief. For a moment I was so happy to be breathing again that I completely forgot what was going on. My mind seemed to be filled with heavenly white light.

Then I remembered the mermaids.

Fear impaled me again, shattering my relief. I looked around quickly but saw nothing—underwater, they were invisible. Not that it mattered. If they attacked, I'd be helpless. I started swimming toward the cliff, trying to go both quickly and quietly, constantly expecting to be yanked underwater.

I was about ten feet from the cliff when something whooshed over my head from behind and splashed into the water a few feet in front of me. Just before it sank, I saw what it was.

A sword.

Gaping in horror and disbelief, I looked back.

The Girl was standing on the rock, apparently as alive as ever, completely expressionless despite the fact that her jaw had been torn half off and now hung askew. She had pulled my sword out of her own head and thrown it at me.

We stared at each other for a moment. Then she dove into the water.

A fresh surge of adrenaline slammed through my veins, and I started tearing frantically toward the cliff, feeling nightmarishly slow. I wasn't sure how far the Girl's dive had taken her, but I knew she was extremely close. Finally I reached the cliff and heaved myself up out of the water—

Her hand gripped my ankle and yanked down. I cried out and dug my fingers and free foot into the pitted rock, then looked down, right into the Girl's face. It was horribly skull-like, the skin bone-white and tightly drawn. Her jaw was grotesquely twisted, one cheek split, revealing rotten, brown teeth. But her eyes were the worst. Sunken and milky, they were alive yet lifeless.

But I only saw her face for a second. Then suddenly she was sucked underwater, her hand ripped from my ankle, and the water below me erupted into a cyclone of thrashing, screeching mer-maids.

I immediately started scrambling up the cliff. A mermaid leapt up and grasped at my foot but couldn't get a grip. I crested the cliff and took off sprinting along the beach. Nigel had said mermaids posed little threat on land, and the Girl was surely doomed, but I wasn't taking any chances.

I sprinted for as long as I could, then jogged the rest of the way, coasting on adrenaline, glancing behind me every few seconds. I found the burrow on my first pass—which I thought was delightfully chuckalicious on God's part. The burrow was empty. I figured someone had noticed that Hooke and I were gone and so now they were out searching.

As I half lay, half fell down on my quilts, the last of my adrenaline seeped away, and I started shaking. I felt as if I were coming out of a drug-induced haze. Only now did I fully realize how sore my body was, especially my legs. Only now did I fully realize how nightmarish that whole ordeal had been: sprinting frantically through the black jungle; being trapped in the cove as the corpselike Lost Girl walked slowly around it; the mermaids gliding unseen under the black surface; the Girl holding me under water; feeling my blade grind sickeningly through her skull; staring into her ghastly face as she gripped my ankle.

Only now did I fully realize how infinitesimally close I'd come to dying, again, and again, and again.

"SAY SOMETHIN', LAD! ARE YE DEAD?!"

I'd dozed off. Now my eyes opened, and Hooke's anxious, wide-eyed face filled my view.

"Satan?" I mumbled, feigning delirium. "Is that you?"

"No," I heard Alex say, "she's back here."

I snorted laughter; I couldn't help it. Mariah said nothing.

Hooke let out a sharp sigh of relief and stepped back. "Bloody hell, lad, we thought ye was *dead*!"

I smiled thinly. "Yeah, well, I came pretty close."

I told them the story. I said that the reason I'd been outside was that I'd been going to the bathroom—not stalking Hooke. But I wondered if Hooke wondered.

"Well," Hooke said grimly when I'd finished the story, "hopefully Peter or his Boys'll find that Girl's body in the cove—then they'll pro'ly figure she just fell in there by accident. But if they don't find it, Peter'll pro'ly figure the Girl ran into one of us. Which means we migh' be seein' even more Boys round here soon. So just watch your arses, lads."

"And just to be clear, Dread," Alex said, "that doesn't mean you literally watch my ass."

"But it's so firm and sexy," Nigel said sarcastically.

Hooke gave a snort of laughter.

I'm not sure if it was because I was thinking about Peter's search for the burrow or because I heard the words "firm and sexy," but I suddenly remembered Lily. I gave the others a summary of my talk with her last night, leaving out most of the stuff about Panther. Alex and Nigel were clearly thrilled at the idea of having another fighter on board; even Mariah looked like her interest had been piqued.

And Hooke seemed appropriately pleased at first. But after we'd finished discussing Lily, once he thought no one was paying attention to him, I noticed that his pleased expression quickly faded—and even became faintly disgruntled.

He knew something we didn't.

I had to confront him. Soon.

Chapter 17

When I awoke the next morning, it was fully light out.

"We figured you could use the rest," Alex said to me. "But don't worry, I managed to save you some fish before Dread ate it all."

Nigel had no comeback. At least partly because his mouth was full.

As I ate, I asked Hooke what we were doing today.

"Today is our day off," he proclaimed regally.

"Why's that?" I asked.

"'Cause I feel like it."

"So what do we do on our day off?"

"We go to the beach."

"The beach, huh?"

"Aye—why not? I mean, hell, as long as we're stuck in a bloody tropical paradise, we might as well go to the bloody beach."

Hooke grabbed some quilts, Nigel grabbed a bunch of bananas, and Alex grabbed a pot of water. Mariah, however, remained sitting in the corner, staring at the floor. The others paid no attention to her, clearly having assumed she wouldn't come. Even though I knew this was entirely her choice, imagining her sitting there in the corner all by herself while the rest of us were having fun at the beach made my heart feel heavy.

Now, for me, like many guys, talking to girls had always been a little bit of an uphill struggle. Talking to Mariah was like climbing fucking Everest. (The risk of being stabbed isn't particularly conducive to eloquence.) Today, however—perhaps because of what Hooke called my "dance with Davy Jones" last night—I was feeling courageous. Or perhaps just reckless.

At any rate, I decided I was going to talk to Mariah. Or die trying.

I wanted to do it alone, however, so when we left for the beach, I "forgot" my sword in the burrow; after we'd walked for a minute, I "remembered" suddenly and ran back.

When I entered, Mariah stiffened and her head snapped toward me. Seeing that it was me, her eyes narrowed suspiciously.

"Hey," I said.

"Wow, Ricky, that was quite the conversation starter. You think of that all by yourself?"

"It started a conversation, didn't it?"

"No, it didn't," she said, and looked away.

I ignored that. "You coming to the beach?"

She cocked an eyebrow at me. "Does it look like I'm coming to the beach?"

"Looks can be deceiving."

"Wow, Ricky, that's deep."

"That's what she said."

She narrowed her eyes in disdain. "Ya know, that's so pathetically immature, it's actually almost funny."

"Okay, *that's* what she said."

For an instant, the corners of Mariah's mouth twitched up in a tiny, involuntary smile of amusement. Then she squelched it and looked away.

"So why aren't you coming to the beach?" I asked.

"*This* is why. Why are you here, anyway? Aren't *you* going to the beach?"

"I forgot my sword, so I came back to get it."

"Then why don't you just get your sword and get out."

"'Cause I didn't really forget my sword. I left it here on purpose so I could talk to you alone." I smiled the biggest, stupidest smile I could.

Very subtly—so subtly I might have been imagining it—Mariah's demeanor seemed to soften. Actually, "soften" might be the wrong word—it was more like a single crack in her stony shell. Nevertheless, I felt a thrill of hope.

"What do you want, Ricky?" she asked.

"I just wanna talk."

"About what?"

"Well, about you, incidentally."

"What about me?"

I paused a beat, crafting my answer. "Well . . . I guess I'd just like to know why you seem to, uh . . . loathe every aspect of my being. And why you loathe the others, although that's much more understandable."

She looked away, and I think the crack widened. "I don't loathe you," she said somewhat grudgingly—yet I could distinctly sense her sincerity. "Any of you."

I smiled a bit. "You have a funny way of expressing non-loathing then."

"Look, none of you, like . . . did anything wrong or anything, it's just . . ." She hesitated for a long moment, groping for words, then sighed in frustration, closed her eyes, and pinched the bridge of her nose. "Look, it's hard to explain—"

"Try," I said earnestly. "Please. If you explain why, maybe I can do something about it, I can . . . change, or something. 'Cause I really don't like that you don't like me."

She shook her head faintly, looking somewhat bitter. "You can't change it."

"Then there is something."

"It doesn't matter. I just told you, you can't change it."

"You can't hold something against me if you won't tell me what it is."

She smiled slightly. "Of course I can. I'm a girl."

"At least tell me why you won't tell me."

"'Cause I don't want to, how's that?" she said, an edge suddenly back in her voice.

"But why not?"

She looked away, her expression surly. I waited a few seconds, but she didn't respond.

I sighed. "Ya know I'm not just doing this for my own sake."

She scowled at me. "Stop worrying about *me*, all right? I'm fine."

"You have a funny way of expressing fineness then."

"I'm as fine as I can be. So stop trying to help me, 'cause you can't."

"I think I can help in at least—"

"No you fucking can't," she snarled furiously. "If this was something you could just fix, I'd fix it myself. I'm not stupid, I'm not helpless, I'm not your fucking damsel in distress."

"I'm not saying I can magically fix all your problems, all right? I don't even know what the hell they are. Except one."

"You have no fucking—" she started indignantly.

"I know what it's like to not have friends," I said forcefully, and she fell silent. "I know what it's like to be lonely. I know it sucks."

I paused for a few seconds, staring at her. She looked away and down, and her surly expression seemed to waver.

"I'm not trying to be your Prince Charming," I said quietly. "I'm just offering to be your friend."

After a long moment, she said quietly, perhaps to herself, "Sometimes one problem is the solution to another."

I narrowed my eyes curiously. "What do you mean?"

She looked at me, and suddenly her face was filled with an emotion I'd never seen on her before—bitter anger tinged with what seemed like soul-deep sorrow. "Get out," she said. Her voice was icy, but trembled a tiny bit, as if she was close to tears.

For some reason I automatically said, "No."

Her eyes narrowed. "Fine. Then I'll leave." She got up and started stalking toward the tunnel.

"Mariah," I said. She didn't respond. As she came closer, I stepped in front of her. "Mariah, please—"

My stepping in front of her was an instinctive and purely symbolic protest; I didn't intend to physically prevent her from leaving. She could have simply gone around me.

Instead, she put both her hands on my chest and shoved me seemingly as hard as she could. Caught completely off guard, I stumbled backward a few steps and then fell, hard. Just before I landed, the back of my head cracked against the wall behind me.

For a moment I just lay there, too shocked to do anything else, a throbbing spike of pain driven into my head. Mariah just stood there, looking fairly shocked herself.

Then the anger came. Not Mariah's this time—mine. It seemed to start in the pain in my head, then rapidly radiated outward like tentacles, coiling around me. I slowly got to my feet, my whole body seeming to throb in beat with my head. I had no idea what I was going to do; I wasn't thinking—anger was.

I saw Mariah see my anger. I saw her realize it was far beyond mere annoyance or anything petty like that. I saw the fear wash over her. For an instant, seeing her fear gave me an intoxicating sense of power.

But then I saw her take a step back, and that suddenly made it real to me: She was actually scared I was going to hurt her.

My anger shattered instantly. And then I just felt absolutely disgusted with myself—partly for getting so angry, but mainly for that one instant that I'd actually enjoyed seeing her scared.

I looked away from Mariah and down—I couldn't look at her. Uncomfortable silence followed. I had no idea what to say or do. I felt like apologizing, but for what? For getting angry that she'd assaulted me?

Finally, after maybe five seconds, I said, "Well, this went well."

Mariah didn't laugh. God knows why. I glanced at her. She was staring at me, her expression growing surly again but still just a tiny bit nervous.

There was only one thing I could think to do. I turned around and walked to the tunnel. At the entrance, however, I stopped, hesitated a moment, then turned back to Mariah. "If there's ever anything I can do for you," I said, "just let me know, okay?"

Mariah just kept staring at me.

I couldn't help Mariah. For one thing, Hooke, Alex, and Nigel had all tried to help her too, and had all failed—why should I think I was any different? But more important, as Mariah had said herself, she wasn't stupid or weak—if anyone could help her, it was her.

The notion that Mariah truly wanted to be alone was significantly harder for me to accept, much less understand. But again, if anyone knew what she wanted, it was her.

I had to respect that.

I was thinking about this after lunch, sitting on a sand dune with my chin propped in my palm. I faintly heard Alex's voice beside me, but didn't realize he was talking to me until he waved a hand in front of my eyes.

"Huh?" I said, looking over at him. "Sorry, what'd you say?"

"I asked you what you were thinking about. You looked like that Michelangelo statue of the thinking dude."

Nigel frowned thoughtfully. "I don't think that was Michelangelo."

Alex waved him off. "Michelangelo, Donatello, Leonardo DiCaprio, they're all dead, so what's the difference?"

Nigel gave a burst of laughter; Alex gave him his patented *wtf* look.

"So what were you thinking about?" Alex asked me.

I shrugged. "I don't know. Nothing in particular." I knew he knew that was bullshit, so I wanted to change the subject before he pressed me—and since Hooke had just gone out for a swim, I said, "Hey, I've been meaning to ask you guys something. I keep seeing this really weird scar on Hooke's leg—like right here, on the thigh—and I was wondering how he got it."

Alex and Nigel both started laughing.

"What's so funny?" I said.

"A crocodile bit him," Nigel said.

That seemed so random, so absurd, I couldn't help laughing myself. "A *crocodile*? Are you serious?"

"Yep," Alex said. "A frickin' *huge* crocodile too. I've seen it a few times, and I think it's gotta be some kinda mutant or something."

"How big is it?"

"Well," Alex said, "remember when I first took ya to the burrow, and you asked if it was some kinda giant gopher hole? Well, it wasn't a gopher."

My eyes widened. "You mean . . . ?"

"Yep," Nigel said. "The crocodile dug the burrow."

I thought about that for a moment, my mouth hanging open—the burrow was roughly the size of a bus. But then I looked at Nigel skeptically. "How do you know the crocodile dug it?"

"'Cause when Cap first found the burrow—er, fell into it by accident—there were eggshells still in it," Nigel said. "Eggshells as big as your head."

My eyes widened in mildly horrified disbelief. "You're saying we're *living* in its *nest*?"

"Its *old* nest," Alex said. "It's been like four years. It's obviously not coming back."

"Christ," I said, looking away. "As if I didn't have enough trouble sleeping at night." After a moment, I looked back at Alex and Nigel. "So this giant crocodile *bit* Cap?"

"Yeah," Nigel said. "About three or four months ago, he and Alex and I were spearfishing at the swamp, and the crocodile just swam up behind us. I have no idea how something that big could just sneak up on us like that, but it did. It bit Cap on the thigh and started swimming away. But Cap got lucky. He pulled out his knife and started stabbing the croc in the head, and he just happened to get it right in the eye. The croc let him go and he got away."

I shook my head wonderingly, smiling a little. "Jesus."

"You wanna hear the crazy part now?" Alex said.

I cocked an eyebrow at him. "That wasn't the crazy part?"

Alex smiled darkly. "Not even close. Now the crocodile's out to get Cap."

"'*Out to get*' him?"

"I know," Alex said, "it sounds crazy—it *is* crazy—but it's true. Since the croc bit him that one time, it's attacked him twice more. *Twice.*"

"Did Cap tell you that? 'Cause he might not be the most reliable source—"

"Alex and I saw both attacks," Nigel said.

I paused a moment, still skeptical. "Maybe it's just coincidence. If the croc lives somewhere around—"

"It's not coincidence," Alex said with finality. "That's three times the croc's attacked in just a few months. And it didn't attack *us*, it attacked *him*—me and Dread were both there for the second attack, me, Dread, *and* Oscar were there for the third one, and even if one of us was closer, the croc always went straight for Cap."

"So, what, you think it just loves how Cap tastes or something?"

Alex shrugged. "I dunno. Maybe it wants revenge for its eye. Maybe it just hates when prey gets away. Maybe it fell in love with Cap and wants to marry him."

"What does Cap say about all this?"

"Oh, Cap thinks the whole thing's hilarious," Nigel said, "but then again, Cap also thinks the tree over the burrow is a mast. Personally, I think it's scary. A giant crocodile's scary enough—and now I'm starting to think this one's about as crazy as Cap."

"It's like *Moby Dick*," Alex said, "except the whale's after Moby."

Chapter 18

Something woke me in the night—I didn't know what. I couldn't get back to sleep, so I went outside.

Emerging from the tunnel, I found Mariah sitting with her back against the tree, looking at me expressionlessly.

"Oh," I said. "Sorry." I turned and started ducking back into the tunnel.

"Ricky?"

I stopped and looked back at her over my shoulder. "Yeah?"

She was staring forward expressionlessly. "I, uh . . . I wanted to . . . tell you something."

I turned to face her completely. "Yeah?"

She looked down and opened her mouth, but hesitated—then abruptly looked to the right, past me—then in one explosive instant she shot to her feet and ripped her sword out. I scrambled to my feet and reached for my sword—

"Ricky?" said a timid, anxious voice from a few yards away.

I froze instantly, but it took me another beat to consciously recognize the voice. Then I blinked and said in surprise, "Lily?"

Lily melted out of the darkness, stepping timidly forward.

I looked back at Mariah and held up a hand in a calming gesture. "It's all right, it's Lily." As Lily came up to us, I said, "I didn't expect you to be back so soon."

Lily smiled excitedly. "I'm sorry to disappoint you. But I thought you might like to know: I think I know a way to capture Peter."

My heart shot up like a firework. "Seriously?" I said with desperate, breathless eagerness. "How?"

"Could I tell the others, too, all at once?"

"Uh, yeah, sure," I said, already spinning around and lunging for the tunnel. "Oh—" I stopped and spun back, "Lily, this is Mariah, Mariah, Lily." I didn't wait to see them greet each other. I practically dove down the tunnel, burst into the burrow going so fast I had to jump over someone before I stopped, then said loudly, "Hey you guys, wake up!"

I might have said it a bit too loudly. Limbs and quilts went flying as everyone scrambled to their feet, looking around wildly, reaching for weapons, and Hooke cried hysterically, "ALL HANDS, BATTLE STATIONS!"

"No no no!" I said quickly. "It's all right, it's just me!"

Hooke looked at me like he wasn't sure I was real. "Ricky?" he said groggily. "What is it, lad, what's wrong?"

"Nothing, nothing at all. Lily just came again—and she says she might know how to capture Peter."

Hooke's eyes widened. "What? How?"

Just then Mariah emerged from the tunnel, followed by Lily. Mariah looked vaguely distraught, but I barely noticed. Lily came forward slowly, tentatively, her head slightly down. I went to her side and put my hand on her upper back. "You guys," I said, "this is Lily. Lily, that's Cap, that's Alex, and that's Nigel."

"So ye say ye might know how to capture Peter, is that righ'?" Hooke said to Lily, staring at her intensely.

"I think so, yes," Lily said. "I hope so."

"Well then fuck the formalities, let's hear it," Hooke said.

"Okay." Lily seemed a tiny bit intimidated. "Well, are you familiar with the Rare Singer, the bird?"

"I know a little 'bout it, aye."

"Do you know that Rare Singers sing so rarely because Peter loves to hunt them?"

"Aye."

"Well, about a week ago, our village heard a single Rare Singer singing, and—"

"Aye, Prince Jaguar told us 'bout this. That's how ye got captured, righ'?"

"Yes, that's right. But what Panther may not have mentioned is that we caught the Rare Singer." Lily paused a beat. "And we still have it."

She paused again—and then, all at once, I put it together. My mouth fell open as my mind raced. After a moment, Hooke murmured, as if from a daze, "Bloody hell."

Lily continued: "The Rare Singer was singing because its nest had been attacked by some kind of animal and it had gotten separated from one of its chicks. It had also been injured in the attack, and we've been nursing it back to health. It's sitting right there in our village. I don't know how I didn't think of it right away, it's so simple."

"What is?" Alex asked, frowning in puzzlement.

"The Never-bird sings, Peter comes looking for it, and we jump him," I said.

A long moment passed in seemingly awed silence.

Then Alex said, "Oh that."

"Wait a sec," Nigel said. "How are we supposed to make the Never-bird sing? Never-birds never sing when Peter's on the island, remember?"

"*Almost* never," I said, and looked at Lily. "You've got the chicks, too, don't you?"

Lily nodded, smiling.

Another few seconds passed in that awed silence. My mind raced around the idea, searching for a major flaw. It seemed too simple to be possible, it seemed like there *had* to be a flaw. But if there was one, I couldn't find it.

I looked around at the others; they were all thinking too. "So can anyone think of any reason we shouldn't do this?" I asked.

Alex, Nigel, and Mariah glanced at me—then looked at Hooke. I looked at him too. Hooke was staring very intently at the wall across from him, as if the wall was explaining something very complex and important. I found myself holding my breath in anticipation of his verdict—and I doubt I was alone. The burrow itself seemed to be holding its breath. There was no movement, no sound. The silence was so total that after a moment my ears started ringing faintly, as if to assure themselves they were still working.

About five endless seconds passed.

Then Hooke abruptly blinked and looked around at us questioningly. "I'm sorry, did someone say somethin' to me?"

I let out a sharp breath, half in relief of the tension, half in impatience. "Can you think of any reason we shouldn't do this?" I asked again.

"Oh," Hooke said. He looked away for a moment, frowning, then shook his head. "Seems like a pretty good idear to me."

My excitement, which I'd been holding back with an effort, now burst free, and relieved, delighted laughter bubbled out of me.

"There is one complication," Lily said, somewhat uncomfortably. "Rare Singers are sacred to my people. That is why we went to find this Rare Singer in the first place, and why we've been nursing it back to health. Panther will not give it to you. So—"

"What if we tell him we're usin' it to capture Peter?" Hooke asked.

"That might work," Lily said, even more uncomfortably. "But I think Panther might worry that Peter would suspect that the Rare Singer came from my people, and so if you failed to capture him, it could cause trouble between us and him. And you don't want to just try asking Panther first, because if he does say no, he will probably then place the Rare Singer under guard. Right now there are no guards, and I know where all of our lookouts are—so I think it would be safest to simply steal the Rare Singer."

"Stealin' from the natives," Hooke murmured musingly, and grinned. "Brings back memories."

Lily smiled, no doubt in relief that Hooke hadn't objected. "There's also one favor I must ask. Once you're done with Peter, if you could just hand him over to my people. Dead or alive, it doesn't matter."

"A' course, lass," Hooke said.

"Thank you," Lily said, smiling again. "So, if it's not a problem for you, I think it would be best to steal the Rare Singer right now."

"Brilliant," Hooke said with the hint of a roguish grin.

"All right then. You'll need one person to carry the bird and another to carry the chicks; I'll help you steal them, of course, but I can't risk taking the time to help you carry them back here."

As the others started talking about which of them would make the best thief, I met Lily's eyes and nodded toward the tunnel. She got the signal and followed me outside.

As soon as we emerged, I turned to Lily and looked at her worriedly. "Don't you think Panther might assume you had something to do with the Rare Singer being stolen?"

"He might," Lily said. "But he will have no proof."

I raised an eyebrow skeptically. "Does he need proof?"

"He needs proof to punish me publicly. He may still try to punish me in private, but I'm quite used to that." She smiled at me half gratefully, half reassuringly. "Don't worry about me, Ricky."

I hesitated a moment, wanting to express my gratitude but not knowing how I could do so adequately. "Thank you for this," I said finally, unable to think of anything else, hoping my tone conveyed the depth of the sentiment.

She smiled. "You can thank me by getting Peter." Then she stepped forward and hugged me. I hugged her back, mildly and pleasantly surprised. "Good luck," she said.

She withdrew just as Hooke emerged from the tunnel, followed by Mariah.

"Alrigh', lass," Hooke said to Lily. "Let's go commandeer that bird."

When I went back inside, it took all my willpower to keep from dancing. I reminded myself that the plan was far from fail-safe, and that even if we did capture Peter, we still weren't sure we could get home. Nevertheless, I don't think I'd ever been more excited in my life. I remember that when I was flying with Peter I'd felt intoxicatingly buoyant, as if my body were made of bubbles. That's how I felt now.

I felt like I could already fly.

Within ten minutes, though, at least half of all that excitement had morphed into suffocating anxiety that Hooke, Lily, and Mariah were going to get caught.

Two or three hours later, I was so restless I was trying to stand on my head while chatting with Alex, who was doing sit-ups, when Hooke and Mariah finally strode in. I toppled over for something like the two hundredth time—though for the first time on purpose—and scrambled to my feet, beaming with relief and excitement. Alex did a couple more sit-ups, then casually kicked Nigel in the side, rousing him from a nap. (How he could sleep now is beyond me.)

Before Nigel could start ranting about proper waking techniques, he saw Hooke—and what Hooke was carrying—and drew his head back with a quizzical frown. "Is that a turkey?"

"Aye, lad," Hooke said. "I figured, rather than seize the extraordinary opportunity to go home after bein' stranded on this miserable, godforsaken island for all these years—we should have Thanksgiving."

I could almost hear Nigel's salivary glands kick into overdrive at the word "Thanksgiving," and he continued staring at the "turkey."

"I swear to God, Dread," Alex said warningly, "if you eat the Never-bird . . ."

The Never-bird really did look like a turkey—the only differences were that it looked somewhat smaller and sleeker, less ball-shaped, than a domestic turkey, and it didn't have that red fleshy thing dangling from its head. It was sitting in a shallow basket that Hooke was holding. A thin rope was tied to one of its scrawny legs; the other end was tied around Hooke's wrist. Mariah was holding a covered basket, which I assumed contained the chicks.

They set the baskets down, and Hooke untied the rope around his wrist and tied it to a tree root protruding from the wall. Then he led us through the jungle for about a half hour to the spot he'd picked out where we were going to carry out the plan. Here he went over the plan in detail.

We were doing it tomorrow night.

For some reason I hadn't expected to do it for at least a couple of days, so when I heard this, my excitement stomped on the gas. But another emotion also popped up in my rearview mirror: dread.

It was so far back it was barely detectable—but it seemed to be catching up.

We practiced for the next two or three hours, with Hooke "playing" Peter and the rest of us trying to capture him. (The one time Alex played Peter, he and Nigel wound up wrestling for ten minutes—which is why it was only one time.)

We returned to the burrow and had breakfast, and I spent the rest of the morning spearfishing with Alex and Nigel. The time went very fast, helped along by Alex and Nigel's protracted, fiery argument over who would win in a fight, Chuck Norris or God. Their ability to find something to argue about and to argue the living crap out of it was amazingly reliable. They should have been married.

After lunch, Hooke insisted we take a nap because we hadn't gotten much sleep last night (except perhaps for Nigel, but he was already fast asleep again). My thoughts and emotions were still in high gear, and the last thing I remember thinking as I lay in my quilts was that there was no way in hell I was going to be able to sleep—then Hooke was waking me and the others up, just before nightfall.

We made dinner. Hooke told us to eat lightly so we wouldn't feel lethargic for the ambush (he had to tell Nigel about seventeen times). I wouldn't have eaten much anyway—I was starting to feel nauseous. The dread had caught up to excitement and was starting to pull ahead—dread not only that the plan wouldn't work, but that somehow one of us would get hurt. Or worse. I felt like we were doing this too soon, even though I couldn't see any benefit in waiting.

After dinner, Hooke brought out a pot of black war paint he'd stolen from the natives long ago, and we rubbed it over most of our exposed skin. Then we set off for the spot Hooke had picked.

The spot consisted of three short, thick trees standing in a triangle of which each side was about twenty feet long. The trees' branches reached over the interior of the triangle, forming a dense, snarled canopy about ten feet high. Probably because of the canopy, the interior of the triangle was sparsely vegetated compared to the exterior. Hooke had picked this spot because the canopy would force Peter to enter the triangle from the sides and low to the ground and because the sparse vegetation would allow a clear shot at him.

Hooke shortened the Never-bird's leash to make it less visible and tied it to a tree root that bulged from the ground in a small loop. He'd also brought some ropes for binding Peter; he tossed these by one of the trees.

We took our positions—Alex and Nigel perched in the canopy, Mariah and I each by one of the trees of the triangle. Hooke, who would take the third tree, came around to each of us and made sure we were well hidden. Then he went to the center of the triangle, put his hands on his hips, and looked around at us. "E'eryone ready?"

We all said yes.

Hooke took a deep breath and blew it out slowly. "Alrigh' then," he said, at least partly to himself. "Here we go." Then he picked up the basket of chicks and started jogging away. He would stash the chicks somewhere in the jungle and then return to the triangle.

As Hooke jogged away, the Never-bird started scurrying after him, but the rope jerked it to a stop. For a few seconds it strained to pull its leg free, leaning its whole body into the effort. Then it started flapping its wings and hopping up and down, growing more and more frenzied. After about five seconds, it stopped struggling, reached its head down and back, and opened its beak, apparently trying to bite the rope—but its neck was about six inches too short. It tried for a few seconds anyway, straining its neck, looking half laughable, half pathetic (for some reason I pictured Alex trying desperately to bite his own ear).

Then the Never-bird pointed its head straight up, opened its beak wide, and started "singing."

At first, the only thing I really noticed was the volume. From my position, I'd say it was about as loud as someone screaming their lungs out right in your ear—plenty loud enough to cause discomfort. I immediately winced and plugged my ears.

With the noise thus muffled, I could actually listen to it. The "song" was an endless series of wails, ranging from barely a second long to almost ten, spaced about two seconds apart. The wails varied wildly in pitch and reverberated eerily, simultaneously beautiful and strident, an unearthly cross between the songs of a peacock and a humpback whale.

After about a minute, I gradually withdrew my fingers from my ears; another minute, without my ears plugged, and I was pretty much used to the noise. I couldn't block it out, certainly, but I could at least tolerate it.

I started scanning the jungle for Peter.

Almost immediately, to my shock, I saw a shadowy figure slipping swiftly through the underbrush. For an instant my heart shot into my throat and adrenaline shot through my body—

Then I realized it was just Hooke, returning from dropping off the chicks. I inwardly called myself a dumbass and relaxed. Hooke slid into his position by the tree, melting into the foliage.

I went back to scanning the jungle. Moonlight streamed through the canopy, bathing the jungle in an unearthly, bluish-white glow. The air was cool and perfectly still; not a leaf stirred. The gentle light and the stillness somehow made the Never-bird's song seem even louder. In the pauses between wails, I could hear the song echoing faintly in the distance.

Five minutes passed.

Ten.

I started getting worried—not so much that Peter wouldn't come, but that he'd come in like six hours. Six hours of waiting, stuck in the same uncomfortable position, unable to sleep or talk or do anything except watch and listen, did not sound like fun. It sounded like school.

I'd intended to stay one hundred percent focused on watching for Peter, but as the minutes dragged on, my mind wandered off. Not for the first time, I wondered what exactly would happen when we got home. Should we tell our parents the truth, or make up stories? There were issues with both options. The only plausible story I could think of was that I'd run away, and I really didn't want my parents to think that. If we told them the truth, though, we'd have to show them we could fly—otherwise they'd just think we were crazy. And did we really want anyone to know we could fly? What would happen if—

Suddenly the Never-bird's song broke off. The silence was startling—somehow it seemed almost deafening, even louder than the song.

I looked back into the triangle. To my shock, the Never-bird was sprawled on its side in a heap, its wings and legs twitching.

A spear was sticking up out of its side.

I looked back into the jungle, and suddenly Peter was there, about thirty feet away and closing, gliding toward the triangle with his feet dangling a couple feet off the ground. I automatically gauged his direction and speed and figured he was going to pass within a few feet of me within a few seconds.

A panic of indecision seized me—my heart seemed to stop as my mind raced furiously: Should I grab him as he's passing, or let him by and then get him from behind? How exactly should I tackle him—should I aim for his torso, waist, or legs? What if I tackle him and he breaks free? What if he sees or hears me coming? What if—

He was just about to enter the triangle, and I could see that the closest he'd come to me was about five feet. I wouldn't be able to just reach out and grab him; I would have had to jump out at him. So I made a split-second decision to let him pass.

I waited just a beat after Peter had broken the perimeter of the triangle, so that he was turned away from me but was still close. Then, adrenaline suddenly surging through my limbs, I lunged out of the brush, took two fast, bounding steps, and dove at his waist.

He must have heard me coming, because the instant before I hit him he started rising quickly, and instead of his waist, I caught him around the knees. As I hit the ground, he continued struggling to ascend—his legs started slipping out of my grasp, and gut-wrenching panic—

Then one of the others streaked in from the side and slammed into him. Peter's legs wrenched out of my grasp as they crashed to the ground and rolled. I scrambled to my feet and jumped on Peter's back, locking my arms around his chest. He was struggling so violently that all three of us rolled once again. Then another one of the others jumped on the pile, and another jumped on *my* back, apparently mistaking me for Peter, and got me in a headlock, but I was too focused on holding on to Peter to bother doing anything about—

"HELP!" Mariah screamed suddenly from several yards away. "HELP, YOU DUMB FUCKS, *HEEELLLPP!*"

Everyone in the pile froze and looked around. What I saw took me almost three seconds to comprehend:

Mariah was hugging Peter's legs as Peter tried to fly away, dragging her toward the edge of the triangle.

For one dumbstruck moment, Hooke, Alex, Nigel, and I looked back at one another, eyes wide, mouths open, still clutching each other tightly.

Then Alex voiced the sentiment we all shared: "Oh *SHIT!*"

172

We burst apart and scrambled toward Peter. A second later, Peter wrenched his leg out of Mariah's grasp and started flying. I was sure he was gone—but Hooke, still almost twenty feet away, made a spectacular leap, over Mariah, practically flying himself, and just managed to catch one of Peter's shins. Peter tried to pull away, but the next instant Alex and Nigel hit him simultaneously and drove him into the ground.

I waited outside the pile, ready to jump on Peter if he broke free again—but that wasn't going to happen. Hooke was firmly hugging both of Peter's legs, Alex had him in a full nelson, and Nigel was on top of both of them, squashing Peter into the ground. Peter thrashed his head, but otherwise he couldn't move.

"Ye got him?" Hooke asked, breathing a bit hard.

"Yeah, I got him," Alex said.

"You sure it's Peter?" Mariah said acidly.

Before anyone could respond, Peter, who had suddenly stopped struggling, said in a muffled, impatient, almost bored voice, "Would ya get off already? This is gettin' painful."

"That's what she said," Alex said.

"Oh, and before we get started," Peter said, "I'd just like to remind ya all, ya can't kill me."

"*Yet,*" Hooke corrected. "We can't kill ye *yet.*"

"Well, now, that doesn't give me much incentive to cooperate, does it? Ya na much of a negotiator, James."

"This ain't a negotiation, it's an interrogation."

"When it comes righ' down to it, really, what's the difference?"

Hooke cocked his arm and slammed his elbow into Peter's side; Peter grunted and writhed in pain.

"That's the difference," Hooke said. He nodded at Mariah. "Get the ropes, lass. And let's move him into the moonlight. I wanna see his face."

"I'm flattered," Peter said through gritted teeth, still in pain, as we lifted him up and carried him outside the triangle. "Did ya eva consida just askin'?"

"Askin' what?" Hooke said.

"'Use ya words.' Didn't ya parents eva teach ya that?" Peter looked at Hooke with a knowing smile. "Didn't ya *dad* eva teach ya that, James?"

"No," Hooke said darkly as we set Peter down, "but he did teach me not to bite the hand that feeds—and that included knuckle sandwiches."

Hooke drove his fist into Peter's stomach. Peter doubled up, gasping for breath.

Nigel cocked an eyebrow at Hooke. "Knuckle sandwiches? Really?"

Hooke just shrugged.

Mariah handed Hooke the ropes, and he started binding Peter's wrists and ankles while the rest of us held him down. I was pinning his right leg, with one of my hands above and the other below his knee.

"Hittin' me really isn't necessary," Peter said breathlessly.

"Perhaps not," Hooke said lightly, "but it sure is fun."

"None a' this is necessary," Peter continued. "I want you lads off this island just as much as you do."

"Splendid," Hooke said. "Then ye won't mind tellin' us how."

"I just take ya hand and fly ya back—same way I brought ya here."

"Besides that."

"What ya mean, besides that?"

"Ye ain't flyin' us back, lad. We ain't gonna let ye."

"*What?!*" Peter exclaimed. "Why na?!"

"We got our reasons."

"Like what?!" Peter demanded.

174

"You're a dick. How's that?"

"Tha's na a—!"

Hooke, looking almost bored, slugged him in the stomach again. Peter squeezed his eyes shut in pain.

"Let's cut the bilge, ay?" Hooke said casually. "Now, first things first: Why d'ye do it? Why d'ye bring lads to the Island, what d'ye do with 'em?"

Peter smiled thinly through his pain. "I'm curious," he wheezed. "What do ya think?"

"Personally," Hooke said, "I think ye should answer the bloody question."

Peter just kept staring at Hooke, and I got the impression he was thinking fast.

"Stop thinkin' and start answerin'," Hooke growled.

Suddenly Peter's right leg, the one I was holding, bent upward a little. I felt a jolt of adrenaline, thinking he was about to try to escape, and I quickly put my hands on his knee and slammed it back down—but he made no other movement. I looked at his face; his expression hadn't changed. Had it been a nervous twitch?

I only thought about it for a moment, though, because the next moment Peter said, "I suck their souls out."

My mind seemed to trip over itself.

"Their *souls?*" Hooke said quizzically.

Peter gave a dismissive wave. "Soul, spirit, life energy—I'm really na sure exactly what it is or what ya'd call it."

"And ye *suck* it out of 'em?" Hooke said, seeming half horrified, half fascinated.

"Yeah."

"Like . . . with a straw?" Alex said.

Peter smiled. "Na exactly. I just gotta be touchin' 'em, and other than that it's all mental. Or at least, nonphysical."

175

My mind was still racing to catch up.

"Why?" Hooke said.

"Why what?"

"Why d'ye suck their souls out? Do they taste good or somethin'?"

Peter smiled again. "No. They . . . well . . . they keep me young."

Nigel cocked an eyebrow. "Like Botox?"

Peter's smile widened. "No, mate. They don't just keep me *looking* young, they keep me *actually* young—they keep me from aging."

"Wait a sec," Hooke said, his eyes narrowed skeptically but his mouth gaping, "are ye sayin'—does that mean ye . . . ye live fore'er?"

"As long as I get a soul every so often, yeah."

My mind, which had just finally caught up, ate shit. And this time it had a lot more trouble getting back up.

About five seconds passed in silence as we all gaped at Peter.

Then Nigel looked over at Hooke. "Do you believe him?"

Hooke nodded slowly, his eyes still fixed on Peter, looking like he was in a trance. "Aye. I always wondered why he ne'er seemed to look any different, any older—he looks exactly the same now as he did all them years ago. And it explains the Lost Boys, too. Why there's so many of 'em. They're your—"

"'*Lost* Boys'?" Peter interrupted, looking derisively amused. "Ya call my children '*Lost* Boys'?"

"Ye call 'em your *children*?" Hooke said, looking appalled.

"They are."

"Bloody hell," Hooke murmured almost wonderingly. "You're even sicker 'n I thought."

Peter shook his head, smiling disdainfully. "Ya don't understand. I told ya all ya should come to the Island so ya could get away from all ya troubles. That wasn't a lie. My children are literally carefree— they get all the benefits of life and death, consciousness and uncon- sciousness, and none a' the drawbacks."

"What the hell are the benefits of death?" Nigel asked coldly.

"Ignorance," Peter said. "Numbness. Peace."

"Uh-huh," Hooke said drily. "So how d'ye pick your victims?"

"They're na '*victims*,'" Peter said testily, "they're—"

"Whate'er. How do ye pick 'em? I figured out that they all wanna leave home for some reason, but there's gotta be somethin' else, too."

As Hooke was saying this, Peter's right leg bent upward again; again I jammed his knee back down, and Peter neither resisted nor made any other movement. Alex noticed the knee jerk and looked at me, frowning questioningly. I shrugged.

Peter nodded in response to Hooke. "There's only a tiny number a' people in the world who have the mental capacity to come to the Island."

"Mental capacity?" Nigel said skeptically, and glanced at Alex.

"Na mental capacity like intelligence," Peter said. "There ain't really a name for what this is. See, ya gotta truly, fully believe in the Island to get here, and that's a lot easier said than done. Most people can *say* they believe and even *think* they believe, but they really can't. The older ya get, the harder it gets to believe in the unbelievable. Young children can do it just fine, but ya also gotta be able to fully *conceive* a' the Island to get here, to *realize* it in ya head, and they can't do that. That's why all the lads I bring out here are all round the same age."

"Why d'ye gotta bring 'em out here at all?" Hooke asked. "Why can't ye just suck their souls out while they're at home, in bed, sleepin'?"

"'Cause they'll resist. They'll only give up their souls when they're extremely weak and miserable—basically, when they lose the will to live. So I just put 'em in my cave for a few days. Or weeks."

Yet again Peter's knee jerked up and I pressed it back down.

Peter didn't even seem to notice he was doing it. I decided it must be involuntary.

"Now, ye say you're the only one that can fly," Hooke said thoughtfully, "but obviously, ye can make other people fly, like when ye took us here."

"Yeah. When I touch someone, I can share my powers with 'em, if they let me. As soon as I stop touchin' 'em, though, they lose 'em."

"So is there any way ye can gimme the powers permanently, so I'll have 'em even after ye stop touchin' me?"

"No."

An alarm immediately went off in my head—he'd said it just the tiniest bit too casually and gave no explanation, as though wanting to brush the topic aside, and he was staring at Hooke just the tiniest bit too intently, as though deliberately not looking away.

Hooke noticed too. He stared at Peter for several seconds, his eyes widening.

"You're lyin'," he said softly.

"No I'm na—"

"Ye can do that, can't ye?" Hooke said, speaking faster as his excitement rose. "Ye can gimme your powers, permanently."

"No, I can't," Peter said firmly. "It just do—"

"How d'ye do it?" Hooke pressed eagerly. "What d'ye gotta do?"

"I *can't* do it!"

"I bet ye lose your own powers when ye do it, don't ye?"

"No, I—"

"That's why you're lyin'."

"I'm na lyin'!" Peter shouted.

"It's too late, lad, I saw it in your face—"

"You saw what you wanted to see!" Peter said vehemently.

"Well, there's only one way to be sure." Hooke drew his knife and twirled it in his hand. Peter's eyes nearly burst out of their sockets.

178

Mine widened a little too. "Ye gimme your powers, or I start takin' your fingers."

"*NO!*" Peter screamed frantically. "Please, no, I *can't* give ya my powers, I *swear* I can't!"

"Well ye best wave good-bye to your fingers then." Hooke grinned. "They can even wave back." The casualness of his voice made the back of my neck prickle. "Alex, hold his hand open."

"NO!"

Peter clenched both his hands into fists, but Alex pried one of them open, pressed it to the ground, and knelt on his forearms, pinning them.

"I'll be nice and start with your pinkie," Hooke said, kneeling down over Peter's hands.

"NO!" Peter was screaming hysterically. "PLEASE, NO! I CAN'T DO IT, I'M NA LYIN', I SWEAR, IF I COULD I WOULD BUT I CAN'T, I JUST CAN'T, I—"

Peter continued screaming like this, but I barely heard him— my attention was fixed on Peter's pinkie and the knife. I kept thinking about the blade hitting the bone, about what it would feel like for both Peter and Hooke. Morbid curiosity overran my rising nausea—I couldn't look away.

Hooke spread Peter's pinkie and ring finger and placed the blade on the web of skin between them. Then, very slowly, he started sliding the blade back and forth, sawing into the web. Blood streamed down Peter's hand, and his pleas turned into screams of pain. Hooke's face remained nonchalant; he could have been whittling wood. He continued sawing, now twisting the blade toward the bone—

"OKAY, OKAY!" Peter shouted suddenly. "I'll do it, alrigh'?! I'll do it."

His voice was brusque, his expression hard; there was no trace of pleading, just frustrated anger.

He'd been acting.

"Splendid," Hooke said cheerily, and withdrew the knife. Peter squeezed his eyes shut and moaned as he gingerly curled his bleeding hand into a fist and covered it with his other hand. "So how's it work?" Hooke asked.

Peter didn't respond for a long moment, breathing shakily, his eyes still closed. Just as Hooke opened his mouth to press him angrily, Peter said, "I just gotta put my hands on ya head." His voice was resignedly flat.

The corners of Hooke's lips flirted with a wolfish grin. "Alrigh'. Now, if ye do it like you're s'posed to, we'll let ye live afterward. We really got no reason to kill ye, other than ye bein' a dick—and we'll just let that one slide. Mind ye, though: If ye try anythin' tricky, you're gonna lose a lot more 'n a pinkie. Got it?"

Peter gave a barely perceptible nod, his eyes still closed.

Hooke looked around at the rest of us. "Alrigh', lads," he said gravely—but I could just detect the almost childlike blend of excitement and apprehension in his voice. "Just hold on to him real tight, okay?" We all readjusted ourselves to make sure we had a firm grip; Mariah and I had his legs, Nigel and Alex his arm. "Ye all ready?" Hooke asked. We all nodded. "Alrigh'," he half murmured. Then he knelt astride Peter's chest and nodded at Alex and Nigel. "Bring his hands up. But don't let go."

Peter's eyes finally slid slowly open—they looked dead—as Alex and Nigel, gripping his forearms, guided his hands to the top of Hooke's head. Peter's fingers slid into Hooke's tangled hair. Blood from Peter's hand got on Hooke's hair and scalp, but Hooke either didn't notice or didn't care.

Then abruptly Peter's eyes rolled back and his eyelids flickered shut—and for a fleeting moment, I heard an extremely faint clinking or jangling, the same sound I'd heard just before I'd flown off to the Island. Then—

180

It felt like trillions of infinitely tiny cords shot up through my arms, coiled around something deep inside me, tightened viciously, then yanked back toward Peter, ripping that something loose—ripping *me* loose—from my body. I felt myself being sucked down into a bottomless black hole that somehow seemed to be contracting and expanding at the same time, almost like a funnel.

Then, instinctively, I resisted. I'm not sure how exactly, but I pulled back. For a moment I fully counteracted the cords and stopped my descent, or whatever it was—then it resumed. But now I knew I was stronger than the cords. I gathered all my strength and yanked back as hard as I could—

And then suddenly I was falling backward—actually, physically falling—my gaze sweeping over the canopy and the starry sky beyond it. I felt a moment's blissful relief at being back in my body—I felt like I'd just sucked in my first breath after almost drowning—

—then my back slammed into the ground, knocking the wind out of me. For a moment I just lay there, too dazed to even think, much less move, staring up at the canopy and the sky, which both seemed to be rotating slowly.

Then I heard a desperate shout—then a grunt of pain and a body hitting the ground—and I dragged my head up just in time to see Peter streak up through a hole in the canopy and disappear.

Chapter 19

Hooke lost it. I'm not sure what or how much he'd had left to begin with, but he sure as hell lost it. For almost five minutes he screamed obscenities, lurching in circles, clawing at vegetation. It was simultaneously amusing and frightening. The rest of us just watched in awe. Had Ms. Fulsom been here, she probably would have exploded.

Hooke's voice reached a dramatic crescendo as he screamed, "FUCKITY FUCK FUCK FUCK-A-DOODLE-*DOOOO!*"

Then abruptly he stopped screaming. For a few seconds he just stood there, breathing hard, glaring at a tree.

Then Nigel started clapping.

Hooke looked over at us with an expression of mild surprise, as though he hadn't known we were there. After a moment, he asked, "Ye lads alrigh'?"

"Well," Alex said, "we're *sane*, at least."

"Sorry," Hooke murmured, looking away distractedly. "I'm just . . . upset."

"Yeah," Nigel said drily, "I picked up on that around the eightieth 'fuck.'"

Hooke looked around at us grimly. "I'm assumin' he tried to suck your souls out too?"

We all nodded.

Hooke shook his head stiffly, looking furious with himself. "I shoulda seen it comin'," he muttered. "He *told* us all he needed was physical contact."

"I think he really can transfer his powers, though," Nigel said.

"Oh, he can," Hooke said softly with almost fervent conviction. "When I first asked him, and he said no, I'd bet me arse he was lyin'."

"Maybe he just wanted us to think he was lying," I said.

"No," Hooke said simply.

"So what are we gonna do next time we capture him?" Alex asked. "How do we keep him from just doing the same thing, trying to suck our souls out again?"

"Well, he said he needs physical contact," Hooke said, "so I figure we could make him a leash or somethin' and have one of us stand back and hold it, not touchin' him. And just in case he can suck souls through a rope, we'll have someone else stand completely separate.

"But I really don't think any a' that's even necessary. Peter said he can only suck someone's soul out when they're weak and miserable and lose the will to live. We ain't like that at all. We can resist—and pretty easily, I reckon. When he was tryin' to suck me soul out, I knew I's much stronger 'n him, I could just feel it. I think the main reason it worked so good this time was that it surprised us; if he does it again, now that we're expectin' it, I don't think it'd have nearly as much effect."

Hooke smiled very slightly, very darkly. "And besides all that . . . next time we get him, we ain't gonna be nearly so gentle with him."

"If there is a next time," Mariah said.

A few seconds passed in bleak silence.

Then Nigel said, "Well, look on the bright side: We're having turkey for breakfast."

We walked back to the burrow in crushingly somber silence—it felt like we were walking for hours. I desperately wanted to start a conversation, but I could think of nothing to talk about—nothing remotely happy, anyway. Every part of my being felt heavy. Even the air felt heavy. And when we finally got back to the burrow, it had never felt more like a coffin.

We cooked the Never-bird for breakfast. It tasted almost exactly like turkey. Nigel was speechless with delight. Actually, he was speechless because his mouth was stuffed. But in Nigel's case, what's the difference?

At first, Nigel's insistence on calling this breakfast "Thanksgiving" seemed so bitterly ironic that, paradoxically, it lightened my mood a tiny bit. But then, at some apparently random point during the meal, I found myself looking around at all the others. Alex was bagging relentlessly on Nigel's eating habits. Nigel didn't seem to be aware Alex existed—nuclear warfare couldn't have broken his turkey-induced trance (although no doubt a bucket of fried chicken would have). Hooke, sitting to one side of the burrow, was quietly discussing the ramifications of the night's events with Mr. Mullins. Mariah was sitting at the edge of the firelight, eating by herself. And even after looking at Mariah—or perhaps especially after looking at Mariah—I found myself smiling.

It wasn't a realization but a re-realization, the retrieval of a nugget of wisdom whose value is rivaled only by its slipperiness. This "Thanksgiving" was not ironic—I don't think Nigel had meant it to be ironic, and even if he had, it really wasn't. Yeah, Peter had gotten away—but we were all alive and unharmed. And we were still together. And that was more than enough reason to be thankful.

"So do you have any ideas on how to capture Peter?" I asked Hooke without preamble as he was taking a drink from the pot of water (or "grog," as he called it). He and I had been chopping wood. It wasn't until we'd gotten back to the burrow that I'd recognized the opportunity. Hooke and I were rarely alone together in the burrow. And it was well past time for me to start taking more control.

Hooke finished drinking and wiped his mouth. "Oh, I got shiploads a' idears. But idears ain't worth bilge."

"What do you mean?"

"Well, the difference between an idear and a fully developed plan with a decent chance a' actually workin'—well, that's the difference between lumber and a ship."

"So do you have a plan?"

"I'm workin' on one."

Even though I'd expected him to say this, my heart still hopped a little. "So what is it?"

Hooke smiled wryly. "A ship ain't worth talkin' 'bout till it can sail."

"Well, a ship's also a lot easier to build with more than one person," I said pointedly.

Hooke's smile faltered a bit. After a beat he said, "If ye wanna help, lad, focus on your combat trainin'."

"I will. And while I'm resting, I'll think about the plan."

"I appreciate the offer, lad, but ye can't help me. There's nothin' ye know 'bout Peter or the Island that I don't."

"That doesn't mean I can't help. I could still think of something you don't. And telling me couldn't hurt."

"Aye it could," Hooke said darkly.

"How?"

"I work alone, lad," he said, a hint of menace creeping into his voice.

"Not anymore," I said, a hint of that thrill of defiance seeping into my voice.

We locked eyes, all pretense of friendliness cast overboard, as Hooke might say. A long moment passed in silence so tense that it felt like the air itself might snap.

"Why don't you wanna tell me?" I asked.

"'Cause it's my responsibility. It'll only worry and distract ye, and ye can't help anyway."

"It sounds like you really don't have a plan, and you just don't want to admit it," I said, my tone taunting him, challenging him.

"I ne'er talk 'bout my plans till they're completely done. Ask the others."

"Well look," I snapped impatiently, "if you don't tell me what the plan is, I'm gonna assume you don't really have one. So if you're worried about my morale, you might as well tell me."

Hooke closed his eyes and pinched the bridge of his nose. "I promise ye, lad—I'm workin' on a plan."

"Then either tell me what it is or give me a legitimate reason why you won't."

"I already told ye—"

"Those weren't legitimate," I snapped fiercely. I paused a few seconds, but Hooke didn't respond. "You don't have a legitimate reason, do you?" I said, sneering with disgust. "This is about you being leader, isn't it? You just don't want the others to see me helping you. Don't wanna risk me thinking of something you didn't, 'cause then—"

"I told ye afore, lad," Hooke said loudly with sudden anger, "I didn't *choose* to be leader, but—"

"Well I didn't choose you, either," I said loudly.

"But *they did*!" he shouted passionately, stabbing a finger in the direction of the tunnel. "They put their faith in me! They put their *hope* in me! And I try me bloody best to deserve it—but I ain't God. I don't got an unlimited number a' idears, and most a' the plans I try to make I end up scuttlin'. I've had this plan in mind for more 'n a year, and now it looks like it's dead in the water. But I don't want the others to know that. I'm their leader. They believe I'm gonna get 'em home. If they see me gettin' frustrated, they'll lose faith in me. If they lose faith in me, they'll lose hope. And once ye lose hope, lad . . . there ain't much left."

Almost ten seconds passed in silence. Our eyes remained locked. Hooke was breathing a bit hard, a vein standing out in his forehead. My body was still in fight mode, my adrenaline pumping hard, and my anger clawed at me, trying to hold on—but then it slipped away. After that little speech, I couldn't help but see Hooke in a new light—one in which anger couldn't survive.

"I won't tell the others," I said quietly. "I promise."

Hooke continued staring at me for a few long seconds, and I got the impression he was gauging me in some way.

Then he nodded slightly. "Alrigh'." After a moment, he drew a long breath and blew it out through his nose. "Well, first of all, like I said, the plan's a tad dead in the water at the moment. But I'm still holdin' out for some wind."

He took another breath. "So, here it is: First, we sneak up Peter's mountain and wipe out the guards at the main entrance. That's by far the hardest part—or, at least, the riskiest. There's somewhere between ten and fifteen guards outside the entrance at all times. But we're all much better fighters than any Boys—well, ye will be soon enough—and we'd have the element of surprise. It's pretty far from easy, but it's a lot farther from impossible.

"And once we secure the entrance, we're gold. Ye 'member the entrance from when Peter took ye there? It's just that one tiny openin'—barely even one person could fit through it at a time."

Suddenly it hit me. "And other than that secret back entrance," I said slowly, thinking quickly, "that's the only entrance, isn't it?"

Hooke grinned. "Aye, lad. And more importantly, the only exit."

Peter would be trapped inside.

"But what about the other Lost Boys?" I asked. "Isn't Peter's mountain like swarming with Boys?"

"Aye. There's ones round the base a' the mountain and inside the caves. But they'll be like fish in a barrel. The Boys inside the caves will all have to squeeze out one at a time through that tiny openin'. All we gotta do is stand to the side, and soon as they stick their heads out, we slice 'em off. They'll ne'er know what hit 'em. The ones round the base a' the mountain will come up and fight too, but we'll be on the ledge—they'll have to climb up onto the ledge, which takes both hands and a bit a' time. All we really gotta do is step on their fingers. And 'member, lad, Lost Boys are 'bout as strategically inclined as a bloody plank. Without Peter, the Boys from the base a' the mountain will be completely unorganized—they'll just throw themselves at us one at a time, one righ' after another, till they're all gone. Hopefully we can take out some a' the ones from inside the caves too, but Peter'll realize pretty quick that that ain't doin' much good, an' he'll have 'em stop and regroup."

"So I don't get it," I said, "why's the plan dead in the water? You don't think we have enough people?"

"No, actually—I was plannin' on doin' it righ' after we rescued ye, soon as ye got a few weeks a' combat practice in. And now it looks like we got Lily, too, so we're doin' even better 'n I's hopin' on numbers.

"Here's the problem: When I came up with this plan, Peter just had lookouts hidden round the base a' the mountain. It certainly wasn't easy to sneak by 'em, but in the jungle, at night, with a bit a' patience, we could do it—we'd done it afore.

"But after we rescued ye, Peter musta got paranoid. I've gone and scouted out the mountain a few times in the past few days, and even just scoutin' is bloody—"

"So that's what you were doing all those times, huh? All those times you left without saying where you were going?"

"Aye, lad. And I found out Peter's been beefin' up his defenses like crazy. He had his Boys clear a strip a' jungle 'bout ten yards wide round the entire mountain, so there's no way ye can get to the mountain without crossin' it and bein' exposed. He's got some Boys who patrol back and forth along that strip and others hidden round the jungle as lookouts. The lookouts move round periodically, so they're real hard to pin down, and the patrols check in with the lookouts and the other patrols on each pass, so if even one Boy goes down, it gets noticed pretty quick.

"Obviously, the plan don't work if we can't get onto the mountain without bein' seen—and with five or six people and those defenses, that's pretty much impossible. I've thought 'bout it o'er and o'er again, and I can only see one way to do it: A diversion. But I've thought 'bout that o'er and o'er again too, and I can't think a' one that would work. The diversion would have to be pretty big, 'cause it's gotta completely distract all the guards in a pretty big area. But more important, it's gotta be somethin' that Peter would ne'er even think to suspect came from us. And knowin' how savvy and paranoid Peter is . . . well, we basically gotta think up the unthinkable."

Chapter 20

That night, at least an hour after we'd all lain down to sleep, I was still trying to think of a diversion (and mentally head-butting a wall in frustration) when a figure glided past me, startling me a little, and slipped into the tunnel. Mariah. I felt a rekindled tingle of curiosity, as well as a pang of guilt—I'd completely forgotten she wanted to tell me something. Or at least, she *had* wanted to tell me something. I had a feeling it might have been a limited-time offer.

I crawled up the tunnel. Mariah didn't seem to notice me when I emerged. She was sitting with her back against the tree, hugging her knees to her chest and gazing skyward. She looked small somehow, and I suddenly had an odd desire to give her a hug. However, I had a stronger desire to not be disemboweled.

"Hey," I said softly.

I'd expected her to start, but she didn't even blink. "You know I was kidding about that being a good conversation starter," she dead-panned, still looking skyward.

"And yet it continues to succeed." I paused a moment, waiting for her to pointedly disagree with me, but she didn't respond. "So, uh . . . a couple nights ago you told me you wanted to tell me something, but then Lily showed up so you never did, remember that? So now I'm curious: What did you wanna tell me?"

She opened her mouth but paused for a long moment, thinking— then shook her head. "I don't remember."

I was almost sure she was lying, but that didn't matter. Challenging her would be pointless, probably counterproductive, and possibly fatal. My heart sank. I waited another few seconds, hoping she'd speak again. She didn't.

"All right, well . . . good night, Mariah," I said.

Sighing inwardly, I turned around and—

"Wait," Mariah said. It sounded half like a command, half like a plea.

I stopped and looked back over my shoulder at her. "Yeah?"

She was facing forward and staring at the ground, her expression sullen. "I'm sorry, all right?" she said, somewhat grudgingly, but with a hint of genuine remorse. "That's what I was gonna say the other night. That's all."

I slowly turned to face her completely, my mouth slightly open in shock, blinking a few times as if to make sure I wasn't hallucinating. I'm not sure what I'd expected she'd wanted to tell me, but it sure as hell wasn't "sorry." "Sorry for what?" I asked.

"For . . . pushing you . . . and yelling at you, and . . . everything."

"Everything?" I said in surprise. "You don't have to apologize for *everything*, Mariah. I mean, I don't think anyone really blames you for the crisis in Darfur." She didn't laugh. Quite unsurprisingly. Even someone who wasn't Oscar probably wouldn't have laughed at that. "Well, I'm sorry too," I said.

She cocked an eyebrow at me skeptically. "For what?"

"For that joke. That was appalling."

There was an uncomfortable pause.

I hesitated a moment, then cleared my throat and said, "Do you, uh . . . do you mind if I stay up here for a while?"

She gave a barely perceptible head shake, staring ahead. "I don't mind."

I stared at her uncertainly. "Like . . . within a few feet of you?"

"Yards," she deadpanned. "Don't push it."

I smiled. Then I leaned against the tree and tilted my head up, pretending to stargaze but actually watching Mariah out of the corner of my eye. I was hoping she would speak first, but after thirty seconds of awkward silence, I asked conversationally, "You come up here a lot, huh? At night, I mean."

She gave a barely perceptible nod.

"You just like it up here or what?"

Now a barely perceptible shrug. "Yeah, I guess." Then, after a couple seconds, she looked down and said, "I don't usually sleep very well, either."

"Yeah, me neither. I always get homesick at night. It's always worst at night, I don't know why—maybe 'cause I'm not doing anything, ya know, so there's nothing to distract me. But yeah, I don't sleep well when I'm homesick." I paused a beat. "So what about you? You scared of the dark or something?"

Mariah didn't respond, just kept staring at the ground. I waited several seconds. Nothing.

I remembered Mariah saying she didn't sleep well when we met outside the burrow my second night on the Island. Her saying it again and her apparent unwillingness to say *why* she wasn't sleeping well made me think the "why" was somehow significant. But it was probably best not to push her.

I was just about to ask her, out of random, genuine curiosity, if she had a favorite *Sesame Street* character and, if so, who it was, when she said softly, "Not of the dark."

For a moment I didn't understand that at all. Then I realized she was responding to the last thing I'd said—*You scared of the dark or something?*—and my confusion deepened. I frowned, thinking I must have misheard or misunderstood. "You mean . . . you're not scared of the dark . . . but you're scared of something else?"

Very slightly, she nodded.

I eyed her quizzically. "Scared of, like . . . Peter and the Lost Boys or something?"

"No, not—nothing like that . . . It's . . . " She hesitated for a long moment, groping for words, her expression reflecting some deeper frustration. Then she bowed her head, suddenly looking weary. "Ya know what, just forget it. I don't even know—"

"I can't just forget it," I said incredulously. "I mean, hell, if *you're* scared of something, I should be fucking terrified."

"No, see, it's not actually—" She seemed to stop herself, closed her eyes for a moment, then shook her head. "You wouldn't understand."

"Well I couldn't possibly understand any less than I understand right now, so telling me couldn't hurt."

"It's just—it's really hard to explain, all right? It's a long story."

"Then I'll just have to clear my schedule." I paused a beat. "C'mon, Mariah . . . stories are meant to be told." *Damn,* I thought, smiling inwardly, *I should write that down.*

"Look, just forget about it, really, it's not important."

"Then why'd you bring it up in the first place?"

She put a hand across her eyes. "I don't wanna talk about this," she said softly.

I smiled. "You brought it up 'cause you don't wanna talk about it?" She didn't smile back. Shocking, I know. I looked away and paused for a few seconds. "I think you do wanna talk about it," I said thoughtfully. "If you really didn't wanna talk about it, we wouldn't even be *talking* about talking about it."

193

"Why do you care so much, anyway?" she asked abruptly, her voice and expression suddenly suspicious and aggressive.

Ah crap, I thought. I'd pushed her.

"What do you mean?" I said.

"I mean why do you keep trying to talk to me? Why are you so interested?"

I shrugged. "I dunno. Does it really matter?"

"Yeah, it does."

I narrowed my eyes curiously. "Why?"

"Do you think I'm hot, Ricky?"

That was so out of the blue and shamelessly blunt that I almost lost my balance and fell over from shock. *"What?!"*

"You heard me. Do you think I'm hot?"

"You mean, like, do you have a fever? 'Cause you do seem kinda delirious, now tha—"

"Answer the question."

I hesitated a moment. I think I'd always kind of wanted to tell her I thought she was hot—but not in this particular context. Nevertheless, I had to answer. "Yeah, I do. I think you're hot. Now would you mind—"

"What if you didn't think I was hot? Would you still care as much?"

And then suddenly I understood. "Wait," I laughed, "are you just trying to determine how shallow I am? 'Cause, I hate to break it to you, Mariah, but I'm a teenage guy."

Mariah looked up at me, and my grin vanished instantly—her expression was stony yet fierce, her eyes narrowed menacingly. "You didn't answer the question. If you didn't think I was hot, would you still care as much?"

I hesitated. The short answer was no, but that wasn't really fair—I *would* still care, just not quite *as much*—and this only applied when using the word "care" to mean "be interested," not "feel compassion." But how could I explain all that without sounding like an asshole?

I couldn't. Which is why I should have just said "Yes."

Instead I went with: "Well—I mean—that's not really—I mean, it depe—"

"That's what I thought," she said disgustedly, sneering. "You don't really give a shit about me, do you? You're just pretending to give a shit 'cause you think that'll make me like you, and then—"

"That is not true," I said with strong, genuine indignation. "Look, I admit, I think you're hot—I can't help that. And for some dumbass reason, that makes me a little more eager to be nice to you—I can't help that either. But that's not why I care about you."

"Why, then?" she asked, her tone challenging, almost taunting. "Why would you still care, if I wasn't hot?"

"I don't need a reason," I said scornfully. "When someone needs help, I try to help them—that's all there is to it. I'd be here right now even if you were a guy, even if you *looked* like a guy."

"*Bullshit!*" she snapped fiercely. "If I looked like a guy you wouldn't have given me a second chance, not even a second fucking *thought!*"

"How the fuck would you know?!" I exclaimed, outraged by her totally baseless assumptions—even as doubt tugged at the back of my mind. "You barely even know me!"

"I know enough. I know enough to know you're just like the others. You say you care, you act like it, but it's all bullshit—deep down you're just another shallow, selfish piece of *shit.*"

"Fuck you," I said, almost softly, before I realized what I was saying.

"Yeah, fuck me," she said bitterly. "That's all you really want, isn't it?"

My ballooning anger felt like it was going to split my body in half. "Ya know, Mariah," I said, my voice shaking slightly, "just 'cause I think you're hot doesn't mean I like you. I'm not so shallow that I can overlook your personality, you fucking bitch."

I turned around and ducked into the tunnel—but then stopped. I'd expected a retort, but Mariah remained silent. I glanced back.

Mariah looked like a whole different person: There was absolutely no indication that she'd been ranting furiously just seconds before. Now her body looked deflated, shoulders slumped and head bowed—and though her face was turned away, I could make out her expression.

She looked like she wanted to cry.

Something pierced my heart like an icy, steel lance, shattering my anger. Only then did I fully realize what I'd just said—and I could scarcely believe I'd said it. It didn't matter that Mariah was always so horrible to me and the others. That she'd called me a shallow, selfish piece of shit just moments before. That she was, in fact, the epitome of a bitch. On my list of "Shit You Just Don't Do," saying something like that to a girl was up there with hitting a girl, or making fun of a disabled person, or playing hacky sack with a kitten.

"I'm sorry," I said, wishing there was a more meaningful phrase. "I didn't mean to say that, I . . . I didn't mean it—"

"It's true, though, isn't it?" she said softly. "I am a fucking bitch."

"Don't say that," I said quietly, shaking my head. "I only said it 'cause I—"

"I'm a fucking bitch," she said a little louder and a little bitterly. "Only I'm not."

I had no idea what that meant, but it seemed inappropriate for me to ask. There was only one thing that did seem appropriate for me to do. Actually, it seemed cowardly, even heartless—but everything else I could think of seemed worse. Besides, I knew it was what Mariah wanted. What she'd *always* wanted. What I should have done a long time ago.

"I'm sorry, Mariah," I said. "For everything. Except, ya know . . . Darfur and shit." I took a breath and let it out in a silent sigh. "I won't bother you again."

I turned around and—

"I never told you, did I?" Mariah said.

I looked back over my shoulder at her. "Told me what?"

"Why I'm scared."

I slowly turned back around, my mouth ajar. I'd spent days struggling to be as nice as I could to Mariah. Then I call her a fucking bitch and suddenly she wants to chat. What the *fuck*. "No," I said. "No, you didn't."

"Do you still wanna know?"

I immediately opened my mouth to say yes, but then hesitated a moment. "Do you wanna tell me?"

She also opened her mouth—to say yes, too, I think—but hesitated, looking almost pained, as if the word was stuck in her throat.

"Well, just think about it, okay?" I said. "I don't wanna pressure you. And if you decide you want someone to talk to, I'll be around." Adding quietly to myself: "God knows I'm not going anywhere."

I ducked into the tunnel.

"Wait," Mariah said abruptly, almost desperately.

I looked back again. "Yeah?"

She opened her mouth, hesitated a long moment, then said quickly, "I do."

I cocked an eyebrow. "You do . . . take me to be your lawfully wedded husband?"

"You wish. I wanna tell you."

I stepped out of the tunnel and studied her for a couple seconds. "All right," I said. "Right now?"

This time she didn't hesitate. She nodded.

197

Chapter 21

"I've never met my real dad—and I don't want to." Mariah's arms were crossed in front of her stomach, her knees pulled up toward her chest, her head down. She looked faintly ill. "He left my mom before I was born. From what she tells me, he was . . . well, a major-league asshole.

"Which I could have guessed. My mom is the sweetest, most caring, selfless person I know—but she has horrible taste in men. And she's a total pushover, which is a really shitty combination. It probably doesn't help that she's pretty, either.

"So . . . she dated a bunch of guys over the years. None of 'em lasted more than a few months. Almost all of 'em were assholes in one way or another. Shallow, unfaithful—even just plain mean. Or crazy. Or, hell, all of the above.

"Anyway . . . when I was thirteen, my mom started dating my stepdad. And, I dunno, maybe it was just 'cause all the other guys were such assholes, but . . . I liked him. He was . . . sweet, charming, funny—all that shit. The only thing bad I could say about him was that once in a while he drank way too much. But he only got friend-lier when he got drunk, so what did I care, ya know.

"So, as usual, my mom fell in love with him in like three days. But this time it lasted longer than three weeks. A lot longer. We moved in with him after about a year, and after about another year they got married. And I guess at some point during all that I started loving him too. I never really saw him as my dad—I never called him Dad. But he was like a really close family friend. Or maybe like an uncle or something, I dunno.

"Anyway . . . they had fights once in a while. Ya know, just the kind of fights any relationship like that has. Nothing too serious. Like, I never worried they'd split up or anything like that.

"But then this one night, like a few months after they got married—they threw this party at our house for a bunch of their friends. My step-dad was already wasted when I went to bed, and there were still quite a few people there, so I'm sure he drank even more.

"I woke up like an hour and a half later 'cause he and my mom were shouting at each other. I couldn't really make out what they were saying, so I have no idea what the fight was about, but it was obviously serious. It went on pretty much nonstop for like half an hour. Just kept getting louder and louder. I just laid in bed the whole time . . . tried to . . . shut it out, ya know.

"Then I heard my mom get in her car and drive off. Just to get away for a bit, not to like leave for good or anything like that."

Mariah paused for a few seconds, staring somberly at the ground.

"For a while, after that night . . . I was really pissed at her for leaving like that. But I don't think I have any right to be pissed. Not at her. If she had thought there was any chance at all I might not be safe, I know she would never have left—or she would have taken me with her. I mean, he was her husband. She trusted him. She loved him. Fuck, so did I."

A knot of horror started forming in the pit of my stomach. My heart started beating a little faster.

Mariah continued: "But right after my mom left—just like a minute after I heard her drive away—he came to my room. I heard him coming up the stairs, and I figured he just wanted to check on me—ya know, see if I was awake, ask if I was all right. Maybe talk about the fight.

"But as soon as he opened the door"—she shook her head slightly—"I don't think I've ever been so scared in my life. He just kinda threw the door open as hard as he could. I remember it bounced off the wall and smashed back into him and it was like he didn't even notice. He started coming toward my bed—I don't know how the hell he managed to walk, he could barely stand. I could smell the alcohol on him from all the way across the room. I started . . . saying his name, asking him what he was doing, but . . . he didn't say a thing. It was like he wasn't there.

"I realized what was going on pretty quick—it wasn't that hard to figure out. But it was really fucking hard to believe. At first I was just so . . . shocked and scared . . . I just had no idea what to do. At first I barely even resisted—I just kinda cried and . . . I dunno, pleaded, I guess. He started trying to take my clothes off. Trying to hold me down and climb on top of me."

"Jesus Christ," I said, my head swimming.

"But that's as far as he got. Then I finally came to my senses a little and got the fuck outta there—he was so drunk, it wasn't hard to get away. And I ran outta the house. I should have gone to a neighbor's and called the police, but . . . I was scared, and . . . embarrassed, and . . . just . . . fuck, I don't know. So I just kept running. I had no idea where I was going, I just ran as far as I could. I ended up collapsing in some park.

"At some point I fell asleep—or at least blacked out or something.

And when I woke up, outta nowhere, this kid came walking up to me. Peter. We must have talked for hours. He knew what had happened. He told me about the Island, showed me he could fly. And then he offered to take me to the Island, and . . . I just . . . God, I don't know why. I don't remember my thought process. But I said yes.

"So he flew me over here, landed on his mountain . . . and the next thing I knew I was in some cave, tied up, with a bitch of a headache. After a while, Cap, Alex, and Nigel came and rescued me."

Suddenly her voice strengthened, as if in defiance. "So that's it. That's why. Right after that night, I got stuck on this godforsaken Island with three teenage guys, and that's it, no one else—and I saw the way they looked at me, I knew—"

"Oh Jesus!" I burst out, suddenly understanding. "You—you were scared they were—?"

"Of course I was fucking scared!" she snarled furiously. "Just think about it, Ricky! *Any* girl should have been scared!"

I narrowed my eyes, a sudden swell of black rage building inside me. "Have they ever done anything to you?"

"Not yet."

"I mean *any*thing, Mariah," I said intensely. "Anything at all?"

"No—but—"

The rage evaporated instantly, and an obvious realization suddenly exploded in my head. "So you thought—you thought *I* might do something like that?"

"I thought you might try, yeah." She looked at me coldly. "And I still do."

I recoiled as if she'd slapped me, my mouth falling open in a silent cry. In the back of my mind I understood that her distrust wasn't personal and was more than justified—but especially because of how she'd said it, it felt like an accusation. "You honestly think I'd fucking *rape* you?" I asked weakly.

"I'm not saying you *would* do anything—I'm saying you *could*."

"Well you're wrong," I said gravely and a little resentfully. "I could never do anything like that."

"Oh, well, that's a relief," she said with acid sarcasm. "'Cause I'm sure, if you intended to rape me, you'd let me know."

"Look, I get that you don't know me, but—"

"I *can't* know you."

"But you can't just assume I'm a rapist. The probability that any given guy—"

"The probability depends on the circumstances. Look at my circumstances, Ricky. I'm the only girl, trapped on some island in the middle of nowhere with a bunch of teenage guys, no civilization, no cops, no legal system, no one to protect me but myself. So that's what I did—I protected myself. I tried to stay away from the others as much as I could. I made sure I never got caught alone with just one of 'em. I cut off my hair, tried to make myself look ugly. I got good at fighting." She paused a moment and looked at me. "And I acted like a bitch. *Acted*. I tried to act as . . . as *formidable* as I could, so they'd respect me, they'd be *scared* of me, so—"

"Whoa, wait a sec," I said, my eyes narrowed skeptically but my mouth hanging open. "You're saying . . . all this time, you—'Oscar'— that was all just an *act*?"

"Well, I don't know if I'd say 'just' an act. I mean, my intentions were real, ya know? But at first it was pretty hard for me, 'cause I'm really not a bitch at all. After a while, though . . . I just . . . got lost in the character, I guess."

I felt like a lightbulb had gone off in my head but it was too bright. *An act.* It almost seemed like it could be a made-up excuse for her behavior. But I thought about how different she seemed when she thought no one was watching, how abruptly she could go from hostile to downcast, how I'd always thought there was a missing piece to the puzzle—and the more I thought about it, the more it made sense.

"Well damn, Mariah," I said. "That was an Oscar-worthy performance."

She looked up at me the way you look at someone when they tell a really bad joke. But after a moment, seemingly despite her best efforts, she smiled. It was the first happy smile I'd ever seen from her—and it filled me with a kind of warmth I'm not sure I'd ever felt before.

"So why now?" I asked curiously. "After, what, like, two months?—Why'd you suddenly open up?"

She gave a small, weary shrug. "I don't know. I guess . . . when I first got here, I was . . . terrified. But that's pretty much worn off. None of the guys have ever done anything to me. I guess I'm starting to . . . well, maybe not exactly trust them, but distrust them a little less. And I was lonely, too. You wouldn't believe how hard it is, going for two months without talking to anybody. I can understand why Cap went crazy."

Suddenly something occurred to me. I looked at her a little worriedly. "You are going to tell the others about all this, aren't you?"

She nodded faintly. "Yeah." She clearly wasn't looking forward to the idea. "Well . . . probably not . . . *all* of it."

I eyed her curiously. "So why'd you tell me first?"

She looked down in embarrassment. The emotion was alien and surprisingly endearing on her. "I dunno. For some reason I . . . I wanted to tell one person before I told the whole group. And . . . I guess it just seemed easiest to tell you 'cause you haven't known me as long." She paused a moment, then shrugged. "Or, I dunno, maybe I just felt more comfortable with you 'cause I know I can kick your ass."

I laughed.

"No offense," she said.

"None taken." Suddenly I thought of something. "Hey—you think you could do me a really big favor?"

She looked at me sideways, somewhat suspiciously. "What?"

"The next time you see Alex, look him right in the eye and show him your biggest, brightest, most dazzling smile. You'll scare the living shit out of him."

She laughed. I'd never heard her laugh before, and I thought it was the most beautiful sound I'd ever heard.

Chapter 22

The next morning, Mariah awoke last. She sat down with the rest of us by the fire, took a deep breath, and said in an affably businesslike manner, "Morning, guys."

Hooke missed the fish he was trying to skewer, poked his hand, and yelped in pain. Nigel choked on the water he was drinking and spewed it all over Alex, who didn't even seem to notice—he was gaping at Mariah, the skewer he was holding over the fire drooping in his limp hand. He looked like Chuck Norris had just round-house-kicked him in the stomach.

Mariah cleared her throat. I could just detect her discomfort. "All right. So, there are two things I need to tell you. The first thing is: Alex, your fish is on fire."

"Wha . . . ? Oh *shit*—"

"The second thing's a bit more complicated."

Mariah explained her front as Oscar, her anxiety at being the only girl in a situation with "*Lord of the Flies* potential" ("Are you calling us Orcs?" Alex said, looking confused and slightly offended).

She said nothing about her stepdad. The others reacted much as I had, and she had to defend herself a little, just as she'd had to do with me. But they came around quickly enough.

Afterward, Mariah left to take a bath.

Alex still seemed flustered. "Oscar *can't* be nice!" he exclaimed to no one in particular. "First Oscar turns nice, then the pigs start flying, and before you know it, it's the end of the fucking world!" Suddenly he looked at Nigel anxiously. "You haven't grown wings, have you?"

Nigel ignored that and looked at me shrewdly. "You knew about this already, didn't you?"

I nodded. "She told me last night."

"I figured you had something to do with it," he said. Before I could say that my role had been mostly incidental, he shook his head wonderingly and clapped me on the shoulder. "You should be a therapist, man."

Alex snorted. "Fuck that. You should be an exorcist."

That night, I waited about ten minutes after we'd all lain down in our quilts, then went and sat outside, hoping Mariah would come up. After fifteen or twenty minutes, though, my only company was disappointment. If she hadn't come up by now, she probably wasn't going to.

I stayed outside anyway. I didn't feel like sleeping. I had a lot to think about.

"Ricky?"

I gasped, my head snapping to the right—then immediately relaxed. Lily was walking toward me. She looked confused.

There was suddenly a sinking feeling in my chest, as if my heart had dropped out of my body like a rock. Peter's getting away had been more than horrible enough by itself; I hadn't even thought about having to tell Lily about it. Having to tell her I'd let her down. It hadn't been my fault at all, of course, but that didn't make me feel any better.

"Hey," I said dejectedly.

"I heard the Rare Singer two nights ago," Lily said, "what ha—"

Suddenly there was a figure right behind Lily—it was like it had stepped out of thin air. Shock hit me like a battering ram to the chest, but before I could shout a warning to Lily, the figure grabbed Lily's hair and wrenched her backward against its body. Lily cried out in shock; I reflexively jumped to my feet. Still gripping her hair, the figure turned its face so that its mouth was almost touching her ear.

"You stupid, selfish whore," Panther snarled.

Then he threw her forward, hard. Lily stumbled but caught an overhanging bough, stopping her fall; then in one fast, fluid motion, she pushed off the bough, spun around, and whipped her fist across Panther's face. Panther, caught off guard, tottered sideways. Going with the momentum of the punch, Lily did a swift 360 and swung her foot into Panther's side. Already off balance, Panther stumbled several steps and crashed to the ground.

Lily remained where she stood in a boxing stance, her face burning with a hunger for combat. Panther got slowly to his feet, holding his side, blood trickling from his nose. He looked annoyed, as though Lily were wasting his time with childish insolence.

"You're going to get us all killed," he said angrily.

"None of your beloved subjects are here, *Prince*," Lily spat, sneering. "Must you still pretend you care about anyone's life but your own?"

Panther gave a bark of harsh laughter. "You of all people have no right speculating that *my* motives are selfish."

"I'm not speculating, I—"

"But my motives are irrelevant," Panther snapped, his smile vanishing instantly. "My argument is sound regardless. You're risking every one of our people's lives."

"You know the risk is insignificant."

"Any risk is too great when you can have no risk at all."

"'No risk at all'?" Lily said in outraged disbelief. "Peter has just proven he's willing to flagrantly violate the agreement and you say there's '*no risk at all*'?"

"Tell me, Lily: Would you object if I sent a team of warriors on a retaliatory mission to kill or capture Peter, even if they were all killed?"

Lily's eyes narrowed suspiciously. "What does that have to do with anything?"

"You wouldn't object. Because their sacrifices would be for the good of the majority. And if—*if*—Peter kidnaps one or two or even ten more of our people, that is what they will be: Sacrifices for the good of the majority."

"If you care so much about the will of the majority, why don't you tell them the truth? Let them have their say?"

"I care nothing about the will of the majority; I care only about the *good* of the majority." Lily opened her mouth, looking indignant, but Panther pressed on impatiently: "There's a reason people need a leader. It's not just tradition. It's because people cannot be trusted to lead themselves. They don't always think things through. They are too likely to make a decision based on some popular passion rather than reason. I am not selfish, I am detached, as a leader should be. And you are not selfless, you are overly emotional." Lily opened her mouth again, but Panther snapped, "I've had enough of this nonsense. You—"

"So have I," Lily said.

"Think whatever you'd like," Panther said carelessly, "but know this: If you come here again, I will banish you from my village."

"Then you might as well banish me now."

"Oh, shut up, you bullheaded bitch," Panther said in annoyance. "Now come. We're going back."

Panther started to turn around, but Lily didn't budge.

"You can go back," Lily said. "I'm staying here."

Panther slowly turned back, his eyes narrowing. I could almost feel his anger building, feel the air crackle as if with electricity. "You are coming back with me right now," Panther said, "even if I have to drag your unconscious body."

"That is the only way I'll go," Lily said.

She drew her sword, the *sssing* seeming to reverberate in the still air, the blade glinting in the moonlight. She held it at her side, a defensive warning, not an offensive threat. Panther barely reacted—his eyes narrowed a bit further, his jaw tightened, and that was it—yet the effect was frightening. Like a gun being cocked.

"If you will not fulfill your duty," Lily said, "if you will not protect our people, not just the majority but ev—"

Panther moved so fast it was like my eyes couldn't quite keep up. One instant he was standing a few yards away from Lily, hands at his side, his sword in its scabbard across his back; the next he was streaking toward her like a bullet, his sword agleaming, arcing blur over his head.

And the next instant they were dueling with all the unrestrained ferocity of wild animals, a whirlwind of darting bodies and flashing blades. It almost looked like they were in fast-forward—I wouldn't have thought it possible for humans to react so fast. Their blows were all very short, and yet so hard that the clang of the blades clashing hurt my ears.

As soon as the fight had begun, I'd instinctively started toward Panther and whipped out my sword—but they were moving so fast, and it was so dark, I could barely even tell who was who. If I jumped in, not only would I likely be killed instantly, I could easily hurt Lily. So I remained where I was, watching anxiously for a good shot at Panther.

After maybe ten seconds—which seemed like an eternity for such ferocious combat—Lily stumbled over something, and Panther took immediate advantage. His blade flashed at her and her sword went flying out of her hand—I couldn't see how he did it, his blade moved too fast. In almost the same instant, he grabbed the front of Lily's shirt and flung her to the ground. Before she could move, Panther stamped his foot down on her chest, pinning her to the ground—and touched the point of his blade to her throat.

Terror wrenched my heart, and before I could think about it I started sneaking quickly toward Panther. I'd thought he hadn't known I was there, but I'd only gone a few steps when he looked straight at me without any hint of surprise. I froze, his glare seeming to pin me. His expression was hair-raisingly cool.

"Back off, boy," he said evenly. "This is not your affair."

"Just stay out of this, Ricky," Lily said, glaring up at Panther, "I can—"

Her voice broke off in a strangled gasp; Panther was pressing his foot harder into her chest, the muscles in his leg standing out. Lily gritted her teeth in helpless fury—with Panther's blade at her throat, there was nothing she could do. Panther's eyes never left mine.

And suddenly rage was boiling up inside me. "Get off of her," I said.

"You and I have no quarrel, boy," Panther said.

"I might have a small one, actually," I said.

Panther's eyes narrowed, and he spoke a little louder: "Sheathe your sword."

"I will if you will," I said, feigning nonchalance. Reason was screaming at me to shut up, but rage was drowning it out.

"Ricky, stop it," Lily wheezed, and now she was looking at me, her voice and expression streaked with anxiety. "Just stay back."

But for some reason this only fueled my rage.

"Sheathe your sword," Panther said quietly—which was a lot scarier than loudly—"or I'll take it from you."

"Go ahead and try," I said.

And instantly, every bit of my mental and emotional activity screeched to a halt except for a single flabbergasted thought that slammed into me like a bus: *Holy shit—did I really just say that?*

Panther's lips curled into a black smile. "Did you happen to overhear what I was just saying about passion versus reason?" he said in a mock conversational tone.

He lifted his foot from Lily's chest and slammed it down into her stomach. Her head and shoulders curled up off the ground, her mouth springing open in a silent, breathless cry of agony. He swiped the side of his foot across her face, and she rolled onto her side, either dazed or unconscious.

Then he stepped over her and started walking calmly toward me.

I automatically started backing up but also raised my sword. Rage and terror clashed inside me, canceling each other out so that I neither fought nor fled. I had no idea what I thought I was going to do, or *could* do against Panther—but I had an idea what I *wanted* to do to him, and I couldn't just run away and leave Lily.

I kept backing up and mentally gridlocking for about three seconds. Then Panther made the decision for me.

He lunged at me with catlike quickness and bombarded me with a blinding flurry of blows—right, down, left, thrust, left. I stumbled back, somehow managing—just barely—to parry or dodge them all. Finally I sidestepped to dodge another downward chop and Panther overbalanced just enough that I had time to sneak in my first strike, a chop at his neck. Panther jerked his sword up, and our blades clashed and held for a beat.

Then Panther snapped his knee up, striking the bottom of the hilt of my sword and popping it out of my hand. Before I could even think *FUCK!* Panther cracked the hilt of his sword against my temple.

Searing pain exploded in my head, my vision went haywire, and I toppled onto my side. Blood washed over my face—it felt just like tepid water except it burned my eyes.

Panther stepped over me. The very back of my mind screamed frantically that he was going to kill me, but the rest of my mind was tripping drunkenly over itself and didn't seem to hear. Though even if I had been lucid, there probably wouldn't have been anything I could do.

"If you weren't trying to get Peter . . ." Panther said. "Well, you're lucky you're valuable to me."

Then he turned around and started walking toward Lily.

But suddenly a bolt of insane rage pierced my haze, and just as he started walking away, I swung my leg as hard as I could into his shins. Caught completely by surprise, Panther fell flat on his stomach. I started struggling to quickly get up, fighting dizziness—but then Panther shot his foot back like a piston into my stomach. I slumped back to the ground, sick pain spreading through my midsection, completely unable to breathe.

"You're insane, aren't you?" Panther laughed as he got to his feet, sounding genuinely amused. "Well, I suppose that just makes you more valuable."

"Then that must make me a bloody treasure chest."

Both Panther's and my head snapped toward the voice—and such relief flooded through me that if I'd been able to breathe I think I would have howled with laughter. Hooke, Alex, Nigel, and Mariah were standing in a line in front of the tunnel, swords at their sides.

Panther showed no hint of fear, but his aura of authority vanished. He held up his hand in a calming gesture. "We are all on the same side here."

Hooke looked at me—on the ground, my face literally dripping with blood—then back at Panther. "Needless to say," he said drily.

"He took the offensive first," Panther said.

"Without any provocation whatsoe'er, I imagine," Hooke said.

There was a rustle of vegetation off to the side, and everyone's head whipped that way. Lily was standing there, sword at her side, glaring at Panther. One side of her face was covered in blood.

Anger flared in Panther's expression. "Drop your sword," he growled at Lily.

"Why don't ye lead by example, lad," Hooke said.

Panther looked at Hooke sharply. "This is not your affair."

"This is not your territory," Hooke said icily.

"I mean none of you any harm," Panther said with rising irritation. "I was only def—"

"Drop your sword," Hooke said loudly, "or I'll make ye drop it."

Panther's eyes narrowed, and I could almost hear a metallic click—the gun was cocked. "I have trained with a sword since the month I could walk," he said. It was half warning, half challenge.

"I have trained with a sword for centuries," Hooke said.

Panther blinked, and his coldly fierce expression took on a dash of puzzlement. Alex suddenly had a small coughing fit. For a moment, Panther didn't seem to know how to respond.

"Stop bluffing, Panther," Lily snapped with disdainful impatience. "You and I both know you're not going to fight."

Panther looked at Lily and just stared at her for a long moment, his face becoming grim—but also, very faintly, regretful. "You have defied me and put my people at risk too many times," he said, his tone matching his expression. "I am banishing you from my village. I will announce it at dawn. And in the interest of my people's safety, I will have to inform Peter that you have become a renegade."

Lily didn't react at all, just kept glaring at Panther.

Panther looked back at Hooke and sheathed his sword, his expression now purely grim. "I am sorry for all this." He looked at me. "And I'm sorry for attacking you; I did not wish to. You are a brave man." Then he looked around at all of us, including Lily. "You are all my allies and I yours. I wish you the very best of luck. And I hope with all my heart that you get that bastard."

Then he turned on his heel and strode away.

Chapter 23

So in one day, our crew lost one member (Oscar) and gained two news ones (Mariah and Lily).

Those first few days were bizarre—but in a very good way.

Everyone quickly came to like Lily; it was hard not to, she was so sweet. She was shy at first, but in an endearing way, not an antisocial one. The vast majority of the time, she seemed remarkably upbeat considering she'd just been banished from her home and life. But a few times, when she wasn't talking to anyone, I saw her looking downcast. She basically never talked about her past life—about Panther, her village, her people, nothing—and no one ever asked her about it.

Alex and Nigel seemed markedly eager to hang out with Lily. And not to hit on her or anything like that. It was just that it had been a year since they'd interacted nonantagonistically with a girl—and a hot one at that—and they seemed enthralled by the novelty of it. They did flirt with her, I think, but just for fun. I think.

Lily got along particularly well with Hooke, which wasn't surprising since he was so familiar with the Island, at least relative to the rest of us; she and Hooke seemed to share the comforting connection of that of two strangers in a foreign country who discover they're from the same town.

What *did* surprise me—although it probably shouldn't have—was how well Mariah and Lily got along. From the first time they talked, they seemed to be best friends. No doubt Mariah was more comfortable with Lily than with anyone else, not only because Lily was female but because she was the only one of us who'd never known Oscar.

Lily was an incredible fighter. She was extremely well trained and conditioned, and when she was practicing fighting, her shy, sweet demeanor was replaced by a sort of controlled ferocity. She was better than all of us except Hooke, with whom she was about evenly matched (though if I had to say, I'd say Hooke was better). Watching Hooke and Lily duel was spellbinding.

"They're like freakin' Jedi, man," Nigel once said wonderingly.

After which he and Alex began arguing about what the proper plural of "Jedi" is.

Also rather spellbinding, for a completely different reason, was watching Mariah and Lily duel.

"It's like Island porn," Alex said, grinning.

To which Nigel replied drily, "Is that the kind of porn you like? Sword-fighting?"

Alex didn't call it that again.

Things between Mariah and Hooke, Alex, and Nigel remained awkward. The guys treated her kindly but hesitantly, as if afraid the old Oscar might pop back out of her trash can at any moment. They tended to avoid her. Which Mariah didn't mind—she was equally hesitant toward them.

I didn't mind either—it just meant I had Mariah more to myself.

She and I spent far more time with each other than with anyone else. I loved being with her. I could talk with her as easily as with the others, much more easily than with any other girl I'd ever known. I could make her smile and laugh without trying at all, and I loved doing so. I remember that the first time I'd ever made her genuinely smile (with that "Oscar-worthy performance" joke) it had filled me with an extraordinary sense of warmth, satisfaction, almost accomplishment. And every time I made her smile or laugh, I still felt that exact same way.

Mariah and I were walking to the tide pools one morning, and I was talking about how I'd been "popular" in school yet hadn't felt I had any real friends, when she asked, "Did you have a girlfriend?"

"Pff," I said with dismissive disdain. "*A* girlfriend? I had like twelve."

She smiled at me with a sort of knowing, taunting skepticism. "Have you *ever* had a girlfriend, Ricky?"

"I've had two, for your information," I said indignantly. "And only one of them was imaginary."

She laughed. "How long did the one last?"

"Almost two years."

Her eyes widened. "Oh my gosh, really?"

"Well, two years in high-school-relationship years. Which is about two months in normal time."

She rolled her eyes but smiled a little. "So what happened? How'd it end?"

I shrugged. "Nothing dramatic. I just broke up with her."

"Why, though?"

"Well, I was never really sure I actually liked her. And I guess eventually I just decided that meant I didn't. I mean, I really liked her as a friend—we'd been good friends for a long time—but—"

"Was she hot?"

I laughed a little, reminiscently. "Well, she was way the hell outta my league. Hell, she wasn't even in my sport."

She cocked an eyebrow at me skeptically, smiling teasingly. "And *you* broke up with *her*? I'd like to see you back that up."

"I'd like to see your mom back that up."

She ignored that. "Well anyway, if ya ask me, friendship and physical attraction are the main ingredients of a relationship."

"The main ones, yeah," I said thoughtfully. "But there's a secret ingredient too."

She looked at me curiously. "What's that?"

"Well, see, the thing about a secret ingredient is that it's usually *secret*."

"Well what do you think it is?"

I frowned a little. "I don't know. But I know there is one. 'Cause I mean, I've known quite a few girls who I liked as friends *and* who I thought were hot—but I never really wanted a relationship with them. I mean, friends with benefits, sure, but not boyfriend–girlfriend. That takes something extra. But hell if I know what it is."

Mariah remained silent for a few seconds in thought. "I don't think you *can* say what it is," she said, a little quietly. "And I don't think you're supposed to. I think you just know it when you feel it."

Chapter 24

Hooke, Alex, and I were spearfishing. A lazy week had passed since the confrontation with Panther, and this day seemed like yet another lazy one. In the muted sunlight of early morning, the swamp seemed almost divinely tranquil. Tendrils of fog still clung to the water. The air was perfectly still and refreshingly cool, the water comparatively warm. The only sound was that of our legs stirring the water as we waded slowly through it. Everything was so serene, the silence so soothing, it seemed almost sacrilegious to speak.

Suddenly Hooke stopped and raised his head, his body and expression tense. "Listen," he whispered.

Alex and I froze. My heart rate spiked with alarm.

"What is it?" I asked anxiously.

Hooke held a finger to his lips. "Shhh . . ."

Alex and I were silent for several seconds, listening. I was holding my breath and looking around apprehensively. I heard nothing but my pulse booming dully in my head.

"I don't hear anything," Alex whispered.

"Exactly," Hooke whispered back.

Only then did I realize the silence had changed—it had become *too* silent. It wasn't soothing at all anymore, it was eerie. Background noises I'd been only subconsciously aware of—birds singing, frogs croaking, crickets chirping, the occasional splash of a fish jumping or a bird stabbing for underwater prey—all that had abruptly ceased. The whole swamp seemed to be holding its breath, just as I was.

"What the hell's going on?" I whispered.

We all heard it at the same time, and our heads snapped toward the shore. About fifty yards inland, the foliage was rustling loudly (though it seemed soft from so far away).

Hooke looked around quickly, then hissed urgently, "Here lads!" and rushed into a dense patch of reeds a few yards away; Alex and I hurried after him. We all crouched down so that only ours heads and shoulders were above water, then peered through the reeds toward shore.

"Lost Boys?" I whispered. My heat was hammering so hard it seemed to make my voice shake.

"I dunno," Hooke said. "If it is, it must be a pretty big group."

Whatever it was, it was heading straight toward us at about a walking pace, I estimated. If it *was* Lost Boys, they must not have cared at all about stealth, because even for a pretty big group the rustling was loud.

And now, amid the rustling, I could hear loud cracks and snaps. Branches breaking. *Large* branches.

Maybe they're just really clumsy, I thought.

Then I looked up slightly, and a horrible sinking feeling filled my chest.

The treetops were stirring.

"I don't think it's Lost Boys," I heard myself say.

Hooke and Alex glanced over at me and then followed my

gaze to the treetops. After a moment, Alex said, "Oh shit."

A couple seconds later the crocodile emerged, crashing through the jungle like a tank, flattening bushes, snaking between large trees but carelessly trampling small ones.

Alex had been right—it must have been a mutant or something, maybe even a different species altogether—Croczilla, perhaps. It was by far the biggest crocodile I'd ever seen. It must have been at least thirty feet long from snout to tail, almost as long as a bus; its head was as big as my whole body, and its teeth were the length of my fingers. Its tree trunk–like legs held its bulging underbelly two feet off the ground. Its ridged, armor-like scales were an ugly, dark, grayish-green. Its left eye socket was a mangled, empty pit.

The croc stopped at the water's edge, about twenty yards away, its snout pointing straight at us. It seemed like it was watching us, even though I thought we were well hidden. Out of the corner of my eye I noticed Hooke moving his head around very subtly—probably looking for an escape route.

After about five seconds, the croc still hadn't moved.

"Does it see us?" Alex breathed, barely moving his mouth.

"I dunno," Hooke breathed back. "But it only wants me. If it comes at us, ye two just run like hell and tr—"

With frighteningly explosive speed for such a massive animal, the croc launched itself into the water like a torpedo—straight toward us.

"RUN!" Hooke screamed, and pushed me to the side. I stumbled but kept my feet and started scrambling toward the shore at an angle, feeling nightmarishly slow and awkward in the nearly waist-deep water, my whole being consumed with panic. I heard loud splashing behind me, gaining on me, I could almost feel the croc's fetid breath, and I looked back, wanting to scream, fully expecting the jaws of death to fill my view—but the splashing was just Alex rushing after me. As Hooke had predicted, the croc was heading for him.

Hooke was running perpendicularly away from the shore, floundering in the waist-deep water; the croc, fully submerged except for its eye sockets and nostrils, glided swiftly after him. It looked like Hooke had nowhere to go. There was a small island with a few trees about twenty yards ahead of him, but there was no way in hell he was going to get there before the croc got him.

He was dead.

But just as the croc was about to overtake him, he leapt up and grabbed onto a bough extending horizontally from a short tree. At almost the same instant the croc exploded from the water, pulling the front half of its massive body into the air, reaching its jaws up and snapping, just barely missing Hooke's feet as he swung himself atop the bough.

The croc crashed back into the water. Hooke stood up on the bough, one hand touching the trunk for balance, and screamed with triumphant, jeering laughter. "Ye missed me again, ye fat scaly bastard!" he shouted delightedly.

"But what the hell are you gonna do now, Cap?" Alex wondered aloud to himself. He and I were standing at the water's edge, watching.

The croc starting swimming away from the tree, moving parallel to the shore.

"It's going away," I said, letting out a breath of relief.

Alex's eyes narrowed suspiciously. "The croc never just goes away." No sooner had he said this than his eyes widened. "Oh shit."

The croc was turning toward the shore.

Toward me and Alex.

"Why ye runnin', huh?!" Hooke called. "Can't take an insult?! That's funny—ye don't strike me as the *thin-skinned* type!"

Hooke threw his head back and laughed so hard he almost fell off the bough. Despite the side-splitting stand-up, Alex and I were stepping back, about to run, thinking the croc was coming ashore.

But it kept turning.

"It's circling around," Alex said.

I narrowed my eyes in apprehensive puzzlement. "But why such a wide circle?"

"Speakin' a' skin," Hooke called, "ye oughta get your arse back here—I been wantin' me a new pair a' shoes!"

Hooke started laughing again. But then the croc veered toward the tree, going into the final leg of its circle—and started swimming very fast.

Hooke's laughter broke off and his delighted expression turned to one of terror. "I's just kiddin'!" he shouted frantically as the croc barreled toward the tree. "I don't even wear shoes! I mean I don't wear shoes 'cause I don't want to, not 'cause I need new ones, I didn't even wear shoes back in oh bloody *fuck*!"

The croc threw itself at the tree, pulling the front half of its body up and back so that its underside slammed against the trunk—it looked almost like the croc was giving the tree a hug. There was a huge, rending crack, and the whole tree bent about thirty degrees; Hooke hugged the trunk to keep from flying off.

A long moment of stillness followed. The croc was still "hugging" the tree, halfway out of the water, looking almost comically awkward.

Then there were several loud cracks in rapid succession, and, with a groan, the whole tree toppled over. Hooke jumped off, and the momentum of the falling tree sent him flying. The tree crashed into the water, Hooke landed several yards beyond it a second later.

He immediately got up and started scrambling toward the island, which was now only about ten yards away. The croc struggled to go over the fallen tree. The island was roughly circular, maybe fifty feet across, and bare except for three trees and some scattered ferns.

Hooke ran to the largest tree and started climbing it. He was

223

about fifteen feet up when the croc rushed ashore, moving with the brute power of a bull elephant and yet the alien sinuousness of a snake. Hooke immediately stopped climbing and hugged the trunk.

The croc launched itself at the tree just as it had the last one, arching its front half up and back so that its underside slammed against the trunk. The tree bent maybe twenty degrees, but there were no cracks or groans, and when the croc awkwardly backed up, the tree bounced right back. This tree was bigger and sturdier than the last one—but as the croc launched another body slam (Hooke still hanging on for dear life), I wondered if the tree could withstand sustained blows.

"Cap!" Alex called with his hands cupped around his mouth. I saw Hooke's head turn toward us. "What are we gonna do?"

"If I knew that, lad, d'ye really think ye'd have to ask?"

As the croc struck again, I called, "I don't think that tree's gonna stay up forever."

"Thank ye, lad," Hooke said, feigning surprised gratitude. "Any other helpful suggestions?"

"What can we do?" Alex called.

"Get me a bloody helicopter."

"Should we come over there?" I called.

The croc struck again.

"Well that's a splendid idea," Hooke said as the tree swayed. "Ye and Paul Bunyan here can have tea together."

I turned to Alex and said to him, "Maybe we should go over there. Maybe we can distract it, or even—"

"No. Me and Dread and Oscar tried to distract it both the last times. It completely ignored us. And unless you have a bazooka handy, you can forget about trying to hurt it."

"Well how'd Cap get away the other times?"

"Well, the first time, he stabbed it in the eye, but that was when he was already in its mouth. The next time it was chasing him around the jungle and got stuck between two trees. And the last time Cap ran all the way to a mountain a couple miles from here and ran up it."

I think it was the word "mountain" that sparked the idea. My heart seemed to catch for a moment, then started beating even faster than it had been; I completely forgot about the present situation as my mind raced around the idea, inspecting it.

"Cap can't outrun the croc?" I asked.

"That croc's a lot faster than you'd think," Alex said. "It's 'cause its stride is so long, and it doesn't have to dodge through the jungle like we do, it just smashes right through it."

"And it'll actually follow Cap through the jungle for, like, miles?"

"That croc would follow Cap to hell and back."

And, with a mix of wonder, skepticism, and exhilaration, I thought: *Perfect.*

"But that's kind of irrelevant at the moment," Alex said. "Maybe you haven't noticed, but Cap's in a tree."

It happened almost immediately after Alex had said this.

The bough Hooke was standing on was somewhat thin and wobbly—I could tell he was having trouble keeping his balance. So, as the croc backed up, Hooke tried to step onto a bigger bough on the opposite side of the trunk. Still hugging the trunk, he reached one leg around the trunk and planted his foot on the new bough. Then he let go of the trunk, grabbed hold of a branch above him, and swung his other foot onto the bough.

But just as he was putting his foot down, the branch he was holding onto snapped, throwing him off balance—his foot slipped—and just as the croc charged at the tree again, Hooke fell. He flailed his arms wildly, trying to grab onto something, but nothing was in reach.

He landed hard on his side—right next to the croc's head. So close he could have reached out and touched one of the croc's hornlike teeth.

That first instant seemed to last an agonizing lifetime. It was as if God had paused His universal TiVo and was leaning forward on His cosmic couch, His mouth open in amazement, to get a better look.

It was indeed a gripping scene—Hooke lying crumpled on his side, just about two feet from the croc's head, the proximity jarringly emphasizing the surreal size difference. Alex and I could do nothing but stand there and watch. I felt no horror yet—the fall had happened so fast, my mind was still blank with shock.

But then that first instant turned into a whole second—and then two—and still the croc hadn't even turned its head toward Hooke. It was still straining against the tree, pressing its underside against it, looking almost like it was humping it. Hooke still hadn't moved—he seemed to be frozen like a deer in headlights. It was as if the croc didn't see him—but that was impossible, Hooke was just two feet away from the croc's *eye*—

Socket.

Its eye *socket.*

Which was a mangled, empty pit.

Hooke had realized this too. When the croc backed up, Hooke scrambled to stay abreast of the croc, on its blind side. The croc finished backing up and was about to charge at the tree again—but then it tilted its head up, looking at the tree's branches, noticing that Hooke wasn't there. After several seconds, the croc slowly swung its head right to left, twice, surveying the island.

Then, with startling suddenness, the croc whipped around to its left, toward Hooke, its jaws snapping open—I'm pretty sure the croc hadn't sensed him, it was just guessing. Hooke had to bound and scramble to stay on its blind side.

Then the croc started marching along the edge of the island, its right side (and thus its eye) facing toward the center of the island. Hooke tiptoed alongside the croc, having to stay within inches of the croc's flank in order to stay out of the water and avoid splashing. The croc circled the island twice, during which time it whipped around to its left twice more—but now Hooke was ready for it and easily kept out of the croc's sight.

Finally the croc slid into the water. Hooke, never taking his eyes off the croc, lowered himself onto his stomach behind a clump of ferns, slipping out of view.

This whole time, Alex and I had been standing there watching, aware of absolutely nothing but the agonizingly tense scene taking place just thirty yards away, but which might as well have been on television for all Alex and I could do about it.

Now, as the croc swam away, parallel to the shore, Alex slowly lay down on his back, took out his coconut, pressed it to his lips, and closed his eyes.

I, however, was watching the croc and thinking fast. I'd just noticed a potentially fatal flaw in my idea: We'd have to be able to locate the croc . . .

"Alex," I said. "I need to follow the croc."

Alex gave a dopey laugh. "What was that, Ricky? You need to swallow the—" Then he bolted upright and stared at me like I was insane. "Wait, what the fuck did you just say?"

"Tell Cap the croc can be the distraction; he'll understand," I said quickly. "He can explain the rest. I gotta go."

I started running, but Alex jumped to his feet and grabbed my upper arm. "Ricky, you're gonna get your crazy ass killed!"

I wrenched my arm out of his grip and took off along the shore. "I won't put myself in danger," I called back over my shoulder.

"Oh, well that's good," Alex called back in mock relief. "I'd hate for you to put yourself in danger while you're harassing the giant man-eating crocodile!"

Chapter 25

It was very possible I'd lose track of the croc or end up determining that it didn't really live anywhere, but it was well worth a shot.

I jogged along the shore as the croc continued swimming parallel to it, about twenty yards out. After about five minutes, the croc crawled ashore and started marching into the jungle; I followed twenty or thirty yards back at a fast walk. Ten minutes later, the croc came to a broad, slow river, tramped along the bank for another few minutes—then abruptly seemed to sink into the ground, disappearing. Proceeding forward, I found what I'd expected: a gaping hole in the ground, about ten feet from the river.

As I was coming down the tunnel, I heard Alex talking loudly. I couldn't make out what he was saying, but he sounded angry.

When I dropped into the burrow, silence fell immediately as everyone looked at me.

"So'd ye find where it lives?" Hooke asked me quickly, his voice and expression desperately eager.

"Yeah," I said. "In another burrow."

Hooke pumped his fist in the air and gave a burst of triumphant laughter.

I grinned. "So does that mean you like the idea?"

"I think it's bloody brilliant, lad," Hooke said, beaming at me.

I glanced at Lily; she smiled back.

"So does that mean we're doing the plan?" I asked Hooke.

Hooke's smile faltered and he hesitated uncomfortably. "Well . . . we've hit a bit of a shoal . . ."

Hooke turned around and looked at Alex. Only then did I realize Alex looked uncharacteristically surly. My uncanny powers of deduction led me to surmise that Alex and Hooke had been arguing.

When Hooke turned and looked at Alex, Alex seemed to take this as a fresh challenge. Anger flared in his expression. "Just look at the goddamn numbers!" he exclaimed, sounding like he was exasperated at having to keep pointing out something painfully obvious. "It's five on at least fifty!"

"No it bloody ain't," Hooke said in a tone almost identical to Alex's. "Once we take the entrance, they'll be comin' at us three at a time at most, and—"

"Even if they come one at a time," Alex said, "each one is another time we risk our lives—and you multiply that risk by forty or more and—"

"And it's still plenty small enough," Hooke said. "With the ledge and that tiny opening, they won't even—"

"You keep talking about taking the entrance like it's a given. Five on, what, ten at the very least? We're not fucking ninjas, Cap."

"Six," I said. "We have six."

"But one's gotta take the back entrance," Alex said.

I frowned. "I thought Peter didn't know about that entrance."

"But there's a chance he found it since we rescued ye," Hooke said to me. "Not a very big chance, I'd reckon, but still too big to ignore." He looked back at Alex. "But still, lad—ye know we're much better fighters than any Lost Boys, and we'll have the element a' surprise."

"This is all assuming the croc thing works," Alex said skeptically, and glanced at me, somewhat apologetically. "No offense, Ricky, but it sounds pretty far-fetched."

"The diversion *has* to be far-fetched so Peter won't suspect we're behind it," Hooke said. "If we did anythin' much less far-fetched, he'd pro'ly have his Boys search the whole mountain just to be safe."

"But there's so much that could go wrong," Alex said. "The Boys could see you, or you might—"

"When a crocodile the size of a bloody galleon is chargin' at ye," Hooke said, "ye tend not to notice much else. In the dark, in the jungle, with that croc ridin' me wake, no Boy's gonna notice little old stealthy me. And besides, lad, the diversion's really a whole separate phase a' the plan, 'cause if it don't work, we can just abort the rest a' the plan afore it gets started."

"But during that 'phase' we could still get killed," Alex said. "It's still one more risk. And if you add all those risks up . . . I think the odds are good we won't all make it out."

A moment passed in grave silence.

Then Nigel said, in a tone that suggested he was fulfilling a grim duty, "Alex—it's time someone said something: You need to stop taking anabolic steroids."

Everyone recoiled a bit and stared at Nigel like he was insane.

"What?" Alex said. "What the fuck are you talking about? I don't take anabolic steroids."

Nigel frowned skeptically. "Are you sure? 'Cause you are a baseball player, and you show all the side effects: extreme aggression, breast enlargement"—he flicked Alex's well developed pecs—"and now, apparently, testicular atrophy. You know what that means?"

"What?"

"It means your balls get smaller."

Alex scowled and turned away. "This isn't a joke, Dread," he said irritably. "I'm not in the mood for your childish little insul—"

"Pussy," Nigel murmured.

Alex stopped and slowly turned back to Nigel. "What'd you say?"

"I said," Nigel said slowly and clearly, "you're a *pussy*."

Alex's eyes narrowed. "Ya know what, Dread, you can—"

"Pussy."

"Just 'cause I—"

"*Pussy.*"

"Would you—"

"*Pussy!*"

"Stop—"

"*PUUUUSSSSSSYYYY!*"

"FINE!" Alex shouted.

Silence.

Alex turned away and glared at a wall, breathing slightly hard. We all knew he wasn't actually agreeing to the plan; he was saying "fine" as in "Fine, don't listen to me. Throw your lives away." And he'd said it with such passion that the subsequent silence was hair-raisingly powerful.

"It's already been a year, man," Nigel said quietly, staring at Alex somberly. "This could be our last shot."

Alex just kept glaring at the wall. But then, slowly, the anger in his expression morphed into something like bitter sorrow. After almost ten seconds—it felt much longer—he closed his eyes.

"All right," he said quietly. "I'm in."

I smiled as a dam-burst of relief and excitement swept through me. Hooke gave a growl of exultant laughter, clapped Alex on the shoulder,

231

and shook him roughly until he cracked a reluctant smile too.

"So when will we do this?" Lily asked.

"Well," Hooke said, looking at me, "that depends on ye, lad. But if ye keep workin' as hard as ye have been, I reckon 'bout two weeks oughta be enough. Forget 'bout fishin' and all that from now on, the rest of us'll handle that—ye do nothin' but practice. E'ery day one of us'll stay here an' practice with ye. Alrigh'?"

I nodded enthusiastically, still smiling. My whole body seemed to be buzzing with excitement.

Hooke took a breath and blew it out. "Alrigh' then—I s'pose that's it for now. We'll go o'er the details later on." He put his hands on his hips and gazed toward the tunnel, jaw set determinedly. After a long moment, he said softly to himself, "Peter or me this time."

As Mariah started asking Hooke about some of the details of the plan, and Alex and Nigel started arguing about who would win in a fight, the crocodile or Steve Irwin on steroids, I noticed Lily slip into the tunnel. I followed her outside and found her walking off into the jungle.

"Hey," I said. She stopped and turned around. "You okay?"

She smiled, and her eyes sparkled—but I thought I also detected a hint of some kind of sadness in her expression. "I'm much more than okay," she said. "I just felt like walking."

"You wanna be alone?"

Her smile widened. "Not at all."

I smiled too. We started walking side by side.

"So what exactly are you gonna do after we get Peter?" I asked curiously.

She shrugged. "I'll just take him back to my village."

"And they'll take you back? Like, you won't be banished any-more?"

She laughed. "They won't just take me back. They'll welcome me back as a hero. Perhaps one of the greatest heroes in my people's history."

"Well that's pretty cool. And Panther won't have a problem with any of that?"

She smiled sardonically. "Not publicly. And that's all that matters."

"Well, you must be pretty eager to get home by now, huh? Now that you've lived with Alex for more than a week?"

"I imagine I might be eager," she said, "if I was going home."

I looked over at her. She was staring forward and down, her face and eyes blank except for that hint of sorrow, which was still very faint yet now somehow overpowering.

"You don't see your village as home?" I asked.

"Home is not a place."

I looked away, and shook my head. "No, it's not," I said, half to myself. After a moment, I looked back at her. "Is it because of Panther?"

She shook her head. "No. Although he certainly doesn't help." She paused and took a slow, deep breath, still staring ahead with that same expression. "Remember I told you that . . . while we were searching for that first boy that went missing, Peter kidnapped one of the searchers, and another searcher saw it happen?"

"Yeah?"

"Well . . . that first searcher—the one he kidnapped—was my best friend. And the second one was me. I saw it happening and . . . I just watched. I choked. And looking back on it, I'm almost certain there was nothing I could have done—they were too far away and it happened too fast. But . . . 'almost certain' isn't certain at all."

I opened my mouth to say I was sorry, wishing I could say something better, something that might actually make her feel better—then she continued: "Prince Red, our leader at the time, was my oldest brother. He as well as one of my uncles died in the rescue attempt. And my mom died when Peter and his braves attacked the village. I tried to protect her—just as she tried to protect me. But . . . Peter's braves . . . there were just so many of them. Swarming everywhere. Killing everyone they could. Several of my friends died as well. I fought back as hard as I could—we all did—but . . . I could only do so much. And I saw so much more. I saw . . . children . . . burn to death."

Her voice and expression still hadn't changed, but now a single tear slipped down her cheek. I didn't even try to think of something to say. I don't think there's anything you *can* say to that.

"My home is dead," Lily said.

But then, after just a few seconds, she said, "But I know I'll find a new one eventually." And her voice, though anything but happy, was confident.

"You will," I said quietly, and smiled to myself. "I did."

We walked in silence for several seconds.

"I think we're going to succeed," Lily said, and now her voice was quiet and grim, but strong. "I think the odds are on our side that we will capture Peter. But I also think Alex is right. No matter how good a plan is, no matter how well you train, in combat, there is always an element of luck. And the more combat there is, the bigger that element is. Cap's plan is good—very clever—but with all that fighting . . . I think Peter's braves are bound to get lucky once or twice.

"But I also think—I *know*—it's worth the risk. And the sacrifice."

Chapter 26

The next day, Mariah and I stood facing each other a few yards apart in the combat-training clearing, holding our wooden swords. She'd volunteered to be the one to practice with me while the others gathered food.

"Now, just so ya know," I said in a deep, suave voice, "I am extremely talented with this long, hard shaft."

Mariah smiled scornfully. "Ricky—you couldn't last one minute with me."

I laughed. "Yeah, well . . . I guess we'll just have to practice a lot then, huh?"

I'd practiced very hard these past couple weeks, and though Mariah could still win almost every duel, I made her work for it. By noon, she seemed almost as exhausted as me—though we were both still fighting hard.

I swung for Mariah's knees; she swatted my blade down, pinning it to the ground, then kicked it out of my hand. It landed a few yards to my right. I turned to lunge for it but Mariah quickly jumped in front of me and pointed her blade at my chest. I stumbled back.

"You can't *kick* my sword!" I exclaimed laughingly. "If that was a real blade you would have cut your foot!"

She laughed. "Ricky, if these were real blades, you would have been dead hours ago."

I stopped and thought about that for a moment. "Well, in that case—"

I lunged forward, grabbed her sword, and yanked it toward me. I was trying to pull it out of her hand, but she managed to hold on and got pulled forward herself. She stumbled into me, and I instinctively caught her in my arms—

And we froze. Time itself seemed to freeze. We were both breathing hard, our hot, sweaty bodies pressed tightly together, our faces inches apart, my arms around her waist, hers slung over my shoulders. After a surprised moment, I laughed uneasily, and she blushed a bit . . . but neither of us pulled away from each other's arms, nor looked away from each other's eyes.

It felt like a dream, like a scene from a particularly corny romance movie, too cliché, too picturesque, too perfect to be real— until someone punched my upper arm. I started and looked over my shoulder. Alex walked by, holding a bunch of bananas, grinning demonically. "Touché," he said, and winked. Without pulling away from me, Mariah swung her sword at him. He jumped out of the way and shuffled off into the jungle, cackling.

I looked back at Mariah and time froze again. She looked exactly how I felt: nervous—but not unpleasantly so—and breathless with desire.

I swallowed hard and said, somewhat hoarsely, "Something witty and romantic."

She smiled quizzically. "What?"

"Isn't that what I'm supposed to say?"

After a moment, she said softly, "I don't think you're supposed to say anything."

Like a lot of guys, I think, I'd often worried I wouldn't have the nerve to kiss a girl even if the opportunity smacked me in the face—or fell into my arms. But now a sudden, powerful impulse seized me, and I acted almost without thinking. My stomach fluttering, I slowly slid my hand up her firm, slender back and cupped her neck. Very slowly, I pulled her head toward mine. Her eyes slid closed and her lips parted a fraction. I leaned my head forward, tilting it a little, and just as our lips were about to meet, I closed my eyes—

Suddenly she stiffened, gave a sort of strangled gasp as if someone had poured freezing water on her, and twisted out of my arms. She half staggered a few paces and stood with her back to me, one hand touching a tree as if to steady herself.

The sensations that had seemed so pleasant a moment ago suddenly seemed jarringly magnified. "What?" I asked almost frantically, thinking I must have done something horribly wrong, my mind scrambling to figure out what it was. "What's wrong?"

No response.

"Mariah, what's wrong?" I pressed louder, my anxiety rising fast. "What did I do?!"

"No, it wasn't you, it's . . . I just . . . I'm sorry."

"Why? Sorry for what?"

"I just . . . I can't . . ."

My anxiety stalled; my mental gears seemed to be struggling to turn. "Can't what? Kiss me?"

She gave a pained sigh. "Look, I just don't wanna start anything like this right now, okay? It's just . . . it's too much pressure."

"What do you mean, pressure?" I said, almost pleadingly. "I'd never pressure you to do anyth—"

She spun around, her eyes pleading for understanding. "You just tried to kiss me, Ricky! You don't think that puts pressure on me?!"

"But you wanted to kiss me too! You closed your eyes and opened your mouth and everything!"

"But what if I hadn't really wanted to, huh? What happens when I don't wanna do something?"

It probably shouldn't have surprised me at all, but the realization hit me so hard I took a step back, my mouth falling open. "Jesus Christ. You still think I might rape you, don't you?"

She opened her mouth but her lips trembled. She pursed them and quickly turned away, looking close to tears.

"Don't you?" I said louder, anger creeping into my voice.

"I'm sorry," she said quietly, miserably. "It's not your fault, I just . . . I'm not ready. Not yet. Not here."

I felt like I should be angry, I *wanted* to be angry—I'd always treated Mariah as best I knew how and had done absolutely nothing to deserve her distrust—but I knew I couldn't hold it against her, and seeing the pain on her cute face pierced my anger like a balloon. I looked away and said sadly, half to myself, "There's only a couple weeks left."

Suddenly her lip curled into a sneer. "Yeah," she said acidly. "Perfect relationship for a guy, isn't it? A built-in two-week time limit. No commitment required."

Now the anger returned full force. "Exactly," I said with furious, disgusted sarcasm. "I'd just fuck you for a couple weeks and never have to see you again. Hit it and quit it, baby. That's my fucking mantra."

She glared at me defiantly. "Do you wanna have sex with me?"

That threw me so off balance that my anger seemed to slide right off of me. I opened my mouth but wasn't sure how to respond. My first instinct was to say no, but I figured that would be blatantly disingenuous. So, after thinking about it for a couple seconds, I told her the truth. "I think you're very attractive, Mariah, so yeah, I guess that means I'd like to have sex with you. But I never expected to. I always figured you wouldn't want to."

"Well if you know I won't have sex with you, why do you wanna be with me so bad?"

"'Cause being with someone isn't just about sex!"

"Then what is it about, Ricky?" she asked challengingly. "What's the difference between 'being with' someone but not having sex, and just being friends?"

I opened my mouth—but then realized I didn't know the answer. At least not one I could articulate offhand. I looked away, thinking. After a moment, I said, "It's that secret ingredient."

"Ah," she said sarcastically. "So you don't know what it is. How convenient."

"But I know it's there," I said earnestly. "You said yourself, you're not supposed to know what it is, you just know it when you feel it."

"I did say that. But under the circumstances . . . I want something more concrete."

I smiled tentatively. "I don't suppose you'd accept a penis joke?"

She didn't laugh. "What do you really want, Ricky?" she asked softly. "If it's not sex, what is it?"

For close to a week I'd been thinking a lot about whether I wanted to "be with" her—but I'm not sure I'd ever really thought about what exactly that meant. What I wanted specifically.

What I wanted most was her friendship—but I already had that. On an undeniable biological level, I wanted to have sex with her—but I'd always known that wasn't going to happen. I wanted to hold her hand, hug her, kiss her—but that was relatively minor.

I looked down at my feet, thinking hard. It was like I could *feel* the answer, I just couldn't verbalize it. Finally, though, after almost ten seconds, I gave it a shot.

"I guess what I want more than anything is for you to be happy,"

I said, still looking at my feet. "'Cause I like seeing you happy. I like seeing you smile and laugh and . . . ya know . . . otherwise express being happy. And if we were together—even though I'm not exactly sure what that means—I think—or at least, I thought—you'd be happy. But . . . if you really, truly don't want to be together . . . well, then . . . I don't either."

Mariah said nothing. After a few seconds, I hesitantly looked up at her. She was gazing at me almost lovingly—and maybe she did love me, at least in some way, at least in that moment. But the love in her expression was mixed with pain and helplessness, as though she hated doing what she was doing, but she had to do it.

"Thank you," she said softly, almost whispering. And a well-timed tear slipped down her cheek.

Then, taking a shaky breath, she turned around and walked off into the jungle.

I couldn't move. I couldn't think. I could barely even breathe, due to a lump in my throat. I could only stand there, staring helplessly after her. It felt like there was an aching void in my chest, as if she'd physically ripped my heart out, or at least a chunk of it.

After maybe five minutes, Alex strode into the clearing, whistling cheerily. When he saw me and my expression, he recoiled a bit and stopped whistling, taken aback. He turned in a circle, presumably looking for Mariah, then cocked an eyebrow at me. "She dump you already?"

I smiled thinly. "We were never together."

"You two looked pretty damn 'together' when I walked up. What the hell happened?"

"Long story short . . . she rejected me."

He pursed his lips and clapped me on the shoulder sympathetically. "Sorry, man. But look at it this way—would you really want a girlfriend who knows how to handle a sword?"

I smiled to myself. "You prefer to handle your own sword?"

"Definitely."

He didn't get it. My smile widened. "Well, after a year on an island with two other guys, I'm sure you're a . . . *master*."

He nodded proudly. "Damn right I am. And what the hell are you smiling about? I'll beat you any day."

I guffawed. "You'd like that, wouldn't you?"

"Yeah, actually, I wou—" He broke off, understanding finally dawning on his face. His eyes narrowed. "You're an asshole."

"Does that turn you on?"

His eyes narrowed more. "You keep laughing I'm gonna stab you."

"Yeah, you'd like to penetrate me with your sword, wouldn't you?"

He opened his mouth, hesitated a moment, then grudgingly closed it—he knew he couldn't recover. "You're just lucky you're in a fragile emotional state," he said finally, and then he walked away, leaving me slumped against a tree, howling with laughter.

When my laughter finally faded, I found that some of my shock and pain had faded as well. Thus, no longer jammed by emotional overload, my mental gears started turning.

How would Mariah act when she got back? How should I act? How did she want me to act? Should I pretend like nothing had happened, or talk to her about it? Or maybe just keep my distance for a while? None of these options jumped out at me as the right way to go. So I decided to just wait to see how Mariah acted and then go from there.

I wondered, with a mix of apprehension and dejection, what would become of our relationship in the next couple of weeks. In my mind, there was no question there would be permanent damage—the question was, how much? At best, our relationship would go back to *almost* what it had been before, only now the specter of today's incident would hang between us, a sheer yet impervious veil of awkwardness. At worst, things between us would be or grow so awkward that we wouldn't even like being around each other, and our friendship would largely crumble.

Awkwardness—that was the primary adversary.

How to beat it?

I trudged back to the burrow, and was talking to Hooke and Lily about an hour later when Mariah dropped in. Our eyes locked immediately. She half opened her mouth, hesitated a beat, looking faintly anxious, then looked away and down. My heart drooped.

Mariah walked across the burrow and sat down on a quilt not far from Nigel, who had a half-eaten banana in each hand, the rest of the bunch sitting beside him. Nigel said something to Mariah, she laughed and said something back, and they started chatting. For what felt like an hour, I continued talking to Hooke and Lily while Mariah continued talking to Nigel. (In between pitches of his coconut, Alex, ever the asshole, kept looking back and forth between me and Mariah, looking mildly amused, as if watching a tennis match.) I couldn't help glancing over at Mariah once or twice or maybe thirteen times a minute, and though our eyes never met, I had a feeling she was periodically glancing at me too.

Finally, Hooke got up and said it was time to "stop prattlin' and start battlin'." I said I wanted just a few more minutes of rest; as I'd hoped, Mariah said likewise; my heart perked up a little. The others all went with Hooke.

As soon as they'd disappeared up the tunnel, Mariah got up, walked over, and sat next to me.

I reached over and patted her left shoulder, the one closest to me. "I like this shoulder."

She smiled at me slightly, quizzically. "As opposed to the right shoulder?"

"No. As opposed to the *cold* shoulder."

She looked away and lightly elbowed my upper arm. "You were giving it right back."

"I was just waiting for you to come talk to me."

"Well I was just waiting for *you* to come talk to *me*."

I grinned at her. "Last time I took the initiative it didn't turn out that great."

She hung her head as though chastened. After a moment, she said, "Are you mad at me?"

Her voice was jokingly cute and childlike, but I knew the question was serious.

I put my arm around her shoulders. "I'm way too shallow to be mad at a girl this cute."

And already I thought I'd found the right way to go, the way to beat the awkwardness: that teenage cure-all—or at least treat-all—humor.

And the next few days proved me right. Rather than discuss the incident or try to pretend to forget about it, I made fun of it. I teased her about rejecting me—always in completely good humor, being very careful never to seem bitter (which I really wasn't at all) or be hurtful. For example, that first day, when she and I joined the others at the clearing and were preparing to duel, I said, "Now, just so you know, now that you rejected me, I'm not gonna let you win anymore." And she laughed.

She also reciprocated. While we were fighting, my foot slipped into a hole in the ground and I fell flat on my face, and she immediately said, "See, you don't need me to kiss, Ricky, you got the ground."

Alex and Nigel, who had stopped fighting to see if I was all right/laugh at me, snickered.

"The ground's better than you anyway," I said, wincing and getting up.

Mariah gave a knowing, condescending smile. "Let me guess. It can only break your bones, not your heart?"

"It lets you walk all over it?" Nigel suggested.

"It never talks?" Alex said.

"No," I said. "As I've just proven, it lets me in its holes."

Alex and Nigel burst into laughter.

"Wow," Mariah said, smiling despite herself. "And to think I almost kissed that mouth."

I also made fun of my liking her. I often mock-flirted with and hit on her, either acting ridiculously over-romantic or using crass sexual innuendo. And again, much to my enjoyment, she reciprocated.

So, at least as far as I could tell, humor proved an effective cure for the awkwardness, and largely as a result, our relationship made a quick, full recovery.

And in fact, in at least one way, I thought our relationship actually got better than it ever had been. I'd always been very comfortable with Mariah, more comfortable than with any other girl I'd ever known—but only now did I realize the extent to which I'd been self-conscious. Now both my feelings for her and her unwillingness to be with me were out in the open, and although that sucked in many ways, it was also liberating.

Beyond our relationship, I decided it was very good that Mariah had rejected me. And that wasn't just something I was telling myself to make myself feel better. In fact, I was kind of pissed at myself for having even considered getting into a relationship. My time, energy, and attention—my life, really—should be devoted to combat training.

And now it was—Mariah's rejection had jump-started my motivation. I practiced fighting every day from the moment it was light enough to see each other to the moment it wasn't; I rested for about an hour at midmorning, midday, and midafternoon; other than that,

I fought almost constantly, never resting more than a few minutes. My conditioning quickly surpassed everyone else's—so much so that by the second week, the others had to take turns fighting me because no one could keep up with me long enough to tire me out. My skills still lagged behind the others', simply because they had so many more total hours of practice. But with every strike, parry, and feint, I got better.

And I got more eager.

Chapter 27

And suddenly it was the night before the raid.

As we lay down in our quilts, fear, excitement, sorrow, joy, and God knows what other emotions got together inside me and decided to have a melee.

Melees, especially when they're inside you, are not conducive to sleep. So after lying there for a while, I went outside and stood leaning against the tree, stargazing absently, waiting to see which emotion would prevail, if any.

A couple minutes later, Mariah trudged out of the tunnel, yawning. "What's up?" she asked.

"Think about that question," I said. "Do you really want me to answer it?"

She rolled her eyes but smiled a little. "Can't sleep?"

I snorted like that was a stupid question. "Why would I wanna sleep when I could be up here with you?"

She cocked an eyebrow. "How'd you know I wasn't sleeping?"

I snorted again. "Why would you wanna sleep when you could

be up here with me? Rhetorical question," I quickly added, because she'd opened her mouth to answer.

She smiled and stood beside me, slipping her arm around my waist. As always, her touch and closeness gave me a bit of a heady rush.

"So how ya feel?" she asked.

I blew out a breath and frowned thoughtfully. "Kinda hard to explain. My heart's beating too fast, my spine's tingling, I feel kinda breathless and dizzy . . . but I always feel like that when I'm around you."

She pushed me away in playful disgust. "God, Ricky, you're so *sappy*."

"I am not *sappy*," I said with the utmost indignation. "I'm *romantic*."

"You say tomato—"

"And so do you, 'cause if you ever actually said 'tuh-*mah*-toe,' you'd deservedly get punched in the face for sounding like a snooty prick."

"Or a British person."

I shrugged. "You say tomato, I—"

"Shut up," she said, smiling thinly and pushing me away again with one hand. Then she pulled me back by my forearm, rested her chin on my shoulder, and gazed at me with sweet concern. "Seriously, though. You all right?"

"It's my last night with you, how the hell could I be all right?"

She punched me in the chest. "I'm not kidding, Ricky."

"Neither am I." Suddenly there was a lump in my throat. I pulled Mariah in front of me and just looked at her, wanting so badly to kiss her—I'd accepted that I had no chance with her and I'd stopped feeling down about it, but that didn't mean I'd stopped wanting her. If anything, I wanted her even more. That was one thing I couldn't control.

Mariah's lips trembled and her luminous green eyes filled with tears. I hugged her tightly, pressing the side of her head against my chest, feeling her tears on my skin. The lump in my throat grew bigger

247

and bigger, making it harder and harder to breathe. Tears nipped at my eyes but I blinked them back.

I dragged in a breath and managed to speak: "Well, it's not like we're dying. We'll still be able to talk to each other whenever we want. And we'll see each other again eventually."

She nodded faintly. After a long moment she said softly, "It won't be the same, though."

I stared forward. She was right, of course—I knew from experience. It wouldn't be the same at all. Our lives would essentially be completely separate, linked only superficially by phone, Facebook, and fading memories. Soon we'd have nothing to talk about; our conversations would grow progressively more shallow, awkward, and infrequent. In a year or two—maybe even sooner—we'd be little more than acquaintances.

Mariah looked up at me, opening her mouth to say something—but then she blinked in surprise and her face filled with compassion. "Ricky," she said softly, and touched my cheek.

I smiled weakly. "I must have something in my eye."

She smiled too, but only for a moment.

I looked away, feeling a tear slide down my cheek. "Ya know," I said thoughtfully, my voice surprisingly even, ". . . I know—I know now—it's stupid to be bitter. But . . . I'll tell ya . . . I'm getting really fucking sick of losing friends."

Mariah wiped my tears away and kissed my cheek. "We're not losing each other," she said quietly.

And I'm sure she meant it with all her heart.

But I was also pretty sure she was wrong.

"Ya know what I'm gonna be doing my first day home?" Nigel said the next morning.

"Lemme take a *wild* guess," Alex said drily. "Eating."

Nigel nodded, beaming. "Damn right. I'm gonna eat and eat and eat till I can't *possibly* eat another bite. And then I'm gonna eat some more." He closed his eyes, smiling dopily. "I had a dream about it last night."

"Wow," Alex said soberly. "That is the saddest thing I've ever heard."

"Ever heard the Jonas Brothers?" I said.

Alex tipped his head toward me. "Touché."

Nigel didn't seem to hear us. "I'm gonna have pizza, cheeseburgers, hot dogs, fried chicken, French fries, onion rings, nachos—"

"Heart disease, diabetes, cancer," Alex said. "Seriously, Dread, do you have the slightest idea how bad for you that crap is?"

"So what's the first thing *you're* gonna eat?" Nigel said, and smirked. "A protein shake?"

Alex gave a *not-my-problem* shrug. "Joke all you want, but you're gonna get fat again."

"I was never *fat*," Nigel said hotly. "Just 'cause I wasn't quite as skinny as *you* doesn't—"

"I am not *skinny*," Alex exclaimed, seeming utterly scandalized. "I'm *fit*. You, on the other hand, could barely *fit* in the tunnel."

"I could barely fit in your mom's tunnel."

Alex shook his head sadly. "Always changing the subject. You're in denial, Dread."

"I'm not in *denial*, you pretentious little—"

"So now you're denying that you're in denial? That's bad, Dread. Next you're gonna be denying that you're denying that yo—"

"Would ye lads shut up already?!" Hooke snapped suddenly, scowling.

Alex and Nigel fell silent, and we all stared at Hooke in surprise. Hooke turned away, muttering to himself. The rest of us exchanged wary glances. I'd never heard Hooke snap like that before, and judging by their reactions, the others hadn't either. Under the circumstances, though, I couldn't blame him for being edgy.

Still, I wished he hadn't silenced Alex and Nigel. Their squabbles always entertained me, and today I needed the distraction—because now, in the grim silence, I inevitably started brooding over the night ahead. As I skewered another piece of fish, I couldn't help wondering whether I would meet a similar fate . . .

Trying to dispel such thoughts, I struck up a conversation with Mariah. Soon Alex, Nigel, and Lily joined in, and we spent the rest of the morning chatting. (Hooke, however, remained rather sullen.) I'd always enjoyed just hanging out together and talking like this, but today I honestly couldn't think of a single thing I'd rather be doing.

After lunch, the conversation died down, and silence reigned. I was restless, alternately lying down, sitting, standing, and pacing, feeling simultaneously light-headed with excitement and leaden with dread.

At nightfall, we cooked our fish. "The Last Supper," Nigel said with a grin. Hooke had to insist we eat, because none of us were hungry—except Nigel, who, if anything, ate even more than usual.

"Jesus, Dread," Alex said wonderingly. "You're like a human black hole."

"Better a black hole than an asshole," Nigel said. At least I think that's what he said. It was hard to tell because his mouth was so stuffed.

After dinner, the silence seemed thick and heavy, almost suffocating. Everyone avoided each others' eyes. I sat alone in a corner, staring blankly ahead. I felt more restless than ever, but whenever I tried to move, my body seemed to refuse—I wondered how the hell I was going to sword-fight when I couldn't even stand. I wanted to know how much longer we'd wait before heading out, but for some reason I couldn't bring myself to ask. My excitement was completely gone—now that the time was so near, I couldn't believe I'd ever been excited. Now only sickening dread remained, intensifying every second. I tried to think of home, of seeing my parents, but the possibility *(probability?!)* of death or serious injury crammed my mind.

Finally, after at least an hour, Hooke slowly stood up. The rest of us looked at him anxiously. In the dying fire's glow, his face looked surprisingly old, his eyes sunken. "Alrigh', lads," he said grimly. "Let's get ready."

We slung our swords and shields over our backs, stuck our knives under our rope belts, and once again covered ourselves in black war paint.

Hooke looked around at us grimly. "We all set to go?"

We nodded.

"Any questions? Concerns? Last words?"

We shook our heads.

Hooke blew out a breath. "Alrigh' then, lads—let's get the hell outta here."

We turned toward the tunnel and—

"Wait a sec," Alex said suddenly, and reached into his pocket. "I think you guys should all kiss my coconut. It'll give us good luck." Hooke, Mariah, Lily, and I kissed the coconut. When Alex thrust it at Nigel, however, Nigel averted his face, grimacing, and tried to push Alex away. Alex's eyes narrowed. "Kiss it, Dread," he said.

"I don't wanna kiss your frickin'—"

"KISS IT, DAMMIT!"

Nigel rolled his eyes and pecked it grudgingly.

Alex kissed it last and stuffed it back in his pocket, murmuring, "C'mon on, baby, don't fail me now . . ."

Chapter 28

The night was pleasantly cool. The crescent moon and the shimmering haze of stars tinged the jungle with a seemingly magical bluish glow. For the first time in weeks, the beauty of this tropical paradise overwhelmed me, and part of me suddenly wished I could stay here for the rest of my life. But that was the part of me that fear was ruling. I think.

No one spoke as we strode briskly toward the swamp in single file. I wanted to scream, *Why the fuck are we walking so fast?!*—but even if I tried to scream, I suspected my vocal cords wouldn't oblige. I tried to savor every second, to make time pass as slowly as possible, but of course, that just made it pass unusually fast.

Right after we passed the swamp, Mariah said, "All right, guys, have fun," and we returned the sentiment as she broke off from the group, angling to the left—she was going to cover the (hopefully) secret entrance. As I watched her melt into the darkness, I couldn't help wondering whether I'd ever see her again.

After maybe ten minutes—it felt more like ten seconds—we

came to the river. We fanned out side by side a couple feet apart and started walking along the bank, scanning the ground for the entrance to the croc's burrow. I was almost hoping the croc wouldn't be there, or that it had decided Hooke wasn't worth the effort and wouldn't pursue him. But as soon as I caught myself thinking this, I mentally bitch-slapped myself. This was no time for testicular atrophy.

"All right, lads," Hooke said a little quietly. "Are ye all sure you're completely ready? 'Cause once that croc's on me arse, we can't exactly call a time-out. So if there's anyth—"

There was an explosive splash just a few yards away, as loud as a thunderclap—cold water spattered my side—and out of the corner of my eye I saw a giant blur of movement. I half dashed, half bounded a few yards away, then ripped my sword out, my adrenaline blazing.

The croc was halfway onto the riverbank, its tail and hind legs still in the water. The next moment, I heard Hooke cackle delightedly and jeeringly. He was several yards off to my right, but I couldn't see him. "What a coincidence!" he called at the croc, feigning pleased surprise. "I's just lookin' for ye!"

The croc started crawling toward Hooke's voice, swinging its head back and forth.

"Wanted to know if ye's up for a stroll!"

As Hooke finished saying this, he jumped out of nowhere and stood right in front of the croc, just about ten feet away. The croc lunged at him, its jaws flying open. Hooke jumped and scurried away with a distinct spring in his step—as if it were a puppy nipping playfully at his heels and not a bus-sized crocodile.

"Splendid, I thought so!" Hooke called back at the croc as he continued running away and the croc pursued him. "C'mon, lads!" he called to us.

We didn't need prompting. All four of us were already hurrying after the croc.

The croc moved at the pace of a brisk jog. Even though obviously I'd known it could keep up with Hooke, its speed still kind of surprised me. It didn't look like it was going that fast. It wasn't really running, it was more crawling quickly. But each of its strides equaled at least several of mine, even at the speed I was running. And whereas we had to dodge constantly through the thick vegetation, the croc had to avoid only large trees, smashing effortlessly through everything else.

I was actually very glad we were going so fast. I had to concentrate intently on dodging through the jungle, and within a few minutes I started getting tired—so I was too distracted to worry much. At the same time, running kept my adrenaline pumping, so I felt ready—maybe even a little eager—for action.

It was like I was racing fear. And I was winning.

Much sooner than I'd expected, I saw the cleared strip around the base of Peter's mountain—it was a little lighter than the surrounding jungle—about a hundred yards ahead. My chest tightened as my heart rate, already high from running, kicked up another notch.

Just a moment later, I heard a Boy somewhere near the strip scream—a single, flat tone about five seconds long. It sounded like it came from the vocal cords of a teenage male human—and yet it didn't sound human at all. It sounded emotionless and somehow primeval, and it made the hairs tingle on the back of my neck. More Boys quickly echoed the first.

The croc was about twenty yards from the strip when I saw a Boy leap out of a low tree onto the croc's head. The croc thrashed its head violently—the Boy slipped and rolled off the side of its head—and the croc, never slowing, ran him over, its massive foot smashing his head into the ground.

The croc continued charging after Hooke—but in the two or three seconds it had taken for the croc to shake off the Boy, Hooke had slipped onto the croc's blind side and started back toward the rest of us.

As Boys started sprinting toward the croc from all directions, we met up with Hooke and started sneaking forward and to the left, giving the croc a wide berth. As we went, I barely breathed, my eyes darting about like a tweaker's, constantly expecting a Boy to leap out at us—but apparently all the guards in the vicinity had already rushed over to the croc. By the time we reached the strip, at least fifteen of them were swarming around and on the croc, which was thrashing and stomping about wildly.

We paused at the edge of the strip; Hooke poked his head out, glanced both ways, then dashed across; the rest of us followed a half step behind. We practically dove into the rocks at the base of the mountain and hid behind them. Just a couple seconds later I heard at least two Boys rushing down the strip toward us. Fear stabbed into my chest, and for one long moment I tensed, ready to bolt— but then they were past us, continuing down the strip, heading for the croc. I realized I'd been holding my breath and let it out in a silent sigh of relief.

We started hiking up the mountain. The sounds of the croc/ Boys battle ceased abruptly after just a couple minutes (the croc had probably fled, though it was possible the Boys had managed to kill it), and in the dead silence that followed, a branch snapping sounded like a gunshot. So we went very slowly. Time, however, still seemed to be in the fast lane. I had to struggle to focus on climbing and not let my anxious mind get ahead of me.

After at least an hour—though again it felt like much less— Hooke somehow determined we were higher than the entrance, and we began moving laterally, circling the mountain. Twenty minutes later the ledge came into view below us, awash with torchlight from the cave. Four Boys stood on the ledge, completely and inhumanly motionless, staring straight ahead, holding swords or spears at their sides; others, I knew, were inside the cave, out of sight.

I tried not to breathe as we crept closer and closer, tiptoeing as though on thin ice. It seemed impossible we wouldn't be detected—but we weren't. Finally we crouched among the rocks over the mouth of the cave, ten feet above the ledge. My heart was beating so fast my whole body seemed to be vibrating. My war paint was running with sweat, even though I felt cold.

We eased the shields off our backs and slipped our forearms through the leather loops, then quietly drew our swords. Hooke turned to us, held up the OK sign, and raised his eyebrows to show he was asking a question. We returned the OK sign in answer—in my case, a tad untruthfully. Hooke then raised three fingers and mouthed, *On three.* I took a deep, tremulous breath and gripped my sword tighter, my arms suddenly feeling like Jell-O. Hooke closed his fist and slowly raised his fingers one at a time, mouthing each number:

One.

Two.

Three.

In rapid succession we dashed forward and leapt over the edge. The instant I jumped, the drop suddenly seemed much higher than ten feet, and I half panicked, instinctively flailing my arms and legs.

The second or two I was airborne seemed to pass in slow motion. I saw Hooke land right behind a Girl, coiling his legs to cushion the impact, then spring back up and slice her head off with a savage howl. I saw Lily falling alongside and slightly below me, arms spread and long hair streaming gracefully, looking a bit like an angel. And I saw the Boy below me spin around and look up just before my feet crashed down on his shoulders. He collapsed and I tumbled forward, rolling frighteningly close to the edge.

The Boy got up first. I scrambled to my feet just as he lunged at me, raising his sword over his head and slicing downward. I recoiled, whipping my sword up. The blades clashed, knocking mine out of my hand. Before he could swing again, I brought my shield up in front of me and rammed into him as hard as I could. He stumbled back and slipped over the edge.

I quickly picked up my sword and looked around. Inside the cave, Hooke, Alex, and Lily were fighting ferociously, tearing through the swarm of Boys like whirlwinds. To my right, two Boys had Nigel backed up against the edge. Nigel dodged a spear thrust and beheaded one with a sharp chop; the other swung his sword at Nigel's neck. Nigel ducked, stepped back—and slipped over the edge.

He barely caught himself, clinging to the ledge by his arms. The Boy stepped over him—

"NO!" I shouted, and lunged at the Boy. He spun around and thrust his blade at my chest. I deflected it with my shield, swung my sword down, and severed his arm at the elbow. He quickly reached down for his sword with his remaining hand, but I easily hacked his head off.

I crouched in front of Nigel, who was struggling to climb back onto the ledge, and offered my hand. "Grab on."

"I'm all right," he grunted, swinging one leg onto the ledge. "You just—LOOK OUT!"

I spun to my left and ducked; the blade whooshed past just inches over my head. I stumbled back and raised my shield just as the Boy swung again. The blade struck so hard it split my shield and threw me onto my butt. I raised my sword defensively but the Boy kicked my arm away and—

Nigel shoved him from behind. The Boy stumbled over me and flew headfirst over the edge.

I started scrambling back to my feet—then realized the battle was over.

My ears rang slightly in the sudden silence. For a moment I just stood there, scarcely able to comprehend that the battle was over and I wasn't dead.

Then Nigel clapped me on the shoulder. "Thanks, man."

My breath escaped in a burst and my whole body slumped with relief. "Yeah, you too," I said hoarsely.

"C'mon," Nigel said.

He strode toward the cave to join the others. I followed slowly, feeling kind of unsteady—after such intense fighting, it felt alien to move in such a relaxed way. I looked around. The floor was littered with swords, spears, and dismembered bodies. The stink of rot clogged the air.

All I could think was: *Holy shit—did that all just happen?*

"E'eryone alrigh'?" Hooke asked, breathing heavily.

We looked around at each other and nodded. Hooke appeared to be completely untouched; the rest of us were bruised and bloody, but nothing serious. A wave of gratitude washed over me. Alex kissed his coconut.

Then I thought of Mariah, and fear squeezed my heart. At the moment, though, I could do nothing for her but pray.

"Alrigh', listen up," Hooke said urgently. "I'm gonna take the entrance. Ye four cover the ledge—they'll be comin' up the mountainside any time now. Got it?"

We nodded. Hooke rushed to the end of the cave and stood beside the small opening, pressing his back to the wall. Just seconds later, a Boy popped out. Hooke stuck out his leg, tripping him. The Boy fell flat on his face. Hooke stamped on his upper back and chopped off his head as casually as though chopping wood.

"You guys!" Alex called. I turned around. Alex was standing on

258

the side of the ledge, looking down. A Girl started clambering onto the ledge right in front of him. He stepped back, let her come half-way up, then swung his sword like a bat and sliced her head off. The body fell; the head landed on the ledge—Alex kicked it off.

Nigel and Lily rushed to the other side of the ledge; I joined Alex and peered over the edge. A few Boys—who had fallen off the ledge during the battle, I assumed—were already within ten yards away. Farther down, hurried movement could be heard in dozens of spots on the mountainside.

Following Alex's example, I let each Boy climb partway up, then easily beheaded him. The climbing required both hands, so the Boys were virtually defenseless. One, however, grabbed my ankle and let himself fall, dragging me halfway over the edge before Alex reached down and severed his wrist. I scrambled back onto the ledge, pried the clammy fingers off my ankle, and flung the hand away. I peered over the brink where I would have fallen and blew out a shaky breath.

Alex clapped me on the shoulder and grinned. "You owe me one, Ricky."

"What do you want, a kiss?" I deadpanned, getting back up.

He snorted. "You'd like that, wouldn't you?"

"Yeah, but I wouldn't want your coconut to get jealous."

We'd decapitated at least thirty Boys before several of them apparently realized the direct approach wasn't working. These Boys climbed past the ledge and then jumped down on us from over the mouth of the cave, just as we had done in the initial attack. The first one blindsided us and would have killed Nigel or Lily if Hooke hadn't shouted a warning; but once we were expecting the attacks from above, it was easy to defend ourselves accordingly.

As Hooke had predicted, the Boys never coordinated them-selves—each Boy simply attacked whenever he happened to reach us. It reminded me of an action movie, where the hero—preferably

Chuck Norris—is encircled by a ridiculous number of bad guys, who conveniently attack one at a time. (Not that it mattered, of course—even if they attacked all at once, Chuck Norris would still roundhouse-kick their collective ass.)

Finally, we killed what we thought was the last Boy. After fifteen Boy-free minutes, we joined Hooke by the entrance.

"How many Boys you get?" Nigel asked Hooke.

"Five," Hooke said. "And all a' them came in the first minute or two."

"You think there's still more in there?" Alex asked.

Hooke shrugged. "No way to know. I been listenin' for a while and I ain't heard nothin', but that certainly don't mean they ain't in there."

"Did Peter ever try to get out?" I asked.

Hooke shook his head.

"Did you see him at all?" I asked. "Or hear him?"

"Nah, but don't worry, lad: He's in there. If he'd escaped, he woulda flown o'er here to lead his Boys."

In my mind I suddenly saw Mariah huddled in that claustrophobic chamber beneath the tunnel, beating back Peter and a horde of Boys, but getting tired . . .

"Well then let's hurry up and get that fucker, huh?" I said.

"Right ye are, lad," Hooke said. "I think ye four should go; I can handle Peter all by meself if I have to, so I'll stay here, cover the entrance."

I removed a torch from its bracket on the wall, and suggested that only I carry a torch so that the others would have both hands free to fight; they agreed.

"Head for the back entrance first," Hooke said. "And be ready for anythin'. I don't know if Peter'll just come righ' at ye or try somethin' tricky, but he ain't gonna go without a fight."

I held the torch out toward the opening and peered into the tunnel, moving my head around to look from different angles. Seeing nothing, I dashed through the opening and quickly looked around again, my sword raised, half expecting Peter or a Boy to leap out at me—but nothing happened, and I saw nothing.

Alex, Nigel, and Lily quickly squeezed in behind me. I held the torch out in front of me, lighting a short stretch of the tunnel. About twenty yards ahead was a dim glow from another torch beyond a bend. In between was a wall of total blackness.

"Christ," I murmured.

"What?" Alex deadpanned. "You scared of the dark, Ricky?"

"When there's fucking *zombies* in the dark, yeah," I said.

"Shall we go?" Lily said pleasantly.

I took a breath and started walking; the others huddled around and behind me. My fear for Mariah easily eclipsed my personal fear, so I walked fast.

I kept the torch out in front of me, my eyes sweeping the edge of the darkness as it crept away from the advancing torchlight. Adrenaline hummed through my veins like a high-voltage electric circuit. My muscles felt like a tightly drawn bowstring, ready if not eager to snap into action. I was constantly expecting something to leap out at me from the darkness—my torchlight only extended about fifteen feet ahead, so I'd have very little warning.

The air seemed to get colder as we plunged deeper into the mountain. That periodic, echoing drip of water somehow emphasized the tunnel's bleakness. There were no sounds of combat—which was either a good sign or an unspeakable one.

A Lost Girl suddenly jumped out of a recess in the wall and lunged at me, swinging her sword at my head. I stumbled back and raised my sword; her blade batted mine away. Before she could swing again I drove the tip of the torch into her head, knocking her off balance, smothering the flame. Instantly darkness swallowed us.

I could still see the Girl's outline, just barely. I dropped the torch, gripped my sword with both hands, and swung wildly, as hard as I could. Largely by luck, the blade hacked straight through her neck. The body collapsed.

"Ricky?!" Alex was shouting frantically. "Ricky, you all right?!"

"Yeah, I'm fine," I gasped. I slumped against the wall and pressed a hand to my chest. My heart was hammering so hard it felt like my rib cage might crack. "Jesus *Christ*, that was close."

"I can't see anything," Lily said nervously.

"Let's go back and—" I started to say, but broke off. It had been so barely perceptible that it took me another beat to consciously process it. A few of my hairs had brushed across my forehead, as if from a very light breeze—as if—

My breath caught.

"LOOK OUT!" I yelled. I flailed my free hand blindly overhead but struck nothing. An instant later Lily cried out, either Alex or Nigel grunted in pain, there was a thud as a body slammed against either the ground or a wall, and a sword clattered to the ground. I looked around frantically, my sword raised, but could see only shifting darkness. Then a body rammed into me, knocking me onto my butt. I quickly scrambled back to my feet, straining to see.

Then Peter spoke, loudly but calmly, from five or ten yards up the tunnel: "I got Nigel. Ya come any closer, I slit his throat."

A huge, horrible sinking feeling filled my chest, as though my heart and lungs were imploding. At that moment, though, I think only a small part of me fully realized just how bad our situation had just become; the rest of me was still jacked up on adrenaline.

"Alex, Lily, you all right?" I said, still looking toward Peter and Nigel.

"I'm fine," Lily said.

"Dread, you all right, man?!" Alex called anxiously.

I heard a faint wheeze, which I assumed was Nigel trying to speak. I could now just make out a dark mass shaped roughly like two humans standing close together, about ten yards ahead. Without thinking about it, I took a step forward; Alex and Lily followed; Peter and Nigel took a step back.

"Nigel's a tad short a' breath at the moment," Peter said lightly. "So allow me to speak for him: You let me get outta here, and I'll let him go."

"All right, fine," I said immediately, trying to sound desperate; I sensed both Alex and Lily look at me sharply; I ignored them. "Just don't hurt him and we'll all get outta your way."

Peter chuckled, seemingly good-naturedly. "Nice try, mate. I daresay James and Mariah are waitin' back at the entrance?"

"No they're not, I swear," I said pleadingly, "they both got killed in the fight!"

"Ya na a bad liar, mate, but na good enough."

I took another instinctive step forward, Alex and Lily followed; Peter took another step back, dragging Nigel with him. I could now see that Peter was standing behind Nigel, gripping his hair and holding a knife to his throat.

Then Nigel spoke, his voice strained and slightly wheezy: "If you let him go, we might never get him again. Even if you ha—"

Peter quickly punched the hilt of his knife into Nigel's stomach—Nigel gave a breathless grunt and fell silent—then snapped the blade back up to Nigel's throat. My hand tightened on my sword in rising fury and frustration. Alex, Lily, and I continued walking slowly forward; Peter continued walking back.

"Here's what's gonna happen," Peter said. "The five a' us are gonna walk slowly back to the entrance. You're gonna call James and Mariah into the tunnel, and ya all gonna put ya weapons down.

263

Then we're all gonna walk slowly back to the fork in the tunnel, and you're gonna go down one a' the branches so I can get past ya. Soon as I get to the entrance, I let Nigel go."

"Bullshit," Nigel spat vehemently with obvious exertion. "You'll just kill me."

"No I won't," Peter said. "I don't wanna antagonize you lot any more 'n I have to, 'cause if ya ever catch me again—and I gotta hand it to ya, that's seemin' more and more likely—I want as much mercy as I can get."

"But if you kill me," Nigel said, "that's one—"

Peter gave Nigel's hair a sharp yank and spoke over him: "But as I'm sure you'll understand, I can only show mercy if ya cooperate. So listen up: I'm gonna give ya 'bout thirty more seconds to decide ya wanna cooperate. If ya still haven't decided by then, I'll have to start cuttin' Nigel up, bit by bit—and I'll just keep cuttin' and cuttin' till either ya decide or he dies."

Still walking back, Peter and Nigel were now moving into the light of a torch on the wall. Peter's tousled blond hair and slitted, glinting blue eyes peeked over Nigel's shoulder. There was a little blood smeared on Nigel's throat from the blade cutting the skin.

But I detected no hint of fear or pain or even anger on Nigel's face. His expression was faintly sad, almost wistful, but otherwise unnaturally serene.

"Think about all the other kids he'd kill, you guys," Nigel said, his voice matching his expression. "Think about their families—and yours."

Peter gave Nigel's hair another yank, pressed the blade harder against his skin, and said through gritted teeth, "Shut up."

Nigel didn't even seem to notice Peter. "This is bigger than us. Bigger than me."

And suddenly I realized where Nigel was going with this—and

every part of me seemed to lock up; suddenly I couldn't move, speak, breathe, think.

"Nigel, take it easy, man," Alex said anxiously, his voice trembling slightly.

As Nigel opened his mouth to speak again, Peter slammed the hilt of his knife into Nigel's stomach again, then quickly returned the blade to his neck. Nigel grunted, but he must have flexed his abs for the blow, because he spoke again right away.

"Just let me go," he said vehemently, speaking to Alex, Lily, and me, his voice hoarse and slightly breathless from the pain. "Rush him."

"Nigel—!" Alex half shouted, half gasped in an agony of terror and helplessness.

"Rush him!"

Peter's hand whipped down and he jammed the blade into the front of Nigel's thigh, then again quickly returned it to his throat. Nigel jerked violently and shrieked, his face contorting in agony, a dark stain spreading rapidly through his shorts.

"NIGEL!" Alex shouted.

"Just do it!" Nigel cried desperately.

"*NO*, NIGEL!"

"Do it *NOW*!"

The next moment seemed to pass in super slow motion. I saw Nigel's hands fly up and grip Peter's forearm, the one with the knife. I felt my whole body explode into motion, launching me down the tunnel toward Nigel and Peter, accelerating as fast as I possibly could but already knowing it wasn't fast enough. I sensed Alex and Lily on either side of me also lunge into desperate, all-out dashes. I saw the muscles in both Nigel's and Peter's arms stand out as Nigel tried to pull the knife away from his throat and Peter tried to plunge it in. I saw them both grimacing fiercely, gritting and baring their teeth, and heard them both half groaning, half howling with desperate exertion.

And I saw the blade slice into the skin of Nigel's throat. Saw the line of blood form.

Then the next moment—when I was on just my second or third stride—I saw a figure burst out of the darkness right behind Peter and slam the hilt of a knife into the base of his skull.

Peter instantly went limp and folded to the floor, unconscious. Nigel slumped against the wall and looked down at Peter, then up at his savior in shock. Alex, Lily, and I sprinted up to them.

"How's that for karma," Mariah said.

Chapter 29

"Jesus Christ, man, your throat," Alex said anxiously, reaching a hand out tentatively toward Nigel's throat.

Nigel shook his head as he pressed both hands against the front of his thigh. "My throat's fine—he just got into the skin, it's not deep. But my *leg*." He fired off a five-second burst of swearing so rapid it would have put Hooke to shame. "He stuck it in fucking *deep*."

Despite his obvious anxiety, Alex grinned. "That's what she said."

Nigel gave him a distinctly not-amused look.

"Oh come on," Alex said. "Laughing will make you feel better."

"What does that have to do with your jokes?" Nigel said.

Alex pushed Nigel's hands off the wound and peered into it, moving his head around to look from different angles.

A few seconds passed in tense silence.

"How's my prognosis?" Nigel said.

"I don't know," Alex murmured, still peering intently into the wound.

Nigel looked like he had a tiny heart attack. "You don't know how bad it is?"

"No," Alex said, "I don't know what a prognosis is. But you should be all right. The bleeding's already slowed way down. Just keep pressure on it."

Nigel let out a breath of relief and looked at Mariah. "You saved my life, Mariah. Thank you."

"Don't mention it," she said. "You're just lucky I heard you guys screaming. By the way, Alex, you scream like a girl."

"Yeah, well, you *are* a girl," Alex retorted.

"Oh snap," Mariah said drily.

"Hey you guys, c'mon," I said, "let's get Peter tie—"

I broke off as I looked at Peter. His wrists were bound, there was a collar around his neck with a leash, and Lily was just finishing binding his ankles.

Alex and I interlocked our arms with Peter's and started dragging him down the tunnel. Lily held the leash, Mariah a torch; they both kept their swords out and watched our tail, just in case. Nigel hobbled along in front of us. With his limp, his scowl, and his occasional rapid-fire bursts of vulgarity, he could have been a rapper.

Coming up to the entrance about ten minutes later, we heard Hooke call anxiously, "That you, lads?"

"No, it's Peter," Alex called back.

"Did ya get him?!"

Nigel ducked out of the opening, followed by me. Hooke didn't even seem to notice Nigel's condition, and seemed to see straight through me. Then I dragged Peter through the opening, and Hooke's wide, gleaming eyes fixed on him. He smiled hungrily, looking like a pirate setting eyes on a treasure chest.

We laid Peter on the floor. Nigel and I sat on his legs; Alex and Lily pinned his arms; Mariah stood several feet away gripping the leash. Hooke knelt astride Peter's chest and started slapping his cheeks and growling, "C'mon, ye little bugger, wake up . . . wake *up* . . ."

After about ten seconds, Peter's eyelids started fluttering open. Immediately Hooke clamped both hands around Peter's throat and squeezed seemingly as hard as he could, the veins in his arms standing out. Peter's eyes bulged in terror and he started struggling—but with five of us holding him down, I barely felt his efforts.

"Well look who's up," Hooke said coolly—then slammed the back of Peter's head against the floor. Peter's eyes rolled a little and appeared to lose focus.

This violence didn't bother me at all. Nor did it appear to bother the others. Peter's pain gave me no pleasure, but I figured, as Hooke and the others presumably did, that the rougher we handled Peter, the less he'd resist. Besides, he certainly didn't deserve any leniency.

Hooke continued choking Peter, his jaw set. After several more seconds, Peter's struggles started weakening.

"Don't kill him, Cap," I said warningly.

Finally Hooke loosened his grip; Peter sucked in a long, wheezing breath, then started coughing violently.

"Let's skip the rest a' the formalities, shall we?" Hooke said courteously. "Ye know the deal: Ye give me the powers, or I start takin' body parts."

"I wasn't lyin' last time," Peter gasped, "I *can't* just *give* ya my—"

Hooke slammed Peter's head against the floor again. Peter gave a soft moan and his eyelids fluttered for a moment as he flirted with unconsciousness.

"Ya're gonna kill me, you idiot," Peter half mumbled, half gasped, his speech slightly slurred.

"Ye'll be wishing that soon," Hooke said, and he drew his knife and pointed it at Peter's face. He moved the blade in little circles, as if teasingly. "I'm gonna give ye ten seconds to decide ye wanna start cooperatin', and if ye don't, I'm gonna surgically remove your eye, ye understand? Good. Ten . . . nine . . . eight . . ."

Hooke started slowly lowering the knife. Peter turned his face away, pressing the side of his head against the floor, and glared forward determinedly. His jaw muscles stood out as he gritted his teeth.

". . . seven . . . six . . . five . . ."

Peter started breathing louder and faster and his head started shaking slightly as though from exertion—perhaps from trying to press his head through the floor. He squeezed his eyes shut. I felt somewhat sick, but didn't look away.

"Four . . . three . . . two . . ."

The tip of the blade touched Peter's eyelid.

"ALRIGH', I'LL DO IT!" Peter shouted. "I'll do it."

"Splendid," Hooke said pleasantly, smiling, and withdrew the knife; Peter let out a small, shaky breath of relief. "Now, it's up to ye, but I'd strongly recommend ye not try anythin' tricky like ye did the last time, 'cause even if—"

"It's in my pocket," Peter said, his voice sullenly flat, his eyes still closed.

Hooke's eyes narrowed suspiciously. "What'd ye say?"

"Just reach into my pocket and you'll get what ya want."

Hooke's eyes narrowed further. "Your powers are in your pocket?"

"The source a' my powers, yeah. My right pocket. It's a little pouch."

We all looked at the right pocket of Peter's shorts. There was a slight bulge in it. I suddenly remembered how, when we'd first captured Peter and I'd been holding his right leg down, he'd kept bending his knee. Now I understood: He'd been drawing my hand toward his knee, away from his pocket.

Hooke got off Peter's chest and peered into the pocket. After several seconds, he very slowly reached his hand into it and pulled out a tan, leather, drawstring pouch, not much bigger than a large tea bag, grasped delicately in his fingers.

"There's something moving in there," Mariah said softly, almost whispering.

For a couple seconds I didn't see what she was talking about. Then, with a jolt, I noticed the pouch bulge very slightly in one spot—as if something had pushed out against the inside of it. After another few seconds, the pouch bulged again in a different spot.

"What is it?" Hooke asked quietly, half suspiciously, half wonderingly.

"There's no word for it in your language," Peter said. "But I s'pose the closest word would be 'fairy.'"

Looking like he was in a trance, Hooke started bringing his other hand toward the pouch, but Peter quickly said, "Don't open it yet. It could get out."

Hooke lowered his other hand and just stared at it, as did the rest of us. All of our mouths were ajar. The pouch continued to bulge slightly in different spots every few seconds.

"And this . . . fairy . . . is the source a' your powers?" Hooke said, never taking his gleaming eyes off the pouch. "All your powers?"

"Yeah," Peter said, his voice thick with bitterness.

"So how exactly d'ye get the powers from the fairy?"

"Well, flyin' to reality takes a lot a' power, so ya need to absorb it more directly. The fairy gives off a kind a' mist or dust that contains the power. So righ' before ya fly to reality, ya need to stick ya hand in the pouch and let some a' the dust seep in."

"We all stick our hands in?" Nigel asked.

"No," Peter said. "Only the fairy's host can absorb the dust. If anyone else sticks their hands in, nothin'll happen. But the host can share the power through touch."

"And what 'bout the other powers?" Hooke asked. "How d'ye get them?"

"The host gets all the other powers just by bein' the host—just by havin' possession a' the fairy."

Hooke's eyes widened a little more. "So does that mean—" Then he looked down—and his feet lifted slowly off the ground.

A moment passed in speechless silence as we all watched Hooke hovering a foot in the air.

Then Alex leapt to his feet, clenched his hands into fists, opened his mouth as wide as he could, and screamed like his team had just won the World Series. He pounced at Hooke and half hugged, half tackled him. Hooke caught him and fell back a little with a look of surprise, then started laughing.

The rest of us just watched this, smiling. I did feel some of the explosive excitement Alex was showing—but more than anything I felt a blissfully peaceful sense of relief. It was kind of like what I imagined I'd feel like at the end of high school. Judging by their expressions, I surmised that Nigel and Mariah felt much the same. Lily just looked happy for us—and amused at Alex's antics.

Alex finally released Hooke, plopped down next to Nigel, and slung his arm around Nigel's neck in a rough one-armed hug. Nigel immediately started struggling—I'm not sure whether because he was uncomfortable with such a display of affection, or because Alex was crushing his windpipe. Possibly both. Alex, still beaming, didn't seem to notice Nigel's struggles.

Hooke carefully slid the pouch into his pocket, then said to Lily, "Well, lass—we got e'erythin' we need from him. He's all yours."

"You want us to help you bring him back?" I asked Lily.

"I'll be fine," Lily said, smiling. "Thank you, though."

"You sure?" I said worriedly; I didn't like the idea of Lily escorting Peter all the way to her village all by herself. I glanced at Peter; he was staring at the ceiling like he wanted to kill it, seeming completely unaware of everything going on around him.

"Quite sure," Lily said, her smile widening reassuringly. "He can't fly and he's unarmed and tied up—what could he do?"

I thought of Lily's combat skill on top of what she'd just said, and figured she was right. I nodded, albeit somewhat reluctantly.

Lily looked around at us and opened her mouth but hesitated a moment, looking bashful. "I don't know how to thank you all," she said quietly.

"Well I'm sure we could all say the same to ye, lass," Hooke said. "So let's just call it even, ay?"

Lily nodded and looked down at her feet. After a long moment, she said, "I don't know how to say good-bye, either."

There was just a second or two of sad silence. Then I hopped to my feet, went up to Lily, and gave her a rather epic hug, lifting her off the ground and spinning around three times. Lily laughed delightedly and hugged me tightly back.

As I put her down and we released each other, I said, "Have fun being a hero."

She smiled at me. "You too."

Then she hugged Nigel, then Alex, then Hooke, then Mariah.

While she and Mariah were hugging, Alex gave a loud sneeze that sounded suspiciously like "make out."

"Bless you," Mariah said to Alex. "And by that I mean 'fuck you.'"

"Same difference," Alex murmured, a tad wistfully.

Lily hugged Mariah longer than anyone else. When they finally broke apart, Lily grabbed the collar around Peter's neck and hoisted him roughly to his feet. Peter continued staring murderously into space.

Lily smiled around at us sadly. "Hopefully I'll see you again sometime."

Then she drew her knife and, pushing Peter along in front of her, walked out onto the ledge. She turned back and waved goodbye one last time; we waved back. Then she and Peter clambered down over the side of the ledge and were gone.

We remained standing there (except for Hooke, who was hovering a few inches off the ground) gazing out of the cave in silence. I'm not sure what the others were waiting for—perhaps they were reflecting on Lily, or were apprehensive about flying home, or just wanted to savor one of the last moments we'd have together on the Island. I was thinking about the last thing Lily had said, and wondering if I'd ever see her again. Presumably, with the fairy, we'd be able to fly back and forth between reality and the Island just as Peter had, so . . .

"Uhh," Nigel said, ". . . how exactly do we get back?"

We all looked at him.

"Well," Alex said, "I figured we might try flying."

"Thanks, Madden," Nigel said. "But, like—where do we aim? I don't see any signs for reality, do you?"

"Well hey Cap," I said, "didn't you say you saw Peter fly back once?"

"Aye," Hooke said. "Far as I could tell, he just flew straight up and eventually he disappeared."

"I think we should try that," I said, nodding. "Just flying straight up. 'Cause that's what he did when he flew me here too."

"Yeah, same here," Alex said, and Nigel and Mariah nodded.

Then a few seconds passed in silence. I think everyone was reluctant to be the one to set the final launch sequence into motion.

But finally Nigel said, "Well, I don't know about you guys, but I've already been waiting for about a year, so I think I'm pretty much—"

I was looking at Nigel, so I didn't see what happened, but I heard Mariah give a sort of half grunt, half cry. My head snapped to the right and I saw Mariah toppling into Alex, who caught her and fell back with a startled cry of "What the *fuck*—"

Then I saw Hooke lunging toward them, his feet dangling several inches off the ground, and sweeping his sword out.

I had no time to think; I just acted. I dove forward desperately and just managed to shove Hooke as he was bringing his sword forward and down. He hit the wall but immediately kicked off it, streaking toward me, and I had no time to do anything but stumble back—

"NO!" Alex roared, and Hooke spun around as Alex thrust his sword at Hooke's midsection. Hooke deflected it with a seemingly effortless flick of his blade and almost simultaneously swung his free hand and socked Alex in the face. Alex staggered sideways and slumped against the wall, blood spilling from his nostrils.

With a furious scream I threw myself at Hooke, ripping my sword out and driving it at his chest. He twisted out of the way—the blade missed by centimeters—and kicked my feet out from under me. I took a flying fall forward, and my temple cracked against the wall.

Pain hacked into my head like an ax, my vision doubled and went gray, and my mind seemed to go blank. It only took me three or four seconds to come to my senses and to start frantically, groggily dragging myself to my feet, but by then it was too late—Hooke had slung Mariah's limp body over his shoulder and was gliding swiftly toward the ledge, and he was already too far away. I could do nothing but watch in agonizing despair. Nigel, crippled by his hurt leg, lurched at Hooke and flailed his sword at him, but Hooke simply gave him a wide berth and kept flying.

And then there was nothing in his way. In just another second or two he'd be out of the cave, on the ledge, in the open air, and then he could simply fly away, and we'd have no way to track or catch him, we'd probably never catch him, never see Mariah again, never get home, never—

Something about the size of a baseball suddenly streaked past me from behind and slammed into the back of Hooke's head with a sharp *THUNK*. Hooke dropped to his feet, staggered forward a couple steps, then crashed to the floor, just a few feet from the end of the ledge.

Beside him, rolling in a pool of milky liquid, was a split coconut.

Chapter 30

A long moment passed in stunned silence. I just stood there, my ears ringing as though an explosion had gone off nearby, my eyes flicking back and forth between Alex's well-named lucky coconut and the not-so-lucky Hooke. I knew why Hooke had done it—I think I'd known as soon as I saw him lunging toward Alex and Mariah—but it was still very hard to believe.

Hooke's arm moved.

"*Shit!*" I said, and started sprinting toward him as fast as I could, half certain he was going to fly away before I could get to him—but as I approached, I saw that his eyes were closed. I pounced on him anyway, pinning him down. He grunted when I hit him, but apparently remained unconscious.

An instant later Alex slid to a stop alongside me. He took the pouch out of Hooke's pocket and slid it into his own, then grabbed Hooke's wrists.

As Nigel came hobbling and swearing after us, Mariah dragged herself into a sitting position with a soft moan, looking bewildered. "What the hell just happened?"

"Cap knocked you out and tried to fly away with you," I said.

"*What?!* What the hell's going on?!"

Before I could answer, Hooke started stirring.

"Mariah," I said urgently, "come over here and hold his legs down. Nigel, you too."

Mariah and Nigel sat on his legs. I drew my knife and cocked my arm, ready to smash Hooke with the hilt if necessary.

Hooke's eyes slid halfway open, and he peered at me blankly for a long moment. Then his eyes snapped wide. He stared at me another moment, then slowly raised his head and looked around at the others, his expression uncertainly anxious, as if he thought he might be hallucinating.

"You wanted to live forever, didn't you?" I said, cold anger starting to churn inside me. "That's why you did this, isn't it?"

"Jesus Christ," Mariah said softly. "You were gonna suck my soul out, weren't you?"

Suddenly Hooke's face seemed to crumble—from remorse? Or was he just acting? "I'm sorry, lads," he said, his voice hoarse with emotion, "I swear I am. I wish it didn't have to be this way but I knew ye wouldn't—"

"Wouldn't what?" Alex spat as though he had acid in his mouth. "Let you suck the souls out of innocent kids just like Peter did?"

"Just hear me out, lads, please," Hooke said anxiously. "Just think about it for a moment." His voice dropped slightly and became filled with an almost childlike combination of wonder and excitement. "Now that Peter's gone, the Island's e'erythin' ye dreamed of afore ye got here—it's paradise, it's freedom, it's—"

"But what about reality, Cap?" Nigel said.

Hooke's face darkened and his lip curled. "What about it?" he

278

said bitterly, scornfully. "I ain't nothin' in reality. None a' ye are." Then his voice dropped again, conspiratorially, and this time became filled with a chilling sort of hunger. "But out here, lads—out here . . . we could rule the Island." A wolfish smile tugged at his lips, and a maniacal gleam entered his eyes. "This whole world could be *ours*."

"I don't want a world," I said. "I want a home."

The hunger and excitement faded from Hooke's face, and his expression became black. "This is home," he said quietly.

Then suddenly he screamed savagely, wrenched his hands out of Alex's grip, and lunged at me, reaching for my throat. I jumped back, startled. Alex quickly grabbed Hooke's hair and yanked him back down. Hooke reached back and started clawing at Alex's face.

"HIT HIM!" Alex screamed. *"HIT HIM!"*

I lunged forward and smashed the hilt of my knife into the center of Hooke's face, both hearing and feeling a sickening crunch. Hooke slumped back to the floor, eyes closed, apparently unconscious.

Silence.

We all stared at Hooke's mutilated face. Much of it was already starting to discolor and swell, and blood flowed from his smashed nose and trickled from his lacerated upper lip. He didn't even look much like Hooke anymore.

After almost ten seconds, I said, "Well . . . if he didn't have brain damage before, you can bet he does now."

Silence again.

First had come shock—shock so extreme it had felt like someone was gripping my brain and shaking it violently. When the shock had started receding, pain and anger had started surging in.

Now, though the pain was still rising, the anger was rising much faster. And I think this was because my mind was starting to distinguish between the concepts of betrayal and deception. Betrayal is when someone who is actually your friend hurts you. Deception is when someone pretending to be your friend hurts you.

What Hooke had tried to do to us was far worse than anything one friend could do to another. We hadn't lost a friend today; we'd merely exposed a fake one. Perhaps Hooke *had* been our friend at some point—but that Hooke must have already died.

"What are we gonna do with him?" Mariah asked, her voice flat.

No one responded for a moment as we all thought about that.

"Well," Alex said, "if we take him back with us, we'd have to turn him in to the police."

Nigel cocked an eyebrow at him. "And tell 'em what? He tried to steal our fairy?"

"Yeah," Alex said soberly. "We'd have to tell the truth."

Another moment passed in gravely thoughtful silence.

"I don't think we wanna do that," Mariah said.

Alex, Nigel, and I all shook our heads in agreement.

"So we'll hand him over to the natives," I said. "That's the only other option. 'Cause we can't just let him loose on the Island, he's too dangerous."

"You guys," Nigel said grimly, his eyes fixed on Hooke's face. "I think maybe we should kill him." After a moment, Nigel looked up at us; we all just stared back. I think the idea had been lurking in the back of all of our minds. "Think about this," Nigel said. "We can tell the natives to keep him locked up forever, but he could still get out somehow. And we're thinking this fairy's the only way to get back to reality, but . . . we really don't know that. And if, somehow, he did get away from the natives and found some way back to reality . . . he'd come after the fairy. It's not likely—not at all—but . . . do you really wanna have that little bit of uncertainty, for the rest of your life?"

There was yet another moment of silence, the longest and gravest yet.

"He saved all of our lives," Mariah said, staring at Hooke with a hard expression. "Some of 'em more than once. And, I dunno, maybe the Cap that did that is already dead, but . . . in case he's not . . . I think we should give him a little bit of mercy."

We looked around at each other and nodded, albeit uneasily. Nigel looked the most uneasy—but I think he knew he didn't have the heart to kill Hooke.

"So we'll give him to the natives?" I said.

More nods.

"Yeah," Alex said, "except I don't like the idea of walking him all the way to their village ourselves. I'd rather keep him unconscious. Why don't we get the natives to come pick him up?"

"I like that idea even less," Mariah said. "We'd have to wait here with Cap until they got here, and that'd probably take at least an hour."

"So?" Alex said.

"So, I doubt every single one of Peter's Boys was at the mountain when we attacked. He probably had some around the Island searching for us. Probably quite a few, actually. At some point they'll be coming back."

"All right, here," I said, "we got some extra rope, right? Let's see if there's enough to tie Cap up to a tree or something. Then we could leave as soon as we tell the natives."

The others agreed. There was just enough rope to very securely bind Hooke's hands behind him and tie him to a tree on the mountainside. He remained, apparently, unconscious. I would have wondered if he was dead if I couldn't hear his ragged breathing.

Alex flew off to find Lily; we'd decided he shouldn't go to the village as we weren't sure how the natives would react without Lily present. The rest of us stood around Hooke in silence, swords at our sides. I was in a minor agony of anxiety—after Mariah had pointed out that there might still be Boys out there, I felt almost sure something horrible was going to happen.

But nothing did. After about fifteen minutes, Alex returned, successful.

We climbed back onto the ledge. I went to the tip of it and stood there, taking in the view, listening to the gentle rumble of the surf. A light breeze lifted my hair, carrying the fresh, salty scent of the ocean. I closed my eyes and breathed deeply. I completely forgot about Hooke as I remembered standing here several weeks ago—it seemed like years—and felt a pang of sadness, almost nostalgia.

Alex clapped me on the shoulder. "You're not thinking of jumping, are you?"

I smiled. "Nah."

"Darn. I could have pulled a Superman and saved your ass."

I laughed a little and looked down; Alex was hovering a couple inches off the ground.

A few seconds passed in silence as we both took in the Island seascape.

"Ya know what?" I said.

"What?" Alex said.

"I'm gonna miss this place."

After a beat, Alex nodded slowly. "Yeah. Me too."

"Would you two mind joining us," Nigel said from a few yards behind us, "or were you gonna kiss good-bye?"

Alex snorted as he turned around. "You'd like to see us kiss, wouldn't you?"

"Well," Nigel said drily, "I do like seeing you happy, my dear friend."

Alex took the pouch out of his pocket, and the rest of us gathered in front of him. For a moment he just held it and we all stared at it. Then, very carefully, he cracked the pouch open a tiny fraction. Wisps of what looked like luminous white powder puffed out and immediately seemed to evaporate into the air. Alex opened the pouch a little more and we all peered in.

An orb of pulsing light, about the size of a large marble, was lazily bouncing around inside the pouch like a trapped bee, continuously secreting a cloud of the powder, which continuously swirled and evaporated.

After we'd all gaped at the fairy for ten or fifteen seconds, Alex slowly lowered his left pinkie into the pouch. After several uneventful seconds, he squeezed his whole hand in, held it there for several more seconds, then pulled it out and held it up. His hand and wrist were covered in the fairy dust—it looked like there was a swirling white glow just beneath the skin.

"Looks like I just jacked off a ghost," Alex said.

We all joined hands in a circle.

"Test it out, Alex," I said. "See if you can make us hover."

Immediately I felt like my insides dropped out of my body as my weight vanished, and I felt the distantly familiar mixture of nausea and exhilaration as my feet floated up off the ground. I looked around; the others were all floating too. Alex lifted us about three feet up, then set us back down; Nigel, Mariah, and I all tottered a little as gravity seized us again.

"Well," Mariah said, "I guess we're all set then, huh?"

A few seconds passed in silence. Again it seemed everyone was reluctant to set the final launch sequence into motion. The air was thick with emotions, many of them conflicting. Joy and sadness. Relief and regret.

"All right, let's hurry up," Nigel said. "Holding Alex's hand is making me nauseous."

Alex looked around at us earnestly. "You guys ready?"

We glanced around at each other and nodded.

Alex grinned excitedly and nodded too. "All right then. Here we go."

I took a somewhat shaky deep breath, my spine tingling, my heart starting to pound.

Alex licked his lips and opened his mouth, but then hesitated a long moment. "You guys sure you're ready?"

"Yes, Alex, we're sure," Nigel said impatiently.

"All right," Alex said, nodding. "Just checking." He took a deep breath. "Here we go. Again." He swallowed hard. "Five . . . four . . . three . . . two . . . hold on a sec." He spun around and walked away from the circle.

"Alex!" Nigel exclaimed exasperatedly. "What the hell are you—oh, Christ," he rolled his eyes.

Alex picked up both halves of his lucky coconut, fitted them together, and returned to the circle. "One more kiss, you guys. For good luck." Mariah and I kissed it. Nigel rolled his eyes again but pecked it without resisting. Alex walked to the end of the ledge, kissed it loudly, then chucked it as far as he could. The halves separated and spiraled away into the darkness.

"That's sad," I said pensively. "The coconut gets a kiss good-bye and I don't."

Alex looked at me quizzically, warily. "You want one?"

"Well not from *you*, dumbass," I said.

"From me?" Mariah said with a sexy smile.

"Actually I was talking about Nigel—"

I'd been purely joking about not getting a kiss—I hadn't been trying to pressure Mariah into kissing me, and would never have expected or even hoped she might do so. So I was completely flabbergasted when Mariah stepped up to me, placed her hands below my ears, and pulled me into a kiss—and not just a peck. Her lips were warm and soft and seemed to melt into mine. I closed my eyes and put my hands on her back, holding her against me. Her tongue brushed my lips teasingly a couple times, then slipped deeper into my mouth. I slid my own tongue forward and brushed the underside of hers.

I honestly don't know how long we kissed—it might have been twenty seconds, it might have been several minutes. For me, time seemed to have stopped. Eventually, though, Alex yawned loudly and Nigel started snoring.

Mariah slowly pulled away, sucking on my bottom lip a little as she did. We stayed in each other's arms for a moment, our eyes locked. Mariah was smiling crookedly; I was gaping like a jackass, my head spinning so fast I thought I might faint.

"You're pretty good at good-byes," I said a bit hoarsely.

Mariah's smile suddenly turned sad and very faintly bitter. "Not really," she said quietly. And then, rather abruptly, she pulled away from me.

And suddenly I knew—I was quite certain—that Mariah would never have kissed me if we hadn't been about to part ways.

After Mariah withdrew, we all just stood there for a long moment in very awkward silence.

Then Alex turned to Nigel, opened his arms, and tilted his head, raising his eyebrows invitingly. Without even glancing at him Nigel deadpanned, "If you touch me I'll stab you."

"Let's get the hell outta here, huh?" Mariah said.

"Sure thing, Miss Hit-It-And-Quit-It," Alex said.

We joined hands again. I still felt dazed from the kiss; it took me a few seconds to remember what we were doing.

"You guys ready?" Alex asked, looking around at us.

We nodded.

He grinned excitedly. "All right, then. Here we go. Again. For real this time." He took a deep breath and blew it out slowly. "All right. Five . . . four—"

"Alex, just go," Nigel said impatiently.

Alex shrugged. "All right." He bent his knees, tilted his head up, and shouted, "BLAST OFF!"

Alex looked like he tried to jump—his legs snapped straight and he went up on his toes. But he didn't leave the ground. None of us did.

The residual daze from the kiss vanished instantly as horror seized me. It felt like an icy fist clenched around my insides with crushing force. Alex tried to jump again, and again, and again, each time straining harder, his expression growing more and more frantic—but he couldn't seem to leave the ground. He stopped trying and looked around at us, and we stared back at him, all of our mouths open in speechless, anguished, disbelieving pleas.

Then suddenly Alex grinned hugely. "Gotcha bitches!" he cried delightedly.

There was an instant of the most stunned and incredulous silence.

And in that instant I heard that sound again—like the softest tinkle of bells.

Then—

"You *ASSHOLE!*" Nigel screamed hysterically. "I AM GONNA FUCKING—"

But I didn't get to find out what Nigel was going to fucking do, because suddenly I was rocketing skyward at mind-blowing speed, cold air blasting my body. I looked down. Thousands of feet below, the ocean was flecked with white and glistened faintly in the moonlight; the island was solid black except for the thin, curving white line of the beach. I looked around at the others. Alex looked like he was riding a roller coaster, grinning hugely, his head thrown back. Nigel was squinting uncomfortably in the rushing air, looking almost bored. Mariah's eyes were closed, her hair streaming.

I closed my eyes too, savoring the feel of the wind buffeting my skin and whipping my hair, and the sort of physically hollow feeling inside me, as though we were going so fast that my insides had been left behind.

"I LOVE YOU GUYS!" Alex shouted suddenly over the thundering wind. Then, after a beat: "PLATONICALLY, OF COURSE."

And Nigel shouted back incredulously, "YOU KNOW WHAT 'PLATONIC' MEANS?!"

Then suddenly their hands vanished; my fingers squeezed shut on empty air. Shock and terror ripped through me as I continued rocketing skyward. I pried my eyes open and looked around frantically, but the others had vanished.

"MARIAH!" I screamed.

No response.

"ALEX! NIGEL!"

Nothing.

I looked skyward, but to my shock, the sky was gone, replaced by a dense field of countless pinpoints of orangish, artificial light. It took me a couple seconds to realize what I was seeing.

A city.

I was back in reality.

And without feeling any change in speed or direction, I was no longer rocketing skyward but plummeting straight down, headfirst.

My terror exploded into panic, and my whole body seemed to fill with adrenaline. I tried to will myself to fly, tried to *believe* I could fly as Peter had instructed so long ago, but not surprisingly, none of it worked. I even flapped my arms and legs like wings, but even less surprisingly, this just set me to tumbling sickeningly.

I couldn't fly without the fairy. Without Alex.

"AAALLEEEXX!" I screamed as loud as I could, looking around again. "HEEEELLLLLPP, AAALLEEEXX!"

I kept screaming and looking around, even knowing it was useless. There was nothing else I could do. I was now low enough that I could see I was headed straight for a large, gray, L-shaped roof, and on the short leg of the L was a lighted helipad. I realized this building must be a hospital.

I was going to die crashing through the roof of a hospital.

And to my amazement, despite my all-consuming horror, I felt my lips crack into a smile.

Maybe I'd even hit the helipad.

I started to laugh.

And then I started laughing harder. And I kept laughing harder and harder even as I curled into a ball, squeezed my eyes shut, and—

Chapter 31

Blinding white light filled my eyes. I squinted and tried to bring my hand up to shield my eyes, but my arm and shoulder didn't seem to hear my brain quite right, and the back of my hand smacked against my forehead. Every muscle in my body felt stiff almost to the point of rigidity. For a couple seconds my mind was as blank as the light.

Then suddenly, with a jolt—quite possibly the biggest jolt of my life—I remembered:

I'd died.

Holy shit, I thought groggily. *This must be heaven.*

Then, after a dumbstruck moment: *Heaven is freakin' cold.*

But then my eyes started to adjust, the light started to recede, and my surroundings started to take shape. I looked around, moving only my eyes because my neck was so stiff. I was lying on my back in a bed with white sheets in a small, square, white room. To my right, a window showed a starless night sky tinged orange by city lights unseen below. On my left, an IV stood next to the bed; it didn't appear to be hooked up to me, though.

It came from straight ahead, a few yards away—a faint rustle of fabric.

My chest tightened and I jerked my head up despite my neck muscles' grinding resistance—

Then froze. Every part of my being seemed to freeze.

A woman sat in a chair against the far wall, legs crossed, reading a book in her lap.

I smiled. And my extremely chapped lips felt like they split open in a hundred different places. But for some reason, this just made me smile wider.

"Hey Mom," I rasped. "You got any ChapStick?"

Chapter 32

"So how do you feel?"

"Well rested."

She smiled. "I imagine, after twenty-seven days. It's probably never felt better simply to be awake, huh?"

"Yeah. Although I kinda wish they would put me back on a feeding tube. Or else serve the food with a side of painkillers."

She smiled again and studied me for a moment. "You know, Ricky, you seem a lot . . . different than the last time I saw you."

"You mean I'm not being an insufferable jackhole?" She hesitated uncomfortably. I grinned. "It's all right. I should seem different. I feel different."

"Why do you think that is?"

"It's amazing what a good month's sleep can do. Honestly, you should consider prescribing comas to your patients."

"My patients are teenagers. Most of them are practically comatose already."

I laughed a little. "So, uh . . . why are you here, exactly? You just couldn't get enough of me the first time?"

"Not nearly enough. But I was also curious. You're a medical mystery, you know—a perfectly healthy sixteen-year-old goes into—"

"'—goes into a coma for no apparent reason, the doctors can't find anything wrong with him besides the fact that he's unconscious, and suddenly, after almost a month, for no apparent reason, he wakes up!' The doctors seem to feel it's necessary to explain this to me every time they come in here. 'Medical mystery' is practically my nickname."

"Well, it is quite a mystery. Do you have any theories?"

"*Me?*" I said, eyeing her quizzically. "Why, did someone give me an M.D. while I was out?"

"Well, sometimes the patient knows things the doctors don't."

I shrugged. "I dunno. Maybe I was just really, really tired."

She smiled. "That's as good an explanation as anyone else has come up with." She crossed her legs and cleared her throat. "Do you mind if I ask you a few questions about what happened?"

"There's not much to tell, really, but sure, go ahead."

"All right." She looked down at the notepad in her lap. "So . . . you opened the window in your room before you went to bed, is that right?"

"Yeah. I was hot."

"And then you got into bed, you were lying there, and that's the last thing you remember?"

"Yup."

"So you don't remember getting out of bed and going over to the window?"

"No."

"Do you remember anything from while you were in the coma? Remember hearing or feeling anything?"

"No, thank God—the memory of lying on this mattress for a month . . . well, this mattress and your chair should get married."

"I'll be sure to introduce them. What about dreams? Any dreams you remember?"

"No."

"Did you have any sense of time, of how long had passed?"

"No—it felt like an instant, just like regular sleep."

"So when you woke up, you didn't know you'd been in a coma?"

"No. I kinda suspected something was wrong, though, 'cause usually when I go to bed I don't wake up in the hospital."

"I see."

"You know, I've already answered all these questions."

"More than once, I imagine, huh?" She smiled apologetically. "I hope you don't mind. I just thought I might be able to help you remember something."

But I didn't buy that. She wouldn't have come all the way out here just to ask the same questions I'd already answered multiple times unless she had a specific, compelling reason. And I couldn't shake the feeling that it was because she suspected I was lying. She was asking me all these old questions again because she was looking for inconsistencies in my story, and she wanted to witness my answers personally so that she could try to tell if I was lying by my behavior.

I told myself I was being ridiculous. How the hell could she have any idea I was lying?

Dr. Komori looked down at her notebook again, flipped the page, and read for several seconds. Then she cleared her throat and looked back up at me. "I, uh . . . I have a friend who's a pediatric neurologist at Mercy General Hospital in Sacramento. 'Pediatric' means she deals with kids, so our fields kind of overlap—and sometimes, when one of us gets an interesting case, we'll talk about it. Sometimes we can help each other. So yesterday, when I heard you'd woken up, I figured I'd give her a call." She paused a moment, her eyes narrowing just slightly. "Do you recognize the name Mariah Bell, by any chance?"

Epilogue

From: Nigel Mason
Date: Friday, November 29, 2009 1:33 AM
To: Mariah Bell, Ricky Darlin, Alex Starkey
Subject: holy shit

Miami Herald Archives
Section: METRO
Published: Thursday, July 25, 1991

THIRTEEN-YEAR-OLD POSSIBLE MURDER
SUSPECT IN COMA

A thirteen-year-old Westchester boy under investigation for murdering his father with a kitchen knife has gone into a coma.

The boy was found unconscious yesterday morning outside a family friend's house where he and his mother were living.

Miami Children's Hospital, where the boy is being cared for, said in a written statement that doctors have yet to determine the cause of the coma and are still running tests. They have found no signs of head trauma, brain tumors, or metabolic abnormalities, three of the most common causes of comas.

The boy made headlines Monday when it was reported that he had become a focus of the Miami-Dade police investigation.

Neighbors found the boy's father, Stuart Hooke, 48, dead in his south Westchester home on the evening of July 19. Police estimated he had been dead for at least a day.

Police say it appears Hooke was sleeping on a couch when he was stabbed repeatedly in the face, neck, and chest with a chef's knife with an 8-inch blade. The knife, which was left at the scene, had been taken from Hooke's kitchen. Police found no sign of forced entry into the house.

Hooke and his wife separated earlier this year and shared custody of the boy, the couple's only child. The wife was cleared of suspicion in the murder after police verified her alibi.

Police questioned the boy Monday, with his lawyer present, and executed a search warrant Tuesday at the house where he and the mother were living.

The boy has not been officially named a suspect in Hooke's murder.

About the Author

Dan Elconin was born in Milwaukee in 1989 and moved to San Diego at age eight. He is currently a sophomore at UCLA.

From fantasy to crazy reality, here's a look at Peter Lerangis's

9:09 P.M.

"Jesus, it's still alive!"

Byron's voice. From the backseat.

Byron was okay.

Jimmy jumped up from the road. He struggled to keep upright, his leg numb. He spat his mouth clean as he made his way around the car. Through the side window he could see Byron's silhouette, peering over the front seat. Jimmy looked through the front window. The deer's back was enormous, matted with blood and flecks of windshield. Under it he could make out only the right side of Cam's body from the shoulder down, but not his face.

Cam was completely smothered.

"Oh God, Jimmy, what did you do?" Byron said.

"I—I don't know. . . . It just, like, *appeared*!" Jimmy

had to grip the side of the car to keep from falling, or flying away, or completely disintegrating. He blinked his eyes, trying desperately to find the right angle, hoping to see a sign that Cam was alive. "Push it, Byron—push it off!"

"It's a monster—how the fuck am I supposed to push it? *Shit, Jimmy, how could you have not seen it?*"

"*I did!*" Jimmy screamed. "I braked. I tried to get out of the way—"

"Dickwad! You tried to outmaneuver a *deer*? You don't *brake*! That makes the grill drop lower—lifts the animal right up into the car, like a fucking spoon! You just *drive*. That way you smack it right back into the woods."

"*If you know so much, why weren't you driving?*"

"With what license?"

"*I don't have one either!*"

"You told me you did!"

"I never told you that! I just said I knew how to drive. I never took the test—"

"Oh, great—the only person in Manhattan our age who knows how to drive, *and you don't bother to get a license.*" Byron leaned closer, suddenly looking concerned. "Jesus Christ, what happened to your mouth?"

"It's what I get for applying lipstick without a mirror—"

"Awwww, *shit!*" Byron was looking at something in his hand. "My BlackBerry's totaled."

"How can you think about your BlackBerry while Cam is under the deer?"

Byron looked up with a start, then immediately leaped out of the car. "Oh fuck, Cam. Is he dead?"

"'*Oh fuck, Cam*'? You just noticed him? You're yelling at me, and you just thought of Cam?" Jimmy's hands trembled as he pulled his cell phone out of his pocket. "I'm calling 911."

"No, don't!" Byron said, snatching the phone from Jimmy's hand.

"Are you crazy?" Jimmy said. "What's wrong with you?"

"We're in East Dogshit and the GPS is busted—do you even know what road we're on? What are you going to tell the cops? *Um, there's this tree? And, like, a ditch? And a road?* And then what, we wait? We don't have time, Jimmy!"

"But—"

"Think it through, Einstein. What's your story? One, you wrecked a car that's not yours. Two, you don't have a license. Three, you killed a deer. And four, look at Cam. You planning to go to Princeton and room with Rhodes scholars? How about a guy with three teeth who can't wait for you to bend over? Because if we don't stop talking, dude, you're facing murder charges."

"He's not dead, Byron—"

"Just put the fucking phone away and let's get Bambi off Cam." Byron threw Jimmy the phone and raced to the back of the car. "Throw me the keys. I'll get a rope out of the trunk. When I give you back the keys, get in the car."

Jimmy reached into the car, tossing the phone onto the dashboard. Quickly removing the keys from the steering column, he threw them to Byron. He eyed the driver's seat. The deer was still moving, still trying to get away. *No way* was he going back in there.

But he couldn't abandon Cam.

If only he could think straight. His brain was useless. In that moment, he was picturing a cloud of small, hungry ticks hovering over the front seat. He tried to shake it off, but it was like some weird psychological hijacking brought on by his mother's perennial vigil over the mortal threat posed by proximity to deer, which turned every suburban outing into a preparation for war.

"What are you fucking worried about, Lyme's disease?" Byron shouted. "Get in there!"

Jimmy cringed. "It's *Lyme*," he muttered, grabbing the door handle. "Not *Lyme's*."

"What?" Byron shouted.

"Nothing. What am I supposed to do—in the car?"

"What the fuck do you think you're supposed to do?"

As if in response, the deer gave a sudden shudder. Jimmy jumped back, stifling a scream. "I—I'm not sure . . ."

"When I give the word, put it in reverse, Jimmy. And gun it."

Byron yanked open the trunk and threw the keys to Jimmy, who kept a wary eye on the deer as he opened the door. It was motionless now, its snout resting just below the gear shift.

As Jimmy climbed inside, the car rocked with Byron's efforts to shove stuff under the rear tires for traction.

Breathe in. Breathe out.

Jimmy tried to stop himself from hyperventilating. He eyed Cam's feet, blinking back tears. He had never liked Cam, or any of the smart-ass jocks who treated the Speech Team kids like they were some kind of lower life-form. Since freshman year he had devoted a lot of time conjuring horrible fates for most of them, fates not unlike this.

In . . . Out . . .

Jimmy hadn't wanted to go on this drive. It was Byron who'd pushed the idea. *Cam* wants us to go, *Cam* says suburban parties are the best ever, *Cam* says Westchester chicks are hot for NYC guys. *Cam* wants to be friends. It would be stupid to miss a chance at détente between the worlds of sports and geekdom.

In . . .

Until this time, Jimmy couldn't imagine that Byron would be friends with a guy like Cam. Byron the potty-mouthed genius, Cam the football guy. Was this some kind of crush? Was *that* the reason for—

"Wake up, douche bag!" Byron shouted. "Now! *Go!*"

With his foot on the brake, Jimmy threw the car in reverse. The accelerator was touching the bottom of the caved-in dashboard. Carefully, he wedged his foot in and floored it.

The engine roared to life, the tires gripping the debris. As the car lurched backward, the deer's head rose slowly off the seat with the force of the rope. Something warm spattered against the side of Jimmy's face.

"AAAGHH!" he screamed, yanking his foot away from the accelerator.

"WHAT?" Byron cried, running around the side of the car. "Why'd you stop? We almost had it!"

"It puked on me!"

Byron shone a flashlight into the front seat. "It's not puke. It's blood."

"Oh, great . . ." Jimmy's stomach flipped. *This couldn't be happening!*

"Here. This'll protect you." Byron was throwing something over the animal's head—a rag, a blanket, it was impossible to see. "Don't think about it, Jimmy. Just step on it! And put on your seat belt."

Jimmy felt a lightness in his head. His eyes were crossing. *Focus.*

He buckled his belt and put the car in reverse again, slipped his foot under the wreckage of the dashboard. As he floored it, the car began to move, the engine roaring. The animal's hulk rose up beside him, away from him— scraping across the bottom of the windshield, slowly receding out of the car and onto the hood.

The blanket fell off the deer's head, and as the carcass finally slipped off, the car jerked backward.

SMMMMACK!

Jimmy's head whipped against the headrest. He bounced back, his chest catching the seat belt and knocking the wind out of him.

"Are you okay?" Byron cried.

"Fah—fah—" Everything was white. Jimmy struggled to breathe, his eyes slowly focusing on the image in the rearview mirror, the twisted metal of a guardrail reflecting against the taillights.

Byron was leaning in the open passenger window, training a flashlight on the dim silhouette of Cam's lifeless body, now freed from the deer. "This does not look good . . . ," he said.

"Is his chest moving?"

"I don't know! I don't think so, but I can't—" In the distance a muffled siren burst through the rain's din. Byron drew back, shutting the flashlight. "Shit! Did you call them?"

"No!" Jimmy said.

"Then how do they know?"

Jimmy thought about the red pickup. "Someone drove past us, just after the accident. Maybe they called."

"Someone saw us?"

"This is a New York suburb. Occasionally people drive on the roads."

"Oh, God. Oh, God. Oh, God. Oh, shit. Oh, God." Byron was backing away from the car, disappearing into the darkness.

"I'm the one who's supposed to be freaking out, not you!" Jimmy leaned toward Cam's inert body, his hands

shaking. The cold rain, evaporating against his body, rose up in smoky wisps. *Don't be dead don't be dead please please please please don't be dead.*

"C-C-Cam?" Jimmy slapped Cam's cheek and shook his massive shoulders, but Cam was limp and unresponsive. His body began to slip on the rain-slicked seat, falling toward the driver's side. Jimmy tried to shove back, but he was helpless against the weight. Cam's head plopped heavily in Jimmy's lap.

"Aaaaghhh!" He pushed open the door, jumped out, and looked around for Byron. "I think he's . . . he's . . ."

The siren's wail was growing closer. How would he explain this? *You see, officer, in New York City no one gets a license until they're in college. But my dad taught me to drive on weekends, on Long Island. No, I don't have the registration either. The car belongs to—belonged to . . . him . . . the deceased.*

He'd have to get out of here before they came. He looked past the car. There was a gully, a hill. It was pitch-black. He could get lost in the night.

Asshole! No, the cops would figure it out. Fingerprints. Friends knew he was driving—Reina Sanchez, she had to know. She was all over Cam. She'd tell them. So it wouldn't only be manslaughter. It would also be leaving the scene of the crime. What was that? Life in prison?

Stay or go, he was screwed either way. Because of a deer. A fucking stupid deer. Without the deer, everything would have been all right.

"BYRON!" he shouted.

In the distance he heard Byron retching, with characteristic heroism.

Cam was now slumped into the driver's seat, his right shoulder touching the bottom of the steering wheel.

He used me. He convinced Byron to get me to drive, so he could go to a party. And now he will never, ever be accountable. Because he's ...

Dead. He was dead. He would never move again, never talk.

And that opened up several possibilities, some of which were

Unthinkable.

An idea was taking shape cancerously fast among his battered brain cells. If you were thinking something, it wasn't unthinkable—that was Goethe, or maybe Wittgenstein, or Charlie Brown. The idea danced between the synapses, on the line between survival and absolute awfulness, presenting itself in a sick, Quentin Tarantino way that made perfect sense.

It was Cam's dad's car. It would be logical that Cam would be driving it.

No one will know.

He grabbed Cam's legs. They were heavy, dead weight. He pulled them across the car toward the driver's side, letting Cam's butt slide with them—across the bench seat, across the pool of animal blood and pebbled glass.

Jimmy lifted Cam into an upright position, but his body fell forward, his torso resting hard against the steering wheel.

HONNNNNNNNNNNK!

The sound was ridiculously loud. Around the bend, distant headlights were making the curtain of rain glow. No time to fix this now.

Jimmy bolted for the woods.

"What are you doing?" Byron called out of the dark. He was standing now, peering into the car. "Jesus Christ! You're trying to *make it look like Cam drove*? What if he's alive? He'll tell them you were driving!"

Jimmy stopped, frantically looking around for something blunt. He stooped to pick up a rusted piece of tail-pipe, maybe a foot long. It would do the trick. He knelt by the driver's door and drew it back.

"JIMMY, ARE YOU OUT OF YOUR FUCKING MIND?"

Byron's eyes were like softballs. He grabbed Jimmy's arm and pulled him back.

Jimmy let the tailpipe fall to the ground. He felt his brain whirling, his knees buckling. He felt Byron pulling him away.

As the cop cars squealed to a halt near the blaring car, he was moving fast but feeling nothing.

LEVIATHAN

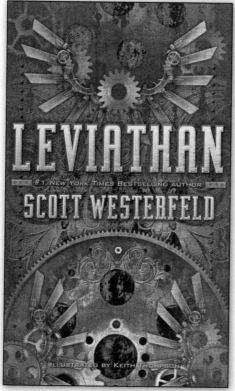

— FROM —

SCOTT WESTERFELD

THE BESTSELLING AUTHOR OF THE UGLIES SERIES

FROM SIMON PULSE
PUBLISHED BY SIMON & SCHUSTER

NEED
A DISTRACTION?
READ ON THE EDGE WITH SIMON PULSE.

DAN ELCONIN

TOM LOMBARDI

TODD STRASSER

LYAH B. LeFLORE

HANNAH MOSKOWITZ

ALBERT BORRIS

PETER LERANGIS

THOMAS FAHY

Published by Simon & Schuster

Check
Your
Pulse